Caine wrapped his arms around Jade and pulled her up against him. "Jade, do you want me to touch you now?"

She struggled out of his arms and took a step back. "It doesn't matter if I want you to touch me or not, Caine. You're my protector. You have to leave me alone."

She suddenly found herself pulled back up against his chest, his thighs . . . Her flimsy night-gown proved scant protection against his body, his incredible heat. "It doesn't work that way, Jade."

"Why not?"

"I want you."

The huskiness in his voice was her undoing. The urge to let him touch her was such a sweet torment . . . Ah, but only a fool would let a man like Caine close . . . only a fool . . .

Thunder rumbled in the distance. Neither Jade nor Caine was aware of the weather now. They were too consumed by the heat flowing between them.

They stared into each other's eyes for what seemed an eternity. And in the end, it was inevitable. When Caine slowly lowered his head toward her, she leaned up to meet him halfway. . . . His mouth took absolute possession. Jade wrapped her arms around his neck, threaded her fingers through his soft, curly hair. . . . When he finally pulled away, she felt as though he'd taken her heart . . .

Books by Julie Garwood

Gentle Warrior
Rebellious Desire
Honor's Splendour
The Lion's Lady
The Bride
Guardian Angel
The Gift
The Prize

Published by POCKET BOOKS

Julie Garwood

Guardian Angel

POCKET BOOKS

New York   London   Toronto   Sydney   Tokyo   Singapore

An *Original* Publication of POCKET BOOKS.

POCKET BOOKS, a division of Simon & Schuster Inc.
1230 Avenue of the Americas, New York, NY 10020

ISBN: 0-671-67006-9

First Pocket Books printing May 1990

10 9 8 7 6 5 4

POCKET and colophon are registered trademarks of
Simon & Schuster Inc.

Printed in the U.S.A.

This one's for you, Elizabeth.

Guardian Angel

Chapter One

T he hunter waited patiently for his prey.

It was a dangerous deception the Marquess of Cainewood was playing. The infamous Pagan of Shallow's Wharf would certainly hear of his impersonator; he'd be forced out of hiding then, for his pride, monstrous by all whispered accounts, wouldn't allow another to take credit for his own black deeds. The pirate would certainly try to extract his own form of revenge. Caine was counting on that possibility. Once Pagan showed himself, Caine would have him.

And then the legend would be destroyed.

The Marquess had run out of choices. The spider wouldn't leave his web. Bounty hadn't worked. No, there wasn't a Judas among the seamen, which was surprising given that most ordinary men would have sold their mamas into bondage for the amount of gold he'd offered. It was a miscalculation on Caine's part, too. Each seaman voiced loyalty to the legend as his own personal reason for refusing the coins. Caine, a cynic by nature and past sour experiences, guessed fear was the real motive. Fear and superstition.

1

Mystery surrounded the pirate like the wall of a confessional. No one had ever actually seen Pagan. His ship, the *Emerald,* had been observed countless times skimming the water like a pebble thrown by the hand of God, or so it was reported by those who'd boasted of seeing the ship. The sight of the black beauty sparked terror in the titled gentlemen of the *ton* with fat purses, snickers of glee from the downright mean-hearted, and prayers of humble thanksgiving from the deprived, for Pagan was known to share his booty with the less fortunate.

Yet as often as the magical ship was sighted, no one could describe a single shipmate on board the vessel. This only increased the speculation, admiration, and awe about the phantom pirate.

Pagan's thievery extended beyond the ocean, however, for he was a man who obviously enjoyed variety. His land raids caused just as much consternation, perhaps even more. Pagan was discriminate in robbing only from the members of the *ton.* It was apparent the pirate didn't want anyone else taking credit for his own midnight raids on the unsuspecting. He therefore left his own personal calling card in the form of a single long-stemmed white rose. His victim usually awakened by morning light to find the flower on the pillow beside him. The mere sight of the rose was usually quite enough to send grown men into a dead faint.

Needless to say, the poor idolized the legend. They believed Pagan was a man of style and romance. The church was no less effusive in their adoration, for the pirate left trunks of gold and jewels next to the collection plates in their vestibules, topped by a white rose, of course, so the leaders would know whose soul they were supposed to pray for. The bishop was hard put to condemn the pirate. He knew better than to saint him, though, for to do so would incur the wrath of some of the most influential members of society, and therefore settled on calling Pagan rogue instead.

The nickname, it was noted, was always said with a quick grin and a slow wink.

The War Department held no such reservations. They'd set their own bounty on the pirate's head. Caine had doubled that amount. His reason for hunting down the bastard was a personal one, and he believed the end would justify whatever foul means he employed.

It was going to be an eye for an eye. He would kill the pirate.

Ironically, the two adversaries were equally matched. The Marquess was feared by ordinary men. His work for his government had earned him his own dark legend. If the circumstances had been different, if Pagan hadn't dared to prod Caine's wrath, he might have continued to leave him alone. Pagan's mortal sin changed that determination, however; changed it with a vengeance.

Night after night Caine went to the tavern called the Ne'er Do Well, situated in the heart of London's slums. The tavern was frequented by the more seasoned dock workers. Caine always took the corner table, his broad back protected by the stone wall from sneak attack, and patiently waited for Pagan to come to him.

The Marquess moved in and out of such seedy circles with the ease befitting a man with a dark past. In this section of the city, a man's title meant nothing. His survival was dependent upon his size, his ability to inflict pain while defending himself, and his indifference to the violence and crudity surrounding him.

Caine made the tavern his home in less than one night. He was a big man, with muscular shoulders and thighs. His size alone could intimidate most would-be challengers. Caine was dark haired, bronze skinned, and had eyes the color of a dark gray sky. There'd been a time when those eyes had had the power to spark a rush of flutters in the ladies of the *ton*. Now, however, those same ladies recoiled from the coldness

3

lurking there, and the flat, emotionless expression. They whispered that the Marquess of Cainewood had been turned into stone by his hatred. Caine agreed.

Once he'd decided to play the role of Pagan, his pretense hadn't been difficult to maintain. The storytellers all agreed on the fanciful notion that Pagan was actually a titled gentleman who took to pirating as a means of keeping up with his lavish lifestyle. Caine simply used that bit of gossip to his advantage. When he first entered the tavern, he'd worn his most expensive clothing. He'd added his own personal touch by pinning a small white rose to the lapel of his dinner jacket. It was an outrageous, silently boastful addition, of course, and gained him just the right amount of notice.

Immediately, he'd had to cut a few men with his sharp knife to secure his place in their group. Caine was dressed like a gentleman, yes, but he fought without honor or dignity. The men loved him. In bare minutes, he'd earned their respect and their fear. His Herculean size and strength gained him immediate loyalty, too. One of the more fearless asked him in a stammer if the talk was true. Was he Pagan then? Caine didn't answer that question, but his quick grin told the seaman his question had pleased him. And when he remarked to the tavernkeeper that the seaman had a very cunning mind, he forced the inevitable conclusion. By week's end, the rumor of Pagan's nightly visitations to the Ne'er Do Well had spread like free gin.

Monk, the bald-headed Irishman who'd won the tavern in a crooked game of cards, usually sat beside Caine at the close of each evening. Monk was the only one who knew about the deception. He was in wholehearted agreement with Caine's plan, too, as he'd heard all about Pagan's atrocity to Caine's family. Just as significant, business had picked up considerably since the deception had begun. Everyone, it seemed, wanted to get a good look at the pirate, and Monk, a man who put profit above all other matters, charged exorbitant prices for his watered-down ale.

The tavernkeeper had lost his hair years before, but his bright orange-colored eyebrows more than made up for any lack. They were thick, curly, and crept like determined vines of ivy halfway up his freckled forehead. Monk rubbed his brow now in true frustration for the Marquess. It was almost three o'clock in the morning, an hour past time to shut down the tavern for the evening. Only two paying customers were lingering over their drinks now. When they'd belched out their sleepy farewells and taken their leave, Monk turned to Caine.

"You've got more patience than a flea waiting on a mangy dog, coming here night after night. I'm praying you don't get too discouraged," he added. He paused to pour a full goblet of brandy for the Marquess, then swallowed a hefty portion directly from the bottle. "You'll flush him out, Caine. I'm sure of it. The way I see it, he'll send a couple of his men first to try to waylay you. That's why I'm always warning you to protect your back when you leave each night."

Monk took another drink, and snickered. "Pagan's a mite protective of his reputation. Your pretense must be turning his hair gray. He'll show himself soon enough. Why, I'll wager that tomorrow will be the night."

Caine nodded agreement. Monk, his gaze piercing with promise, always ended his nightly speech with the prediction that tomorrow the prey would show himself.

"You'll pounce on him then, Caine, like a duck on a bug."

Caine swallowed a long drink, his first of the evening, then tilted his chair back so he could rest his shoulders against the wall. "I'll get him."

The harshness in Caine's tone sent a shiver down Monk's spine. He was about to give hasty agreement when the door suddenly flew open, drawing his attention. Monk half turned in his chair to call out that the tavern was closed for the night, but the sight standing in the center of the doorway so stunned him, he could only gape in astonishment. When he was finally able to regain his voice, he whispered, "Holy Mother of God, has an angel come calling on us?"

From his position against the wall, Caine faced the entrance and had a clear view. Though he didn't move or show any outward reaction, in truth, his surprise was just as great as Monk's. His heart started slamming a wild beat and he couldn't seem to catch his breath.

She did look like an angel. Caine didn't want to blink, certain his vision would vanish into the night if he closed his eyes for just a second or two.

She was an incredibly beautiful woman. Her eyes captivated him. They were the most magnificent shade of green. The green of his valley, he thought to himself, on a clear, moonlit night.

She was staring at him. Caine stared back.

Several long minutes passed while they studied each other. Then she started walking toward him. As soon as she moved, the hood of her black cape fell to her shoulders. Caine quit breathing. The muscles in his chest constricted painfully. His vision was blessed with lush, auburn-colored hair. In the candlelight, the color was as brilliant as fire.

Caine noticed the pitiful condition of her clothing when she neared the table. The quality of her cloak indicated wealth, yet the expensive material had been shredded halfway up one side. It looked as though someone had taken a knife to it. Part of the green satin lining hung in tatters around her hem. Caine's curiosity intensified. He looked back up at her face, saw the faint bruises on her right cheekbone, the small cut below her full lower lip, and the splotch of dirt marring her forehead.

If his vision was an angel, she'd just been forced to pay purgatory a visit, Caine decided. Yet even though she looked like she'd just lost the battle with Satan, she was still very appealing, too appealing in fact for his peace of mind. He grew tense as he waited for her to speak.

She stopped when she reached the other side of the round table. Her gaze was now directed on the rose pinned to his lapel.

His angel was obviously frightened. Her hands were shaking. She clutched a small white bag to her bodice and he noticed several faded scars on her fingers.

He didn't know what to make of her. Caine didn't want her to be afraid of him, though. That admission made his frown intensify.

"You're all alone?" he asked, his tone as brisk as the rising wind.

"I am."

"At this time of night, in this section of the city?"

"Yes," she answered. "Are you Pagan?"

Her voice, he noticed, was husky, whisper soft.

"Look at me when you ask your questions."

She wouldn't comply with his command but stubbornly continued to stare at the rose. "Pray, answer me, sir," she returned. "Are you Pagan? I have need to speak with the pirate. It is a terribly important matter."

"I am Pagan," Caine said.

She nodded. "It's said that you'll do any task if the price be enough. Is that true, sir?"

"It is," Caine acknowledged. "What is it you want from me?"

In answer to his question, she dropped the bag onto the center of the table. The drawstring tore open and several coins spilled out. Monk let out a low whistle.

"There are thirty pieces in all," she said, her gaze still downcast.

Caine raised an eyebrow in reaction to that statement. "Thirty pieces of silver?"

She timidly nodded. "Is that enough? It's all I have."

"Who is it you wish to betray?"

She looked startled by that assumption. "Oh, no, you misunderstand. I don't want to betray anyone. I'm not a Judas, sir."

He thought she looked insulted by his comment. "It was an honest mistake to make."

Her frown indicated she didn't agree. Caine vowed he wasn't going to let her get his temper riled. "Then what is it you ask from me?"

"I would like you to kill someone, please."

"Ah," he drawled out. His disappointment was almost painful. She looked so damned innocent, so pitifully vulnerable, yet sweetly asked him to murder someone for her.

"And who is this victim? Your husband, perchance?" The cynicism in his voice was as grating as a nail scraping down a chalkboard.

She didn't seem to mind his biting tone. "No," she answered.

"No? You're not married then?"

"Does it matter?"

"Oh, yes," he countered in a whisper to match hers. "It matters."

"No, I'm not married."

"Then who is it you want killed? Your father? Your brother?"

She shook her head again.

Caine slowly leaned forward. His patience was wearing as thin as the ale Monk watered down. "I tire of having to question you. Tell me."

He'd forced a belligerent tone, certain he'd intimidate her into blurting out her full explanation. He knew he'd failed in that endeavor, however, when he caught the mutinous expression on her face. If he hadn't been watching her so intently, he knew he would have missed the flash of anger. The frightened little kitten had a little spirit inside her, after all.

"I would like you to accept this task before I explain," she said.

"Task? You call hiring me to kill someone a task?" he asked, his voice incredulous.

"I do," she announced with a nod.

She still refused to look him in the eye. That fact irritated him. "All right," he lied. "I accept."

Her shoulders sagged in what Caine surmised was acute relief. "Tell me who my victim is," he instructed once again.

She slowly lifted her gaze to look at him then. The torment Caine saw in her eyes made his chest ache. The urge to reach out, to take her into his arms, to offer her comfort very nearly overwhelmed him. He suddenly felt outraged on her behalf, then had to shake his head over such a ludicrous, fanciful notion.

Hell, the woman was contracting him to murder someone.

Their gazes held a long while before Caine asked again, "Well? Who is it you want killed?"

She took a deep breath before answering.

"Me."

Chapter Two

"Holy Mother of God," Monk whispered. "You cannot be serious, dear lady."

She didn't take her gaze away from Caine when she answered the tavernkeeper. "I'm very serious, my good man. Do you think I would have ventured out into this part of town in the middle of the night if I weren't serious?"

Caine answered her question. "I think you've lost your mind."

"No," she replied. "It would be much easier if I had."

"I see," Caine said. He was trying to keep his temper controlled, but the urge to shout at her made his throat ache. "When would you like this . . . this . . ."

"Task?"

"Yes, task," Caine asked. "When would you like this task done?"

"Now."

"Now?"

"If it's convenient, mi'lord."

"If it's convenient?"

"Oh, dear, I'm so sorry," she whispered. "I didn't mean to upset you."

"Why do you think you've upset me?"

"Because you're shouting at me."

He realized she was right. He had been shouting. Caine let out a long sigh. For the first time in a good long while, his composure was completely shattered. He excused his shameful condition by telling himself that anyone with half a mind would have been caught off guard by such an outrageous request. She looked so sincere and appeared to be terribly fragile, too. Hell, the woman had freckles on the bridge of her nose, for God's sake. She should be home under lock and key with her loving family protecting her, not standing in this seedy tavern calmly discussing her own murder.

"I can see how distressed I've made you," she said. "I really do apologize, Pagan. Have you never killed a woman before?" she asked. Her voice was filled with sympathy.

She looked as if she felt sorry for him now. "No, I've never killed a woman before," he grated out. "But there's always a first time for everything, now isn't there?"

He'd meant the comment to be sarcastic. She took it to heart. "That's the spirit," she rushed out. She actually smiled at him then. "It really shouldn't be too difficult for you. I'll help, of course."

He wanted to throw his head down on the table. "You're willing to help?" he strangled out.

"Certainly."

"You have lost your mind."

"No, I haven't," she countered. "But I'm very desperate. This task must be done as soon as possible. Do you think you could hurry and finish your drink?"

"Why must it be done so soon?" he asked.

"Because they're going to come for me sometime soon, perhaps even yet tonight. I'm going to die, Pagan, by their

11

hand or yours, and I'd really rather determine my own end. Surely you can understand that."

"Then why don't you just kill yourself?" Monk blurted out. "Wouldn't that be much easier than hiring someone else?"

"For God's sake, Monk, don't encourage her."

"I'm not trying to encourage her," Monk rushed out. "I'm just trying to understand why such a pretty would want to die."

"Oh, I could never kill myself," she explained. "It would be a sin. Someone else has to do it. Don't you see?"

Caine had taken about all he could handle for one evening. He bounded to his feet, upsetting the chair in his haste, then planted the palms of his big hands on the tabletop. "No, I don't see, but I promise you I'm going to before this night is over. We're going to start at the beginning. First you'll begin by telling me your name."

"Why?"

"It's a little rule I have," he snapped. "I don't kill anyone I don't know. Now tell me your name."

"It's a stupid rule."

"Answer me."

"Jade."

"Damn it, I want your real name!" he commanded in a near roar.

"Damn it, that is my real name," she replied. She had a thoroughly disgruntled look on her face.

"You're serious, aren't you?"

"Of course, I'm serious. Jade is my name," she added with a shrug.

"Jade's an unusual name," he said. "Fitting, though. You're proving to be a rather unusual woman."

"Your opinion of me isn't at all relevant, sir. I hired you to complete an assignment and that is all. Is it customary for you to interview your victims before you do them in?"

He ignored her glare. "Tell me the rest of your name, or I may strangle you."

"No, you mustn't strangle me," she replied. "I don't want to die that way and I am the one doing the hiring, if you'll remember."

"What way did you have in mind?" he asked. "Oh, hell, never mind. I don't want to know."

"But you have to know," she argued. "How can you kill me if you don't know how I want it done?"

"Later," he interjected. "You may instruct me in the method you've chosen later. First things first, Jade. Are your parents waiting at home for you?"

"It's doubtful."

"Why?"

"They're both dead."

He closed his eyes and counted to ten. "So you're all alone?"

"No."

"No?"

It was her turn to sigh. "I have a brother. I'm not going to tell you anything more, Pagan. It's too much of a risk, you see."

"Why is it a risk, miss?" Monk asked.

"The more he knows about me, the more difficult the task will become. I believe it would be very upsetting to kill someone you liked. Don't you, sir?"

"I ain't never had to kill someone I liked," Monk admitted. "As to that, I ain't never killed anyone. Still, your theory makes sense to me."

It took all Caine had not to start bellowing. "Jade, I assure you that won't be a problem. At this moment, I don't like you at all."

She took a step back. "Well, why not?" she asked. "I haven't been half as insulting as you have. Are you just a cranky person by nature, Pagan?"

"Don't call me Pagan."

"Why not?"

"It's a danger, miss, if anyone overhears," Monk blurted out when he saw how infuriated Caine was becoming. The muscle in the side of his jaw had started flexing. Caine had a fierce temper and she was innocently shaking him into a real froth. Why if he let loose, he might very well give her her wish and frighten her to death.

"What should I call him then?" she asked the tavernkeeper.

"Caine," Monk answered with a nod. "You can call him Caine."

She let out an inelegant snort. "And he thinks I have an unusual name?"

Caine reached out and grabbed hold of her chin. He forced her to look at him again. "What is your brother's name?"

"Nathan."

"Where is Nathan now?"

"He's away on pressing business matters."

"What business?"

She slapped his hand away before answering. "Shipping business."

"When will he be back?"

Her glare could melt a lesser man. "Two weeks," she snapped. "There, I've answered all your questions. Now will you please quit pestering me and get on with your assignment?"

"Where do you live, Jade?"

"Sir, your endless questions are giving me a pounding headache. I'm not at all used to having men scream at me."

Caine glanced down at Monk and let him see his exasperation. "The daft woman wants me to kill her, yet now complains about a headache."

She suddenly reached out, grabbed hold of his chin, and nudged him back to look at her. It was a deliberate imitation

14

of his earlier action. Caine was so surprised by her boldness, he let her have her way.

"Now it's my turn," she announced. "I'll ask you my questions and you will answer them. I'm the one giving you the silver coins, sir. First, and most important, I want to know if you're really going to kill me. Your hesitation alarms me. That and this endless inquisition."

"You're going to have to satisfy my curiosity before I decide," he told her.

"No."

"Then I won't kill you."

"You scoundrel!" she cried out. "You promised me before you knew who your victim was. You gave me your word!"

"I lied."

Her gasp of outrage nearly knocked her over. "You are a real disappointment to me. A man of honor wouldn't so easily break his word. You should be ashamed of yourself."

"Jade," he answered. "I never said I was a man of honor."

"Nay, miss, he didn't," Monk interjected.

Her eyes turned the color of green fire. She was apparently furious with him. Her hands joined his on the tabletop. She leaned forward and whispered, "I was told Pagan never, ever breaks his word."

"You were misinformed."

They were almost nose to nose now. Caine tried to concentrate on their conversation, but her wonderful scent, so clean, so fresh, so utterly feminine, kept getting in the way.

She was shaking her head at him now. Caine was literally at a loss for words. He'd never had a woman stand up to him before. No, the ladies of the *ton* usually cowered when he showed the least amount of displeasure. This one was different, however. She wasn't just standing up to him either. She was actually matching him glare for glare. He suddenly felt like laughing and didn't have the faintest idea why.

Her insanity was obviously the catching kind.

"You really should be hanged," she said. "You certainly had me fooled. You don't look like the sort to act so dastardly."

She tried to move away from the table but Caine's hands covered hers, trapping her. He leaned down again, until his mouth was just a scant kiss away. "I'm a pirate, madam. We're known to be dastardly."

He waited for another angry rebuttal. She burst into tears instead. Caine wasn't at all prepared for that emotional display.

While he reached for his handkerchief, Monk jumped to his feet and rushed over to comfort her. The barkeep awkwardly patted her on her shoulders. "There, there, miss, don't cry now."

"It's all his fault," she sobbed. "All I asked was a simple little favor. Just one quick task that wouldn't take him any time at all; but, no, he couldn't be bothered. I even offered to wait until he'd finished his refreshment," she continued with a wail. "I was willing to pay good coins too."

By the time she'd finished her pitiful tirade, Monk was glaring at Caine. "You've upset the pretty," he told the Marquess. "Why, you've broken her heart."

The tavernkeeper grabbed the handkerchief out of Caine's hand and began to awkwardly mop the tears away from her cheeks. "It will be all right, miss," he crooned.

"No, it won't," she argued. Her voice was muffled by the linen cloth Monk had shoved under her nose. "Do you know I've never asked anyone for anything in all my days? Yet the very first time I do ask, I'm denied my request. No one wants to make an honest living anymore. No, they'd rather steal than earn their way. It's a shame, isn't it, Monk?"

Caine was too incredulous to speak. He didn't know if he should take her into his arms and comfort her or grab her by the shoulders and shake some sense into her. One thing was certain, however. If Monk continued to frown at him, he was going to break his nose.

"Mi'lady, it really ain't honest work to take coins from a lady and kill her," Monk argued. He patted her shoulder in a bid to soften his gentle rebuke.

"Of course it's honest work," she replied. "As long as the lady wants the killing done."

Monk paused to rub his brow. "She's got a true point there, don't she?" he asked Caine.

"For the love of . . . now what are you doing?" Caine asked Jade when she began to collect her coins.

"I'm leaving," she announced. "I'm sorry I bothered you, Pagan, or Caine, or whatever your real name is," she whispered.

She tied the string into a knot, then tucked the bag in her pocket.

When she turned and started for the door, Caine called out. "Where do you think you're going?"

"That's none of your concern," she answered. "Still, I'm not half as insolent as you are and so I shall tell you I'm going to find someone more cooperative. Have no fear, sir. I won't give up. Before this black night is over, I'll find someone willing to kill me."

He caught her at the door. His hands settled on her shoulders and he slowly forced her around to look at him.

The minute he touched her, she started crying again. Caine was exasperated, unsettled too. He gave in to his overwhelming urge though, and roughly pulled her into his arms.

His bear hug seemed to be all the prodding she needed. She wept against his chest, whispering her apology for her unladylike behavior in between her loud sobs.

Caine was content to wait until she'd regained a bit of control. He couldn't possibly reason with her now. She was making so much noise she wouldn't have been able to hear a word he said anyway. And she kept blaming her current condition on him too. She was, without a doubt, the most confusing woman he'd ever encountered.

Lord, she was wonderfully soft. She fit him nicely too. He usually disliked women who cried, yet found he didn't want to let go of this one.

She was hiccupping just like a drunken peasant now, the aftermath of the quick storm.

It was high time he reasoned with her. "Jade, it can't possibly be as terrible as you now believe," he told her in a low, husky voice. "Surely, come morning, you'll be thankful I didn't give in to your request."

"I'll be dead come morning," she wailed.

"No, you won't," he replied. He gave her an affectionate squeeze. "I won't let anything happen to you. I promise. You can't really want to die just yet."

"My brother's bound to be disappointed if I die," she said.

"I would imagine so," he answered dryly.

"Still, I'm not strong enough to fight them. They're very mean-hearted men. I fear they'll use me before they kill me. I don't want to die that way. There's no dignity in it."

"Death with dignity?" he asked. "You speak like a soldier preparing for the battlefield."

"I don't want to be remembered as a coward."

"Will your brother be able to take care of your problem once he returns?"

"Oh, yes," she answered. She rested her cheek against his chest. "Nathan wouldn't let anything happen to me. Since our papa died, he's become my protector. My brother's a very strong man."

"Then I'll keep you safe until your brother returns. I give you my word."

A long, silent minute passed before she showed any reaction to that promise. Caine thought she might be too overcome with gratitude to speak. Then she moved away from him and looked up into his eyes. He realized she wasn't overcome at all. Hell, she looked downright irritated. "You've already broken your word to me, sir. You promised you'd kill me and then changed your mind."

"This is different," he argued.

"You really mean what you say?"

"Yes, I mean what I say," he answered. "You just explained that you'll be safe once your brother returns in two weeks. It is two weeks, isn't it?"

Her expression was solemn. "Perhaps even sooner. But you're a pirate. You cannot be taking such chances keeping me safe for two long weeks. There's a bounty on your head. I won't be responsible for getting you killed."

"You don't have much faith in my ability."

"I don't have *any* faith in your ability," she qualified. "Why should I? You've just admitted that the rumors about you aren't at all reliable. You probably don't even leave a white rose on your victim's pillow, do you?"

Caine was exasperated with her again. "You don't have to sound so damned disappointed in me."

"But I am disappointed!" she cried out. "You aren't even honorable. That's the real pity. Besides, you don't look at all strong enough to take on my enemies. You'd be an easy target, Caine. You're such a . . . big man. No, I'm sorry. I'm afraid you simply won't do."

He wanted to throttle her.

She turned her back on him again and tried to leave. Caine was so astonished by her attitude he almost let her get away. Almost. He caught her just as she reached the walkway outside the door.

His hold wouldn't allow her any freedom as his arm was anchored around her shoulders. He tucked her into his side with as much care as he'd give an old blanket, then turned to speak to Monk. "I don't want you telling anyone what happened here tonight. Give me your word, Monk."

"Why should he give you his word when you so freely break yours? A gentleman only asks as much as he can give in return, sir. Didn't your mama teach you any manners?" she asked.

"Ah, Jade," he said. "That's the rub." He looked down at her and slowly stroked the side of her cheek with his fingertips. "I'm not a gentleman. I'm a pirate, remember? There's a distinct difference."

She went completely still the second he touched her. Caine thought she looked quite stunned. He didn't know what to make of that odd reaction. When his hand dropped away, she came out of her stupor and shoved against him.

"Yes, there is a difference," she muttered. "Tell me this, Caine. If I make you angry enough, will you kill me in vexation?"

"The idea's beginning to have merit," he answered.

"Let go of me. You must never touch me."

"I mustn't?"

"No. I don't like to be touched."

"Then how in God's name was I suppose to kill you?"

She obviously hadn't realized he was jesting. "You were going to use a pistol," she told him. She paused to give him a suspicious look. "You do own one, don't you?"

"I do," he answered. "And where was I suppose to . . ."

"One clean shot, directly through my heart," she explained. "You'd have to be accurate, of course. I wouldn't want to linger."

"No," he agreed. "Lingering would definitely be out of the question."

"How can you find this amusing? We happen to be discussing my death!" she cried out.

"I'm not amused," he argued. "Fact is, I'm getting downright angry again. Tell me, do I get to ravage you first?"

She took a deep breath before answering. "You certainly do not."

"That's a pity," he replied, completely ignoring her outraged expression.

"Sir, do your parents happen to be first cousins? You're

acting like a complete simpleton. You're either an idiot or the most cold-hearted man I've ever met. I find your conduct disgraceful."

Her eyes were flashing with indignation. Caine had never seen such a dramatic shade of green before. It was as though the purity and the sparkle of a thousand emeralds had all been squeezed dry of their color and given to her.

"I'm not at all convinced you're in any real danger, Jade," he announced. "This could very well just be a product of your overactive imagination."

"I dislike you intensely," she whispered. "And as for your ignorant opinions, well I . . ."

"Jade, save the bluster for later. I'm not in the mood. Now, I don't want to hear another word about killing you. And if you continue to glare up at me so prettily, I swear I'm going to kiss you just to take your mind off your foolish worries."

"Kiss me?" She looked stunned. "Why in God's name would you want to kiss me?"

"I haven't the faintest idea," he admitted.

"You'd kiss someone you disliked?"

"I guess I would," he replied with a grin.

"You are arrogant, overbearing . . ."

"You're sputtering, my sweet."

She didn't have a quick comeback. Caine continued to stare down at her when he spoke to Monk again. "Well, Monk, do you give me your word?"

"I do. I won't be telling anyone about this night, Caine, but we both know your friend, Lyon, will surely find out before the sun sets again. He'll wring the truth out of me. I'm giving you warning ahead of time."

Caine nodded. The Marquess of Lyonwood was a good friend. Caine trusted him completely. The two had worked on several missions together for their government. "Yes, he will find out," he predicted. "But his new wife and son keep him occupied. Besides, when he learns what I'm up to, he'll keep it to himself. If he inquires, you may speak freely to him. No one else though, not even Rhone," Caine added, referring to Lyon's closest friend. "For all his merits, Rhone does talk too much."

Monk nodded. "I'm begging you, Caine, to let me know how it all ends up with the little lady."

"Monk?" Jade asked, drawing both men's attention. "You wouldn't happen to own a pistol, would you?"

She sounded too damned eager to him. Caine knew what she was thinking. His angel was as easy to read as a Latin text. "He doesn't and he won't," he announced.

"I don't and I won't what?" Monk asked.

"You don't own a pistol and you won't kill her," Caine answered in a clipped tone of voice.

"No, no, of course not," Monk agreed. "Caine, you aren't forgetting your trap, are you?" he asked, when he was finally able to pull his gaze away from the beautiful woman.

"No, I'm not forgetting," Caine answered. He turned to Jade and asked, "Is your carriage returning for you?"

Her exasperation was obvious. "I hired a hack," she told him. "I didn't think I'd be returning to my lodgings tonight." She pushed away from his hold and picked up the large gray satchel from the walkway. "All I own is in here. I came directly from the country," she added, almost as an afterthought.

"You left your possessions on the street for anyone to snatch?"

"It was my intention to have my things stolen," she answered. She sounded like a tutor instructing a deliberately obtuse student. "I was hoping my clothing could benefit some poor soul. I wasn't supposed to have further need once you . . ."

"Enough!" he nearly growled. "You aren't going to mention murder again. Have you got that?"

She didn't answer him quickly enough. Caine tugged on her hair. She let out a shrill cry just as he noticed the large swelling above her ear. "Good God, Jade, when did you get that?"

"Don't touch it," she demanded when he tried to prod the edges of the bump. "It still stings."

"I would think so," he said. His hand dropped back to his side. "Tell me what happened."

"I caught the heel of my boot on the carpet loop in my brother's house and tumbled down the stairs," she explained. "I hit the side of my head on the banister knob. It fairly knocked the wind out of my sails."

The wind out of her sails? Caine thought that was a rather odd remark to make, but he didn't take time to reflect upon it. "You could have killed yourself," he stated. "Are you always so awkward?"

"No, I'm never awkward," she countered. "I'm usually very ladylike. Lord, you're rude," she ended with a mutter.

"What happened after you fell?" Monk asked.

She shrugged. "I went for a walk to try to clear my head. Then they started in chasing after me, of course."

"Of course?" Monk asked.

"They?" Caine said at the very same time.

She paused to give both men a frown. "The men I saw kill the finely dressed gentleman," she explained. "For heaven's sake, do pay attention. I'm certain I mentioned that fact earlier."

Monk shook his head. "I'm just as certain you didn't, miss," he confessed. "I'm sure I would have remembered."

"You witnessed a murder? No, Jade, you sure as hell didn't mention that fact."

"Well, I meant to mention it," she muttered. She folded her arms across her chest and looked disgruntled again. "I would have explained it all to you if you hadn't turned my attention by arguing with me. So you see, this is your fault because I lost my train of thought. Yes, you're to blame."

"Did you witness the murder before or after you hit yourself in the head?" Caine asked.

"Do you suppose it was a titled gentleman she saw murdered?" Monk asked Caine.

"I did not hit myself," Jade snapped. "And it was before . . . no, it was after. At least I think it was after I fell down. Oh, I don't remember now. My head's pounding again. Do quit your questions, sir."

Caine turned back to the tavernkeeper. "Now I'm beginning to understand," he said. He looked at Jade again. "Were you wearing your cloak at the time of this mishap?"

"Yes," she answered. She looked perplexed. "But what does that . . ."

"You tore your cloak and bruised your face when you fell down, didn't you?"

His tone was a little too condescending for her liking. "Tell me exactly what it is you think you're beginning to understand."

"It's really very simple," he answered. "Your head suffered a trauma, Jade. You aren't thinking logically now, though I must admit that most women aren't ever logical. Still, with plenty of rest and care, in a few days you'll realize your mind was just playing tricks on you. You'll be worrying about what gown to wear to your next ball then."

"My mind isn't playing tricks on me," she cried out.

"You're confused."

"I am not confused!"

"Quit shouting," Caine ordered. "If you'll only think about what I'm . . ."

He gave up when she shook her head at him. "You're too addled to be reasoned with now. We'll wait until you're feeling better."

"He's right, miss," Monk whispered. "If you'd seen a titled gentleman murdered, the news would have hit this section of town right off. The men who'd done the deed would have boasted of their cunning. Listen to Caine now. He knows what's best."

"But if you believe I'm just imagining I'm in danger, then you don't need to protect me, do you?"

"Oh, yes, I do," he replied. "Only now I know who I'm protecting you against."

Before she could ask another question, he continued. "Like it or not, you're a menace until you've recovered. In all good conscience, I can't leave you on your own." His smile was gentle when he added, "I guess you could say I'm protecting you from yourself, Jade. Now give me your satchel. I'll carry it for you."

She tried to lift the bag before Caine could and ended up in a tug of war. Caine won. "What in God's name do you have in here?" he asked. "This thing weighs more than you do."

"Everything I own," she answered. "If it's too much for you, I'll be happy to carry it."

Caine shook his head. He took hold of her hand. "Come along. My carriage is waiting two blocks over. You should be home in bed."

She drew to an abrupt stop. "Whose bed, Caine?"

His sigh was loud enough to wake the drunks littering the alleys. "Your very own bed," he snapped. "Your virtue's safe. I never take virgins to my bed and I sure as certain don't want you."

He thought she would be relieved by his vehement promise not to bother her. It was only a half lie, of course. He did want to kiss her, yet he wasn't sure if it was merely out of the need to have a few minutes of blissful silence.

"Is that a little rule of yours?" she asked. "Not to bed a virgin?"

She looked highly insulted. Caine didn't know what to make of that reaction. "It is," he answered. "I also don't bed daft women I don't particularly like, sweet, so you're safe enough with me."

He dared to grin at her when he made those shameful

remarks. "I do believe I'm beginning to hate you," she muttered. "Well, you're bloody safe with me, too, Caine. I would never let you touch me, either."

"Good."

"Yes, good," she replied, determined to have the last word. "If you don't quit dragging me, I'm going to scream your name over and over again until the authorities come and take you away, Pagan."

"I'm not Pagan."

"What?"

She almost fell down. Caine grabbed her. "I said, I'm not Pagan."

"Just who in thunder are you then?"

They'd reached his carriage but she refused to let him assist her inside until he'd answered her question. She kept slapping his hands away.

Caine gave in. He tossed her satchel up to the driver, then turned back to her. "My name really is Caine. I'm the Marquess of Cainewood. Now will you get inside? This is neither the time nor the place for a lengthy discussion. When we're on our way, I'll explain everything to you."

"You promise?"

"I promise," he answered with a low growl.

She didn't look like she believed him. Jade folded her arms across her chest. "Shame on you, Caine. You've been pretending to be the noble pirate all this time . . ."

"That bastard's a lot of things, Jade, but he sure as hell isn't noble."

"How can you know if you speak truth or fancy?" she demanded. "I'll wager you never even met the man. Is your own life so unhappy that you must pretend to . . ."

The look on his face turned as stinging as his hard grip on her arm, interrupting her speech. While she watched, he tore the flower from his lapel and tossed it on the ground. He wasn't at all gentle when he half lifted, half tossed Jade inside the vehicle.

Once the carriage started moving, the interior was thrown into darkness. She couldn't see his scowl and was most relieved.

He couldn't see her smile either.

They rode in silence a short while. Jade used the time to regain her composure. Caine used the time to calm his frustration.

"Why were you pretending to be Pagan?"

"To hunt him down," Caine answered.

"But why?"

"Later," he snapped. "I'll tell you all about it later, all right?"

He was sure his hard tone of voice would discourage her from asking any more questions. He was mistaken.

"You're angry because I made you quit your hunt, aren't you?"

His sigh indicated his impatience. "You didn't make me quit my hunt. I might have failed thus far, but when we've taken care of your problem, I'll go back to my hunt. Don't worry, Jade. I won't fail."

She wasn't at all worried, but she couldn't very well tell him that. Caine hadn't failed at all. No, he'd gone into the tavern to draw Pagan out.

And that's exactly what he'd done.

She'd done her task well. Her brother was going to be pleased.

Chapter Three

T he tears had been a nice touch. Jade had been almost as surprised as Caine appeared to be by the spontaneous show of emotion. It hadn't been in her plans to use such a weak ploy to get him out of the tavern. Yet once she saw how upsetting it was for him to see a woman in such a pathetic condition, she'd cried all the more, of course. Caine had looked so helpless. Jade had no idea she had such a talent. Wailing on command took concentration, however, but she quickly adapted herself to the problem, and thought she'd conquered it rather quickly, too. Why, she could probably burst into a full fit of tears before a gentleman could drop his hat if she really put her mind to it.

She didn't feel at all ashamed of her conduct. Desperate times always called for desperate measures. At least that's what Black Harry liked to say. Her adopted uncle would have a good laugh too. In all their years together, he had never seen her cry, not even when his enemy, McKindry, had used a whip on her back. The lash had hurt like fire, but she hadn't let out a single whimper. McKindry only got in one good lash before Harry tossed him over the side. Her uncle had been in such a spitting rage, he'd jumped overboard to finish the bloke. McKindry was a much stronger swimmer, however, and was last seen backstroking his way to France.

Of course, Black Harry would be in another good rage if he knew what she was up to now. He'd have her hide, he would. Yet it hadn't been possible to explain her plan to him. No, there simply hadn't been enough time to sail all the way to their island to inform him of her decision. And time was of the essence. Caine's life was at stake.

Jade knew all about the Marquess of Cainewood. He was a bit of a contradiction, too. Caine was an earthy, downright lusty man, but he was also honorable. She'd read his file through from start to finish, and every bit of it was memorized in her mind. She had the uncanny knack for recording everything in her mind the first time she read it. Although she thought that was a rather odd ability, she had to admit that the gift had certainly come in handy upon occasion.

Obtaining Caine's impressive record from the War Department had been tricky, but not impossible. The information had of course been sealed and locked away. It was a point of pride with Jade that she could undo any lock ever fashioned. She'd succeeded in getting Caine's file on her third attempt.

It was a shame that none of the information in his records mentioned the disturbing fact that he was such a handsome devil. The term "ruthless" had been sprinkled liberally throughout each account of his activities, yet never was "compelling" or "appealing" put to his name. The file didn't mention what a big man he was either.

Jade remembered how uneasy she'd felt when she read his operative name. He was called Hunter by his superiors. After reading the file in full, she understood why he'd been given that name. Caine never gave up. In one incident, when the odds had been overwhelmingly against him, he continued to stalk his adversary with the patience and the tenacity of an ancient warrior. And in the end, he had succeeded.

Caine had quit his duties the day he'd been informed of the death of his brother Colin. According to the last entry made by his senior advisor, a man by the name of Sir Michael Richards, the resignation had Caine's father's full support. The Duke of Williamshire had just lost one son to his country and wasn't about to lose another. It was also noted by Richards that until that day, Caine had had no idea his younger brother also worked for the government.

Both Colin and Caine came from a large family. Caine was their eldest child. In all there were six children: two sons and four daughters.

The children were all very protective of each other and of their parents. The one fact that kept repeating itself in his file was that Caine was a protector by nature. Whether he considered that fact a flaw or a virtue wasn't significant to Jade. She simply used it to get what she wanted.

She'd been prepared to like Caine, of course. He was Colin's brother, after all, and she was very fond of Colin, since the moment she'd fished him out of the ocean and he told her to save her own brother first. Yes, she'd been prepared to like Caine, but she hadn't been at all prepared to find herself so physically drawn to him. It was a first for her, a worry too, for she knew he could overwhelm her if she gave him the opportunity.

She protected herself by pretending to be everything she thought he disliked. When she wasn't crying like an infant, she tried to remember to complain. Most men hated ill-disciplined women, didn't they? Jade certainly hoped so. She would be forced by circumstances to stay by Caine's side for the next two weeks, and then it would be over. She'd return to her way of life and he'd probably return to his womanizing.

It was imperative for him to think he was protecting her. It was the only way she could keep him safe. His views on the inferiority of women, no doubt enhanced by four little sisters, made her plan much easier. Yet Caine was also a very perceptive man. His past training had polished his predatory instincts. For that reason, Jade had ordered her men to wait for her at Caine's country home. They were going to hide in the woods that surrounded his house. When she arrived, they would take over the task of watching Caine's backside.

The letters were at the heart of this treachery, of course, and she wished to God she'd never found the things now. What was done was done, she reminded herself. It certainly wouldn't do her any good to have regrets. It would be wasted effort and Jade never, ever wasted anything. It was all very clear-cut to her. When she'd shown her brother, Nathan, their father's letters, she'd started this mess, and she would now be the one to mop it up.

Jade forced her worries aside. She'd inadvertently just given Caine quite a little time to think. Silence, she decided, could very well be her enemy now. She had to keep Caine off guard . . . and occupied. "Caine? What do you . . ."

"Hush, sweet," Caine ordered. "Do you hear . . ."

"That odd squeak? I was just about to mention it," she replied.

"It's more like a persistent grinding noise . . . Miller," Caine shouted out the window. "Stop the carriage."

The vehicle came to an abrupt stop just as the left rear wheel snapped. Jade would have been tossed to the floor if Caine hadn't caught her in his arms. He held her tightly for a long minute, then whispered. "Damned bad timing, wouldn't you say?"

"I'd say it's probably trickery," she whispered.

31

Caine didn't comment on that remark. "Stay inside, Jade, while I see what can be done."

"Do be careful," she cautioned. "They could be waiting for you."

She heard his sigh when he opened the door. "I'll be careful," he promised.

As soon as he'd shut the door behind him, Jade opened it and climbed out. The driver came to stand beside his employer. "I can't fathom it, mi'lord. I'm always checking the wheels to make certain they're sound."

"I'm not faulting you, Miller," Caine returned. "We're far enough on the side of the street to leave it here for the night. Unleash the horse, Miller. I'll . . ."

Caine stopped when he noticed Jade. She was clutching a wicked-looking dagger in her hand. He almost laughed. "Put that away, Jade. You'll hurt yourself."

She slipped the knife back into the seam pocket of her gown. "We're fair targets, Caine, standing out here for anyone to grab."

"Then get back inside," he suggested.

She pretended she hadn't heard him. "Miller? Was the wheel tampered with, do you suppose?"

The driver squatted down next to the axle. "I'd say it was," he whispered. "Mi'lord, it was tampered with! Have a look here, at the cuts made in the side bar."

"What are we going to do now?" Jade asked Caine.

"We'll ride the horse," he announced.

"But what about poor Miller? They might do him in when we leave."

"I'll be all right, miss," the driver interjected. "I got me a big flask of brandy to keep me warm. I'll sit inside the carriage until Broley comes to fetch me."

"Who is Broley?" Jade asked.

"One of the tigers," Miller returned.

Jade didn't know what he was talking about. "You have a friend who is an animal?"

Caine did smile then. "Broley works for me," he explained. "I'll explain it all to you later."

"We should just hire a hack," she announced then. She folded her arms across her chest. "Then we could all ride together and I wouldn't have to worry about Miller."

"At this time of night? It's doubtful we'd find a hack."

"What about Monk's lovely tavern?" she asked. "Couldn't we go back there and wait until light?"

"No," Caine answered. "Monk has certainly locked up and gone home by now."

"We're a fair distance away from the Ne'er Do Well now, mi'lady," Miller interjected.

When the driver moved to unstrap the horse, Jade grabbed hold of Caine's hand and moved closer to his side. "Caine?" she whispered.

"Yes?"

"I think I know what happened to your fine carriage wheel. It was probably the very same men who . . ."

"Hush now," he whispered back. "It's going to be all right."

"How can you know it's going to be all right?"

She sounded so frightened. Caine wanted to comfort her. "My instincts," he boasted. "Sweet, don't let your imagination get out of hand. It's . . ."

"Too late," she countered. "Oh, Lord, my imagination's at it again."

The pistol shot rang out just as she threw herself into his side, knocking him off balance.

The shot flew past the side of his head, narrowly missing him. He could hear the whistle in his ear. Though he was certain it wasn't intentional, Jade had actually just saved his life.

Caine tightened his hold on Jade's hand, shouted a warning to Miller as he pushed her in front of him, and then started running. He forced her to stay directly in front of him so he could shield her with his broad back.

Several more pistol shots rang out. Jade could hear the thundering of men chasing them. It sounded like a herd of wild horses were about to trample them down.

Jade soon lost all track of where they were. Caine seemed to know his way around the area well enough. He pulled her through a maze of alleys and back streets, until she had a horrid stitch in her side and couldn't catch her breath. When she stumbled against him, he lifted her into his arms without breaking his stride.

He continued the grueling pace long after the sounds of pursuit had stopped. When they reached the center of the old bridge spanning the Thames, he finally paused to rest.

Caine leaned against the rickety railing, holding her close against him. "That was close. Damn, my instincts were off tonight. I never saw it coming."

He hadn't sounded a bit winded when he made that remark. She was amazed by his stamina. Why, her heart was still pounding from the exertion. "Do you do quite a lot of running through alleys, Caine?" she asked.

He thought that was an odd question. "No, why do you ask?"

"You aren't at all out of breath," she answered. "And we never once ran into a dead end," she added. "You do know your way around the city, don't you?"

"I guess I do," he answered with a shrug that almost sent her flying over the railing. She threw her arms around his neck and held on. Then she realized he was still holding her in his arms.

"You may put me down now," she announced. "I'm certain we lost them."

"I'm not," Caine drawled out.

"I've already explained that I don't like being touched, sir. Put me down." She paused to give him a hard look, then asked, "You aren't going to blame me for your instincts failing you, are you?"

"No, I'm not going to blame you. Jade, you ask the damnedest questions."

"I'm not in the mood to argue with you. Just apologize and I shall forgive you."

"Apologize?" He sounded incredulous. "What for?"

"For thinking I have an overactive imagination," she explained. "For telling me I'm confused, and most of all, for being terribly rude when you said those insulting things to me."

He didn't apologize, but he did smile at her. She noticed the wonderful dimple in the side of his left cheek then. Her heart took notice and started pounding in a wild beat again.

"We're standing on a bridge in the middle of London's most disreputable section with a band of cutthroats chasing us, and all you can think about is gaining my apology? You, sweet, really are mad."

"I always remember to apologize when I've done something wrong," she remarked.

He looked downright exasperated with her now. She couldn't help but smile at him. Lord, he was a handsome rascal. The moonlight softened his harsh features, and she barely minded his frown now.

In truth, she wanted him to smile at her again.

"Jade? Can you swim?"

She was staring intently at his mouth, thinking to herself that he had the most beautiful white teeth she'd ever seen.

He shook her. "Can you swim?" he asked. There was a little more urgency in his tone now.

"Yes," she answered with an unladylike yawn. "I can swim. Why do you ask?"

In answer to that question, he tossed her over his right shoulder and started climbing the rail.

Her long hair brushed the back of his boots. The wind was knocked out of her when he slammed her against his shoulder, but she soon recovered. "What in bloody hell are you doing?" she cried out. She clutched the back of his jacket. "Put me down."

"They've got the exits blocked, Jade. Take a deep breath, sweet. I'll be right behind you."

She only had enough time to shout her denial at him. Then she let out a bellow of outrage. The sound echoed off into the inky blackness when he threw her away from the railing.

She was suddenly flying like a disc into the biting wind. Jade kept right on screaming until her backside hit the water. She remembered to close her mouth just as the frigid water closed over her head. She came up sputtering, but immediately closed her mouth again when she got a good whiff of the stench surrounding her.

Jade vowed she wouldn't let herself drown in this filth. No, she was going to stay alive until she found her new protector and drowned him first.

Then she felt something brush against her leg. She became absolutely terrified. In her confused mind, she was certain the sharks had come for her.

Caine suddenly appeared at her side. He wrapped his arm around her waist, then let the swift current drag them under the bridge and away from the enemy stalking them.

She kept trying to climb up on his shoulders. "Hold still," he ordered.

Jade wrapped her arms around his neck. "The sharks, Caine," she whispered. "They're going to get us."

The terror in her voice and her grip told him she was close to losing all control. "There aren't any sharks," he told her. "Nothing could live in this water long enough."

"You're certain?"

"I'm certain," he returned. "Just hold on a little longer, sweet. We'll be out of this muck in no time at all."

His soothing voice did calm her a little. She was still trying to strangle him, but her grip had lessened. It was only a halfhearted attempt now.

They floated at least a good mile down the winding river before he finally pulled her out of the water and onto the grassy slope. Jade was too cold, too miserable, to blister him with her opinion of his conduct.

She couldn't even get in a decent whimper. Her teeth were chattering too much. "I smell like dead fish," she stammered out in a pitiful wail.

"Yes, you do," Caine agreed. He sounded amused.

"So do you, you . . . pretender."

"Pretender?" he repeated while he tore his jacket off and tossed it on the ground behind him. "What do you mean by that?"

Jade was trying to wring the water out of the hem of her gown. Her hair covered most of her face. She paused to toss the clumps out of her vision. "You needn't act so innocent with me," she muttered.

She gave up her task and accepted the pitiful fact that her gown now outweighed her, then wrapped her arms around her waist and tried to hug some warmth back into her bones. Her voice took on her shivers when she added, "Pretending to be the pirate, Pagan. He would never throw a gentle lady in the Thames."

"Jade, I did what I thought was best under the circumstances," he defended.

"I lost my cloak." That announcement came out in a loud gasp.

"I'll buy you another one."

"But my silver coins were in that cloak," she said. "Well?"

"Well, what?"

"Go fetch it."

"What?"

"Go fetch it," she ordered again. "I'll wait here."

"You can't be serious."

"I'm perfectly serious," she countered. "We only drift-ed a mile or so, Caine. It shouldn't take you any time at all."

"No."

"Please?"

"I'd never find it," he returned. "It's probably at the bottom of the river by now."

She mopped at the corners of her eyes with the backs of her hands. "Now I'm a pauper and it's all your fault."

"Don't start," he commanded. He knew she was on the verge of tears again. "Now isn't the time for hys-terics or complaints, even though they seem to be the only two things you're any good at," he continued. He caught her gasp and smiled. She was getting her temper back. "Do you still have your shoes on or do I have to carry you?"

"How would I know?" she asked. "I've lost all the feeling in my feet."

"Look, damn it."

"Yes, damn it," she muttered when she'd done as he ordered. "I'm still wearing them. Well?" she added. "Are you going to apologize or not?"

"No," he answered in a clipped voice. "I'm not going to apologize. And lower your voice, Jade. Do you want every cutthroat in London after us?"

"No," she whispered. She moved close to his side. "Caine? What would you have done if I didn't know how to swim?"

"The same thing," he answered. "But we would have jumped together."

"I didn't jump," she argued. "Oh, never mind. I'm cold, Caine. What are we going to do now?"

He took hold of her hand and started up the bank. "We're

going to walk over to my friend's town house. It's closer than mine."

"Caine, you're forgetting your jacket," she reminded him.

Before he could tell her to leave it, she rushed back, lifted the jacket, rung as much of the water out of it as she could manage with her numb fingers, and then hurried back to his side. She tossed the hair out of her eyes again, just as he put his arm around her shoulders. "I look terrible, don't I?"

"You smell worse," he told her quite cheerfully.

He gave her an affectionate squeeze, then remarked, "I'd say it's more like rotten meat than dead fish though."

She started to gag. Caine slapped his hand over her mouth. "If you lose your supper, I'll become very angry with you. I have enough to contend with now. Don't you dare complicate matters by getting sick."

She bit his hand, gaining both her freedom and another blasphemy from him. "I didn't have any supper," she announced. "I wanted to die on an empty stomach."

"You still might," he muttered. "Now quit talking and let me think. Why the hell did you want to die on an empty stomach?" he couldn't help but ask.

"Some people become ill when they're frightened. I thought I might, you see, right before you . . . oh, never mind. I just didn't want to go to my Maker in a messy gown, that's all."

"I knew I shouldn't have asked," he replied. "Look, when we get to Lyon's place, you can have a hot bath. You'll feel better then."

"Is Lyon the interfering friend Monk mentioned?"

"Lyon isn't interfering."

"Monk said he'd find out what happened to you this black night," Jade replied. "Those were his very words. That certainly sounds interfering to me."

"You'll like Lyon."

39

"If he's your friend, I have my doubts," she returned. "Still, I will try to like him."

They lapsed into silence for several blocks. Caine was on his guard now and Jade wasn't nearly as worried as she pretended to be.

"Caine? After we've had our baths, what will we do?"

"You're going to sit down and tell me everything that happened to you."

"I've already told you what happened to me. You didn't believe me though, did you?"

"No," he admitted. "I didn't."

"Besides, your mind is already set against me, Caine. You won't believe anything else I tell you. Why should I make the effort?"

"My mind isn't set against you," he answered. His irritation was obvious in his tone.

She let out a rather inelegant snort. Caine vowed he wouldn't let her draw him into another argument. He led her through another maze of back streets. She was so exhausted by the time they'd reached the steps to the impressive, redbrick town house, she wanted to weep real tears.

A giant of a man with a rather sinister-looking scar creasing his forehead opened the door on Caine's insistent pounding. The man had obviously been asleep. He wasn't happy about being awakened, either. Jade took one look at the stranger's dark scowl, and edged closer to Caine.

The man she assumed was Lyon wore only a pair of black britches. The frightening scowl quickly turned to a look of true astonishment as soon as he saw who his visitor was. "Caine? What in God's name . . . come inside," he rushed out. He moved forward with the intent of clasping Caine's hand, then abruptly changed his mind. He'd obviously just gotten a good whiff of the two of them.

Jade was horribly embarrassed. She turned to glare at Caine, a silent message that she still believed her foul condition was all his fault, then walked into the black and white tiled foyer. She saw a beautiful woman hurrying down the winding staircase then. The woman's long, silvery blond hair flew out behind her. She was so lovely, Jade felt all the worse.

Caine made hasty introductions while Jade stared at the floor. "This is Lyon, Jade, and his wife, Christina."

"What happened to you two?" Lyon asked.

Jade whirled around, raining drops of sour water in a wide circle. She lifted her hair out of her eyes and then announced, "He threw me in the Thames."

"He what?" Lyon asked, a hint of a smile in his expression now, for he'd only just noticed what looked very like a chicken bone dangling from her hair.

"Caine threw me in the Thames," she repeated.

"He did?" Christina asked. Lyon's wife sounded astonished.

Jade turned to her. "He truly did," she announced yet again. "He didn't apologize afterward either."

After making that remark, she burst into tears. "This is all his fault," she sobbed. "First he lost his carriage wheel and then he lost his instincts. My plan was really so much better. He's just too stubborn to admit it."

"Don't start on that again," Caine warned.

"Why did you throw this poor dear in the Thames?" Christina asked again. She hurried over to Jade, her arms outstretched. "You must be chilled to the bone," she said in sympathy. Christina came to a quick stop when she got close to Jade, then backed up a space.

"It was necessary," Caine answered. He was trying to ignore Jade's glare.

"I believe I hate him," Jade told Christina. "I don't care if he's your friend or not," she added on another sob. "The man's a scoundrel."

"Yes, he can be a scoundrel," Christina agreed. "But he does have other nice qualities."

"I've yet to see them," Jade whispered.

Christina wrinkled her nose, took a deep breath, and then put her arm around Jade's waist. "Come with me, Jade. We'll have you cleaned up in no time. I think the kitchen will serve us better this night. Lyon? You best wake up the staff. We'll need help heating the water. My, you do have an unusual name," she told Jade then. "It's very pretty."

"He ridiculed my name," Jade whispered, though loud enough for Caine to overhear.

Caine closed his eyes in vexation. "I did not ridicule your name!" he shouted. "I swear to God, Lyon, that woman's done nothing but complain and weep since the moment I met her."

Jade let out a loud gasp, then allowed Christina to prod her along toward the back of the house. Both Caine and Lyon watched the pair depart.

"Do you see how insulting he is, Lady Christina?" Jade asked. "All I asked was one little favor from the man."

"And he refused?" Christina asked. "That certainly doesn't sound like Caine. He's usually very accommodating."

"I even offered to pay him silver coins," Jade announced. "I'm a pauper now. Caine threw my cloak in the Thames, too. The coins were in the pocket."

Christina shook her head. She paused at the corner to look back at Caine so he could see her displeasure. "That was terribly ungallant of him, wasn't it?"

They rounded the corner on Jade's fervent agreement.

"What was the favor she asked of you?" Lyon asked.

"Nothing much," Caine drawled out. He bent over to pull off his water-soaked boots. "She just wanted me to kill her, that's all."

Lyon let out a shout of laughter, but stopped when he realized Caine wasn't jesting.

"She wanted it done before morning," Caine said.

"She didn't."

"She was willing to let me finish my brandy first."

"That was thoughtful of her."

The two men shared a grin. "Now your wife thinks I'm an ogre because I've disappointed the woman."

Lyon laughed again. "Christina doesn't know what the favor was, friend."

Caine dropped his boots in the center of the hall, then added his socks to the pile. "I could still change my mind and accommodate the little woman, I suppose," he remarked dryly. "Damn, my favorite boots are ruined."

Lyon leaned against the archway, his arms folded across his chest, while he watched Caine pull off his shirt. "No, you couldn't kill her," he replied. His tone was mild when he added, "She wasn't really serious, was she? She seems quite timid. I can't imagine . . ."

"She witnessed a murder," Caine interjected. "Now she has several unsavory men chasing after her, obviously intent on silencing her. That's all I know, Lyon, but as soon as possible, I'm going to find out every detail. The sooner I can solve her problem, the sooner I'll be rid of her."

Since Caine was glaring so ferociously, Lyon tried to hide his smile. "She really has you rattled, doesn't she?" he asked.

"The hell she does," Caine muttered. "Why would you think a mere woman could get me rattled?"

"You just took your britches off in the middle of my foyer, Caine," he replied. "That's why I think you're rattled."

"I need some brandy," Caine countered. He grabbed his pants and started to put them back on again.

Christina strolled past him, smiled at her husband, and then continued on up the stairs. She didn't mention his near naked condition, and neither did he.

Lyon thoroughly enjoyed Caine's embarrassment. He'd never seen his friend in such a state. "Why don't you go inside the library. The brandy's on the side bar. Help yourself and I'll see about your bath. God, you do smell rank."

Caine did as Lyon suggested. The brandy warmed him a little and the fire he started in the hearth took the rest of his chills away.

Christina left Jade alone once the tub had been filled with steaming hot water. She'd already helped her wash her hair in the bucket of warm, rose-scented water.

Jade quickly stripped out of her soggy clothing. Her fingers were numb from cold, but she took the time to remove her dagger from the hidden pocket in the lining. She put the weapon on the chair beside the tub as a precautionary measure in case someone tried to sneak up behind her, then climbed into the hot water and let out a long sigh of pleasure.

She scrubbed every inch of her body twice before she felt clean again. Christina came back into the kitchen just as Jade was standing up. Since her back was to her, Christina immediately noticed the long, jagged scar along the base of her spine. She let out a gasp of surprise.

Jade grabbed the blanket from the back of the chair, wrapped it around herself, and then stepped out of the tub to face Christina. "Is something the matter?" she asked, daring her to mention the scar she knew she'd seen.

Christina shook her head. She saw the knife on the chair then and walked over to have a closer look at it. Jade could feel herself blush with embarrassment. She tried to think of a logical explanation to give her hostess as to why a gentle lady would be carrying such a weapon, but she was simply too weary to come up with a believable lie.

"Mine's much sharper."

"I beg your pardon?" Jade asked, certain she hadn't heard correctly.

"My blade is much sharper," Christina explained. "I use a special stone. Shall I fix yours for you?"

Jade nodded.

"Do you sleep with this by your side or under your pillow?" Christina asked very matter-of-factly.

"Under my pillow."

"So did I," Christina said. "It's much easier to grasp that way, isn't it?"

"Yes, but why did you . . ."

"I'll take your knife upstairs and put it under your pillow," Christina promised. "And in the morning, I'll sharpen it for you."

"That's very kind of you," Jade whispered. "I didn't realize other ladies carried knives."

"Most don't," Christina replied with a dainty shrug. She handed Jade a pristine white nightgown and matching wrapper, then helped her dress. "I don't sleep with a dagger under my pillow any longer. Lyon protects me. In time, I think you'll give up your dagger, too. Yes, I do believe you will."

"You do?" Jade asked. She was desperately trying to make sense out of the woman's remarks. "Why is that?"

"Destiny," Christina whispered. "Of course, you'll have to learn to trust Caine first."

"Impossible," Jade blurted out. "I don't trust anyone."

From Christina's wide-eyed expression, Jade assumed she'd been too vehement in her reply. "Lady Christina, I'm not at all certain I know what you're talking about. I barely know Caine. Why would I have to learn to trust him?"

"Please, you needn't call me Lady Christina," she countered. "Now come and sit by the fire while I brush the crinkles out of your hair."

She dragged the chair across the room, then gently pushed Jade down into the seat. "I don't have many friends in England."

"You don't?"

"It's my fault," Christina explained. "I don't have enough patience. The ladies are very pretentious here. You're different, though."

"How can you know that?" Jade asked.

"Because you carry a knife," Christina explained. "Will you be my friend?"

Jade hesitated a long minute before answering. "For as long as you wish me to be your friend, Christina," she whispered.

Christina stared down at the lovely woman. "You believe that once I know all about you, I'll change my inclination, don't you?"

Her new friend shrugged. Christina noticed her hands were tightly clenched in her lap.

"I haven't had time for friends," Jade blurted out.

"I noticed the scar on your back," Christina whispered. "I won't tell Caine about it, of course, but he'll notice when he takes you to his bed. You carry a mark of honor, Jade."

Jade would have bounded out of the chair if Christina hadn't grabbed her shoulders and held her down. "I meant no insult," she rushed out. "You shouldn't be ashamed of . . ."

"Caine isn't going to take me to his bed," Jade countered. "Christina, I don't even like the man."

Christina smiled. "We are friends now, aren't we?"

"Yes."

"Then you cannot lie to me. You do like Caine. I could see it in your eyes when you looked at him. Oh, you were frowning, but it was all bluster, wasn't it? At least admit that you think he's handsome. All the ladies find him very appealing."

"He is that," Jade answered with a sigh. "He's a womanizer, isn't he?"

"Lyon and I have never seen him with the same woman twice," Christina admitted. "So I do suppose you could call him a womanizer. Aren't most until they're ready to settle down?"

"I don't know," Jade replied. "I haven't had many men friends either. There just wasn't time."

Christina finally picked up the brush and began to give order to Jade's lustrous curls. "I've never seen such beautiful hair before. There are threads of red fire shining through it."

"Oh, you have beautiful hair, not me," Jade protested. "Men have a preference for golden-haired ladies, Christina."

"Destiny," Christina countered, completely changing the topic. "I have a feeling you've just met yours, Jade."

She didn't have the heart to argue with her. Christina sounded so sincere. "If you say so," she agreed.

Christina noticed the swelling on the side of her head then. Jade explained what had happened to her. She felt guilty because she was deceiving the woman, for she was telling the same lie she'd told Caine earlier, but her motives were pure, she reminded herself. The truth would only upset her new friend.

"You've had to be a warrior, haven't you, Jade?" Christina asked, her voice filled with sympathy.

"A what?"

"A warrior," Christina repeated. She was trying to braid Jade's hair, then decided it was still too damp. She put the brush down and waited for her friend to answer.

"You've been alone in this world for a long time, haven't you?" Christina asked. "That's why you don't trust anyone."

Jade lifted her shoulders in a shrug. "Perhaps," she whispered.

"We should go and find our men now."

"Lyon is your man, but Caine isn't mine," Jade protested. "I'd rather just go to bed, if you please."

Christina shook her head. "Caine will have had his bath by now and must feel refreshed again. I know both men will want to ask you some questions before they let you rest. Men can be very stubborn, Jade. It's better to let them have their way every now and again. They're so much easier to manage that way. Do trust me. I know what I'm talking about."

Jade tightened her sash on her wrapper and followed Christina. She tried to clear her mind for the inevitable sparring ahead of her. As soon as she walked into the library, she saw Caine. He was leaning against the edge of Lyon's desk, frowning at her. She frowned back.

She really wished he wasn't so handsome. He had bathed and was now dressed in clothes Lyon had given him. The fit was true, the fawn-colored britches indecently snug. A white cotton shirt covered his wide shoulders.

Jade sat down in the center of the gold-colored settee. Christina handed her a full goblet of brandy. "Drink this," she ordered. "It will warm your insides."

Jade took a few dainty sips until she became accustomed to the burning sensation, then emptied the glass.

Christina nodded with satisfaction. Jade felt immensely better, sleepy, too. She leaned back against the cushions and closed her eyes.

"Don't you dare fall asleep," Caine ordered. "I have some questions to put to you."

She didn't bother to open her eyes when she answered him. "I won't fall asleep, but when I keep my eyes closed, I don't have to see your mean frowns, Caine. It's much more peaceful this way. Why were you pretending to be Pagan?"

She'd slipped in that question so smoothly, no one reacted for a full minute.

"He was what?" Lyon finally asked.

"He was pretending to be Pagan," Jade repeated. "I don't know how many other famous people he's pretended to be in the past," she added with a nod. "Still, it seems to me that your friend has an affliction of sorts."

Caine looked as if he wanted to throttle her. Christina held her smile. "Lyon? I don't believe I've ever seen our friend this upset."

"Neither have I," Lyon returned.

Caine successfully glared him into quitting his comments. "This isn't a usual circumstance," he muttered.

"I doubt he's ever pretended to be Napoleon though," Jade interjected. "He's too tall to pull it off. Besides, everyone knows what Napoleon looks like."

"Enough," Caine bellowed. He took a deep breath, then continued in a softer tone. "I'll explain why I was pretending to be Pagan after you've told me everything that led up to this black night."

"You make it sound as though everything is my fault!" she cried out.

He closed his eyes. "I do not fault you."

"Oh, yes, you do," she argued. "You're the most exasperating man. I've been through a terrible time and you've shown me as much compassion as a jackal."

Caine had to count to ten before he could trust himself not to shout at her.

"Why don't you just start at the beginning?" Lyon suggested.

Jade didn't pay any attention to Lyon's request. Her full attention was centered on Caine. He was still a little too controlled for her liking. "If you don't start giving me a little sympathy and understanding, I'm going to start shouting."

"You're already shouting," he told her with a grin.

That statement gave her pause. She took a deep breath, then decided to take a different tack. "Those terrible men ruined everything," she announced. "My brother had just finished renovating his lovely home and they ruined it. I cannot tell you how disappointed Nathan is going to be when he finds out. Oh, quit staring at me like that, Caine. I don't care if you believe me or not."

"Now, Jade . . ."

"Don't talk to me."

"You seem to have lost control of the conversation," Lyon pointed out to Caine.

"I was never in control," Caine answered. "Jade, we're

going to have to talk to each other," he announced then. "Yes," he added when he thought she was about to interrupt. "You have been through a trying time. I'll give you that much."

He thought his tone had been filled with understanding. He wanted to appease her, yet knew he'd failed when she continued to frown at him. "You're the most galling man. Why do you have to sound so superior all the time?"

Caine turned to Lyon. "Did I sound superior?"

Lyon shrugged. Christina nodded. "If Jade thinks you sounded superior," she said. "Then perhaps you did, just a little."

"You treat me like an imbecile," Jade said. "Doesn't he, Christina?"

"Since you are my friend, I will of course agree with you," Christina answered.

"Thank you," Jade replied before turning her attention back to Caine. "I'm not a child."

"I've noticed."

His slow grin infuriated her. She could feel herself losing ground in her bid to keep him off balance. "Do you know what the very worst of it was? They actually torched my brother's beautiful carriage. Yes, they did," she added with a vehement nod.

"And that was the worst?" Caine asked.

"Sir, I happened to be inside at the time!" she cried out.

He shook his head. "You actually want me to believe you were inside the carriage when it caught fire?"

"Caught fire?" She bounded out of her seat and stood there with her hands on her hips, glaring at him. "Not bloody likely. It was torched."

She remembered her audience and whirled around to face them. Clutching the top of her wrapper against her neck, she lowered her head and said, "Pray forgive me for losing my temper, please. I don't usually sound like a shrew."

She resumed her seat then and closed her eyes. "I don't

care what he believes. I can't talk about this tonight. I'm too distraught. Caine, you're going to have to wait until morning to question me."

He gave up. The woman was certainly given to drama. She put the back of her hand up against her forehead and let out a forlorn sigh. He knew he wasn't going to be able to reason with her now.

Caine sat down on the settee beside her. He was still frowning when he put his arm around her shoulders and hauled her up against his side.

"I specifically remember telling you that I cannot abide being touched," she muttered as she snuggled up against him.

Christina turned to her husband and let him see her smile. "Destiny," she whispered. "I think we should leave them alone," she added. "Jade, your bedroom is the first on the left at the top of the steps. Caine, you're next door."

Christina tugged her reluctant husband to his feet. "Sweetheart," Lyon said, "I want to know what happened to Jade. I'll just stay down here a few more minutes."

"Tomorrow will be soon enough for you to satisfy your curiosity," Christina promised. "Dakota will be waking us in just a few more hours. You need your rest."

"Who is Dakota?" Jade asked, smiling over the affectionate way the happy couple looked at each other. There was such love in their expressions. A surge of raw envy rushed through her, but she quickly pushed the feeling away. It was pointless to wish for things she could never have.

"Dakota is our son," Lyon answered. "He's almost six months old now. You'll meet our little warrior in the morning."

The door closed softly on that promise and she and Caine were once again all alone. Jade immediately tried to move away from him. He tightened his hold.

"Jade? I never meant to sound like I was ridiculing you,"

JULIE GARWOOD

he whispered. "I'm just trying to be logical about this
situation of yours. You have to admit that tonight has
been . . . difficult. I feel like I'm spinning around in circles.
I'm not used to ladies asking me so sweetly if I could kill
them."

She turned to smile up at him. "Was I sweet?" she asked.

He slowly nodded. Her mouth was so close, so appealing.
Before he could stop himself, he leaned down. His mouth
rubbed against hers in a gentle, undemanding kiss.

It was over and done with before she could gather her wits
and offer a protest.

"Why did you do that?" she asked in a strained whisper.

"I felt like it," he answered. His grin made her smile. He
pushed her back down on his shoulder so he wouldn't give in
to the urge to kiss her again, then said, "You've been
through hell, haven't you? We'll wait until tomorrow to talk.
When you've had a proper rest, we'll work on this problem
together."

"That is most considerate of you," she replied. She
sounded acutely relieved. "Now will you please tell me why
you were pretending to be Pagan? You said earlier that you
wanted to draw him out, but I don't understand how . . ."

"I was trying to prick his pride," he explained. "And
make him angry enough to come after me. I know that if
someone was pretending to be me, I'd . . . oh, hell," he
muttered. "It sounds foolish now." His fingers were slowly
threading through her soft curls in an absentminded fashion. "I tried everything else. Bounty didn't work."

"But why? Did you want to meet him?"

"I want to kill him."

Her indrawn breath told him he'd stunned her with his
bluntness. "And if he sent someone else in his place to
challenge you, would you kill that man too?"

"I would."

"Is your work killing people then? Is that how you make
your way in this world?"

She was staring into the fire but he could see the tears in her eyes. "No, I don't kill for a living."

"But you've killed before?"

She'd turned to look at him when she asked that question, letting him see her fear. "Only when it was necessary," he answered.

"I've never killed anyone."

His smile was gentle. "I never thought you had."

"Yet you really believe it's necessary to kill this pirate?"

"I do." His voice had turned hard, a deliberate choice that, for he hoped to get her to quit her questions. "I'll kill every one of his damned followers, too, if it's the only way I can get to him."

"Oh, Caine, I really wish you wouldn't kill anyone."

She was on the verge of tears again. Caine leaned back against the cushions, closed his eyes, and said, "You're a gentle lady, Jade. You can't possibly understand."

"Help me understand," she implored. "Pagan's done so many wonderful things. It seems a sin that you . . ."

"He has?" Caine interrupted.

"Surely you know that the pirate gives most of his booty to the less fortunate," she explained. "Why, our church has a new steeple, thanks to his generous donation."

"Donation?" Caine shook his head over her ludicrous choice of words. "The man is nothing but a common thief. He robs from the rich . . ."

"Well, of course he robs from the rich."

"What's that supposed to mean?"

"He takes from the rich because they have so much, they won't miss the paltry amount he steals. And it wouldn't do him any good at all to take from the poor. They don't have anything worth stealing."

"You seem to know quite a lot about this pirate."

"Everyone keeps up with Pagan's adventures. He's such a romantic figure."

"You sound as if you think he should be knighted."

53

"Perhaps he should," she answered. She rubbed her cheek against his shoulder. "Some say Pagan's never harmed anyone. It doesn't seem right for you to hunt him down."

"If you believe he hasn't ever killed anyone, why did you come looking for him? You wanted him to kill you, remember?"

"I remember," she answered. "If I explain my true plan, will you promise not to laugh?"

"I promise," he answered, wondering over her sudden shyness.

"I was hoping . . . that is, if he didn't want to kill me, well then, perhaps he might consider taking me away on his magical ship and keeping me safe until my brother came home."

"Heaven help you if you'd gotten that wish," Caine said. "You've obviously been listening to too many fanciful stories. You're wrong, too. That bastard pirate has killed before."

"Who has he killed?"

He didn't speak for a long minute but stared into the fire. When he finally answered her, there was ice in his voice. "Pagan killed my brother, Colin."

Chapter Four

"Oh, Caine. I'm so sorry," she whispered. "You must miss him terribly. Was Colin older or younger than you?"

"Younger."

"Did he die very long ago?"

"Just a few months," Caine answered.

"Your family must be having a difficult time of it," she whispered. "Are both your parents still living?"

"Yes, though of the two, my father's having a much more difficult time accepting Colin's death. He's all but given up on life."

"I don't understand," she countered.

"Father used to be very active in politics. He was known as the champion of the poor, Jade, and he was able to force through many substantial measures that eased their burdens."

"Such as?"

She'd taken hold of his hand and was holding it against her waist. Caine didn't think she was aware of her action. It was just an instinctive attempt to give him comfort, he guessed, and he found he didn't dislike the touch or her motive.

"You were explaining how your papa helped the poor," she reminded him.

"Yes," Caine returned. "He was responsible for defeating the tax increase, for one example."

"But he quit these important duties?"

"He quit everything," Caine said. "His politics, his family, his friends, his clubs. He doesn't even read the dailies now. He just stays locked inside his study and broods. I believe, once Pagan has been punished, that my father might . . . hell, I don't know. He's such a defeated man now."

"Are you like your father? Are you also a champion of the poor? I believe you must be a protector by nature."

"Why do you say that?"

She couldn't very well tell him she'd read his file. "Because of the way you took me under your wing," she answered. "And I think you would have offered your help to any defenseless, poor person. Of course, I wasn't poor when I met you."

"Are you going to start in about the silver coins again?"

Because he was smiling at her, she knew he wasn't irritated with her. "No, I'm not going to start in, whatever that's suppose to mean. I was just reminding you. You are like your father then, aren't you?"

"I suppose we share that trait."

"Yet your father retreated from the world while you immediately went after vengeance. Your reactions were just the opposite, weren't they?"

"Yes."

"I understand why your father gave up."

"You do?"

"It's because fathers aren't supposed to lose their sons, Caine."

"No," Caine agreed. "They should die first."

"After a long, happy life, of course," she added.

She sounded so sincere, he didn't want to argue with her. "Of course."

"And you're absolutely certain it was Pagan who killed Colin?"

"I am. I have it on high authority."

"How?"

"How, what?"

"How did Pagan kill him?"

"For God's sake, Jade," he muttered. "I don't want to talk about this. I've already told you more than I intended."

"I'm sorry if I've upset you," she replied. She leaned away from him and looked into his eyes.

The worry in her expression made him feel guilty for his biting tone. "Colin was killed at sea."

"Yet someone was thoughtful enough to bring him home for burial?"

"No."

"No? Then how can you know if he's really dead? He could have washed up on a deserted island, or possibly . . ."

"Proof was sent."

"What proof? And who sent it?"

He couldn't understand her interest in this topic and determined to end the conversation. "Proof came from the War Department. Now will you quit your questions?"

"Yes, of course," she whispered. "Please accept my apology for intruding upon such a personal matter."

She let out a yawn, then begged his forgiveness for that unladylike action.

"Caine? We can't stay here long. I fear we would be putting your friends in danger."

"I agree," he answered. "We'll only stay one night."

He stared into the fire while he formulated his plans. Jade snuggled up against him and fell asleep. He told himself he was thankful for the blessed quiet. Yet he resisted the urge to go up to bed, for he liked holding the impossible woman in his arms too much to move.

He kissed her brow just for the hell of it, then kissed her once again.

Only when the fire had burned down to glowing embers and a decided chill settled in the room did he finally get up.

She came awake with a start. Jade jumped to her feet, but was so disoriented, she started walking in the wrong direction. She would have walked right into the hearth if he hadn't stopped her. He tried to lift her into his arms. She pushed his hands away. He let out a sigh, then put his arm around her shoulders and guided her up the stairs. He kept trying not to think about how lovely she looked now. Her hair was almost dry and had regained its enchanting curls. He also tried not to think about the fact that she was wearing only a thin nightgown and wrapper.

He opened the bedroom door for her, then turned to find his own.

"Caine?" she called out, her voice a sleepy whisper. "You won't leave me, will you?"

He turned back to face her. The question was insulting, yet the fearful look in her eyes softened his initial reaction. "No, I won't leave you."

She nodded, looked like she was about to say something more, and then abruptly shut the door in his face.

Christina had prepared the adjoining bedroom for Caine. The bed covers on the large bed had been turned back, and a full fire blazed in the hearth.

As inviting as the bed was, sleep still eluded Caine. He tossed and turned in the giant bed for almost an hour, all the while damning himself for his own lack of discipline. Yet no matter how valiantly he tried, he couldn't get the red-haired, green-eyed enchantress out of his mind.

He couldn't understand his own reaction to her. Hell, he wanted her with an intensity that made him burn. That didn't make any sense at all to him. He disliked bad-tempered, illogical, cry-at-the-sight-of-a-frown young ladies, didn't he?

He was simply too exhausted to think straight now. He wasn't used to being restrained either. Caine was a man who took what he wanted when he wanted it. He'd gone soft over the last few years, though. He didn't have to bother with the chase any longer. The women always came to him. They gave themselves freely. Caine took what each offered without feeling a qualm of remorse. He was always honest with his women, and he never, ever spent a full night with any of them. Mornings, he knew, would bring false hopes and foolish demands.

Yet he wanted Jade. Lord, he wasn't making any sense. Jade's sneeze echoed in the distance then. Caine immediately got out of bed. He put on his pants but didn't bother with the buttons. He now had an excuse to go into her room. She probably needed another blanket, he told himself. The night air had a chill to it. There was also the possibility of a fire, for the light coming from beneath the door indicated she'd fallen asleep with the candles burning.

He wasn't at all prepared for the sight he came upon. Jade was sleeping on her stomach. Her glorious hair was spread like a shawl on her back. Her face was turned toward him. Her eyes were closed, and her deep, even breathing indicated she was fast asleep.

His enchantress was stark naked. She'd taken off her nightgown and placed it on the chair beside the bed. She'd also kicked the covers off the bed.

The little lady had a decidedly sensual streak hidden inside her, if she preferred sleeping in the nude, as he did.

She looked like a golden goddess to him. Her legs were long, beautifully shaped. He suddenly pictured those silky legs wrapped around him and almost groaned in reaction.

He was fully aroused and aching by the time he walked over to the side of the bed. He noticed the long thin scar across her spine then. Caine immediately recognized the mark, as he had a similar one on the back of his thigh. There was only one weapon that could inflict such a jagged line. It was the thick lash from a whip.

Someone had used a whip on her. Caine was stunned, outraged too. The scar was old, by at least five years or so, judging from the faded edges, and that fact made the atrocity all the more repugnant. Jade had been a child when she'd been so mistreated.

He suddenly wanted to wake her up and demand the name of the bastard who'd done this to her.

She started moaning in her sleep. The restlessness in which she moved made him think she was in the throes of an unpleasant dream. She sneezed again, then let out another whimper of distress.

With a sigh of acute frustration, he grabbed the nightgown and turned back to the angel he'd been foolish enough to promise he'd protect. He tried to see the humor in this bleak situation. For the first time in his life, he was actually going to put a nightgown back on a woman.

Caine was just leaning over her when he saw the flash of steel out of the corner of his eye. His reaction was instinctive. He moved to block her attack with a forceful sweep of his left arm. She was already stopping herself when his arm slammed into her wrist. The dagger went flying across the room and landed with a loud clatter on the base of the hearth.

She'd turned into a hellion. Jade was on her knees now, facing him. Her breathing was harsh, her anger apparent in her dark expression. "Don't you ever sneak up on me like that again," she shouted up at him. "Good God, man, I could have killed you."

Caine was just as furious with her. "Don't you ever try to use your knife on me," he roared. "Or good God, woman, I will kill you!"

She didn't appear to be the least intimidated by that

threat. Caine decided she just didn't understand her own peril, or she certainly would have tried to act a little contrite. She'd also forgotten she wasn't wearing any clothes, either.

He hadn't forgotten. Her full, round breasts were only partially concealed by her long dark curls. Her nipples were pink, hard. Her anger made her pant, forcing her slender ribcage to rise and fall in a rhythm he found hypnotic.

He felt like a cad for noticing until she started prodding his temper again.

"You're not going to kill me," she announced. "We've already had this discussion, remember?"

He was staring down at her with the most astonished look on his face. "You aren't at all afraid of me, are you?"

She shook her head. Her long hair swayed gracefully over her shoulders.

"Why would I be afraid of you?" she asked. "You're my protector, sir."

Her irritated tone of voice was the last provocation he was going to take. Caine grabbed hold of her hands and roughly shoved her back against the mattress. He followed her down, spreading her thighs with one of his knees wedged between so she couldn't lash out at him with her legs and do real damage. He wouldn't put it past her to try to make a eunuch out of him if she had the opportunity. "I think it's high time you understood a few basic rules," he grated out.

She let out a loud gasp when his bare chest touched her breasts. Caine guessed she'd finally realized she wasn't wearing a nightgown. "Exactly," he said on a low groan.

Damn, but she was soft, wonderfully so. He wanted to bury his face in the crook of her neck and make slow, sweet love to her. He would have her, he vowed, but she'd be hot and begging for him, not muttering unladylike obscenities against his ear as she was now doing.

"Where in God's name did you learn those blasphemies?" he asked when she threatened to do him in, in the most amazing way.

"From you," she lied. "Will you get off me, you . . . wart from hell."

She was full of bravado. Yet there was a tremor of fear in her voice, too. Caine immediately reacted to it. It took extreme discipline, but he slowly moved away from her. His jaw was clenched tight and a fine sweat covered his brow. Her nipples rubbed against his chest when he moved. Caine groaned low in his throat. Her breasts were ready for him, even if the rest of her wasn't. Ready for him to take into his mouth, to kiss, to suck, to . . .

"Caine?"

He propped himself up on his elbows so he could see her expression. He immediately wished he hadn't bothered. Her intense frown was already making him angry again.

She was filled with the most conflicting emotions. She knew she should feel outraged, but the opposite was really the full truth. The dark hair on his chest, so crisp, so warm, tickled her breasts into responding. He was so warm all over, so exciting. And hard, she added to herself. The sleek bulge of muscle in his upper arms made her breath catch in her throat. She knew better than to let him know how much he was affecting her. Outrage, she remembered. I must be outraged, and frightened, too.

"Is this how you plan to protect me?" she asked, affecting just the right amount of fear in her voice.

"No, this isn't how I plan to protect you," he answered in a husky voice.

"Caine?"

"Yes?"

"You look like you want to kiss me. Do you?"

"Yes," he admitted. "I do."

She started shaking her head, but he stopped that action by cupping the sides of her face and holding her still.

"But you don't even like me much." Her voice was a breathless whisper. "You said so, remember? Have you changed your mind, then?"

He found himself smiling over the bewildered look on her face. "No," he answered, just to goad her temper.

"Then why would you want to kiss me?"

"I can't explain it," he said. "Perhaps it's because you're stark naked, and I can feel your soft skin beneath me. Perhaps . . ."

"Only once then."

He didn't understand what she meant, but the blush that covered her cheeks indicated her embarrassment. "Only once what, Jade?" he asked.

"You may kiss me, Caine," she explained. "But only once. Then you must get off me and leave my room."

"Jade? Do you want me to kiss you?"

His voice had turned so tender, she felt as though he'd just caressed her. She stared at his mouth, wondering what it would feel like to be properly kissed by him. Would his mouth be as hard as the rest of him?

Curiosity overruled caution. "Yes," she whispered. "I do want you to kiss me, Caine."

The kiss was one of absolute possession. His mouth was hard, demanding. His tongue thrust inside and rubbed against hers. She had no idea that men kissed women in such a manner, yet found she liked the stroke of his tongue very much. It was thoroughly arousing. Only when her tongue timidly imitated his bold action did he gentle the kiss. It was shameful the way he used his tongue in the erotic mating ritual, but she didn't care. She could feel his hard arousal against the junction of her thighs. He pushed against her each time his tongue slid deep into her mouth. A slow heat began to burn inside her belly.

She couldn't seem to stop touching him. His mouth made her wild. His tongue slid in and out, again and again, until she was shivering for more. Caine had wrapped her hair around his fist to hold her still, but that action wasn't really necessary. She was clinging to him now.

It was time to stop. Caine knew he was at risk of losing all control. Jade tried to bring him back to her by digging her nails into his shoulders. Caine resisted the unspoken invitation. He stared down into her eyes a long minute. He liked what he saw there, didn't even try to hide his grin of male satisfaction. "You taste like sugar and honey."

"I do?"

He brushed his mouth over hers once again. "Oh, yes, you do," he said. "Brandy too."

She moved restlessly against him. "Don't push your hips up like that," he ordered. His jaw was clenched tight against the innocent provocation.

"Caine?"

"Yes?"

"Only twice," she whispered. "All right?"

He understood. She was giving him permission to kiss her again. He couldn't resist. He kissed her again, a long, hard, wet, tongue-thrusting kiss, and when he next looked into her eyes, he was thoroughly pleased. She looked completely dazed. He'd done that to her, he knew. The passion inside her more than matched his own.

"Caine?"

"No more, Jade," he growled.

"You didn't like it?" she asked, her worry obvious in her gaze.

"I liked it all right," he replied.

"Then why . . ."

Her hands were caressing his shoulders and it was becoming an agony to maintain his discipline. "I can't promise you I'll stop if I kiss you again, Jade. Are you willing to take the risk?"

Before she could answer him, he started to ease away from her. "That wasn't a fair question to ask in your present state."

The passion began to clear her mind. "What present state?"

He let out a deep sigh. "I think I'm going to make love to

you eventually, Jade," he whispered. "But you'll make the decision before passion clouds your mind." His expression darkened when she started struggling against him. The movement reminded him of her soft breasts waiting for his touch. "If you don't quit wiggling against me like that," he grated out. "I swear it's going to happen now. I'm not made of iron, sweet."

She went completely still.

Though he was reluctant to leave her, he even assisted her in putting her nightgown back on. He refused to let her have her dagger back, even when she fervently promised him she wouldn't try to use it on him again.

"I was sound asleep," she reasoned. "And you were sneaking up on me like a thief. I had to protect myself."

Caine took hold of her hand and dragged her toward his bedroom. "You were having a nightmare, weren't you?"

"I might have been," she replied. "I don't remember now. Why are you tugging at me?"

"You're going to sleep with me. Then you won't have to worry about anyone sneaking up on you."

"Out of the boat and into the ocean, is that it?" she asked. "I really believe I'm much safer on my own, thank you."

"Can't trust yourself to keep your hands off me?" he asked.

"Yes, that's true," she admitted with a feigned sigh. "I'll have to restrain myself, though, or I'll surely be sent to the gallows. Murder's still frowned on in this part of the world, isn't it?"

Caine laughed. "You won't be thinking about murdering me when I'm touching you," he predicted.

She let out a low groan of frustration. "You really aren't going to do. A protector shouldn't be lusting after his charge."

"And what about you?" he asked. "Do you lust after your protector?"

He turned around to wait for her answer. "I don't know,"

she said. "I find you terribly appealing, Caine, yet I've never gone to bed with a man and I don't know if I want you that much. Still, this attraction is becoming too much of a distraction. You aren't going to do at all, sir. Come morning, I'm going to have to find someone else to protect me . . . someone less appealing."

She tried to pull away from him then. Caine caught her before she'd taken a step back toward her own bed. In one quick motion, he tossed her over his shoulder and carried her through the connecting doorway.

"How dare you treat me like this? I'm not a bag of feed. Put me down this minute, you bastard rake."

"Bastard rake? Sweet, you've got quite a vocabulary for a lady."

He dropped her into the center of his bed. Since he fully expected her to bounce right back out and try to escape, he was pleasantly surprised when she began to settle the blankets around herself. After she'd scooted to the far side of the bed, she fluffed the feather pillow behind her head and draped her hair over her shoulder. The alluring blaze of red curls against the pristine white nightgown looked incredibly beautiful to him. The woman who had just called him bastard was now looking like an angel again.

Caine's sigh blew out the candles.

"I am a lady," she muttered when he'd settled himself beside her. "But you've riled my temper, Caine, and that's the reason for my . . ."

"Colorful vocabulary?" he asked when she didn't finish her thought.

"Yes," she replied. She sounded forlorn when she added, "Must I apologize?"

He kept his laughter contained. "I fear you wouldn't mean it," he answered. He rolled to his side and tried to take her into his arms. When she pushed his hands away, he moved onto his back again, stacked his hands behind his head, and stared into the darkness above while he thought about the warm body next to him. She was certainly the most unusual woman he'd ever met. Why, she could have him laughing one second and shouting the next. He couldn't explain his reactions to her, for he didn't understand himself. Only one thing was certain in his mind. He knew she desired him. Her kiss had shown him that much.

"Jade?"

His husky voice sent a shiver down her arms. "Yes?"

"It's damned odd, isn't it?"

"What's damned odd?" she asked.

He could hear the smile in her voice. "You and me sharing this bed without touching each other. You do feel comfortable with me, don't you?"

"Yes," she answered. "Caine?"

"Yes?"

"Is making love painful?"

"No," he answered. "It's painful when you want to and can't."

"Oh. Then I must not want you very much, Caine, because I'm not hurting at all." She made that statement of fact in a gratingly cheerful tone of voice.

"Jade?"

"Yes?"

"Go to sleep."

She felt him turn toward her and immediately tensed in anticipation of another kiss. After waiting a long while, she realized he wasn't going to kiss her again. She was horribly disappointed.

Caine propped himself up on his elbow and stared down at her. Jade forced a serene expression in case he had cat's eyes and could see in the dark.

"Jade? How did you get that whiplash on your back?"

"From a whip," she answered. She rolled to her side and resisted the urge to scoot up against his warmth.

"Answer me."

"How do you know it was a whiplash?"

67

"I have an identical mark on the back of my thigh."

"You do? How did you get yours?"

"Are you going to answer my every question with a question of your own?"

"It worked quite nicely for Socrates."

"Tell me how you got your whiplash," he asked once again.

"It's a personal matter," she explained. "It's almost dawn, Caine. I've had a rather trying day."

"All right," he conceded. "You can tell me all about this personal matter in the morning."

Before she could fend him off, he threw his arm around her waist and hauled her up against him. His chin rested on the top of her head. The junction of his hard thighs was nestled against her backside.

"Are you warm enough?" he asked.

"Yes," she answered. "Are you?"

"Oh, yes."

"You will behave, won't you?" she teased.

"Probably," he replied. "Jade?" he asked, his tone much more serious now.

"Yes?"

"I would never do anything you didn't want me to do."

"But what if you thought I wanted you to . . . and I didn't really want . . ."

"Unless you gave me your approval, your wholehearted approval, I wouldn't touch you. I promise."

She thought that was the nicest promise she'd ever been given. He sounded so sincere, and she knew he really meant what he said.

"Caine? Do you know what I've just discovered? You really are a gentleman, and an honorable one at that."

He'd already fallen asleep hugging her. Jade decided to do the same. She rolled over in his arms, slipped her arms around his waist, and promptly fell asleep.

Caine woke up a bare hour later when Jade cried out in

her sleep. She muttered something he couldn't decipher, then let out a terrified scream. He shook her awake. When he brushed her hair away from her face, he felt the wetness on her cheeks. She'd been weeping in her sleep.

"Sweetheart, you're having a bad dream. It's all right now," he soothed. "You're safe with me."

He rubbed her shoulders and her back, too, until the tension eased out of her. "What were you dreaming about?" he asked, when her breathing had calmed down.

"Sharks." The word came out in a whisper filled with anguish.

"Sharks?" he asked, uncertain if he'd heard correctly.

She tucked her head under his chin. "I'm so tired," she whispered. "I don't remember the nightmare now. Hold me, Caine. I want to go back to sleep."

Her voice still trembled. Caine knew she was lying. She remembered every bit of her nightmare. He wasn't going to prod her into telling him about it, however.

He kissed the top of her head, then complied with her order and pulled her close.

Jade knew the minute he fell asleep again. She slowly eased herself away from him and moved to the side of the bed. Her heart was still slamming inside her chest. He thought she'd only had a nightmare. Was reliving an actual event the same? And would she ever be able to forget the horror?

God help her, would she ever be able to go willingly back in the water again?

She felt like crying. It took all her discipline not to give into her urge and hold on to him now. Caine was such an easy man to trust. She could get used to depending on him, she knew. Yes, he was the dependable type, but he could also break her heart.

She was thoroughly confused by her reaction to him. In her heart, she trusted him completely.

Why then didn't his own brother?

Chapter Five

Caine woke up ravenous . . . for her. Jade's nightgown was tangled up around her thighs. She had cuddled up against his side and had thrown her right leg over his thighs sometime during the short night. Her knee now covered his throbbing arousal. Out of deference to her feelings, he'd slept with his pants on. The clothing proved to be a paltry barrier against her softness, though, and Caine could feel the scorch of her body branding him with hot desire.

The side of her face rested on his bare chest. Her lips were softly parted, her breathing deep, even. She had long, black-as-night eyelashes and a healthy sprinkle of freckles across the bridge of her nose. The woman was utterly feminine. Caine continued to stare at her lovely face until he was so hard, so hurting, he was clenching his teeth.

It was a battle to move away from her. When he tried to ease her onto her back, he realized she was holding his hand. She didn't seem inclined to let go, either.

He had to pry her fingers loose. Then he remembered she'd called him a bastard rake the night before. Yet she was clinging to him now. Caine was certain she'd be wary of him once again when she was wide awake. She couldn't hide her vulnerability from him when she was sleeping, however, and that fact pleased him considerably.

A fierce wave of possessiveness consumed him. In that moment, while he stared down at his angel, he vowed he would never let anything happen to her, he would protect her with his life.

For as long as he was her guardian . . . or did he want her to stay with him much, much longer . . . Nathan would be home in two short weeks to take up the task of keeping his sister safe. Would Caine be able to let her go then?

He didn't have any ready answers; he knew only that the thought of giving her up made his heart lurch and his stomach tighten up.

It was all he was prepared to admit to himself, all he was willing to give.

It certainly wasn't possible to be logical with a half-naked beauty draped over him. Yes, he thought as he leaned down and kissed her brow, he would wait until later to sort it all out in his mind.

He washed and dressed in clothes that belonged to Lyon, then woke Jade. She tried to hit him when he nudged her awake. "It's all right, Jade," he whispered. "It's time to get up."

She was blushing by the time she'd sat up in bed. Caine watched her pull the coverlet all the way up to her chin. The act of modesty really wasn't necessary considering her state of undress the night before, but he decided against mentioning that to her now.

"Please excuse my behavior," she whispered in a husky, sleep-filled voice. "'Tis the truth I'm not at all accustomed to being awakened by a man."

"I would hope not," he replied.

She looked bewildered. "Why would you hope that?"

"You're not awake enough to play Socrates with me," he told her, his voice gentle.

Jade stared rather stupidly up at him. Caine leaned down and kissed her then, a hard, quick kiss that was over and done with before she could summon a reaction . . . or make a fist.

She had the most astonished look on her face when he pulled away from her. "Why did you do that?"

"Because I wanted to," he answered.

He started for the door, but she called out to him. "Where are you going?"

"Downstairs," he replied. "I'll meet you in the dining room. I imagine Christina left some clothes for you in the other room, sweet."

"Oh my God . . . she must think that we . . . that is . . ."

The door closed on her horrified whispers.

She could hear Caine whistling as he made his way down the corridor. Jade fell back against the pillows. The brief kiss he'd given her had left her shaken. That, and the fact that his friends now thought she was wanton.

And just what did she care what they thought? When this deception was over, she wouldn't ever see them again. Still, Christina wanted to be her friend. Jade now felt as though she'd just betrayed her in some way.

"I'll simply explain that nothing happened," she whispered to herself. She's going to understand. A true friend would, wouldn't she?

Since Jade hadn't had any true friends in the past, she couldn't be certain what rules applied.

She got out of her bed and rushed back into her own room. Caine had been correct, for Christina had left a pretty dark blue riding outfit. Dark brown boots with nary a mark on them were on the floor beside the chair. Jade prayed they were close to her size.

She couldn't quit thinking about Caine while she dressed. The man was going to be a challenge to her peace of mind. He was so dangerously attractive. The damned dimple made her want to swoon. Lyon had loaned him a pair of indecently snug deerskin-colored britches. The pants accentuated the sleek bulge of muscles in his thighs . . . and his crotch. Black Harry would throttle her if he knew she'd taken the time to notice a man's body. Caine's sexuality, so raw, so appealing, made her notice, though. She might be innocent of men, but she certainly wasn't blind.

A scant fifteen minutes later, she was ready to go downstairs. The white silk blouse was a bit too tight in the bosom, but the jacket hid that fact. The boots scrunched her toes, too, but only just a little.

She'd tried to braid her hair, but it was a disaster. She gave up the task when she saw the lopsided mess she was making. Jade had little patience and absolutely no expertise in the area of hair styling. That fact had never bothered her before, yet now it worried her. She was a gentle lady of the *ton* until this masquerade was finished, and it wasn't like her to let any little detail slip her notice.

The dining room doors were wide open. Caine was sitting at the head of a long, mahogany table. A servant was pouring dark tea into a cup from a beautiful silver pot. Caine wasn't paying any attention to the man, however. He seemed to be engrossed in the newspaper he was reading.

She wasn't certain if she was supposed to curtsy or not, then decided it really didn't matter since he wasn't paying any notice. She was mistaken in that belief, however, for as soon as she reached the chair adjacent to his, he stood up and offered her his assistance.

No one had ever held out a chair for her, not even Nathan. She couldn't make up her mind if she liked the fuss or not.

Caine continued to read his paper while she ate her breakfast. When he'd finished with what she decided was probably a daily ritual, he leaned back in his chair, folded the newspaper, and finally gave her his complete attention.

"Well?" she asked as soon as he looked at her.

"Well, what?" he asked, smiling over the eagerness in her expression.

"Was there mention of a finely dressed gentleman being murdered?" She pointed to the newspaper.

"No, there wasn't."

She let out a gasp of dismay. "I'll wager they tossed him in the Thames. Do you know, Caine, now that I reflect upon it, I did feel something slither against my legs. And you did say nothing could live for long in the Thames, didn't you? It must have been that poor . . ."

"Jade, you're letting your imagination get the better of you," he interjected. "Not only was there no mention of your finely dressed gentleman, there wasn't any mention of *anyone* being murdered."

"Then they haven't found him yet."

"If he's a member of the *ton,* someone would have noticed his disappearance by now. It's been two days, hasn't it, since you saw . . ."

"It has been two days, exactly," she interrupted.

Caine thought that if she became any more enthusiastic, she might jump out of her chair.

"Which leads me to my first question," he announced. "Exactly what did you see?"

She leaned back against her chair. "Where are Lyon and Christina, do you suppose?"

"Are you avoiding my question?"

She shook her head. "I just don't want to have to tell it twice," she explained. Even as she gave that lie her mind was racing for another plausible story.

"Lyon went out for a bit," he answered. "And Christina is tending to Dakota. Answer me, please."

Her eyes widened.

"Now what's the matter?"

"You just said please," she whispered. She sounded awestruck. "If you're not careful, you'll soon be giving me the apologies you owe me."

He knew better than to ask her why he should apologize,

guessing she had her list of his faults memorized. Besides, the smile she just gave him was so dazzling, he could barely hold his concentration.

"They pitched him from the roof."

Caine was jarred back to their topic when she made that announcement. "You were on a roof?" he asked her, trying to imagine what in God's name she'd been up to.

"Of course not," she replied. "Why would I be on a roof?"

"Jade . . ."

"Yes?" she asked, looking expectant again.

"You weren't on a roof but you saw "them" throw this man . . ."

"He was a finely dressed gentleman," she interrupted.

"All right," he began again. "You weren't on the roof but you saw several men throw this finely dressed gentleman from the roof? Is that it?"

"There were three of them."

"You're certain?"

She nodded. "I was frightened, Caine, but I could still count."

"Where were you when this happened?"

"On the ground."

"I gathered that much," he muttered. "If you weren't on the roof, I did assume . . ."

"I could have been inside another building, or perhaps riding Nathan's fine horse, or even . . ."

"Jade, stop rambling," he demanded. "Just tell me where you were and what you saw."

"What I heard is just as significant, Caine."

"Are you deliberately trying to make me angry?"

She gave him a disgruntled look. "I was just about to walk into the church when I heard all the commotion. They weren't actually on top of the church. No, they were dragging this poor man across the rectory's roof. It's a bit lower. From my position, I could see the gentleman was trying to get away from them. He was struggling and shouting for help. That's how I knew, Caine. I wasn't just imagining it."

"And?" he prodded when she suddenly quit her explanation.

"They tossed him over. If I'd been just a foot to the left, well sir, you wouldn't be having to protect me now. I'd be as dead as the poor gentleman is."

"Where is this church?"

"In Nathan's parish."

"And where is that?" he asked.

"Three hours north of here," she answered.

"Am I interrupting?" Christina asked from the doorway. Jade turned to smile at her.

"Of course not," Jade answered. "Thank you for the lovely breakfast, and for loaning me your beautiful riding clothes. I shall take good care of them," she added.

Lyon came up behind his wife and put his arms around her. While Caine and Jade watched, Christina's husband nuzzled the top of his wife's head.

"Miss me?" he asked.

"Of course," Christina answered. She smiled up at her husband, then turned back to Jade. "I went into your room . . ."

"Nothing happened," Jade rushed out. "It's all his fault, really. But nothing happened, Christina. I tried to use my knife on him. That's all. He took exception, of course," she added as she waved her hand in Caine's direction. "He was so bloody furious, he dragged me into his room. Oh Lord, I'm making a muddle out of this, aren't I?"

She turned to Caine. "Will you say something, please? My new friend is going to think I'm . . ."

She quit her explanation when she noticed Caine's astonished expression. He wasn't going to be any help at all, she realized. He was back to thinking she was daft.

She could feel herself burning with embarrassment.

"I went into your room to fetch your knife," Christina explained. "You actually tried to cut him with that dull blade?"

Jade wanted to find a place to hide. "No," she answered with a sigh.

"But you just said . . ."

"At first, I did try to cut him," she explained. "He woke me up trying to put my nightgown back on . . ."

"You did?" Lyon asked Caine. His grin was downright shameful.

"Lyon, stay out of this," Caine ordered.

"Well, as soon as I realized who it was, I quit trying to stab him. He gave me a startle. I thought he was a thief."

Lyon looked like he was dying to say something more. Caine glared him into keeping silent.

"Did you find out anything?" Caine called out.

Lyon nodded. He started into the room. "Christina? Take Jade into the drawing room, would you?"

"She'll have to go in there on her own," Christina answered. "I promised to sharpen her knife for her. Jade? I couldn't find it under your pillow. That's what I've been trying to explain."

"He took it," Jade answered with a wave in Caine's direction. "I believe I saw him put it on the mantle, though I'm not absolutely certain. Would you like me to help you look for it?"

"No, I'll find it. You go and keep Dakota company. He's playing on his blanket inside. I'll join you in just a few minutes."

Jade hurriedly followed Christina out of the room. She paused at the drawing room doors when she heard Lyon's booming laughter. She smiled then, guessing Caine had just told his friend what an imbecile he thought she was.

She was feeling quite smug now. It took a certain concentration to be able to ramble on and on so convincingly, and she thought she'd pulled it off quite nicely. She had no idea she was so talented. Still, she was honest enough to admit to herself that there had been a moment when she hadn't really been pretending. Jade straightened her shoulders. Pretense or not, rambling was definitely a plus when dealing with Caine.

She went inside the room then and closed the door behind her. She spotted the quilted blanket in front of the settee right away. Christina's son, however, was quite another matter. She couldn't find him anywhere.

She was about to shout an alarm when she noticed a tiny foot protruding from the back of the settee. She hurried over and knelt down, briefly thought about pulling him out by his one foot, and then decided she'd better find the rest of him first. With her backside in the air, she leaned down until the side of her face rested on the carpet.

The most magnificent blue eyes she'd ever seen were just inches away from her now. Dakota. Jade thought she might have startled him by her sudden appearance. His eyes did widen. He didn't cry, though. No, he stared at her a long, drooling moment, and then gave her a wide, toothless grin.

She thought he was the most amazing infant. Once he'd finished smiling at her, he went back to his main interest. He seemed determined to gum his way through the ornately carved wooden leg of the settee.

"Oh, that can't be at all good for you, little boy," Jade announced.

He didn't spare her a glance as he continued to chew on the wood. "Stop that now, Dakota," she commanded. "Your mama will be unhappy if she sees you eating the furniture. Come out here, please."

It was obvious that she had no experience handling children. It was also a fact that she didn't realize she had an audience watching her either.

Both Caine and Lyon leaned against opposite door frames observing the pair. They were both trying not to laugh.

"You aren't going to cooperate, are you, Dakota?" Jade asked.

The baby gurgled happily in answer to that remark.

"She's innovative, I'll give her that," Lyon whispered to Caine when Jade lifted the edge of the settee and moved it to the side.

She then sat down on the floor next to the little one. He immediately wiggled his way toward her. She wasn't at all certain how to lift a baby. She'd heard that their little necks weren't strong enough to hold their heads up until they were at least a year or so. Dakota, however, had lifted his chest off the carpet and seemed to be strong enough on his own.

He made the most delightful sounds. He was such a happy little boy. She couldn't resist touching him. She gingerly patted the top of his head, then eased her hands under his arms and slowly dragged him up onto her lap.

She wanted to cuddle him against her bosom.

He wanted something else. Dakota grabbed hold of a clump of her hair, pulled on it, hard, while he tried to find his supper.

It didn't take her any time at all to realize what he was trying to do.

"No, no, Dakota," she whispered when he arched up against her and started to fret. "Your mama's going to have to feed you. Shall we go and find her, love?"

Jade slowly gained her feet, keeping the baby close against her. His grip on her hair stung, but she didn't mind.

The baby smelled so wonderful. He was beautiful, too. He had his mother's blue eyes, but his dark curls came from his father. Jade stroked the baby's back and softly crooned to him. She was in awe of him.

She turned and noticed the men then. Jade could feel herself blush. "You have a fine son," she told Lyon in a stammer.

Caine stayed by the door while Lyon went to claim

Dakota. He had to pry his son's hands away from Jade's hair. She stared at Caine, wondering over the odd expression on his face now. There was tenderness there, but something else as well. She didn't have any idea what he was thinking.

"He's the first baby I've ever held," she told Lyon after he'd lifted his son into his arms.

"I'd say that you are a natural," Lyon replied. "Wouldn't you agree, Dakota?" he asked. He held the baby up until they were eye level. Dakota immediately grinned.

Christina breezed into the room, drawing Jade's attention. She hurried over and handed her friend the sharpened knife. The dagger was inside a soft leather carrier. "It's sharp enough now," she told Jade. "I made the pouch so you wouldn't accidentally prick yourself."

"Thank you," Jade replied.

"You aren't going to need a knife," Caine announced. He moved away from his lazy repose and walked over to Jade's side. "Let me keep it for you, sweet. You'll hurt yourself."

"I will not give it to you," she announced. "It was a gift from my uncle and I promised him I'd always have it with me."

He gave in when she backed away from him. "We have to get going," he told her then. "Lyon, you'll . . ."

"I will," Lyon returned. "Just as soon as I've . . ."

"Right," Caine interrupted.

"They seem to be speaking in a different language, don't they?" Christina said to Jade.

"They don't want me to worry," Jade explained.

"Then you understood what they were saying?"

"Of course. Lyon is suppose to start his investigation. Caine's obviously given him a few suggestions. As soon as he's found out anything of consequence, he'll get in touch with Caine."

Lyon and Caine were staring intently at her. "You deducted all that from . . ."

She interrupted Caine with a nod. Then she turned to Lyon. "You're going to try to find out if there's anyone gone missing of late, aren't you?"

"Yes," Lyon admitted.

"You'll need a description, won't you? Of course, the poor man's nose was a bit scrunched from the fall. Still, I could tell he was quite old, almost forty, I would guess. He had gray hair, bushy eyebrows, and cold brown eyes. He didn't look at all peaceful in death, either. He'd gone to fat, too, around the middle. That's yet another reason to suppose he was a member of the *ton.*"

"Why is that?" Caine asked.

"Because he had more than enough to eat for one," she countered. "There weren't any callouses on his hands, either. No, he certainly wasn't a working man. I can tell you that much."

"Come and sit down," Lyon suggested. "We'd like to have descriptions of the other men as well."

"I fear there isn't much to tell," she said. "I barely saw them. I don't know if they were tall or short, fat or thin . . ." She stopped to sigh. "There were three of them and that's all I had time to notice."

She looked distressed. Caine thought she was still frightened of the ordeal she'd gone through. She had seen a man fall to his death, after all, and she was such a gentle woman, she couldn't be used to such horrors.

Jade was upset, yes, and when Caine put his arm around her shoulders, she felt all the more guilty. For the first time in her life, she actually disliked lying. She kept trying to tell herself that her motives were pure. The reminder didn't help at all, though. She was deceiving three very nice people.

"We have to leave," she blurted out. "The longer we stay, the more danger we put this family in, Caine. Yes, we must leave now."

She didn't give anyone time to argue with her but rushed over to the entrance.

"Caine? Do you have a home in the country somewhere?" she asked, knowing full well that he did.

"Yes."

"I think we should go there. You can keep me safe away from London."

"We aren't going to Harwythe, Jade."

"Harwythe?"

"The name of my country estate," he answered. "I'm taking you to my parents' home. Their property borders mine. You might not be concerned about your reputation, but I am. I'll come and see you every day to make certain you're doing all right. I'll place guards around . . . now why are you shaking your head at me?"

"You'll come and visit me? Caine, you're already breaking your word to me," she cried out. "We are not going to involve your parents in this. You promised me you'd keep me safe and by God, you aren't going to leave my side until it's over."

"She sounds determined, Caine," Lyon interjected.

"I am in wholehearted agreement with Jade," Christina interjected.

"Why?" Both Caine and Lyon asked at the same time.

Christina shrugged. "Because she's my friend. I must agree with her, mustn't I?"

Neither man had a valid argument for that explanation. Jade was pleased. "Thank you, Christina. I will always agree with you, as well," she added.

Caine shook his head. "Jade," he began, thinking to draw her back to their original topic. "I am thinking about your safety when I suggest you stay with my parents."

"No."

"Do you honestly believe you'll be safe with me?"

She took exception to his incredulous tone of voice. "I most certainly do."

"Sweet, I'm not going to be able to keep my hands off you

for two long weeks. I'm trying to be noble about this, damn it."

In the blink of an eye, her face turned crimson. "Caine," she whispered. "You shouldn't be saying such things in front of our guests."

"They aren't our guests," he countered in a near shout of obvious frustration. "We're their guests."

"The man's always using blasphemies around me," she told Christina. "He won't apologize either."

"Jade!" Caine roared. "Quit trying to change the topic."

"I don't believe you should shout at her, Caine," Christina advised.

"He can't help himself," Jade explained. "It's because of his cranky nature."

"I'm not cranky," Caine announced in a much lower tone of voice. "I'm just being honest. I don't mean to embarrass you."

"It's too late," Jade countered. "You've already embarrassed me."

Both Christina and Lyon looked absolutely mesmerized by the conversation. Caine turned to his friend. "Don't you have someplace to go?"

"No."

"Leave anyway," Caine ordered.

Lyon raised an eyebrow, then gave in. "Come along, wife. We can wait in the dining room. Caine? You're going to have to let her explain a few more facts before you leave if you want me to . . ."

"Later," Caine announced.

Christina followed her husband and son out of the room. She paused to squeeze Jade's hand on her way past her. "It's best not to fight it," she whispered. "Your fate has already been determined."

Jade didn't pay any attention to that remark. She nodded just to please Christina, then shut the door and whirled around to confront Caine again. Her hands settled on her hips. "It's absolutely ridiculous to worry about keeping your hands off me. You won't take advantage of me unless I let you. I trust you," she added with a vehement nod. Her hands flew to her bodice. "With all my heart," she added quite dramatically.

"Don't."

The harshness in his tone startled her. She quickly recovered. "Too late, Caine. I already do trust you. You'll keep me safe and I won't let you touch me. We have an easy pact, sir. Don't you try to muddy the waters now with last-minute worries. It will all work out. I promise you."

A commotion in the entryway drew their attention. Caine recognized the voice.

One of his grooms was stammering out his need to find his employer.

"That's Perry," Caine told Jade. "He's one of my grooms. You stay inside this room while I see what he wants."

She didn't obey that command, of course, but followed behind him.

When she saw Lyon's dark expression, she knew something foul had happened. Then her attention turned to the servant. The young man had wide hazel eyes and dark crinkly hair that stood up on end. He couldn't seem to catch his breath but kept making a circle with the hat he clutched in his hands.

"Everything be lost, mi'lord," Perry blurted out. "Merlin said to tell you it were a miracle the whole block wasn't set afire. The Earl of Haselet's town house was just a bit scorched. There be smoke damage we would imagine, but the outside walls are still intact."

"Perry, what are you . . ."

"Your town house caught fire, Caine," Lyon interjected. "Isn't that what you're trying to tell us, Perry?"

The servant quickly nodded. "It weren't carelessness," he

defended. "We don't know how it started, mi'lord, but there weren't any candles burning, no fire unattended in the hearths. God be my witness, it weren't carelessness."

"No one is blaming you," Caine said. He kept his voice contained, his anger hidden. What the hell else could go wrong? he wondered. "Accidents happen."

"It wasn't an accident."

Everyone in the foyer turned to look at Jade. She was staring at the floor, her hands clenched together. She seemed to be so distressed, some of Caine's anger dissipated. "It's all right, Jade," he soothed. "What I lost can easily be replaced." He turned back to Perry and asked, "No one was hurt?"

Lyon watched Jade while the servant stammered out the news that all the servants had gotten out in time.

Caine was relieved. He was about to give fresh orders to his groom when Lyon interrupted him. "Let me handle the authorities and the servants," he suggested. "You need to get Jade out of London, Caine."

"Yes," Caine answered. He was trying not to alarm Jade but he'd already guessed the fire had something to do with the men chasing after her.

"Perry, go to the kitchen and get something to drink," Lyon ordered. "There's always ale and brandy on the counter."

The servant hurried to comply with that suggestion.

Lyon and Caine both stared at Jade now, waiting for her to say something. She stared at the floor. She was wringing her hands together.

"Jade?" Caine asked when she continued to hold her silence. "Why don't you believe it was an accident?"

She let out a long sigh before answering. "Because it isn't the first fire, Caine. It's the third they've set. They do seem partial to fires."

She lifted her gaze to look at him. He could see the tears in her eyes then. "They'll try again, and again, until they finally catch you . . . and me," she hastily added. "Inside."

"Are you saying they mean to kill you by . . . ?" Lyon asked.

Jade shook her head. "They don't just mean to kill me now," she whispered. She looked at Caine and started to cry. "They mean to kill him, too."

Chapter Six

Jade wiped the tears away from her face with the backs of her hands. "They must have somehow learned your true identity," she whispered. "When I went into the tavern, I thought you were Pagan . . . but they must have known all along, Caine. Why else would they burn your town house?"

Caine went to her and put his arm around her shoulders. He led her back into the drawing room. "Monk wouldn't have told them," he announced. "I don't know how they could have . . . never mind. Jade, no more half explanations," he ordered. "I have to know everything."

"I'll tell you anything you want to know," she said.

Lyon followed the pair inside the salon. He shut the doors behind him and then took his seat across from the settee. Caine gently forced Jade to sit down beside him.

Jade looked at Lyon. "I think we lost them last night when we jumped into the Thames. Perhaps, if you told Perry to pretend to continue his search looking for Caine, whoever is watching will assume you didn't know where we were."

Lyon thought that was an excellent plan. He immediately agreed and went in search of the servant.

As soon as he left the room, Jade turned to Caine. "I can't stay with you. I understand that now. They'll kill you trying to get to me. I've tried not to like you, sir, but I've failed in that endeavor. It would upset me if you were hurt."

She tried to leave after making that explanation but Caine wouldn't let her move. He tightened his hold around her and hauled her up close to his side. "I have also tried not to like you," he whispered. He kissed the top of her head before continuing. "But I've also failed in that endeavor. We seem to be stuck with each other, sweet."

They stared at each other a long while. Jade broke the silence. "Isn't it peculiar, Caine?"

"What's that?" he countered in a whisper to match hers.

"You've just lost your town house, we're both in terrible danger now, and all I want is for you to kiss me. Isn't that peculiar?"

He shook his head. His hand moved to cup her chin. "No," he answered. "I want to kiss you, too."

"You do?" Her eyes widened. "Well, isn't that the . . ."

"Damnedest thing?" he whispered as he leaned down.

"Yes," she sighed against his mouth. "It is the damnedest thing."

His mouth took possession of hers then, ending their conversation. Jade immediately wrapped her arms around his neck. Caine nudged her mouth open by applying subtle pressure on her chin, and when she'd done as he wanted, his tongue swept inside.

He meant only to take a quick taste, but the kiss quickly got out of control. His mouth slanted over hers with hard insistence.

He couldn't get enough of her.

"For the love of . . . Caine, now isn't the time to . . ."

Lyon had made those half statements from the doorway, then strolled back over to his chair. Caine, he noticed, was reluctant to stop kissing Jade. She didn't have such reservations, however, and shoved herself away from her partner with amazing speed.

She was beet red when she glanced over at Lyon. Since he was grinning at her, she turned her attention to her lap. She realized then that she was clutching Caine's hand against her bosom, and immediately tossed it aside.

"You forget yourself, sir," she announced.

He decided not to remind her that she'd been the one to bring up the topic of kissing in the first place.

"I think it's high time we heard her explanation," Lyon ordered. "Jade?" he asked, though in a much softer tone when he saw the startle his booming voice had caused. Lord, she was timid. "Why don't you tell us about the first fire?"

"I will try," she answered, her gaze still downcast. "But the memory still gives me the shivers. Please don't think me a weak woman." She turned to look up at Caine. "I'm really not weak at all."

Lyon nodded. "Then can we begin?" he asked.

"Jade, before you tell us about the fires, why don't you give us a little background?" Lyon asked.

"My father was the Earl of Wakerfields. Nathan, my brother, has that title now, along with numerous others, of course. Father died when I was eight years old. I remember he was on his way to London to see another man. I was in the garden when he came to say goodbye."

"If you were so young, how can you remember?" Caine asked.

"Papa was very upset," she answered. "He frightened me and I think that must be the reason I remember it all so clearly. He kept pacing back and forth along the path with his hands clasped behind his back and he kept telling me that if anything happened to him, Nathan and I were to go to his friend, Harry. He was so insistent I pay attention to what he was telling me that he grabbed me by the shoulders and shook me. I was more interested in the trinkets I wanted him to bring home for me." Her voice took on a wistful quality when she added, "I was very young."

"You're still young," Caine interjected.

"I don't feel young," she admitted. She straightened her shoulders and continued. "My mother died when I was just an infant, so I don't have any memory of her."

"What happened to your father?" Caine asked.

"He died in a carriage mishap."

"He had a premonition, then?" Lyon asked.

"No, he had an enemy."

"And you believe your father's enemy is now after you? Is that the reason for your fears?" Lyon asked.

She shook her head. "No, no," she blurted out. "I saw someone murdered. The men who killed him did get a good look at me. The only reason I told you about my father was because you asked me to explain to you my . . . background. Yes, Lyon, that was your very word."

"Sorry," Lyon said again. "I didn't mean to jump to conclusions."

"What happened after your father died?" Caine asked. He was suddenly feeling immensely superior to his good friend, as Lyon now looked thoroughly confused and bewildered. It was nice to know he wasn't the only one muddled around Jade. Damned nice.

"After the burial service, Harry came to get us. When the summer was over, he sent Nathan back to school. He knew our father would have wanted my brother to finish his education. I stayed with my uncle. He isn't really my uncle, he's actually more like a father to me now. Anyway, he took me to his island where it's always warm and peaceful. Uncle Harry was very good to me. He'd never married, you see, and I was just like his very own daughter. We got along well together. Still, I missed my brother. Nathan was only able to come and visit us once in all those years."

When she paused and gave Caine such an expectant look,

he gently prodded her into continuing. "And then what happened?"

"I came back to England so I could see Nathan, of course. I also wanted to see my father's house again. Nathan had made several changes."

"And?" Lyon asked when she paused again.

"Nathan met me in London. We went directly to his country home and spent a wonderful week together catching up. Then he was called away on an important personal matter."

"Do you know what this matter was?" Caine asked.

She shook her head. "Not all of it. A messenger arrived with a letter for Nathan. My brother became very upset when he read it. He told me he had to return to London and that he would be back in two weeks. His good friend was in trouble. That's all he would tell me, Caine. Nathan's an honorable man. He would never turn his back on a friend in need, and I would never ask him to."

"So you were left alone?" Lyon asked.

"Oh, heavens no. Nathan had a complete staff in residence. Lady Briars . . . she was a good friend of my father's . . . well, she'd hired the staff and even helped Nathan with his renovation plans. She wanted to raise us, you see, and was going to petition the court for guardianship. Then Harry took us away, and she never could find us. I will have to go and see her as soon as this has been settled. I dared not go before, of course. They'll probably burn her house to the ground if they . . ."

"Jade, you're digressing," Caine interjected.

"I was?"

He nodded.

"I'm sorry. Now where was I?"

"Nathan left for London," Lyon reminded her.

"Yes," she replied. "I now realize I did do something foolish. On my island, I could come and go as I wished. I never had to worry about an escort. I'd forgotten that England isn't at all the same. Here, everyone must lock their doors. Anyway, I was in such a hurry to get outside, I wasn't looking down, you see, and the heel of my boot got caught up in the carpet loop on the way down the stairs. I took quite a tumble," she added. "And hit my head on the knob of the banister."

She paused, waiting to hear their remarks of sympathy. When both men just continued to look at her so expectantly, she decided neither was going to say anything. She gave them both a disgruntled look for being so insensitive, then continued. "About an hour later, after my head quit pounding from my fall, I set out on my own for a brisk walk. I soon forgot all about my aches and pains, and because it was such a glorious day, I forgot the time. I was just about to look inside the pretty church when I heard all the commotion, and that's when I saw the poor man being pitched to the ground."

She took a deep breath. "I shouted and went running," she explained. "I had lost my direction though, and I ended up on the rise directly above my parents' graves. That's when I saw the men again."

"The same men?" Lyon asked. He was leaning forward in his chair, his elbows braced on his knees.

"Yes, the very same men," Jade answered. She sounded bewildered. "They must have decided it wasn't worth their effort to chase after me, and they were very . . . occupied."

"What were they doing?" Caine asked.

She didn't immediately answer him. A feeling of foreboding settled around his heart. Her hands were clinging to his now. Caine doubted she was aware of that telling action.

"The digging," she finally answered.

"They were digging up the graves?" Lyon asked, his voice incredulous.

"Yes."

Caine didn't show any outward reaction. Lyon looked as though he didn't believe her. She thought it odd indeed that she could tell a lie and both men easily accepted it, yet now when she was telling them the full truth, it was quite another story.

"It's really true," she told Lyon. "I know it sounds bizarre, but I know what I saw."

"All right," Caine answered. "What happened next?"

"I started shouting again," she answered. "Oh, I realize I shouldn't have made a sound, for now I'd drawn their notice again. But I was so outraged I wasn't thinking properly. All three men turned to look up at me. The fancy dressed man held a pistol. Odd, but I couldn't seem to move until the shot rang out. I ran like lightning then. Hudson, Nathan's butler, was working inside the library. I told him what happened, but by the time he'd calmed me down and gained the full story, it was too dark to go looking for the men. We had to wait until the following morning."

"Were the authorities notified?"

She shook her head. "This is where it becomes a little confusing," she admitted. "The next morning, Hudson, with several strong men, went to find the body I'd seen pitched from the rooftop. Hudson wouldn't let me tag along. I was still very upset."

"Of course you were," Caine agreed.

"Yes," she replied with a sigh. "When Hudson and the men returned, they were trying to be as kind as you are now being, Caine, but they had to tell me the truth."

"What truth?"

"They couldn't find any body. The graves hadn't been touched either."

"So they believed you were just . . ."

"Imagining, Lyon?" she interrupted. "Yes, I'm certain they did. Because they were in Nathan's employ, they didn't dare tell me they thought I was . . . addled, but their expressions spoke for them. I immediately went back to the grave to see for myself. The wind and rain had been fierce the night before, yet even so, it didn't look as though the ground had been touched by a shovel."

"Perhaps they'd only just begun to dig when you interrupted them," Caine suggested.

"Yes, they had only just begun," she admitted. "I'll never forget their faces."

"Tell us the rest of this," Caine suggested.

"I spent the rest of the day trying to understand what their motives were. Then I went to Hudson and told him not to bother Nathan with this problem. I lied to the butler and told him I was certain it was just the setting sun playing tricks on me. I must tell you Hudson looked very relieved. He was still worried, of course, since I'd taken that fall down the stairs and bumped my head."

"Jade, couldn't this be your . . ."

"Imagination?" Caine asked. He shook his head. "There were at least five men chasing us last night. No, it isn't her imagination."

She gave Lyon a suspicious look. "You don't believe me, do you?"

"I do now," Lyon replied. "If there were men after you, then you did see something. What happened next?"

"I refused to give up," she told him. She tried to fold her hands in her lap and only then realized she was clinging to Caine's hand again. She pushed it away. "I can be a very stubborn woman. And so, the next morning, I once again set out to find proof."

Lyon smiled at Caine. "I would have done the same," he admitted.

"What morning was this?" Caine asked.

"Yesterday morning," she explained. "I set out on horseback. I didn't make it to my parents' graves, though. They shot my horse out from under me."

"They what?" Caine asked in a near shout.

She was pleased with his stunned reaction. "They killed Nathan's fine horse," she repeated with a nod. "I cannot tell you how upset my brother's going to be when he finds out his favorite steed is dead. It's going to break his heart."

Caine reached for his linen handkerchief when he thought she was about to cry again. "And then what happened?" he asked.

"I went flying to the ground, of course. I was very fortunate because I didn't break my neck. I only sustained minor injuries. Surely you noticed the bruises on my shoulders and arms when you snuck into my bedroom last night."

She turned to look at Caine and waited for his reply. "I didn't notice," he whispered. "And I didn't sneak into your room."

"How could you not have noticed my bruises?"

"I wasn't looking at your shoulders."

She could feel herself blushing again. "Well, you should have been looking at my shoulders," she stammered. "A gentleman would have noticed my injuries right away."

Caine lost his patience. "Jade, not even a eunuch would have . . ."

"Do you want to hear the rest of this or not?"

"Yes," he answered.

"After they shot my horse, I ran all the way back to the main house. I don't know if they chased after me or not. I was very upset. This sort of thing has never happened to me before. I've led a very sheltered life."

She seemed to want agreement. "I'm sure you have," Caine supplied.

"I found Hudson again and told him what happened. I could tell right away he was having trouble believing me. The man kept trying to force a cup of tea down me. This time, however, I had proof."

"Proof?" Caine asked.

"The dead horse, man," she cried out. "Pay attention, please."

"Of course," he returned. "The dead horse. And did Hudson apologize to you when you showed him this dead horse?"

She chewed on her lower lip a long minute while she stared up at him. "Not exactly," she finally answered.

"What do you mean by not exactly?"

Lyon had asked that question. Jade turned to look at him. "I know you're going to find this difficult to believe, but when we reached the spot where the horse had gone down . . . well, he'd vanished."

"No, I don't find that difficult to believe," Lyon drawled out. He leaned back against the chair again. "Do you, Caine?"

Caine smiled. "It makes as much sense as everything else she's told us."

"Hudson insisted on returning to the stables," she continued. "He was convinced we'd find the horse had found its way back home on its own."

"And was he correct in that assumption?" Caine asked.

"No, he wasn't. The men searched the grounds for the rest of the morning but they couldn't find him. There were fresh wagon tracks along the south trail, though. Do you know what I think happened, Caine? I think they put the horse in the wagon and carried him away. What do you think of that possibility?"

She sounded so eager he was a little sorry to have to disappoint her. "You obviously don't have any idea how much a fully grown horse weighs, Jade. You can take my word it would require more than three men to lift it."

"Difficult," Lyon interjected. "But not impossible."

"Perhaps the animal only had a flesh wound and wandered off," said Caine.

"A flesh wound between his eyes? I doubt that." She let out a groan of frustration. "Nathan's going to be so upset when he finds out about his house and his carriage, too."

"His house? What the hell happened to his house?" Caine muttered. "Damn, I wish you'd tell this in sequence, Jade."

"I believe she has finally gotten to the fires," Lyon said.

"Why, it burned to the ground," Jade returned.

"When did the house burn down?" Caine asked with another weary sigh. "Before or after the horse was killed?"

"Almost directly after," she explained. "Hudson had ordered Nathan's carriage made ready for me. I had decided to return to London and find Nathan. I was good and sick of the way his servants were acting. They kept a wide berth around me, and kept giving me odd looks. I knew Nathan would help me solve this riddle."

She didn't realize she'd raised her voice until Caine patted her hand and said, "Just calm down, sweet, and finish this."

"You're looking at me the very same way Hudson . . . oh, all right then, I'll finish. I was on my way back to London when the footman shouted that Nathan's house was on fire. He could see the smoke coming over the hilltops. We immediately turned around, of course, but by the time we arrived back at the house . . . well, it was too late. I ordered the servants to go to Nathan's London town house."

"And then you set out for London again?" Caine asked. He was absentmindedly rubbing the back of her neck. It felt too good for Jade to ask him to stop.

"We stayed on the main road, but when we turned a curve, they were waiting for us. The driver was so frightened, he ran off."

"The bastard."

Lyon had made that remark. Caine nodded agreement.

"I don't fault the man," Jade defended. "He was frightened. People do . . . peculiar things when they're afraid."

"Some do," Caine allowed.

"Tell us what happened then, Jade?" Lyon asked.

"They blocked the doors and set the carriage on fire," she answered. "I was able to wiggle out through the ill-framed window. Nathan spent good coins on that vehicle, but it wasn't at all sturdy. I was able to kick the hinges away from the branches easily enough. I don't believe I'll mention that fact to my brother, though, for it would only upset him . . . unless, of course, he thinks to hire the same company."

"You're digressing yet again," Caine said.

Lyon smiled. "She reminds me of Christina," he admitted. "Jade, why don't you go and find my wife for me? She was going to pack a satchel for you to take with you."

Jade felt as though she'd just been given a reprieve. Her stomach was in a quiver of knots. She felt as though she'd just had to relive the terror.

She didn't waste any time at all leaving the room.

"Well, Caine?" Lyon asked when they were alone. "What do you think?"

"There were men chasing us last night," Caine reminded his friend.

"Do you believe her story?"

"She saw something."

"That isn't what I asked you."

Caine slowly shook his head. "Not a damned word," he admitted. "And you?"

Lyon shook his head. "It's the most illogical story I've ever heard. But damn, if she's telling the truth, we've got to help her."

"And if she's not?" Caine asked, already guessing the answer.

"You damned well better watch your back."

"Lyon, you don't think . . ."

Lyon wouldn't let him finish. "I'll tell you what I do know," he interrupted. "One, you're not being objective. I can't fault you, Caine. I reacted to Christina in much the same way you're reacting to Jade. Two, she is in danger and has put you in danger, too. Those are the only facts we can take as true."

Caine knew he was right. He leaned back against the settee. "Now tell me what your gut reaction is."

"Perhaps this has something to do with her father," Lyon suggested with a shrug. "I'll start looking into the Earl of Wakerfield's history. Richards will be able to help."

Caine started to disagree and then changed his mind. "It couldn't hurt," he said. "Still, I'm beginning to wonder if her brother might not be behind all this. Remember, Lyon. Nathan went to London to help a friend in trouble. That's when all this started."

"If we accept the story she told us."

"Yes," Caine answered.

Lyon let out a long sigh. "I only have one question to put to you, Caine." His voice was low, insistent. "Do you trust her?"

Caine stared at his friend a long minute. "If we apply logic to this bizarre situation . . ."

Lyon shook his head. "I value your instincts, friend. Answer me."

"Yes," Caine said. He grinned then. For the first time in his life, he pushed reason aside. "I trust her with my life but I couldn't give you one valid reason why. How's that for logic, Lyon?"

His friend smiled. "I trust her, too. You don't have the faintest idea why you trust her, though, do you, Caine?"

Lyon sounded downright condescending. Caine raised an eyebrow in reaction. "What are you getting at?"

"I trust her only because you do," Lyon explained. "Your instincts are never wrong. You've saved my backside more than once because I listened to you."

"You still haven't explained what your point is," Caine reminded him.

"I trusted Christina," Lyon said. "Almost from the very beginning. I swear to you it was blind faith on my part. She led me a merry chase, too. Now I must side with my wife. Christina, as you know, has some rather unusual opinions. She's on the mark this time, though."

"And how is that?" Caine asked.

"I believe, good friend, that you've just met your destiny." He let out a soft chuckle and shook his head. "God help you now, Caine, for your chase is just about to begin."

Chapter Seven

The ladies were waiting in the foyer for Caine and Lyon. A large gray and white speckled satchel was on the floor between them.

Caine tried to lift it, then shook his head. "For God's sake, Jade, no horse is going to be able to carry this load. The weight will be too much for the animal."

He knelt on one knee, flipped open the catch on the satchel and looked inside. Then he let out a low whistle. "There's a bloody arsenal in here," he told Lyon. "Who packed this thing?"

"I did," Christina answered. "There are just a few weapons I thought Jade might need to protect the two of you."

"Weapons Jade might need to protect *me?*" He looked incredulous. "Lyon, did your wife just insult me?"

Lyon smiled while he nodded. "She certainly did, Caine. You might as well apologize now and get it over with."

"Why in God's name would I apologize?"

"It will save time," Lyon explained. He was trying not to laugh. Caine looked thoroughly bewildered.

"Marriage has made you soft," Caine muttered.

"As soft as milk toast," Lyon announced with a grin.

Caine turned his attention back to stripping the unnecessary items from the bag.

While both ladies gasped in dismay, Caine tossed several long knives to the floor, two pistols, and one mean-looking link of chain. "You aren't going to need all of this, Jade. Besides, you're far too timid to use any of them."

She was already gathering up the weapons. "Leave them there, my little warrior."

"Oh, have it your way," she muttered. "And quit using endearments on me, sir. Save them for the other women in your life. I'm neither your sweetheart, nor your love, and I'm certainly not your warrior. Oh, don't look so innocently perplexed, Caine. Christina told me all about the other women."

He was still trying to make sense out of her earlier comment. "Calling you a warrior is an endearment in your befuddled mind?"

"It most certainly is, you rude man," she replied. "I won't make you apologize for calling me befuddled, but only because you're probably still cranky over the news that your town house was burned down."

Caine felt like growling in frustration. He finished stripping the bag of unnecessary weapons, then clipped the lock shut. "Thank you for going to all the trouble, Christina, but you may need your weapons to keep Lyon safe. Come along, Jade," he ordered. He took the bag in one hand and Jade's hand in the other. His grip stung.

She didn't mind. She was too pleased at how well she had told her stories—how she had at once convinced Caine and confused him. The set of Caine's jaw indicated he wasn't in a reasonable mood. She let him drag her to the back door. Lyon's groom had readied two mounts for them. Just as Jade was passing through the doorway, Christina threw her arms around her and hugged her tight. "God speed," she whispered.

Caine tied the satchel to his mount, then tossed Jade on top of the other horse. She waved farewell as she followed Caine through the back gate.

Jade glanced back again to look at Lyon and Christina. She tried to memorize Christina's smile, Lyon's frown, too, for she was certain she wouldn't ever see them again.

Christina had mentioned destiny more than once to her. She believed Caine was going to become Jade's lifelong mate. But Christina didn't understand the full situation. And when Christina learned the truth, Jade feared her new friend would never acknowledge her again.

It was too painful to think about. Jade forced herself to think only of the one reason she was there. Her duty was to protect Caine until Nathan came home.

And that was that. Her destiny had been determined years ago.

"Stay closer to me, Jade," Caine ordered from over his shoulder.

Jade immediately nudged her mount closer.

Caine certainly took a roundabout way out of London. He circled the outskirts of the city, then backtracked to make certain they weren't being followed.

He refused to take the north road until they were an hour away from the city.

The ride should have taken them approximately three hours. Yet because of his cautious nature, they were only halfway to their destination before he took to the main road.

Jade recognized the area. "If they haven't moved it, Nathan's carriage is just a little ahead of us," she told Caine.

It was further away then she remembered. Jade decided the vehicle had been dragged off when they'd ridden another half hour or so and still not spotted it.

Then they turned yet another crooked bend in the road and saw it on the side of the narrow ravine.

Caine never said a word. His expression was grim, however, when they rode past the carriage.

"Well?" she asked.

"It was gutted, all right," he answered.

She heard the anger in his voice and began to worry that he was blaming her for the destruction. "Is that all you have to say?" she asked. She nudged her mount to his side so she could see his expression. "You didn't believe me, did you? That's why you're angry."

"I believe you now," he countered.

She waited a long minute before she realized he wasn't going to say any more.

"And?" she asked, thinking to gain his apology.

"And what?"

"And haven't you anything else to say?" she demanded.

"I could say that as soon as I find the bastards who did this I'm going to kill them," he replied in a mild, thoroughly chilling voice. "And after they are dead, I'll probably want to set their bodies on fire just for the hell of it. Yes, I could say that, but it would only upset you, wouldn't it, Jade?"

Her eyes had widened during his recitation. There wasn't any doubt in her mind that he meant to do what he said. A shiver passed through her.

"Yes, Caine, it would upset me to hear such plans. You can't go around killing people, no matter how angry you are with them."

He pulled his mount to an abrupt stop next to hers. Then he reached out and grabbed the back of her neck. She was so startled, she didn't try to move away.

"I protect what is mine."

She wasn't about to give him argument. He looked as if he might throttle her if she did. Jade simply stared at him and waited for him to let go of her.

"Do you understand what I'm telling you?" he demanded.

"Yes," she answered. "You will protect what belongs to you. I understand."

Caine shook his head. The little innocent was actually

trying to placate him. He suddenly jerked her to the side of her saddle, leaned down, and kissed her. Hard. Possessively.

She was more bewildered than ever. Caine pulled back and stared into her eyes. "It's time you understood that you're going to belong to me, Jade."

She shook her head. "I'll belong to no man, Caine, and it's time you understood that."

He looked furious with her. Then, in the flash of a moment, his expression softened. Her sweet protector was back in evidence. Jade almost sighed with relief.

"It's time we left the main road again," he said, deliberately changing the topic.

"Caine, I want you to realize . . ."

"Don't argue," he interrupted.

She nodded and was about to nudge her horse down the slope when Caine took the reins from her hands and lifted her into his lap.

"Why am I riding with you?" she asked.

"You're tired."

"You could tell?"

For the first time in a long while, he smiled. "I could tell."

"I am weary," she admitted. "Caine, will Lyon's horse follow us? Your friend will be upset if his mount gets lost."

"She'll follow us," he answered.

"Good," she answered. She wrapped her arms around his waist and rested the side of her face against his chest. "You smell so nice," she whispered.

"So do you," he told her.

He sounded terribly preoccupied to her. He also seemed determined to take the most challenging route through the forest. Jade put up with the inconvenience for a good ten minutes, then finally asked, "Why are you making this journey so difficult?"

Caine blocked another low-hanging branch with his arm before answering her. "We're being followed."

That statement, given so matter-of-factly, stunned her as

much as a pinch in the backside would if given by a stranger. She was immediately outraged. "We're not," she cried out. "I would have noticed."

She tried to pull away from him so she could look over his shoulder to see for herself. Caine wouldn't let her move. "It's all right," he said. "They're still a distance behind us."

"How do you know?" she asked. "Have they been following us since we left London? No, of course they haven't. I really would have noticed. How many do you suppose they are? Caine? Are you absolutely certain?"

He squeezed her into quitting her questions. "I'm certain," he answered. "They've been following us for about three, maybe four miles now. More specifically, since we reached my property line. I believe their number is six or seven."

"But . . ."

"I spotted them the last time I backtracked," he patiently explained.

"I backtracked with you, if you'll remember," she countered. "And I didn't see anyone."

She sounded incensed. Caine didn't know what to make of that reaction.

"Are we very far from your house?"

"About fifteen minutes away," Caine answered.

They broke through a clearing a short while later. Jade felt as though she'd just entered a wonderland. "It's beautiful here," she whispered.

The grassy clearing was circled on two sides by a narrow stream that trailed down a lazy slope adjacent to a small cabin. Sunlight filtered through the branches bordering the paradise.

"Perhaps the gamekeeper is inside the cabin," she said. "He might be willing to help us trap the villains."

"The cabin's deserted."

"Then we'll just have to trap them on our own. Did you leave all the pistols behind?"

He didn't answer her. "Caine? Aren't we going to stop?"

"No," he said. "We're just taking a shortcut."

"Have you chosen another spot to wait for them?"

"I'm taking you home first, Jade. I'm not about to take any risks with you along. Now tuck your head and close your mouth. It's going to get rough."

Since he was back to sounding surly again, she did as he ordered. She could feel his chin on the top of her head as she squeezed her face against the base of his throat.

"Someday I want to come back to this spot," she whispered.

He didn't remark on that hope. He hadn't been exaggerating either when he said it was going to get rough. As soon as they reached the open fields, Caine pushed his mount into a full gallop. Jade felt like she was flying through the air again. It wasn't at all the same feeling as being pitched into the Thames, though, for now she had Caine to hold onto.

Whoever was behind this treachery had sent men to Caine's estate to wait for him. Jade worried about the possibility of an ambush when they neared the main grounds. She prayed her men would be there to take up the battle.

They were just about to reach the crest and the cover of the trees again when the sound of pistol shots rang out. Jade didn't know how to protect Caine's back now. She tried to twist in his arms to see where the threat was coming from, even as she instinctively splayed her hands wide up his shoulders to cover as much of him as she could.

The shots were coming from the southeast. Jade jostled herself over onto his left thigh, just as another shot echoed in the wind.

"Hold still," Caine ordered against her ear at the same second she felt a mild sting in her right side. She let out a soft gasp of surprise and tried to look at her waist. It felt as though a lion had just swatted her with his claws extended. Just as quickly, however, the ache began to dissipate. A rather irritating burning sensation radiated up her side, and Jade decided one of the branches they'd just broken through had cut into her side.

Numbness set in and she put the matter of her paltry scratch aside.

"We're almost home," Caine told her.

In her worry, she forgot to act afraid. "Watch your back when we get near the house," she ordered.

Caine didn't answer that command. He took the back road up to the stables. His men must have heard the commotion, for at least ten hands were rushing toward the forest, their weapons at the ready.

Caine shouted to the stablemaster to open the doors, then rode inside. Jade's mount galloped behind. The stablemaster grabbed the reins and had the mare slapped inside the first stall before Caine had lifted Jade to the ground.

His grip on her waist made the ache in her side start nagging again. She bit her lower lip to keep herself from shouting at him.

"Kelley!" Caine shouted.

A yellow-haired, middle-aged man with a stocky frame and a full beard rushed over. "Yes, mi'lord?"

"Stay here with Jade," he ordered. "Keep the doors closed until I get back."

Caine tried to remount his steed then, but Jade grabbed hold of the back of his jacket and gave it a fierce jerk. "Are you demented? You can't go back outside."

"Let go, sweetheart," he said. "I'll be right back."

He pulled her hands away and gently pushed her back against the stall. Jade wasn't about to give up, however. She dug into his lapels and held on.

"But Caine," she wailed while he was peeling her hands away. "They mean to kill you."

"I know, love."

"Then why . . ."

"I mean to kill them first."

He realized he shouldn't have shared that truth with her when she threw her arms around his waist and squeezed him in a grip that was surprisingly strong.

They both heard two more shots ring out while he pulled her arms away.

Caine assumed his men had taken up the fight. Jade prayed her men had already intervened and chased the villains away.

"Shut the doors after me, Kelley!" Caine shouted as he swiftly remounted and goaded his stallion around.

Another shot sounded just a minute or two after Caine had left. Jade rushed past the stablemaster and looked out the small square window. Caine's body wasn't sprawled out in a pool of blood in the field. She started breathing again.

"There's absolutely nothing to be worried about," she muttered.

"You best get away from the window," Kelley whispered from behind.

Jade ignored that suggestion until he started tugging on her arm. "Mi'lady, please wait for the Marquess in a safer spot. Come and sit over here," he continued. "The Marquess will be back soon."

She couldn't sit down. Jade couldn't stop herself from pacing or fretting, either. She prayed that both Matthew and Jimbo had taken care of the intruders. They were two of her most loyal men. Both were well trained in trickery, too, for Black Harry had personally seen to their education.

This was all Caine's fault, she decided. She certainly wouldn't be in such a state of nerves if he'd turned out to be anything like the man she'd read about in the file. He seemed to have two completely different personalities, however. Oh, she knew the file told the truth. His superiors had referred to him as a cold, methodical man when the task at hand needed his special consideration.

Yet the man she'd encountered wasn't at all cold or

unfeeling. She'd played on Caine's protector instincts, but she believed he was going to be very difficult all the same. He hadn't turned out to be difficult at all, though. He was a caring man who'd already taken her under his wing.

The problem, of course, was the contradiction. Jade didn't like inconsistencies. It made Caine unpredictable. And unpredictable meant dangerous.

The doors suddenly flew open. Caine stood there, his mount still in a lathered pant behind him.

She was so relieved to see he was safe, her knees went weak on her. Every muscle in her body began to ache. She had to sit down in the chair Kelley provided before she could speak.

"You're all right, then?" she managed to ask.

Caine thought she looked as if she were about to burst into tears. He gave her a smile to reassure her, then led his horse inside. After handing the reins to the stablemaster, and waving the men who were following him back outside, he casually leaned against the wall next to her. He was deliberately trying to make her believe nothing much out of the ordinary had happened.

"The fight was over and done with by the time I got to the forest."

"The fight was over? How could it be over?" she asked. "I don't understand."

"They must have changed their minds," he said.

"You don't have to lie to me," she cried out. "And you can quit acting as though we're discussing the crops, too. Now tell me what happened."

He let out a long sigh. "Most of the fight was over and done with by the time I got there."

"Caine, no more lies," she demanded.

"I'm not lying," he countered.

"Then make sense," she ordered. "You're supposed to be logical, remember?"

He'd never heard that tone of voice from her before. God's truth, she sounded like a commander now. Caine grinned. "It was the damnedest thing I ever saw," he admitted. "I got two of them, then turned to the area I thought hid the rest, but when I got there, they were gone."

"They ran away?"

He shook his head. "There was evidence that a fight had taken place."

"Then your men . . ."

"Were with me," he interjected.

Jade folded her hands in her lap, her gaze downcast so he wouldn't be able to see her expression. She feared she wouldn't be able to hide her relief or her pleasure. Matthew and Jimbo had done their jobs well. "No, that doesn't make any sense," she agreed.

"There was evidence of a fight," he said, watching her closely.

"Evidence?" she asked, her voice whisper soft. "Such as?"

"Footprints . . . blood on a leaf," he returned. "Other signs as well, but not a body in sight."

"Do you think they might have had an argument among themselves?"

"Without making a sound?" he asked, sounding incredulous.

"You didn't hear any noise?"

"No." Caine continued to lean against the wall. He stared at Jade.

She stared back. She thought he might be filtering through the information he'd gained over the past hours, yet the strange expression on his face worried her. She was suddenly reminded of a story Black Harry liked to tell about the wonderful, unpredictable grizzly bears who roamed the wilderness of the Americas. The animal was such a cunning breed. Harry said the bear was actually much smarter than his human trackers. Often he would deliberately lead his victims into a trap or circle back to attack. The poor unsuspecting hunter usually died before realizing he'd actually become the hunted.

Was Caine as cunning as the grizzly? That possibility was too chilling to think about. "Caine? You frighten me when you look at me that way," she whispered. "I hate it when you frown."

She underlined that lie by wringing her hands together. "You're sorry you got involved in this mess, aren't you? I can't fault you, sir," she added in a melodramatic tone of voice. "You're going to get yourself killed if you stay with me. I'm very like a cat," she continued with a nod. "I bring people terrible luck. Just leave me here in your barn and go on home. When darkness falls, I'll walk back to London."

"I believe you've just insulted me again," he drawled out. "Haven't I already explained that no one touches what belongs to me?"

"I don't happen to belong to you," she snapped, somewhat irritated he hadn't been impressed with her theatrics. The man should be trying to comfort her now, shouldn't he? "You can't just decide that I . . . oh, never mind. You're shamefully possessive, aren't you?"

He nodded. "I am possessive by nature, Jade, and you will belong to me."

He sounded downright mean now. Jade valiantly held his stare. "You're not only in error, sir, but you're horribly stubborn, too. I'd wager you never shared your toys when you were a child, did you?"

She didn't give him time to answer that allegation. "Still, I didn't mean to insult you."

Caine pulled her to her feet. He put his arm around her shoulders and started toward the doors.

"Caine?"

"Yes?"

"You can't continue to protect me."

"And why is that, love?"

"A father shouldn't have to lose two sons."

The woman certainly didn't put much store in his ability, he thought to himself. Still, she sounded so frightened, he decided not to take exception. "No, he shouldn't," he replied. "Your brother shouldn't have to lose his only sister, either. Now listen to me. I'm not sorry I got involved, and I'm not going to leave you. I'm your protector, remember?"

Her expression was solemn. "No, you're more than just my protector," she said. "You've become my guardian angel."

Before he could answer her, she leaned up on tiptoe and kissed him.

"I shouldn't have done that," she said then, feeling herself blush. "I don't usually show much affection, but when I'm with you . . . well, I find I like it when you put your arm around me or hug me. I do wonder about this sudden change in me. Do you think I might be wanton?"

He didn't laugh. She seemed too sincere and he didn't want to hurt her feelings. "I'm pleased you like it when I touch you," he said. He paused just inside the door and leaned down to kiss her. "I find I love touching you." His mouth captured hers then. The kiss was long, hard, lingering. His tongue rubbed against her soft lips until they opened for him, then slid inside with lazy insistence. When he pulled back, she had a most bemused look on her face again.

"You tried your damnedest to become my shield on that horse, didn't you, love?"

She was so surprised by that question, her mind emptied of all plausible explanations.

"What did I do?"

"You tried to become my shield," he answered. "When you realized the shots were coming from . . ."

"I didn't," she interrupted.

"And the other night, when you threw yourself into me and knocked me off center, you actually saved my life," he continued as though she hadn't interrupted him.

"I didn't mean to," she interjected. "I was afraid."

She couldn't discern from his expression what he was thinking. "If there is a next time, I promise not to get in your way," she rushed out. "Please forgive me for not being very logical, Caine. You see, I've never been chased after before, or shot at, or . . . do you know, I don't believe I feel very well now. Yes, I feel sick. I really do."

It took him a moment to make the switch in topics.

"Is it your head, sweet? We should have asked Christina for something to put on that bump."

She nodded. "It is my head and my stomach and my side, too," she told him as they walked toward the front of the main house.

She was weak with relief, for her aches and pains had waylaid his attention. Jade glanced around her, realizing for the first time how beautiful the landscape was. When they turned the corner, she came to an abrupt stop.

The drive seemed to be unending. It was lined with a multitude of trees, most at least a hundred years old by Jade's estimation. The branches arched high across the gravel drive, providing an enchanting canopy.

The redbrick house was three stories high. White pillars lined the front, adding a regal touch. Each of the oblong windows was draped in white cloth and each was identically held in place with black tiebacks. The front door had been painted black as well, and even from the drive, the attention to detail was very apparent.

"You didn't tell me you were so wealthy," she announced.

She sounded irritated to him. "I live a comfortable life," he answered, a shrug in his voice.

"Comfortable? This rivals Carlton House," she said.

She suddenly felt as out of place as a fish on the beach.

Jade pushed his arm away from her shoulders and continued on.

"I don't like wealthy men," she announced.

"Too bad," he replied, laughing.

"Why is it too bad?" she asked.

Caine was trying to get her to move again. She'd stopped at the bottom of the steps and was now staring up at the house as though it was somehow a threat to her. He could see the fear in her eyes.

"It's going to be all right, Jade," he said. "Don't be afraid."

She reacted as though he'd just defamed her family. "I'm not afraid," she stated in her most haughty tone and with a glare to match.

It had been instinctive, giving him that setdown for daring to suggest such a sin, but she soon realized her blunder. Damn, she was suppose to be afraid. And now Caine was looking at her with that unreadable expression on his face again.

She never would have made that error if she hadn't been in such sorry shape. Lord, she ached.

"You insult yourself by saying I'm afraid," she explained.

"I what?"

"Caine, if I am still afraid, then it would mean I don't have any faith in you, wouldn't it?"

Her sudden smile diverted his attention. "As to that," she continued, "I've already counted eleven men with their weapons at the ready. I assumed they were in your employ, since they aren't trying to shoot us. The fact that you'd already seen to such nice precautions set my mind to rest."

Her smile widened when she guessed he was thinking she was daft again. Then she stumbled. It wasn't another ploy to turn his attention, but a real stumble that would have felled her to the ground if he hadn't caught her.

"My knees are weak," she hastily explained. "I'm not

accustomed to riding. Do let go of my waist, Caine. It aches a bit."

"What doesn't ache, love?" he asked. His tone was filled with amusement, yet there was tenderness in his eyes.

She tried to act disgruntled. "I'm a woman, remember? And you did say all women were weak. Is that the reason you're looking so smug now, sir? Because I've just given your outrageous opinion substance?"

"When you look at me like that, I seem to forget all about how confusing you are. You have the most beautiful eyes, love. I think I know what green fire looks like now."

She knew he was trying to embarrass her. His slow, sexy wink said as much. The man could be a tease all right. When he leaned down and kissed the top of her forehead, she had to catch herself from letting out a telling sigh of pleasure. She forgot all about her aches and pains.

The front door opened then, drawing Caine's attention. With his gentle prodding, she also turned, just as a tall, elderly man appeared in the entrance.

He looked just like a gargoyle. Jade assumed the man was Caine's butler. He was dressed all in black, save for his white cravat, of course, and his austere manner more than matched his formal attire. The servant looked as though he had been dunked in a vat of starch and left out to dry.

"That's my man, Sterns," Caine explained. "Don't let him frighten you, Jade," he added when she moved a step closer to his side. "He can be as intimidating as a king when the mood comes over him."

The thread of affection in Caine's voice told her he wasn't at all intimidated. "If Sterns takes a liking to you, and I'm sure he will, then he'll defend you to the death. He's as loyal as they come."

The man under discussion advanced down the steps with a dignified stride. When he faced his employer, he made a stiff bow. Jade noticed the wings of silver hair on the sides of his temples and guessed his age to be in the middle to late fifties. Both the salt and pepper hair and his grossly unattractive face reminded her of her Uncle Harry.

She liked him already.

"Good day, mi'lord," Sterns stated before he turned to look at Jade. "Did your hunt go well?"

"I wasn't hunting," Caine answered.

"Then the pistol shots I heard were just for sport?"

The servant hadn't bothered to look at his employer when he made that remark but continued to give Jade his full scrutiny.

Caine smiled. He was vastly amused by Sterns' behavior. His man wasn't one to rattle easily. He was certainly rattled now, and Caine knew he was fighting quite a battle to maintain his rigid composure.

"I was after men, not game," Caine explained.

"And were you successful?" Sterns inquired in a voice that suggested he wasn't the least interested.

"No," Caine answered. He let out a sigh over his butler's lack of attention. Still, he couldn't very well fault the man for falling under Jade's spell. He'd already done the same. "Yes, Sterns, she is very beautiful, isn't she?"

The butler gave an abrupt nod, then forced himself to turn back to his lord.

"That she is, mi'lord," he agreed. "Her character, however, is still to be discerned." He clasped his hands behind his back and gave his lord a quick nod.

"You'll find that her character is just as beautiful," Caine replied.

"You've never brought a lady home before, mi'lord."

"No, I haven't."

"And she is our guest?"

"She is," Caine answered.

"Am I making more of this than I should, perchance?"

Caine shook his head. "No, you're not, Sterns."

The butler raised an eyebrow, then nodded again. "It's about time, mi'lord," Sterns said. "Do you require one of the guest chambers made ready or will the lady be occupying your rooms?"

Because the sinful question had been asked in such a matter-of-fact fashion, and because she was still stinging from their rudeness in talking about her as though she wasn't even there, she was a little slow to take insult. Only when the fullness of what Sterns was suggesting settled in her mind did she react. She moved away from Caine's side and took a step toward the butler. "This lady will require a room of her own, my good man. A room with a sturdy lock on the door. Do I make myself clear?"

Sterns straightened himself to his full height. "I understand perfectly well, mi'lady," he announced. Although the man's tone was dignified, there was a noticeable sparkle in his brown eyes. It was a look only Caine had been privy to before. "I shall check the bolt myself," he added with a meaningful glance in his employer's direction.

"Thank you so much, Sterns," Jade replied. "I have many enemies chasing after me, you see, and I won't rest properly if I have to worry about certain gentlemen sneaking into my room at night to put my nightgown back on me. You can understand that, can't you?"

"Jade, don't start . . ." Caine began.

"Caine suggested I stay with his mama and papa, but I couldn't do that, Sterns," she continued, ignoring Caine's rude interruption. "I don't want to drag his dear parents into this sorry affair. When one is being hunted down like a mad dog, one simply doesn't have time to worry about one's reputation. Don't you agree, sir?"

Sterns had blinked several times during Jade's explanation, then nodded when she gave him such a sweet, expectant look.

A clap of thunder echoed in the distance. "We're going to get soaked if we stand out here much longer," Caine said.

"Sterns, I want you to send Parks for the physician before the storm breaks."

"Caine, is that really necessary?" Jade asked.

"It is."

"You're ill, mi'lord?" Sterns inquired, his concern apparent in his gaze.

"No," Caine answered. "I want Winters to have a look at Jade. She's been in a mishap."

"A mishap?" Sterns asked, turning back to Jade.

"He threw me in the Thames," she explained.

Sterns raised an eyebrow in reaction to that statement. Jade nodded, pleased with his obvious interest.

"That isn't the mishap I was referring to," Caine muttered. "Jade has a rather nasty bump on her head. It's made her a little light-headed."

"Oh, that," Jade countered. "It doesn't sting nearly as much as the stitch in my side," she added. "I don't want your physician prodding at me. I won't have it."

"You will have it," Caine replied. "I promise you that he won't prod. I won't let him."

"I'm afraid it isn't possible to fetch Winters for your lady," Sterns interjected. "He's gone missing."

"Winters is missing?"

"Over a month now," Sterns explained. "Should I send for another physician? Your mother turned to Sir Harwick when she couldn't locate Winters. I understand she was pleased with his services."

"Who required Sir Harwick's attention?" Caine asked.

"Your father, though he protested most vehemently," Sterns said. "His loss of weight has your mother and your sisters very concerned."

"He grieves for Colin," Caine said, his tone abrupt, weary, too. "I hope to God he pulls out of this soon. All right, Sterns, send Parks for Harwick."

"Do not send Parks for Harwick," Jade commanded.

"Jade, now isn't the time to be difficult."

"Mi'lady, what happened to you in this unfortunate mishap? Did someone hit you on your head?"

"No," she answered shyly. She lowered her gaze to the ground. "I fell. Please don't become upset on my behalf, Sterns," she added when she peeked up and caught his sympathetic expression. "It's only a little, insignificant bump. Would you like to see it?" she asked as she lifted her hair away from her temple.

The movement made her side start nagging her again. She couldn't quite block the pain this time.

Sterns couldn't have been more interested in her injury, or more compassionate. While Caine watched, his butler turned into a lady's maid. He stammered out all sorts of condolences, and when Jade accepted his arm and the two of them started up the steps together, Caine was left to stare after them.

"We must put you to bed immediately, dear lady," Sterns announced. "How did you take your fall, mi'lady, if I may be so bold as to inquire?"

"I lost my balance and fell down a full flight of steps," she answered. "It was very clumsy of me."

"Oh, no, I'm certain you aren't at all clumsy," Sterns rushed out.

"It is kind of you to say so, Sterns. Do you know, the pain is not nearly as awful now, but my side . . . well, sir, I don't wish to alarm you, nor do I wish you to think I'm a complainer . . . Caine believes I do nothing but complain and cry. Those were his very words, sir. Yes, they were . . ."

Caine came up behind her and grabbed hold of her shoulders. "Let's have a look at your side. Take your jacket off."

"No," she answered as she walked into the foyer. "You'll only prod at it, Caine."

A line of servants waited to greet their employer. Jade breezed past them while she held on to Sterns' arm. "Sir, is my room in the front of the house? I do hope so. I would love to have a window facing the lovely view of the drive and the forest beyond."

Because of her cheerful tone of voice, Caine decided she'd been exaggerating about her aches. "Sterns, take her upstairs and get her settled while I take care of a few matters."

He didn't wait for a reply but turned and walked out the front door again.

"Have Parks fetch the physician," Sterns called down from the top of the steps. The butler turned to Jade. "Don't argue with us, mi'lady. You look terribly pale to me. I cannot help but notice that your hands feel like ice."

Jade hastily removed her hand from his. She hadn't realized she'd held onto him as she climbed the steps. Sterns had noticed, of course. The poor dear was obviously worn out. Why, she was actually trembling.

"The sun will be setting soon. You'll have your dinner in bed," he added. "Did mi'lord really throw you in the Thames?" he asked when he thought she was about to argue with his decisions.

She smiled. "He did," she answered. "And he has yet to apologize. He threw away my satchel, too. I'm a pauper now," she added, sounding cheerful again. "Lady Christina did give me some of her lovely clothes, though, and I thank God for that."

"You don't seem very saddened by your current predicament," Sterns remarked. He opened the door to her room, then stepped back so she could pass through.

"Oh, I don't believe in being sad," she answered. "Why, Sterns, what a lovely bedroom. Gold is my very favorite color. Is the coverlet made of silk?"

"Satin," Sterns answered, smiling over the enthusiasm in her voice. "May I assist you in removing your jacket, mi'lady?"

Jade nodded. "Would you open the window first? It's a bit

stuffy in here." She walked over to look outside, judging the distance to the cover of trees. Matthew and Jimbo would be waiting for her signal come darkness. They'd be watching the windows for the lighted candle, the sign they'd decided upon, to indicate that all was well.

Jade turned when Sterns began to tug on her jacket. "I shall have this cleaned for you, mi'lady."

"Yes, please," she answered. "I believe there's a small tear in the side too, Sterns. Could you have someone patch it up, too?"

Sterns didn't answer her. Jade looked up at his face. "Have you gone ill, sir?" she asked. The servant was suddenly looking quite green in the complexion to her. "Sterns, do sit down. Don't take insult, but I believe you might be in jeopardy of a swoon."

He shook his head when she shoved him into the chair adjacent to the window. The butler finally found his voice. He shouted in a true roar for his lord to present himself.

Caine was just starting up the stairs when he heard Sterns' bellow. "Now what has she done?" he muttered to himself. He rushed through the foyer where the servants were again lined up, passed a wave in their general direction, and then raced up the staircase.

He came to an abrupt stop when he reached the doorway, for the sight he came upon did surprise him. Sterns was struggling to get out of the wingback chair. Jade held him down with one hand on his shoulder. She was fanning him with a thin book she held in her other hand.

"What in God's name . . . Sterns? Are you ill?"

"He's gone faint," Jade announced. "Help me get him to the bed, Caine."

"Her side, mi'lord," Sterns protested. "Dear lady, do quit waving that book in my face. Caine, have a look at her side."

Caine understood before Jade did. He hurried over to Jade, turned her around, and when he got a good look at the god-awful blood soaking her white blouse, he wanted to sit down, too.

"Dear God," he whispered. "Oh, sweetheart, what happened to you?"

Jade let out a loud gasp when she saw the damage. She would have staggered backward if he hadn't been holding her. "Love, didn't you know you were bleeding?"

She looked dumbfounded. "I didn't know. I thought it was a scratch from one of the branches."

Sterns stood on her other side. "She's lost a fair amount of blood, mi'lord," he whispered.

"Yes, she has," Caine answered, trying his best not to sound overly concerned. He didn't want her to become any more frightened.

His hands shook when he gently lifted the garment away from her waistband. She noticed. "It's bad, isn't it?" she whispered.

"Don't look at it, sweetheart," he said. "Does it hurt?"

"The minute I saw all the blood, it started hurting like the devil."

Jade noticed the tear in Christina's garment then. "They ruined my friend's lovely top," she cried out. "They bloody well shot right through it. Just look at that hole, Caine. It's the size of a . . . of a . . ."

"Pistol shot?" Sterns suggested.

Caine had worked the top away and was now using his knife on her chemise.

"She's getting dotty on us," Sterns whispered. "You'd best put her on the bed before she swoons."

"I'll not swoon, Sterns, and you should apologize for thinking I would. Caine, please let go of me. It isn't decent to cut my clothes away. I'll take care of this injury by myself."

Jade was suddenly desperate to get both men out of her room. Since the moment she'd seen the injury, her stomach had been in an uproar. She felt light-headed now and her knees were starting to buckle up on her.

"Well, Sterns?" she asked. "Do I get my apology or not?"

Before the butler was given a chance to answer, Jade said, "Bloody hell. I *am* going to swoon after all."

Chapter Eight

Jade came awake with a start. She was surprised to find herself in bed, for she didn't have the faintest idea how she'd gotten there. After a long moment, the truth settled in. Good God, she really had fainted.

She was trying to come to terms with this humiliation when she realized the breeze coming in through the open window was cooling her bare skin.

She opened her eyes to find Sterns leaning over her from one side of the bed and Caine bending over her from the opposite side. Their deep scowls were almost enough to send her into another faint.

"The shot went clear through," Caine muttered.

"Thank the Lord for that," Sterns whispered.

"Which one of you scoundrels removed my clothing when I wasn't looking?" she asked, her tone of voice as crisp as new frost.

Sterns visibly jumped. Caine merely smiled. "You're feeling better, mi'lady?" the butler inquired after he'd regained his composure.

"Yes, thank you. Sterns? Why are you holding my hand?" she asked.

"To keep you still, mi'lady," he answered.

"You may let go of me now. I won't interfere with Caine's task."

After he'd complied with that request, she immediately tried to push Caine's hands away from her side. "You're prodding, Caine," she whispered.

"I'm almost finished, Jade."

His voice sounded terribly surly to her, yet he was being incredibly gentle, too. It was a contradiction. "Are you angry with me, Caine?"

He didn't even bother to glance up when he gave his curt answer. "No."

"You could sound a little more convincing," she countered. "You are angry," she added with a nod. "I don't understand why . . ." She paused to let out a gasp.

Caine assumed the bandage he was applying to her injury had caused her discomfort. "Is it too tight?" he asked, his gaze filled with concern.

"You think this is all my fault, don't you?" she stammered out. "You think I deliberately . . ."

"Oh, no, mi'lady," Sterns interrupted. "The Marquess doesn't blame you. You didn't mean to get yourself shot. Mi'lord always gets a bit . . ."

"Cranky?" she supplied.

The butler nodded. "Yes, he gets cranky when he's worried."

She turned her attention back to Caine. "I'm sorry if I worried you," she said then. "Are you still worried?"

"No."

"Then the injury isn't as terrible as it looked?"

Caine nodded. He put the finishing touches on his handiwork before giving her his full attention. "A mere flesh wound, Jade," he said. "You should be up and about in no time."

He really looked as if he meant what he said. Jade was immediately relieved.

"Cover my legs, Sterns, and don't look while you're doing it," she ordered. Her voice had regained some of its bite, warming a smile out of the dour-faced man.

Jade was wearing only her chemise now. One side of the lace-bordered garment had been torn wide to expose her injury. She understood the necessity of having her clothes removed, but now that she knew she wasn't in jeopardy of dying, appearances needed to be maintained.

The butler did as she requested, then left to fetch a tray of supper for her. She and Caine were all alone. "I don't care if it's only a paltry flesh wound," she said. "I've decided I'm going to linger, Caine."

He sat down on the side of the bed, took hold of her hand, and gave her a heart-stopping smile. "Why do I get the feeling there's more to this announcement?"

"How astute of you, sir," she countered. "There is more. While I'm lingering, you're going to stay by my sick bed. This is, after all, probably all your fault," she added with a nod.

She had to bite her lower lip to keep herself from laughing. Caine looked thoroughly confused.

"Oh?" he asked when she stared at him expectantly. "How have you come to the conclusion that it's my fault?"

She shrugged. "I haven't quite figured it out yet, but I will. Now give me your word, Caine. I won't rest easy until I know you won't leave my side."

"All right, love," he answered. His wink was slow, devilish. "I won't leave your side day or night."

The significance in that statement wasn't lost on her. "You may take to your own bed at night," she replied.

"May I?" he asked dryly.

Jade decided not to goad him any further, guessing he'd get downright cranky if she persisted with her orders. Besides, she'd won this round, hadn't she?

The inconvenience of getting shot was going to be turned into a nice advantage. She now had a perfectly good reason to keep him at her side. Why, she just might linger until Nathan came to fetch her.

She hadn't realized how exhausted she was. She fell asleep right after dinner, the tray still perched on her lap, and only awakened once during the night. Twin candles were burning a soft light on the night stand. Jade remembered the signal she needed to give to Jimbo and Matthew to let them know all was well, and immediately pushed the covers away.

She spotted Caine then. He was sprawled out in the wingback chair adjacent to the bed, his bare feet propped up on the bed, his white shirt opened to the waist, and was sound asleep.

Jade didn't know how long she watched him. She told herself she was just making certain he was really sound asleep. Lord, he was so appealing to her. He had quickly become far more, however, than merely handsome. He was like a safe haven from the storm, and the urge to lean on him, to let him take care of her, nearly overwhelmed her.

Her guardian angel began to snore, pulling her out of her trance. She eased out of the bed, picked up one of the candles, and went to stand in front of the window.

Light rain cascaded down upon the landscape. Jade felt a bit guilty that her men were getting a good soaking. If she'd given her signal earlier, they could have found dry shelter sooner.

"What are you doing?"

Jade almost dropped the candle, so startled was she by Caine's booming voice.

She turned around and found him just a scant foot away. "I was just looking out the window," she whispered. "I didn't mean to wake you."

His hair was tousled and he seemed to be more asleep than awake yet. A lock of his hair had fallen on his forehead, giving him the appearance of being a bit vulnerable to her. Without a thought as to what she was doing, she brushed his hair back in place.

"You may look out the window tomorrow," he returned, his voice husky from slumber.

After making that statement, he took the candle away from her, put it back on the table, and then arrogantly motioned for her to get back in bed.

"Does your side hurt?" he asked.

She didn't think he was overly concerned about her injury because he'd yawned when he'd asked the question.

Jade started to tell him no, that it didn't pain her much at all, then reconsidered. "Yes," she said. "It stings, but only just a little," she added when he looked a bit too concerned. "Why were you sleeping in the chair?"

He pulled his shirt off before answering her. "You were taking up most of the bed," he explained. "I didn't want to move you."

"Move me? Why would you want to move me?"

Caine blew out the candles, pulled the covers back, and stretched out next to her. Then he gave her a roundabout answer. "I'll just stay with you until you fall asleep again."

"But Caine, it isn't at all proper . . ."

"Go to sleep, love. You need your rest."

She stiffened when he put his arm around her. His hand rested between her breasts. When she tried to ease it away, he captured her hand and held on.

"This really isn't at all . . ." She quit protesting in mid-sentence, realizing it was wasted effort. Caine was already snoring again and certainly wouldn't hear a word she said.

She decided there was little harm in letting him sleep with her for a short while. She had, after all, run the man ragged and he surely needed his rest. She'd already noticed how cranky he became when he was weary. Odd, but she found that flaw a bit endearing.

129

Jade snuggled up against him and closed her eyes. She instinctively knew he would behave himself. He was a gentleman, and he'd given her his word that he'd never take advantage of her.

She was obviously just as exhausted as he appeared to be, for she fell asleep with the most confusing thought rambling through her mind.

She was beginning to wish he wasn't such a gentleman after all.

The physician, Sir Harwick, couldn't be located for two full days and nights. Caine sent messengers to his London home and to his country estate. Harwick was finally located at the residence of Lady McWilliams, attending to a birthing. He sent a missive back to Caine explaining that as soon as his duty there was completed, he would immediately ride over to Caine's estate.

Caine ranted about that inconvenience until Jade reminded him that her condition wasn't life threatening, a fact, she added, that the messenger had related to the physician, and that she was beginning to feel much better anyway and didn't need or want anyone poking at her.

Lingering soon became torture for Jade. She couldn't stand the confinement.

The weather mimicked her mood too. Since the moment she'd arrived at Caine's home, it hadn't quit raining.

Caine's mood was just as sour as her own. He reminded her of a caged animal. Every time he came into her room to speak to her, he paced back and forth, his hands clasped behind his back, while he grilled her about her past, her brother, and all the events leading up to the murder she'd witnessed. Caine always ended each dueling session with the remark that he didn't have enough information yet to draw any substantial conclusions.

His frustration was almost visible. Jade found fencing

with him just as nerve grating. She was careful not to give him too many true facts or too many lies, either, but Lord, it was exhausting work.

They spent quite a lot of time shouting at each other. Jade accused him of being sorry he ever became involved in her problems. He was, of course, insulted by such an accusation. Still, he didn't come right out and deny it.

In her heart, she thought he didn't find her appealing any longer. Why, he didn't even try to kiss her anymore, or sleep next to her, and by the third day, he was barely speaking a civil word to her.

On the fourth night of her confinement, Jade's control snapped. She tore off the fresh bandage that Sterns had changed for her just a few hours' earlier, ordered a bath for herself, and then announced that she was fully recovered.

By the time she finished washing her hair, her frame of mind had improved considerably. Sterns helped her dry the long curls, then sat her in front of the hearth where a full fire blazed.

After Sterns directed the servants in changing the bedding and removing the tub, he nagged Jade back into bed.

As soon as darkness fell, Jade gave the signal to her men, then returned to her bed. She opened one of the books she'd borrowed from Caine's library, and settled down to read to the sound of thunder rumbling in the distance.

The storm proved to be more than just bluster, however. A giant tree, as tall as Caine's three-story house, was felled to the ground by a bolt of lightning that was so powerful, the exposed roots glowed an eerie red for a good long while. The clap of thunder shook the house, and the aftermath, a sizzling, crackling sound of wood burning, snapped and popped in the night air like meat roasting over an open fire.

All the extra hands were needed in the stables to soothe the frightened horses. The scent of fire was in their nostrils, or so Kelley, the head stablemaster, professed. Caine was called when his stallion wouldn't settle down. As soon as he entered the stables, however, his mount immediately quit his tantrum.

It was well after midnight when Caine returned to the main house. Though it was only a short distance from the stables, he was still soaked through. He left his boots, socks, jacket, and shirt in the entryway and went upstairs. Another booming clap of thunder shook the house just as Caine was about to enter his room.

Jade must be terrified, he told himself as he changed direction. He would just look in on her to make certain she was all right. If she was sound asleep, he'd leave her alone. If, however, she was still awake . . . well then, perhaps they could have another shouting debate about the ills of the world and the inferiority of women. That thought made Caine smile in anticipation. Jade was turning out to be anything but inferior. She was making a mockery out of his beliefs, too. He'd go to his grave before admitting that fact to her, though, for it was simply too much fun watching her try to cover her own reactions to his opinions.

It was actually a little stunning when he realized he really wanted to talk to her. Granted, there were several other things he wanted to do as well, but he forced himself to squelch those thoughts.

He did pause to knock on her door. He didn't, however, give her time to tell him to go away, or time either, if she was sleeping, to wake up. No, he had the door opened before she could react.

He was pleased to see she wasn't sleeping. Caine leaned against the door frame and stared at her a long minute. A warm feeling of contentment filled him. In the last few days he had begun to accept that he liked having her in his house, and even when she frowned at him, he felt he'd arrived in heaven. He really must be daft, he thought then, for he was beginning to love her disgruntled expressions. The fact that he could so easily get her riled indicated that she cared, if only just a little.

The woman bewitched him. Caine didn't like admitting that truth . . . yet she was so beautiful, so soft, so feminine. A man could only take so much before surrendering. God help him, he knew he was nearing that point.

It was becoming a torment not to touch her. His mood reflected the struggle he was going through. He felt tied up in knots inside, and every time he saw her, he wanted to take her into his arms and make wild passionate love to her.

And yet he couldn't seem to stay away from her. Hour after hour he kept coming into her room to check on her. God, he was even watching her sleep.

She couldn't possibly know the torment he was going through. She wouldn't look so damned serene if she had any idea of the fantasies he was considering.

She really was an innocent. She was sitting up in bed with her back propped up by a mound of pillows, looking so pure and virginal as she shook her head at him.

Two candles burned on the side table and she held a book in her hands. While he continued to stare at her, she slowly closed the book, her gaze directed on him all the while, and then let out a long sigh.

"I knew I should have bolted the door," she announced. "Caine, I'm simply not up to another inquisition tonight."

"All right."

"All right?"

His easy agreement obviously surprised her. She looked suspicious. "Do you mean it, sir? You won't badger me?"

"I mean it," he answered with a grin.

"You still shouldn't be here," she told him in that husky, sensual voice he found so arousing.

"Give me one good reason why I shouldn't be here."

"My reputation and your near nakedness," she answered.

"Those are two reasons," he drawled out.

"What can you be thinking of?" she asked when he shut the door behind him. "Your servants will know you're here."

"I thought you didn't care about your reputation, Jade. Have you changed your mind, then?"

She shook her head again. The light from the candles shimmered in her hair with the movement. He was mesmerized. "I didn't care about my reputation when I thought you were going to kill me, but now that you've given me hope for continued good health, I've changed my mind."

"Jade, Sterns knows I slept in here the first night when . . ."

"That was different," she interjected. "I was ill, injured, and you were concerned. Yes, that was definitely different. Now I've recovered. The servants will surely tell your mama, Caine."

"My mama?" He burst into laughter. "You needn't worry about the servants, Jade. They're all sleeping. Besides, my motives aren't lascivious."

She tried not to let him see her disappointment. "I know," she said with another mock sigh. "But if you're not up to mischief, why are you here at this hour?"

"Don't give me that suspicious look," he replied. "I thought you might be frightened by the storm, that's all." He paused to frown at her, and then added, "Most women would be frightened. You're not, though, are you?"

"No," she answered. "I'm sorry."

"Why are you sorry?"

"Because you look so disappointed. Did you wish to comfort me?"

"That thought did cross my mind," he admitted dryly. His frown intensified when he realized she was trying not to laugh at him. He pulled away from the door and walked over to the side of her bed. Jade moved her legs out of the way just a second before he sat down.

She tried desperately not to stare at his bare chest. The

mat of dark, curly hair tapered to a line that ended in the middle of his flat stomach. She wanted to run her fingers through the crisp hair, to feel his heat against her breasts, to . . .

"Hell, Jade, most women would have been afraid."

His voice pulled her from her erotic thoughts. "I'm not most women," she replied. "You'd best understand that now, Caine."

He was having trouble understanding much of anything now. He stared at the buttons on the top of her white nightgown, thinking about the silky skin hidden beneath.

His sigh was ragged. Now that he knew she wasn't worried about the storm, he really should leave. His pants, wet from the storm, were probably soaking the covers.

He knew he should leave, but he couldn't seem to move.

"I'm not at all like most of the women you know," she announced, just to fill the sudden awkward silence. Drops of water clung to his muscular shoulders and upper arms. In the candlelight, the moisture made his bronzed skin glisten. She turned her attention to his lap. That was a mistake, she realized. The bulge between his thighs was very evident . . . and arousing. She could feel herself blush in reaction.

"You're soaking wet," she blurted out. "Have you been walking in the storm, you daft man?"

"I had to go to the stables to help quiet the horses."

"Your hair turns to curl when it's wet;" she added. "You must have hated that when you were a child."

"I hated it so much I wouldn't share my toys," he drawled out.

His gaze turned to her chest. He noticed her hardened nipples brushing against the thin fabric of her gown. It took a supreme act of discipline not to touch her. His control was close to snapping, and even a simple goodnight kiss would make him forget his good intentions.

Another bolt of lightning lit up the room, followed by an ear-piercing explosion of thunder. Caine was off the bed and standing by the window before Jade had kicked the covers away.

"That surely hit something," Caine announced. "I don't think I've ever seen a storm as fierce as this one."

He peered into the darkness, looking for signs of a budding fire. Then he felt Jade take hold of his hand. He hid his concern when he turned to look down at her.

"It will wear out very soon," she promised. She nodded when he looked so surprised, squeezed his hand to reassure him, and added, "You'll see."

He couldn't believe she was actually trying to comfort him. Since she looked so sincere, he didn't dare laugh. He didn't want to hurt her tender feelings, and if she felt the need to soothe him, he'd let her.

"Uncle use to tell me the angels were brawling whenever there was a thunderstorm," she said. "He made it sound as if they were having quite a party."

"And did you believe your uncle?" he asked, a smile in his voice.

"No."

He did laugh then, a full booming sound that reminded her of thunder.

"I have grown to appreciate your honesty, Jade. I find it most appealing."

She didn't look as though she wanted to hear that opinion. She let go of his hand and shook her head again. "Everything's always black and white to you, isn't it? There's never any room for deviations, is there? I tried to believe my uncle, but I knew he was lying to soothe my fear. Sometimes, Caine, a lie is all for the good. Do you understand what I'm saying?"

He stared down at her for a long minute. "Give me another example, Jade." His voice was whisper soft. "Have you ever lied to me?"

She slowly nodded.

Several heartbeats later, Caine asked, "And what was this lie?"

She didn't answer him soon enough to please him. His hands were suddenly on her shoulders and he forcefully turned her to face him. Then he nudged her chin up, demanding she look at him. "Explain this lie!" he demanded.

The look in his eyes chilled her. She couldn't find any warmth there. The color had turned the gray of winter mornings.

"You cannot abide a lie then, no matter what the reason?"

"Tell me what the lie was," he instructed again.

"I don't really dislike you."

"What?" he asked, looking incredulous.

"I said, I don't really dislike you."

"That's it? That's the lie you . . ."

"Yes."

She could feel the tension ebb from his grasp. "Well, hell, Jade, I thought it was something serious."

"Like what?" she demanded in a raised voice.

"Like perhaps you were married," he answered in a near shout of his own. "I already know you don't dislike me," he added in a softer tone of voice.

"You're impossible," she cried out. "Unbending, too. If I had other lies, I certainly wouldn't admit them to you now. You get too cranky."

"Jade?"

"Yes?"

"What other lies?"

"I thought about telling you I was married," she said then. "But I'm not any good at fabrications and I didn't think you'd believe me."

"Why would you want me to believe you were married?"

He was rubbing her shoulders now in an absentminded fashion. "Because," she rushed out. "In the tavern, well, you were looking at me very like a tiger planning his next meal, and I thought that if you believed I was married . . . or recently widowed, then I'd gain your compassion."

"So you wanted my compassion and not my lust?"

She nodded. "You must admit that we are attracted to each other. I've never wanted a man to touch me the way I want you to . . . touch me."

"That's nice to know, my love."

"Oh, you already know it," she whispered. "Quit looking so pleased with yourself. It was bound to happen sooner or later."

"What was bound to happen?"

"I was bound to find someone I wanted to get a little closer to," she explained.

"I'm glad it happened with me," he admitted.

He wrapped his arms around her and pulled her up against him. "Jade, do you want me to touch you now?"

She struggled out of his arms and took a step back. "It doesn't matter if I want you to touch me or not, Caine. You're my protector. You have to leave me alone."

She suddenly found herself pulled back up against his chest, his thighs, his hard arousal. Her flimsy nightgown proved scanty protection against his body, his incredible heat. "It doesn't work that way, Jade."

"Why not?"

"I want you."

The huskiness in his voice was her undoing. She knew she should be appalled by her own reaction to him. Yet she actually wanted to melt in his arms. The urge to let him touch her was such a sweet torment. Lord, she was confused. She'd never, ever permitted anyone to get this close to her. She'd always protected herself against involvements of any kind, having learned early in life that loving someone caused more pain than joy. Even Nathan had deserted her. She'd become so vulnerable then. Yes, only a fool would let a man like Caine close . . . only a fool.

Thunder rumbled in the distance. Neither Jade nor Caine was aware of the weather now. They were too consumed by the heat flowing between them.

They stared into each other's eyes for what seemed an eternity.

And in the end, it was inevitable. When Caine slowly lowered his head toward her, she leaned up to meet him halfway.

His mouth took absolute possession. He was as ravenous for her as she was for him. She welcomed his tongue, rubbed against it with her own. Her whimper of longing and acceptance blended with his raw growl of need.

The kiss was openly carnal. Caine was a lusty man whose hunger wouldn't be easily appeased. He wouldn't let her retreat or give half measure. Jade didn't want to draw back. She wrapped her arms around his neck, threaded her fingers through his soft curly hair, and clung to him. She never wanted to let go.

When he finally pulled away, she felt as though he'd taken her heart. She cuddled up against him quite brazenly, resting the side of her face against his warm chest. The mat of hair tickled her nose but she liked the sensation too much to move away. His scent, so wonderfully masculine, reminded her of heather and musk. The earthy fragrance clung to his skin.

Caine's voice was ragged when he asked, "Jade? Are there other lies you want to tell me about?"

"No."

He smiled over the shyness in her voice, then said, "No, there aren't any other lies, or no, you don't want to tell me about them?"

She rubbed her cheek against his chest to try to distract him, then said, "Yes, there are other lies." She felt him tense against her, then hastily added, "But they're so insignificant I can't even remember them now. When I do, I promise to tell you."

He immediately relaxed again. Lying, she decided, was on the top of his list of atrocities.

"Jade?"

"Yes, Caine?"

"Do you want me?"

He didn't give her time to answer. "Damn it, be honest with me now. No more lies, Jade. I have to know," he grated out. "Now."

"Yes, Caine, I want you. Very much."

She sounded as though she'd just confessed a dark sin. "Jade, there should be joy in wanting each other, not despair."

"There is both," she answered. She shivered inside over the knowledge of what she was about to do. She was eager . . . and terribly uncertain. I will not fall in love with him, she promised herself, and knew the lie was a mockery when her eyes filled with tears. Caine had already found his way into her heart.

When she moved back into his arms, he felt her tremble. He tightened his hold around her. "I'll take care of you, Jade," he whispered. "Love, what are you thinking?"

"That I'll survive," she answered.

He didn't understand what she meant, but the fear in her voice made his heart ache. "We don't have to . . ."

"I want you," she interrupted. "But you have to promise me something first."

"What?" he asked.

"You mustn't fall in love with me."

The seriousness in her voice told him she wasn't jesting. Caine was immediately infuriated with her. She was such a confusion to him. He decided he'd demand an explanation for her ridiculous request, but then she started caressing his skin into a fever. She placed hot, wet kisses on his chest, and when her tongue brushed against one of his nipples, his body began to burn for her.

She teased a path up the side of his neck with her sweet mouth, urging him without words to respond. Caine's control disappeared. He'd never had a woman respond to him with such innocence, such honesty. For the first time in his life, he felt cherished . . . and loved.

A low growl escaped him even as he told himself to be gentle with her. He wanted to savor each touch, each caress, to make this night with her last forever. Yet he contradicted his own command when she began to make those erotic little whimpers in the back of her throat. She drove him wild. He roughly pulled on her hair until he'd made a fist of her silky curls, then jerked her head back so he could once again claim her mouth for another searing kiss.

His passion consumed her. His mouth ate at her lips, and his tongue . . . dear God, his tongue made her shake with raw desire. Jade's nails dug into the bulge of muscle in his upper arms. She gave herself over into his care. A deep ache began to spread like wildfire through her stomach, then lower, until it became an excruciating sweet torture.

Caine's hands moved to her buttocks. He pulled her up against his arousal. Jade instinctively cuddled his hardness between her thighs and began to rub against him.

The ache intensified.

When his mouth moved to the side of her neck, when his tongue began to flick her sensitive earlobe, she barely had enough strength left to stand up. He whispered dark, forbidden promises of all the erotic things he wanted to do to her. Some she understood, others she didn't, but she wanted to experience all of them.

"There's no turning back now, Jade," he whispered. "You're going to belong to me."

"Yes," she answered. "I want to belong to you tonight, Caine."

"No," he grated out. He kissed her long, lingeringly. "Not for just one night, love. Forever."

"Yes, Caine," she sighed, barely aware of what she was promising. "Tell me what you want me to do. I want to please you."

He answered her by taking her hand and moving it to the waistband of his pants. "Hold me, sweetheart," he instructed in a husky voice. "Touch me. Squeeze me. Hard."

His size frightened her but his reaction to her touch overrode her initial shyness. His groans of pleasure made her bolder. He made her feel powerful and weak at the same time. Jade sagged against him, smiling when she heard his whispered instructions again, for his voice actually shook. As to that, so did her hand. Her fingers brushed against his flat stomach, then slipped inside the wastband of his pants. Caine inhaled sharply, telling her without words how pleased he was with her aggression. She grew bolder then and slowly began to unbutton the opening of his trousers. She was awkward, yet determined until all the buttons were undone. She hesitated then. Caine took over the task for her. He forced her hand inside the opening. Her fingers splayed downward, into the springy hair, and then lower still, until she was touching the very heat of him. He was so incredibly hot, hard, but Jade had barely caressed him when he pulled her hand away.

"It will be over for me before we've started," he grated out when she tried to touch him again.

"Caine, I want . . ."

"I know," he groaned. He was pulling her nightgown up when he made that gruff statement. Jade was suddenly embarrassed and tried to push her gown back down over her hips. "Can't I have it on?"

"No."

"Caine, don't," she stammered. "Don't . . ."

And then he was touching her there, in her most private place. The palm of his hand cupped her boldly and then his fingers began to weave their magic. He knew just where to stroke and fondle, just how much pressure to exert.

Her nightgown was quickly discarded, his pants as well. His big hands cupped her full breasts. His thumbs rubbed her distended nipples until she was straining against him.

Another bolt of lightning lit the room. When Caine saw the passion in her eyes, he lifted her into his arms and carried her over to the bed. He followed her down on the sheets. One of his knees wedged between her thighs, forcing her to open for him, and when she complied, he pushed his arousal against her moist softness.

"Oh, God, you feel good," he whispered. He propped himself up on his elbows so he wouldn't suffocate her with his weight, then lowered his head to the valley between her breasts. He kissed her there, the undersides of her breasts next, and then slowly circled one of her nipples with the tip of his tongue.

She felt as though she'd just been hit by lightning. She moved against him restlessly. When he finally took her nipple into his mouth and began to suckle, her nails dug into his shoulders. His low grunt was one of pain and pleasure.

"Do you like that, love?" he asked before he turned to take the other nipple into his mouth.

She wanted to tell him how much she liked what he was doing to her, but desire made speech impossible. His mouth captured hers again and his hands gently moved her thighs further apart. His fingers were relentless in their quest to make her ready for him. "Put your legs around me, Jade," he suddenly ordered in a harsh voice. "I can't wait any longer, baby. I have to be inside you."

She felt the moist tip of his sex, then his hands were holding her hips, lifting them. His mouth covered hers and his tongue thrust inside just as he drove inside her. The stabbing pain broke through her sexual haze. She cried out and tried to move away. Caine felt the resistance pushing against his arousal. He hesitated for the briefest of seconds. The look in his eyes when he tilted his head back to look at her showed his determination. And then he drove into her

143

again, until he'd broken through the maidenhead and filled her completely. Jade cried out again and squeezed her eyes shut against his invasion.

He went completely still, trying to give her time to adjust to him, trying, too, to give himself time to gain control.

"You have to stop now," she cried out. "I don't want to do this any longer."

Tears streamed down her cheeks. She opened her eyes to look at him. "Stop now," she pleaded.

His expression showed his concern. A fine sheen of perspiration covered his brow. His jaw was clenched tight. She thought he must be in as much pain as she was.

And then he shook his head at her. "I can't stop now," he grated out. "Just hold me, Jade. Don't move like that . . . it makes me want to . . ."

Caine's forehead dropped to rest on top of hers. He closed his eyes against the sweet torment. "Are you in pain, too?" she asked on a near sob.

"No, love," he whispered. "I'm not in pain."

"I'm not a virgin any longer, am I? We're done now, aren't we?"

She was overwhelmed by the confusing emotions warring inside her. The pain was insistent. She wanted Caine to leave her alone . . . and yet, she wanted him to hold her, too.

"No, baby, you aren't a virgin any longer," he finally answered. "You're mine now. And we sure as hell aren't finished."

He sounded like he'd just run a great distance. The grim expression on his face when he looked at her again actually frightened her.

It was apparent he hated this as much as she did.

She felt devastated by her failure. "I knew I wouldn't be any good at this," she cried out. "Please get off me. You're hurting me."

Caine shuddered for control. "Baby, I can't stop," he said

again. He tried to kiss her, but she turned her face away and began to struggle again.

"If you don't stop, I'm going to start crying," she pleaded. "I hate to cry," she added with a sob against his ear.

He didn't mention the fact that she was already crying. Hell, she made him feel as low as a snake. He wanted to comfort her, yet the fact that he was fully imbedded inside her tight, hot sheath made his discipline all but desert him. "Love, the pain won't last long," he promised. He hoped to God he was right.

His hands roughly cupped the sides of her face, and his mouth ended their conversation.

His tongue swept inside to mate with hers, and when he felt her resistance begin to fade, he moved his hand down, between their joined bodies, to stroke the sensitive bud into arousal again.

Jade didn't forget about the pain, but it didn't seem to matter now. The restlessness came back with building insistence. Caine forced himself to stay completely still until she'd adjusted to him. When she slowly arched up against him, he partially withdrew, then drove back into her again.

Her ragged moan forced him to stop again. "Am I still hurting you?" he asked, all the while praying he wasn't causing her more pain. His body was screaming for release, and he knew, even if she begged him, he wouldn't be able to stop now. "Is it better now?"

"A little," she answered against his neck. Her voice sounded shy, uncertain. "It's a little better."

He continued to hesitate until she bit his earlobe and pushed against him again. It was all the encouragement he needed. His body took over. Though he vowed to be gentle with her, his thrusts became more powerful, more out of control.

Her thighs clenched him tight. Her toes arched against the backs of his legs. Her nails dug into his shoulder blades.

Caine was relentless now in his quest to push her beyond control. He drove into her and then slowly withdrew, again and again. He knew he should withdraw before he reached his own climax, for neither of them had taken any precautions against pregnancy, but she was so hot, so tight, that noble thought became untenable. And somewhere, in the dark recesses of his mind was the honest admission that he wanted to give her his child.

The mating rhythm took over. The bed squeaked with each hard thrust. Thunder blended with their low moans of pleasure, his whispered words of love. Caine wouldn't let her give half measure. Wave after wave of intense pleasure began to spiral through her body until she was shaking with her need for fulfillment. He made her burn for completion. Jade was suddenly terrified of what was happening to her. It was as though he was trying to steal her soul. "Caine, I can't . . ."

He hushed her fear with another long, drugging kiss. "Let it happen, Jade. Hold on to me. I'll keep you safe."

Safe. He would keep her safe. Jade's instinctive trust in him pushed her fear and her vulnerability away. She let the storm capture her until she became one with the wind. And then she felt as though she was splintering through the air toward the sun. Her body squeezed him tight. She cried out his name, with joy, with release, and with love.

Caine buried his seed inside her at the very same moment. His head fell to her shoulder and he let out a low grunt of satisfaction.

His own climax made him shudder in wonder. Never had he felt such blissful surrender. He felt drained . . . and renewed.

He was never going to let her go. That sudden thought hammered through his mind with the same force of his wild heartbeat. He neither fought the truth nor tried to move.

He was content.

Jade was exhausted.

Only when her arms began to ache did she realize she was still clinging to him. She slowly released her hold, then let her arms fall to her sides. She was too astonished by what had just happened to her to speak yet. No one had ever told her it would be like this. Dear heaven, she'd completely lost control. She'd given herself to him completely, body and soul, trusting him absolutely to keep her safe.

No one had ever had such power over her. No one.

Jade closed her eyes to keep her tears hidden. Caine, she decided, was a far more cunning thief than she was. The man had dared to steal her heart. Worse, she had allowed it.

Even when he felt her tense beneath him, he couldn't find the strength or the will to move away from her.

"I think you should leave now," she whispered. Her voice trembled.

Caine sighed against her neck. He wrapped his arms around her and rolled to his side. Jade couldn't resist the urge to cuddle up against his chest for just a minute. Though she didn't understand why, she actually wanted to hear a few words of praise from him before she sent him away . . . just a few little lies about love and honor, that she could pull out and savor in the future on those cold nights when she was all alone. Yes, they would be lies, but she wanted to hear them anyway.

That, of course, didn't make any sense to her. She could feel herself becoming angry with him. This was all his fault because he'd turned her into a blithering simpleton who couldn't make up her mind if she wanted to weep or shout.

"Sweet, are you already having regrets?"

She couldn't detect a shred of regret in his tone. In truth, he sounded downright amused.

When she didn't answer his question, he tugged on her hair, forcing her to look up at him.

He was thoroughly pleased by what he saw. Her face was flushed from their lovemaking, her mouth swollen from his kisses, and her eyes were still cloudy with passion.

Caine felt as though he'd left his brand on her. A wave of raw possessiveness filled him, and he arrogantly nodded. He decided to ignore her disgruntled expression, guessing it was all bluster for his benefit.

He couldn't resist kissing her again. When he slowly leaned down to claim her mouth, she tried to turn away. Caine simply tightened his hold on her hair to keep her still.

The kiss was meant to melt away her glare. As soon as his mouth covered hers, his tongue sank inside her sweet, intoxicating heat. The erotic love play coaxed her response. It was a long, intense kiss and she was clinging to him when he finally lifted his head to look at her again.

"You wanted me as much as I wanted you, Jade," he said. "You made the choice, love, and now you're going to have to live with it."

The man was a cad. Her eyes filled with fresh tears. His attitude was as callous as a hardened blister. And did he have to smile at her after making such a painful statement?

She vowed he'd never know how much his words hurt her. "Yes, Caine, I did make the choice to give you my virginity, and I will live with the consequences of my actions. Now, if you don't mind, I'm really sleepy and I would like . . ."

"That isn't what I'm talking about," he interrupted. His voice was as ragged as lightning. "The choice you made was to belong to me, Jade. We're going to get married, sweet."

"What?"

"You heard me," he replied, his voice softer now. "Don't look so appalled, my love. It isn't as bad as all that."

"Caine, I never made any such choice," she stammered out.

He wasn't in the mood to listen to her denial. He wanted her acceptance. By God, he wasn't going to leave her bed until he had it. He rolled her onto her back, then roughly pushed her thighs apart with one of his knees. His hands held hers captive above her head. He deliberately ground his pelvis against her. "Look at me," he commanded. When she obeyed that order, he said, "What we have just shared can't be undone. You're all mine now. Accept it, Jade, and it will go a hell of a lot easier for you."

"Why should I accept?" she asked. "Caine, you don't know what you're asking."

"I'm a very possessive man," he countered. His voice had taken on a hard edge.

"I noticed," she muttered. "It's a sin, that."

"I won't share what belongs to me, Jade. Understand?"

"No, I don't understand," she whispered. The look in his eyes chilled her. "Is it because I was a virgin and you feel guilty? Is that the reason you want to marry me?"

"No, I don't feel guilty," he answered. "You are going to marry me, though. I'll speak to your brother just as soon as he returns to . . ."

"You are the most arrogant, unbending man I've ever had the displeasure to meet."

A smile tugged at the corners of his mouth. "But you like arrogant, unbending men, love. You wouldn't have let me touch you otherwise."

Odd, but she couldn't fault that argument. "Please get off me. I can't breathe."

He immediately rolled to his side. Then he propped his head up with his elbow so he could watch her expressions. Jade pulled the sheet up over the two of them, folded her hands across her breasts, and stared intently at the ceiling.

"Jade?"

"Yes?"

"Did I hurt you?"

She wouldn't look at him. Caine tugged on her hair to emphasize his impatience. "Answer me."

"Yes, you hurt me," she whispered. She could feel herself blush.

"I'm sorry, Jade."

She shivered over the tenderness in his voice, then realized she needed to get control of her emotions. She felt

149

like weeping and couldn't understand why. "No, you're not sorry," she announced. "Or you would have stopped when I asked you to."

"I couldn't stop."

"You couldn't?" She turned to look at him.

"No, I couldn't."

She was almost undone by the tenderness she could see in his eyes. There was a definite sparkle there, too, indicating his amusement. She didn't know what to make of him now. "Well, it's a good thing you don't feel guilty because you have nothing to feel guilty about."

"And why is that?" he drawled out.

"Why? Because you didn't make me do anything I didn't want to do. This was all my doing."

"Was I even here?" he asked. "I seem to remember being an active participant."

She ignored the laughter in his voice. "Yes, of course you were here. But I allowed you to be . . . active."

If she hadn't looked so damned sincere, if she hadn't been wringing her hands together, he would have shouted with laughter. Her feelings were at issue, however, and for that reason he controlled himself. "All right," he agreed. "You were more active than I was. Happy now?"

"Yes," she answered. "Thank you."

"You're most welcome," he returned. "Now tell me why you wanted me to make love to you."

She looked back up at the ceiling before she answered him. Caine was fascinated by the blush that covered her face. His little innocent was embarrassed again. She'd been wild just minutes before when they'd been making love. His shoulders still stung from her nails. Her passionate nature more than matched his own, but it had also been the first time for her, and he assumed she was still shy and confused by what had happened.

"Because I wanted to," she answered. "You see, I've always known I would never marry and I wanted to . . . Oh, you aren't going to understand. I wager that soon, after I've gone away, you won't even remember me."

She turned to judge his reaction to that statement, certain she'd made him angry.

He started laughing. "You're being very rude," she announced before returning her gaze back to the ceiling. "I do wish you'd go away."

His fingers trailed a shiver down the side of her neck. "Jade? It was inevitable."

She shook her head. "It wasn't."

He slowly pulled the sheet down until her breasts were uncovered. "It was," he whispered. "God, I wanted you for so long."

He tugged the sheet lower until her stomach was in view. "You know what, love?"

"What?" she asked. She sounded breathless.

"I want you again."

He leaned down and kissed her before she could argue with him. Jade let him have his way until his mouth became more insistent. Then she nudged him away. She rolled with him, and when they were facing each other, she kept her gaze directed on his chest. "Caine?" Her fingers toyed with the crisp hair while she tried to find the courage to ask him her question.

"Yes?" he asked, wondering why she was acting shy again.

"Was it all right then?"

He tilted her chin up with his thumb. "Oh, yes, it was all right."

"You weren't disappointed?"

He was touched by her vulnerability. "No, I wasn't disappointed."

His expression had turned so somber, she decided he was telling the truth.

"I wasn't disappointed either."

"I know," he answered with that arrogant grin back in evidence.

JULIE GARWOOD

"How do you know?"

"By the way you reacted to my touch, the way you found your own fulfillment, the way you shouted my name then."

"Oh."

His smile melted away the rest of her worry. "It was a little shattering, wasn't it, Jade?"

She nodded. "I had no idea it would be so . . . splendid."

He kissed the top of her head. "I can smell my scent on you," he said. "I like that."

"Why?"

"It makes me hard."

"I should wash."

"I'll do it for you," he offered.

She rolled away from him and was out of the bed before he could reach for her. "You'll do no such thing," she said before she gave him her back and struggled into her robe.

Her smile was dazzling but it faded quickly when she noticed the spots of blood on the sheets.

"You made me bleed." That accusation came out in a stammer.

"Love, it was your first time."

"I know that," she returned.

"You were supposed to bleed."

She looked taken aback by that statement. "You're serious?"

He nodded.

"But only the first time, Caine? Not that there's ever going to be a second time," she rushed on. "Still, I wouldn't . . ."

"Only the first time," he answered. He decided to ignore her protest about not making love again and asked instead, "Jade? Didn't anyone ever explain these facts to you?"

"Well, of course they did," she replied, feeling like a complete fool now.

He didn't believe her. "Who? Your parents died before you were old enough to understand. Was it your brother? Did Nathan explain?"

152

"Nathan left me." She really hadn't meant to blurt out that truth. "I mean to say, he was away at school all the time and I rarely saw him."

Caine noticed how agitated she was becoming. She was twisting the tie of her robe into knots. "When did Nathan leave you?"

"He was away at school," she said again.

"For how long?"

"Why are you asking me these questions?" she asked. "My Uncle Harry took over my education while Nathan was away. He did a fine job, Caine."

"He obviously left out a few pertinent facts," Caine remarked.

"Uncle is a very reserved man."

"Weren't there any women around who . . ."

He quit his question when she shook her head at him. "There were women but I would never discuss such a personal matter with any of them, Caine. It wouldn't have been proper."

She moved behind the screen before he could question her further. Jade washed with the slivers of rose-scented soap and water from the basin. She only then realized how sore she was. She was thoroughly irritated with him and with herself by the time she returned to her bed.

Caine looked like he was settled in for the night. The pillows were now propped up behind his head. He looked extremely comfortable. She tightened the belt on her robe and frowned at him. "Caine, you really have to understand something," she began in a firm voice.

"What's that, sweet?" he asked.

She hated it when he smiled at her so innocently. It made her heart start pounding and her mind empty of every thought. She had to stare at the floor in order to continue. "This can't happen again. Not ever. It won't do you any good to argue with me, Caine. My mind's set. Now it's time for you to leave."

In answer to her fervent order, Caine lifted the covers and motioned her over with the crook of his finger. "Come to bed, Jade. You need your rest."

She let out a loud groan. "Are you going to be difficult?"

"I'm afraid so, love."

"Please be serious," she demanded when he winked at her.

"I am being serious," he countered. "But realistic, too."

"Realistic?" She moved closer to the side of the bed, nibbling on her lower lip while she thought about the best ploy to get him moving.

Her mistake was in getting too close, she realized a little too late. Caine easily captured her. She suddenly found herself flat on her back next to him. His warm, heavy thigh locked her legs in place and one of his hands held her high around her waist. Jade realized that even in the forceful action, he'd been careful not to touch her injury. He was such an incredibly gentle man. Arrogant, too. She was good and trapped, and he had the audacity to smile over it.

"Now then," he said. "I'm realistic because I know this has only just begun," he explained. "Jade, quit pinching me. You can't honestly believe I won't ever touch you again, can you? Married couples . . ."

"Don't you dare mention marriage to me again," she interjected.

"All right," he agreed. "Since it seems to be so upsetting to you, I'll wait awhile before bringing up that topic. Still, you agree that you'll be staying here for approximately two weeks, right?"

He was back to being logical. Jade actually found that flaw quite comforting now. "Yes, though it surely won't be two weeks now. I've already been here more than half a week."

"Fine," he returned. "Now then, do you think in all the time we have left that I'm going to live like a monk?"

"Yes."

"It isn't possible," he countered. "I'm already hurting."

"You aren't."

"I am," he muttered. "Damn it, Jade, I want you again. Now."

"Damn it, Caine, you have to behave yourself."

Her voice sounded hoarse to her, but it was all his doing, she told herself. He was deliberately provocative. He stared down into her eyes as he slowly untied the belt to her robe. Then his fingers grazed the tips of her breasts. While he continued to hold her gaze, he slowly stroked a path down her belly. His fingers moved lower into the soft curls at the junction of her thighs.

He kissed the valley between her breasts while his fingers slowly stoked the fire in her. Jade closed her eyes and instinctively moved against his hand. His tongue made her nipples hard and when he eased his fingers inside her, she let out a groan of half pleasure, half pain.

He moved upward to kiss her mouth, demanding her response. His tongue wet her lips. When he'd gained her cooperation, he leaned back. "You're already getting hot for me, aren't you, love?"

"Caine," She whispered his name as she tried to pull his hand away. He wouldn't be deterred. She could barely think. "You must stop this torment. You have to fight this attraction. Oh God, don't do that."

"I don't want to fight it," he returned. He nibbled on her earlobe. "I like the attraction, Jade."

He was incorrigible. She let out a ragged sigh, then let him kiss her senseless again. She barely protested at all when he took her robe off and settled himself between her thighs. The hair on his legs tickled her toes and she was suddenly quite overwhelmed by all the wonderful differences in their bodies. He was so hard, so firm all over. Her toes rubbed against the backs of his legs and her nipples strained for more of his touch.

"Caine? Will you promise me something?"

"Anything," he answered, his voice ragged.

"We can have this time together, but when Nathan returns, then it has to be over. We . . ."

"I won't make promises I won't keep," he interrupted.

He sounded angry. "You'll change your mind," she whispered.

"You sound damn certain. Why? What is it you're hiding from me?"

"I know you'll get bored with me," she rushed out. She wrapped her arms around him. "Kiss me, please."

There was a frantic edge to her voice. Caine responded in kind. The kiss was like wildfire, and soon completely out of control.

His full attention was centered on pleasing her. He took his time building the tension by slowly driving her mad. He kissed each and every goose bump on her breasts, suckled both nipples until she was whimpering for release.

And then he slowly moved down her body. His tongue teased her flat stomach, and when he moved lower still, her moans became gasps of raw pleasure.

His teeth deliberately scraped against the soft curls. His tongue stroked the silky petals until they were sleek with moisture. And all the while his fingers caressed her with erotic deliberation.

He couldn't get enough of her. His tongue repeatedly stabbed against her as his fingers slid in and out.

Her hands tore at the sheets. The pleasure he forced on her stunned her. She had no idea a man made love in such a way. It was obvious Caine knew what he was doing. He made her wild with her need for him.

When she felt the first rush of ecstasy, when she instinctively tightened in pleasure and agony around him, he moved up and over her. She couldn't stop the splendor from consuming her. Caine drove inside her, hard, hot, full, just as she found her own release. She squeezed him tight and clung to him in joyful surrender.

He tried to hold back, yet found himself powerless to stop.

She made him desperate for his own release. His seed poured into her in a blazing orgasm that made him forget to breathe.

Until this night, he'd never given himself so completely. A part of him had always held back. He'd always been able to maintain his own rigid control. Yet he hadn't been able to withhold anything from this special woman. Odd, but he didn't look at his acceptance as surrender. In truth, it was a victory of sorts, for in his heart he knew she hadn't been able to hold back either.

He felt cleansed in body and soul. This incredible gift they'd just shared filled him with contentment.

It took all his strength to roll to his side. He was pleased when she followed him and snuggled up against him. He wrapped his arms around her and held her tight.

"I can still taste you."

"Oh, God." She sounded mortified.

He laughed. "I like the taste of you. You're all honey and female, love. It's a sexy combination. A man could become addicted."

"He could?"

"Yes," he growled. "But I'm the only one who's ever going to taste you. Isn't that right?"

He pinched her bottom to gain his answer. "Yes, Caine," she agreed.

"Did I hurt you again?"

"A little," she answered.

"I'm not sorry."

She feigned a sigh. "I know."

"I couldn't have stopped."

She tucked her face under his chin. Long minutes elapsed before she spoke again. "I shall never, ever forget you, Caine."

She knew he hadn't heard her. His deep, even breathing indicated he'd already fallen asleep.

She knew she should wake him and demand that he go

back to his own room. Sterns was bound to be disappointed when he found them together.

He tightened his hold on her when she tried to roll away from him. Even in sleep, the man was as possessive as ever.

Jade didn't have the heart to wake him. She closed her eyes and let her thoughts scatter like the wind. She fell asleep minutes later.

He dreamed of angels.

She dreamed of sharks.

Chapter Nine

The following morning the physician, Sir Harwick, arrived to have a look at Jade. He was an elderly man with dark gray hair and blue eyes that sparkled like the ocean on a calm day. He was impeccable in both his dress and manners. Jade thought he looked like a wily raccoon, for the hair on the sides of his face had been coached into sweeping curves that ended just a scant inch or so away from the edges of his severely pointed nose.

Just as she'd predicted to Caine, Sir Harwick did poke and prod at her. Caine stood at the foot of the bed, his hands clasped behind his back, acting like a sentinel guarding his treasure. When the physician finished his examination, he decreed that rest was the best ticket for her condition. Since Jade didn't believe she was in any special condition, she ignored all his suggestions.

Caine looked as if he were memorizing every dictate. He was determined to make an invalid out of her, she decided. When Harwick suggested a cold compress for the fading bump on the side of her temple, Caine immediately went to fetch it.

Jade was thankful she had the physician all to herself. "I understand you were called upon to examine Caine's father," she began. "I was sorry to hear he wasn't feeling well. Is he better now?"

The physician shook his head. "There's little anyone can do for him," he announced. "It's a pity. He's given up on life since Colin was taken from him. Why, Colin was his favorite son, you understand, and the loss has broken him."

"Why do you say that Colin was his favorite?" she asked.

"He's the firstborn from the second wife," Harwick explained. "Caine's mother died when he was just a youngster. The boy couldn't have been more than five or six."

It was apparent that Sir Harwick enjoyed a good gossip session. He pulled up a chair next to the side of the bed, took his time settling in, and then said in an enthusiastic whisper, "The first marriage was forced, you see, and from what I understand, it was a most unhappy union. Henry certainly tried to make a go of it."

"Henry?"

"Caine's father," Harwick instructed. "Henry hadn't become the Duke of Williamshire yet as his own father was still living. For that reason, he had more time to devote to his marriage. It didn't wash, though. Caine's mother was a shrew. She made life a living hell for both her husband and her son. Why, she tried to turn him against his own father, if you can believe such blasphemy. When she died, no one mourned her long."

"Did you ever meet this woman?"

"I did," he answered. "She was attractive, but her beauty hid a black heart."

"And is the Duke's second marriage happy?"

"Oh my, yes," Harwick answered. He made a sweeping gesture with his hand. "Gweneth's a fine woman. She set the *ton* on its ear, she did, when she first started attending their functions with her husband. Why, the elite follow her lead almost as fervently as they follow Brummel's dress and manners. I must say that Gweneth has been a good wife and mother. The children are all very close to each other—the proof, you see, that she did her job well."

"Do you include Caine, Sir Harwick, when you speak of the children?"

"I do," Harwick replied. "The others look up to Caine, for he is the eldest, but he tends to separate himself from the family. Unless someone tries to harm one of his brothers or sisters, of course. Then Caine involves himself." He paused to lean forward in his chair, then whispered in a conspiratorial voice, "Some say with a vengeance." He wobbled his eyebrows to emphasize that remark.

"Why do they say with a vengeance?" she asked. Her voice sounded worried to her but Harwick didn't seem to notice. Jade didn't want him to quit the conversation just yet. She schooled her expression to show only mild interest and even managed a smile. "You've made me most curious, sir," she added.

Harwick looked pleased by her interest. "My dear, Caine's made it well known he's hunting Pagan. Why, he had his men post the reward notice all over town. The gamblers have given odds. Ten to one favor Caine, of course. He'll get the pirate," he predicted. "And when he does, God have mercy."

"Yes, God have mercy," she agreed. "But Caine's father is ill, you mentioned?" she asked again, trying to pull him back to their initial topic. "Just how ill is he?"

"Gravely so," Harwick announced.

"Is there nothing that can be done?"

Harwick shook his head. "Gweneth's nearly out of her mind worrying about Henry. The man doesn't eat or sleep. He can't go on this way. No, I fear he'll be the next one to die if he doesn't come to terms with Colin's death."

"Perhaps he needs a little assistance," Jade said.

"Who needs assistance?" Caine asked from the doorway.

"Your papa," Jade called out. She turned back to Sir

Harwick then. "What is this I heard about a friend of yours disappearing?"

"Oh, yes, poor Sir Winters," Harwick answered. "A fine physician he was, too," he added with a nod.

When he gave her such an expectant look, Jade said, "You speak as though he's dead."

"I'm certain he is," Sir Harwick stated.

Caine stood on the other side of Jade's bed, trying without much success to force the cold compress on her injury. Jade was far more interested in hearing the physician's opinions than bothering about her puny bump. She kept waving the cloth away. Caine kept pushing it back.

Harwick observed the silent struggle a long minute, trying all the while not to smile. These two were certainly a pair, all right.

Jade's next question pulled him back to their topic. "Why do you think Winters is dead?"

"Has to be," Harwick countered. "His cook was the last to see him alive," he explained. "Winters was strolling through his back gardens. He turned the corner and simply vanished."

"How long ago was this?" Caine asked.

"Near to three months now," the physician answered. "Of course we all know what happened to him."

"We do?" Jade asked, startled by the abruptness in Harwick's tone. "And what is that?"

"I shouldn't be discussing it," Harwick answered. The look on his face indicated just the opposite was really the truth. The man appeared as eager as a little boy about to open birthday gifts.

Sir Harwick leaned forward in his chair. In a dramatic whisper, he said, "White slavers."

She was certain she hadn't heard correctly. "I beg your pardon?"

"White slavers," Harwick repeated. He nodded to emphasize his announcement, then leaned back in his chair.

Jade had to bite on her lower lip to keep herself from laughing. She didn't dare look up at Caine, knowing full well that if he showed the least amount of amusement, she wouldn't be able to control herself. "I didn't realize," she whispered.

Harwick looked as though he was savoring her reaction. "Of course you didn't realize," he rushed out. "You're a gentle lady and certainly wouldn't have heard about such unsavory elements. Pagan's behind the treachery, too. He's the one who snatched Winters and sold him to the slavers."

Jade wasn't amused now. She could feel herself turning red. "Why is it that Pagan is blamed for every sin in England?" she asked before she could stop herself.

"Now, now, don't get yourself upset," Sir Harwick whispered. He patted her hand then and said, "I shouldn't have told you the current speculation."

"I'm not upset," Jade lied. "I just think it's galling the way everyone uses Pagan as a convenient scapegoat. I'm not worried about your friend either, Sir Harwick, for in my heart I know Winters will turn up safe and sound one day soon."

The physician squeezed her hand with affection. "You have such a tender heart."

"Does Caine's father have a strong heart?"

It was Caine who answered her question. "He does."

Jade was surprised by the anger in his voice. She turned to look up at him. "That is good to know," she said. "Why are you frowning? Is it because I asked about your father or is it because he does have a strong heart?"

"Neither," Caine answered. His attention turned to the physician. "My father will begin to feel better when Pagan's been taken care of. Revenge will be his healing balm."

"No, Caine," Jade answered. "Justice will be his salvation."

"In this instance, they are the same," Caine argued.

The rigid set of his jaw indicated his displeasure. His stubbornness, too.

She wanted to shout at him. She thanked him instead. "It was kind of you to bring me this compress." She slapped the cold cloth against her temple. Then she turned to Sir Harwick. "And thank you, sir, for tending to me. I feel ever so much better now."

"It was my pleasure," Sir Harwick replied. He stood, clasped her hand again, and added, "As soon as you're feeling better, you must move in with the Duke and Duchess. I'm certain Caine's parents would be more than happy to have you as their guest until you've fully recovered."

His gaze turned to Caine. "I shall, of course, keep this confidence. There won't be any unsavory gossip attached to this lovely lady."

"What secret?" Jade asked, thoroughly puzzled. Sir Harwick was giving Caine such a piercing stare. It was unsettling.

"He's concerned about your reputation," Caine said.

"Oh, that." She let out a long sigh.

"She isn't overly concerned," Caine said dryly.

Sir Harwick looked startled. "Why, my dear, it simply isn't done. You shouldn't be all alone here with an unattached man."

"Yes, I suppose it isn't done," she agreed.

"But you've been ill, my dear, and certainly haven't been able to think clearly. I don't fault you or Caine," he added with a nod toward the Marquess. "Your host has acted in good faith."

"He has?" Jade asked.

"Most certainly," Sir Harwick replied. "There's a full staff in residence here. Still, the gossipers would have a holiday with this bit of news. Too many people would be hurt by the rumors. Caine's mother . . ."

"My stepmother," Caine interjected.

"Yes, of course, your stepmother," Harwick continued. "She'd be hurt. As to that, his intended would also be quite crushed."

"His what?"

She really hadn't meant to raise her voice but Sir Harwick's casually given remark stunned her. She suddenly felt sick. The color all but drained from her face. "Did you say Caine's intended?" she asked in a scratchy whisper.

"Jade," Caine began. "I believe Sir Harwick is referring to Lady Aisely."

"I see," she replied. She forced a smile for the physician's benefit. "Now I remember. Lady Aisely, the woman you're going to marry." Her voice had risen to a near shrill by the time she'd finished.

She didn't even know this Aisely woman, but she already despised her. The longer she had to mull it over, the more infuriated she was with Caine. God's truth, she hated him, too.

"Lady Aisely wouldn't take the news of your visitation here lightly," Sir Harwick predicted.

"She isn't my intended," Caine interjected. "She's my stepmother's intention for me," he qualified. He couldn't keep the laughter out of his voice. Her reaction to hearing about Lady Aisely couldn't have been more revealing. It told him she cared.

"But your dear stepmother is . . ."

"She's hell-bent on getting Lady Aisely and me together," he interrupted. "It isn't going to happen, Harwick."

Jade could feel Caine's stare. She desperately tried to feign disinterest. She realized she was wringing the compress in her hands and immediately stopped that telling action. "Who you marry doesn't concern me," she announced.

"It should."

She shook her head. "I just wish you'd mentioned your engagement before last night."

"I'm not engaged," he snapped. "And last night would have . . ."

"Caine!" She shouted his name, then lowered her voice when she added, "We have a guest, if you'll remember."

Harwick let out a rich chuckle. He walked by Caine's side over to the door. "I have a feeling about you two. Am I right?"

"Depends upon what the feeling is," Caine answered.

"She's your intended, isn't she?"

"She is," Caine replied. "She just hasn't accepted it yet."

The two men shared a grin. "I can tell she's going to be difficult, my boy."

"Difficult or not," Caine countered, in a voice loud enough to wake the dead, "she will be my wife."

The door slammed shut on her shout of denial. Jade threw the compress across the room and collapsed against the pillows. She gritted her teeth in frustration.

Why did she care who he married? As soon as Nathan returned, she was never going to see Caine again. And why in thunder did everything have to be so complicated? Lord only knew that protecting Caine was work enough. Now she had to add Caine's father to her list.

Was Lady Aisely pretty?

Jade pushed that black thought aside. She really was going to have to do something about the Duke of Williamshire. Colin was certain to be upset when he returned home and found his papa had died from grief.

Had Caine taken Lady Aisely to bed?

I cannot think about her now, Jade decided. There are too many other problems to worry about.

She was going to have to do something about Colin's father. A note, she decided, wouldn't be good enough. She'd have to confront the man and have a firm talk with him.

Had Caine's stepmother already made the arrangements for Caine's wedding? Oh God, she hoped Caine had been telling her the truth. She hoped he didn't want Lady Aisely.

"This is ridiculous," she muttered to herself. Of course Caine would marry. And of course it would be to someone other than her. When he found out the truth about her background, he wouldn't want her anymore.

With a growl of frustration, Jade gave up trying to formulate any plans. Her emotions were like the masts on the *Emerald,* blowing strong in a high wind. It was pointless to try to concentrate now. Caine's papa would just have to despair a little longer.

She avoided Caine for most of the day. They ate a quiet dinner together. Sterns surprised Jade when he pulled out a chair and sat down with them. The butler ate his meal with them, too. He kept his attention on Caine most of the time, but when he did look at her, his expression was kind, affectionate.

She decided he hadn't found out that she slept with Caine, after all. Jade was relieved. She'd already noticed that Sterns' relationship with Caine was far more than employer and employee. They were very like family, and she didn't want a man who Caine cared about to think she was a trollop.

She kept giving Sterns fretful glances until he reached over and patted her hand.

Caine did most of the talking during the meal. The conversation centered on the problems of running such a large estate. Jade was extremely interested. Surprised as well, for Caine showed he had a true concern for the members of his parish. He actually felt responsible for their well-being.

"Do you aid those who need help?" she asked.

"Of course."

"By giving them money?"

"When it's the only answer," he explained. "Jade, a man's pride is as important as his hunger. Once the stomach's been filled, a way to better himself is the next step."

She thought about that statement a long while, then said,

"Yes, a man's self-worth is important. So is a woman's," she added.

"If you take that self-worth away, there's a good chance that he . . . or she will give up altogether. A man can't be made to feel he's been manipulated or made to feel a failure."

"There's a difference between manipulation and failure," she argued.

"Not really," Caine replied. "A man's a fool if he allows either, isn't he, Sterns?"

"He most certainly is," Sterns agreed. The butler reached for the teapot before continuing. "A man's pride is most important. It should matter above all else."

"But surely you two will agree that there are times when pride must be set aside," she interjected.

"Such as?" Caine asked.

"A man's life is one excellent example," she answered.

"But a man's life isn't as important as his self-worth," Sterns said. "Don't you agree, mi'lord?"

Caine didn't answer. He was looking at Jade with that unreadable expression on his face again. Jade didn't have any idea what he was thinking now. She smiled at him just to cover her own unease, then pleaded fatigue and returned to her bedroom.

Sterns had ordered a bath made ready for her. A fire burned in the hearth, toasting the air. Jade lingered in the tub, then went to bed. She tossed and turned for almost an hour before falling into a fitful sleep.

Caine came to her bed sometime after midnight. He stripped out of his clothes, smothered out the candles, and eased into bed beside her. She was sleeping on her side, her nightgown bunched up around her thighs. Caine slowly eased the gown high, then pulled her silky bottom up against him.

She sighed in her sleep. The sound was like a fever to him. God, she was so warm, so sweet. His hand moved beneath her gown. He stroked her skin, her breasts, rubbing her nipples into hard buds. She moved against him restlessly, moaning in her sleep.

She probably thought she was in the throes of an erotic dream, Caine thought. He nibbled on her neck, teased her earlobe with his tongue, and when her backside pushed up against him more insistently, his hand slid down into the heat between her thighs.

He stoked the fire in her until she was hot, wet, ready for him. His other arm held her around the waist. She tried to turn toward him, but he wouldn't let her move. "Open up for me, Jade," he whispered. "Let me come to you."

His knee nudged the back of her thighs until he was wedged between them.

"Tell me you want me," he demanded.

She could feel the velvet tip of his sex. She bit on her lower lip to keep herself from shouting at him to quit his torment. "Yes, I want you," she whispered. "Please, Caine. Now."

It was all the surrender he needed. He gently pushed her onto her stomach, his hand splayed wide across her pelvis, and surged inside her with one powerful thrust. Her tight sheath gloved him, squeezed him. He almost spilled his seed then and there. Caine stilled his movements and took a deep breath. "Easy love," he whispered on a groan when she pushed up against him.

Her hands were making knots out of the sheets. Caine's hands joined hers. His head fell forward to rest in the fragrant hollow between her neck and shoulder.

"Caine, I want . . ."

"I know," he answered. He was determined to go slow this time, to prolong the sweet agony, but her insistent pleas drove him beyond control. He drove into her again and again, until he was mindless of everything but finding fulfillment for both of them. When he knew he was about to pour his seed into her, his hand moved down her stomach. He stroked her into finding her own release.

Their climax was glorious. Caine collapsed on top of her. He was exhausted, and completely at peace. "Love, are you still breathing?" he asked when his heart quit hammering in his ears.

He was teasing her, yet when she didn't answer him, he immediately moved away from her. "Jade?"

She rolled over and looked at him. "You made me beg."

"I what?"

"You made me beg."

"Yes, I did, didn't I?" he answered with a wide grin.

"You aren't the least contrite," she announced. Her fingertips caressed his warm chest. "You're a rake, all right. I don't understand why I find you so appealing."

The dreamy, passionate look was still in her eyes. Caine kissed her forehead, the tip of her freckled nose, and then claimed her mouth for a long, wet, tongue-thrusting kiss. "Do you want more, love?"

He didn't give her time to answer. "I do," he whispered in a low growl.

A long while later, the two lovers fell asleep wrapped in each other's arms.

Chapter Ten

The following eight days were magical for Jade. Caine was such a gentle, loving man. He was so considerate of her feelings, too, and had the uncanny knack of understanding her moods quicker than she did. She liked their evenings most of all. Sterns would light a fire in the hearth in Caine's study, and the three of them would read in companionable silence.

Over the years, Sterns had actually become Caine's substitute father. Jade learned that the servant had been with Caine's family from the time of Caine's birth. When Caine established his own residence, Sterns had followed.

Sterns did let her know he was aware of the new sleeping arrangements. While she blushed with mortification, he announced that he certainly wasn't judgmental. He also added that he hadn't seen Caine so carefree in a good long while. Jade, he decreed, had lightened the Marquess's mood.

A messenger arrived from Caine's mother, requesting his aid in pulling his father out of his present dire circumstances.

Caine immediately went to visit his father, but when he

returned some two hours later, he was in a foul mood. His talk with his father had come to little good.

That night, after Caine had fallen asleep, Jade met with Matthew and Jimbo to give them new orders.

Matthew was waiting for her just a few feet behind the cover of the trees. The seaman was tall, reed thin, and had skin as dark as a panther's. He had the personality to match the magnificent beast, but only when he was riled. He also had an easy smile that could be quite dazzling when he was in the mood to give it.

Matthew wasn't smiling now. He had his arms crossed in front of his chest and was scowling at her just like a man who'd found a thief rummaging through his drawers.

"Why are you frowning so, Matthew?" she asked in a bare whisper.

"I saw Him standing at the window with you the other night, girl," Matthew grumbled. "Has that dandy been touching you?"

Jade didn't want to lie, but she wasn't about to share the truth with her trusted friend, either. "I was injured," she replied. "Now don't give me that look, Matthew. I took a pistol shot in my side. It was a paltry wound. Caine was . . . concerned and he stayed in my chambers that night, watching out for me."

"Black Harry's going to feed my arse to the sharks when he hears . . ."

"Matthew, you aren't going to tell Harry anything," she interjected.

The seaman wasn't at all intimidated by her angry tone. "You got yourself a sassy mouth," he replied. "I seen the fancy man put his arm around you when you were walking to the front door that first day, and I will be telling Harry. That's a fact you can start cringing over now. Jimbo wanted to put a knife in his back. Only reason he didn't is because he knew you'd be put out with him."

"Yes, I would be put out," she answered. "No one's going to touch a hair on Caine's head or he'll answer to me. Now quit frowning, Matthew. We have an important issue to discuss."

Matthew didn't want to let go of their topic. "But is he giving you real trouble?"

"No, he isn't giving me any trouble," she replied. "Matthew, you know I can take care of myself. Please have more faith in me."

Matthew was immediately contrite. He didn't want his mistress to be disappointed in him. "Of course I know you can take care of yourself," he rushed out. "But you don't know your own appeal. You're too pretty for your own good. I'm thinking now Jimbo and Harry were right. We should have cut your face when you was a youngster."

She knew from the sparkle in his handsome brown eyes that he was jesting with her. "None of you would have dared to harm me," she countered. "We're family, Matthew, and you love me as much as I love you."

"You're nothing but a puny brat," came another deep voice. Jade turned toward the sound and watched her friend, Jimbo, silently move to stand directly in front of her. Jimbo's frown matched his giant's size. Like Matthew, he was also dressed in drab brown peasant garb, for brighter colors could easily be spotted through the branches.

In the moonlight, Jimbo's frown looked fierce. "Matthew told me the dandy touched you. I could kill him, just for that. No one's . . ."

"You're both underestimating Caine if you think he'll easily let you put your knives in him," she interjected.

"I'm betting he's as puny as Colin," Jimbo argued.

Jade let him see how exasperated she was with him. "You haven't seen Colin in quite some time and he was half out of his mind because of his injuries then. He's probably as fit as ever now. Besides, you've made a serious miscalculation if

173

JULIE GARWOOD

you believe either brother is weak. Remember, Jimbo, I was the one who read Caine's file. I know what I'm talking about."

"If the man's got blood, he can bleed," Matthew pronounced.

Neither seaman seemed affected by her frown. Jade let out a sigh of frustration.

She turned to Matthew and said, "I must go and have a little chat with Caine's father. You must keep Caine occupied with a diversion while I'm away."

"I don't see any need for you to talk to Caine's father," Matthew protested. "Colin and Nathan are bound to show up any time now."

"The way they're dawdling? No, I dare not wait any longer. Caine's father might very well be on his death bed now. He isn't eating or sleeping. I can't let him die."

"I can see you got your mind set," Matthew muttered. "What kind of a diversion are you thinking of?"

"I'll leave that in your capable hands," Jade countered.

"When you want it done?" Jimbo asked.

"Tomorrow," she answered. "As early as possible."

Jade finally went back to her bed, content with the knowledge that Matthew and Jimbo wouldn't let her down.

The diversion began just bare minutes before dawn the following morning.

She realized then that she should have been more specific with her instructions. And when this was over, she was going to have Matthew's hide. His capable hands, indeed. The man had set the stables on fire. Fortunately, he'd had enough sense to let the horses out first.

Caine was occupied, she'd give Matthew that much credit. The horses were running wild. Three were about ready to drop their foals, and every hand was needed to squelch the spreading fire and chase the animals down.

She pretended to be asleep until Caine left the room.

Then she dressed in quick time and slipped out the back way. Caine had posted guards around the perimeter, but in the chaos, she was easily able to sneak past.

"Jimbo just left for Shallow's Wharf," Matthew told Jade as he assisted her onto the mount he'd chosen for her. "He should be back by sunset tomorrow with word for us. If the winds are strong, don't you suppose Nathan will be here soon? And are you certain you don't want me riding along with you?"

"I'm certain I want you to keep your guard on Caine's back," she replied. "He's the one in danger. I'll be back in an hour. And Matthew? Don't set anything else on fire while I'm gone."

Matthew gave her a wide grin. "It did the trick, didn't it now?"

"Aye, Matthew," she answered, not wishing to injure his pride. "It did do the trick."

She left Matthew smiling after her and arrived at her destination a half hour later. After leaving her horse in the woods adjacent to the property line, she quickly made her way to the front door. The house was monstrous, but the lock was puny by any thief's standards. Jade had it unlatched in bare minutes. There was enough light filtering through the windows for her to make her way up the winding staircase. Sounds radiated from the back of the house, indicating that the kitchen staff was already at work.

Jade was as quiet as a cat as she looked into each of the numerous bedrooms. The Duke of Williamshire couldn't be found in any of them, however. She had assumed he'd be occupying the largest bedchamber, but that giant's room was empty. A blond-headed, rather attractive elderly woman who snored like a sailor occupied the adjacent bedchamber. Jade guessed the woman was the Duchess.

At the end of the long corridor in the south wing, she found the library. It was an out-of-the-way, unusual place to house the study. Caine's father was inside. He was sound asleep in his chair behind the mahogany desk.

After locking the door against intruders, Jade studied the handsome man for a long while. He was very distinguished looking with silver-tipped hair, high, patrician cheekbones, and an angular face very similar to Caine's. There were deep circles under his eyes. The color of his skin was sallow. Even in sleep he looked as though he was in torment.

Jade couldn't decide if she should blister him with a stern lecture or apologize for causing him such needless pain.

Her heart went out to him, though. He reminded her of Caine, of course, though the father certainly wasn't as muscular. He certainly had the height, however. When she touched his shoulder, he came awake with a start and bounded out of his chair with a quickness that surprised her.

"Please don't be alarmed, sir," she whispered. "I didn't mean to startle you."

"You didn't?" he asked, imitating her low tone of voice.

The Duke of Williamshire slowly regained his composure. He ran his fingers through his hair, then shook his head in an attempt to clear his mind.

"Who are you?" he asked.

"It doesn't matter who I am, sir," she answered. "Please sit down, for I have important information to share with you."

She patiently waited until he'd obeyed her request, then leaned against the edge of the desktop close to his side. "This grieving must stop. You've made yourself ill."

"What?"

He still looked confused to her. She noticed, too, that the color of his eyes was the exact shade of gray as Caine's. His frown was similar as well.

"I said that you must stop grieving," she stated again. "Sir Harwick thinks you might well be dying. If you don't stop this nonsense . . ."

"Now see here, young lady . . ."

"Do not raise your voice to me," she interjected.

"Who in God's name are you? And how did you get into . . ."

The bluster went out of him and he slowly shook his head.

Jade thought he seemed more incredulous than angry. She decided that was a good beginning.

"Sir, I simply don't have time for a lengthy discussion. First, you must give me your promise that you'll never tell anyone about our conversation. Do you give me your word?"

"You have it," he replied.

"Good. Now, I believe I must apologize to you, though in truth I'm no good at it. I hate apologizing to anyone." She shrugged, then added, "I'm sorry I didn't come to you sooner. You've been caused needless grief, and I really could have spared you. Do you forgive me?"

"I have no idea what you're talking about, but if it will make you happy, I shall forgive you. Now tell me what it is you want from me."

"Your bark, sir, is just as irritating as your son's."

"And which son is that?" he asked, a hint of a smile coming into his eyes.

"Caine."

"Is this visitation concerning Caine? Has he done something to offend you? You might as well know now that Caine's his own man. I won't interfere unless there's real cause."

"No," Jade answered. "This isn't about Caine, though I'm happy to know you have such faith in your eldest son's ability to make his own decisions. By not interfering, you show your pride in your son."

"Then who is it you wish to discuss?" he asked.

"I'm a friend of Colin's."

"You knew him?"

She nodded. "I know him, yes. You see, he's . . ."

"Dead," he interjected, his tone harsh. "Pagan killed him."

Jade reached out and put her hand on his shoulder. "Look at me, please," she commanded in a soft whisper when he turned his gaze toward the windows.

When Caine's father did as she ordered, she nodded. "What I am about to tell you will be difficult for you to believe. First, understand this. I have proof."

"Proof?"

She nodded again. "Pagan didn't kill Colin."

"He did."

"I'm sick of hearing about Pagan's sins," she muttered. "Colin . . ."

"Did Pagan send you to me?"

"Please lower your voice," she returned. "Pagan didn't kill your son," she repeated. "He saved him. Colin's very much alive."

A long minute elapsed before the Duke reacted. His face slowly turned a blotchy shade of red while he stared at her. His eyes turned so cold, she thought he might cause frostbite.

Before he could shout at her again, she said, "I told you I had proof. Are you willing to listen to me or is your mind so set . . ."

"I will listen," he returned. "Though if this be some sort of cruel jest, I swear I'll hunt Pagan down myself and kill him with my bare hands."

"That is a fair exchange for such cruelty," she agreed. "Do you remember the time when Colin had climbed up a giant tree and couldn't get down? He was four or five years old then. Because he was crying and feeling very cowardly, you promised him you'd never tell anyone. You also convinced him that it was quite all right to be afraid, that fear was not a sin, that . . ."

"I remember," the Duke whispered. "I never did tell anyone. How did you . . ."

"As I just said, Colin told me that story. Many others, too."

"He could have told you these stories before he was killed," the Duke stated.

"Yes, he could have, but he didn't. Pagan fished Colin out of the ocean. Your son was in sorry shape. Do you know the physician, Sir Winters?"

"He's my personal physician," the Duke muttered.

"Don't you think it odd that he disappeared?"

The anger was slowly easing away from the elderly man's expression. "I do think that odd," he admitted.

"We took him," Jade explained. "He was needed to tend to Colin. I thought it important that your son have his family physician. He was in terrible pain, sir, and I wanted him to have as many familiar comforts as possible."

Jade nibbled on her lower lip while she contemplated another way to convince him. He still looked disbelieving to her. "Colin has a birthmark on his backside," she suddenly blurted out. "I know because I took care of him until Jimbo and Matthew could take Winters captive. There! Is that proof enough for you?"

In answer to that question, the Duke slowly leaned back in his chair. "Proof was sent of Colin's death."

"By whom?"

"The War Office."

"Exactly."

"I don't understand."

"I shall explain after Colin comes home," Jade answered. "Will you explain something to me before I continue to try and convince you?"

"What is it?" he asked, his tone weary.

"Do you happen to know why Colin would make me promise not to tell Caine he was alive? I've learned to trust your eldest son, and I don't understand the reason behind this promise. Colin was half out of his mind at the time, however, and perhaps his mumbling about the Bradley brothers wasn't . . ."

Caine's father bounded out of his chair again. "Colin is alive."

"Please lower your voice," she ordered. "No one must know."

"Why? I want to shout it to the heavens. My boy is alive."

"I see I've finally convinced you," she countered with a smile. "Please sit down, sir. You look faint to me."

She waited until he'd resumed his seat, then asked, "What was it that made you realize I was telling the truth?"

"When you said that Colin didn't want Caine to know . . ." He stammered to a stop, then whispered. "Lord, the Bradley brothers. I'd forgotten that incident."

Now it was her turn to look confused. "Why?" she asked, unable to keep the worry out of her voice. "Doesn't he trust his own brother?"

"Oh, no, you misunderstand," he replied. "Colin idolized Caine. I mean to say, he idolizes him. My God, this is difficult to take in."

"But if he idolizes Caine, why would he make me promise not to tell him? You've still to explain. And who, pray tell, are the Bradley brothers?"

The Duke of Williamshire let out a deep chuckle. "When Colin was just eight or nine years old, he came running home with a bloody nose and cut lip. Caine happened to be home. He demanded to know who'd done the damage, and as soon as Colin said that the Bradley brothers were responsible, Caine went charging out the door. Colin tried to stop him, of course. He hadn't told him the number of brothers, you see. A half hour later, Caine came home as bloody as his brother."

"How many brothers were there?" Jade asked.

"Eight."

"Good heavens, do you mean to say all eight brothers attacked Colin and . . ."

"No, only one went after Colin, a boy named Samuel if I remember correctly. Anyway, Samuel must have known Caine would retaliate, and he raced home to get his own reinforcements."

"Caine could have been killed," she whispered.

"Actually, my dear, your sympathy should be for the Bradley brothers. Caine was only going to put the fear of God into the boy who'd hurt Colin, but when they came at him in force, he gave them what for! My boy gave equal measure."

Jade shook her head. She didn't find the horrid story the least bit amusing. Yet Caine's father was smiling like a proud papa.

"And so you see, my dear, it isn't out of mistrust that Colin made you give your promise. It's just that Colin knows Caine very well. Colin must be thinking to protect Caine until he can explain the full situation to him. He doesn't want him charging into another group of Bradleys again. Of the two, Colin's always been the more cautious. Caine didn't know Colin was working for our government," he added. "As to that, I didn't know either. I never would have allowed it, especially when I learned that Sir Richards wasn't his superior."

"Richards," she whispered. "Yes, he was Caine's director, wasn't he?"

Caine's father looked surprised over that statement. "You've gathered quite a bit of pertinent information, haven't you? I cannot help but wonder how you came by it. Will you tell me who gave you such secrets?"

She was a little insulted by that question. "No one gave me anything," she said. "I found out on my own. I'm most resourceful, sir. My brother, Nathan, was helping Colin sort out a rather complex problem for the government. Someone didn't want them to succeed, however. A trap was set. The only reason they're both still alive is that . . . Pagan became suspicious. The pirate was able to intervene in time."

"Does Colin know who is behind this treachery?"

She shook her head. "We only know that it's someone high up in the War Office. Nathan and Colin are safe only as long as they are believed dead. I cannot tell you anything more. When Colin returns . . ."

"Will you take me to see him?"

"He should be home in just a few more days, sir. He cannot stay here, of course, unless you've cleaned your house of the servants . . . the details will have to be worked out." She paused to smile at him. "I wonder if you'll recognize your son. His hair has grown way past his shoulders. Both he and Nathan look like true pirates now."

"That must please Pagan."

"Oh, it pleases Pagan very much."

"Were their injuries severe?" he asked.

"They had been bound and gagged, then shot and tossed into the waters. Their enemies knew they weren't dead yet."

"They left them to drown."

"No, they left them for the sharks. The waters were infested with the predators and the fresh blood . . . drew their notice."

"My God . . ."

"The sharks didn't get them, though I will admit there were several close minutes. Pagan lost a good man in the rescue."

"Pagan went into those waters with this other man?"

"Yes," she answered. "Pagan is the strongest swimmer. Besides, the pirate would never ask others what . . . he could not do himself."

Jade started for the door, but was stopped by his next question. "Are you in love with my Colin?"

"Oh, heaven's no," she answered. She unlocked the door, then turned back to her new confidant. "When we next meet, you must pretend not to know me. I'm keeping Caine occupied for the present. As you know, he's determined to track down Pagan. The hunt has put him at risk, but that soon will be resolved."

"But Pagan wouldn't . . ."

"Pagan's protecting Caine," she said. "The pirate has been blamed for killing Nathan and Colin. Your government put a price on his head. Caine, as you probably know, has doubled that amount. Now consider what would happen if Caine were able to find Pagan and talked to him before he . . ."

"Pagan might be able to convince Caine he didn't kill Colin."

"Exactly," she replied. "Do you see? Whoever is behind this treachery wants to make certain Pagan isn't found."

"Or have Caine killed before he hunts down the truth."

"Yes."

"My God, Caine is at risk. I must . . ."

"Do nothing, sir," Jade announced. "As I've explained, Pagan is watching out for Caine."

"Good Lord, Pagan isn't our enemy," the Duke whispered. "I owe the man a debt I shall never be able to repay. Dear lady, is there nothing I can do for you?"

"I must take care of Caine for now," she answered. "He's a very stubborn man, but a protector by nature. He's occupied by thinking he's taking care of my problems now. When Colin comes home, then the three of you can decide what's to be done."

"Pagan sent you to Caine then?"

"Yes," she replied with a smile.

"Caine won't give up," he interjected. "I pray Colin returns soon."

"Don't worry so," Jade said. "If you tell Caine to quit his

hunt, he'll only try harder to succeed. He's too determined to stop now."

"Then you must confide in him."

"I cannot, sir. I have given my word to Colin. Besides, we've only a few more days before the truth is revealed."

"What if your brother and Colin are delayed?"

"Then we'll have to form a new plan," she announced with a nod.

"But what specifically . . ."

"We'll have to find a way to take the prey away from the hunter. Caine will be furious, but he'll be alive. I must consider this carefully," she added as she opened the door.

"When will I see you again? You mentioned that I must pretend not to know you, but . . ."

"Oh, I'm certain you'll see me again," she answered. "And there is one little thing you could do to repay me," she added. "You did say you would do anything," she reminded him.

"Yes, anything."

"Caine is your eldest son and if there must be a favorite, then he should be the one."

The Duke was clearly astonished by her remarks. "I love all my children. I wasn't aware that I favored one above the others."

"Sir Harwick believes Colin is your favorite," she said. "He also said that Caine keeps himself separate from the family. Don't allow this to continue, sir. Caine needs your love. See that he gets it."

The door closed.

The Duke of Williamshire sat at his desk a long while before his legs felt strong enough to hold his weight. Tears of joy streamed down his cheeks. He said a prayer of thanksgiving for this miracle he'd just been given.

His Colin was alive.

Henry was suddenly ravenous. He went in search of

breakfast. It was going to be difficult, for the Duke wasn't a man given to trickery, but he would have to control his smiles. None of his staff must suspect the true reason for his recovery.

He felt reborn. It was as though someone had reached down into his lonely black abyss of despair and lifted him all the way up to the stars.

The young lady he now considered his savior had the most unusual green eyes. Pagan must have named his ship after the beautiful woman. The *Emerald*. Yes, he decided with a nod. He was also certain he now knew the pirate's true identity, but he vowed he'd go to his death before revealing that truth to anyone.

He wondered, though, what Caine would say when he found out that the woman he was sheltering was actually Pagan's little sister?

There'd be fireworks aplenty, and his only prayer now was that he'd be there to protect his savior when Caine's temper exploded.

The Duke of Williamshire was certain he had it all figured out.

He was filling his plate with a second helping of eggs and kidneys when his wife, Gweneth, came rushing into the dining room. "Cook told me you were eating," she stammered out.

The Duke turned to his wife, a soft smile on his face. Poor Gweneth looked rattled. Her short blond hair was in complete disarray and she couldn't seem to get the sash to her robe tied. "Why, Henry?" she asked, staring at him so intently.

"It's the usual custom each morning," he answered. "And I was hungry."

Her brown eyes filled with tears. "You were hungry?" she whispered.

Henry put his plate down on the side bar and walked over

to his wife. He took her into his arms and kissed the top of her head. "I've given you quite a worry lately, haven't I, love?"

"But you're feeling better now?" she asked.

"I've been advised not to languish any longer," he stated.

"By whom?"

"My conscience," he lied. "In time, Gweneth, I shall explain this sudden turnabout to you. For now, however, I can only say I'm sorry for all the worry I've caused you and the children. I've grieved long enough."

"It's a miracle," she whispered.

Yes, he thought to himself, a miracle with bewitching green eyes. "Come and have a bite to eat, my dear. You look a bit peaked to me."

"I looked peaked?" Her laughter was shaky. "You, my love, look like death."

He kissed her tenderly, then led her over to the table. "After I've cleaned up, I believe I'll ride over to Caine's place."

"He'll be stunned by your recovery," Gweneth announced. "Oh, Henry, it's so good to have you back with us."

"Would you like to ride over to see Caine with me?"

"Oh, yes, I'd like that," she answered. A determined gleam entered her eyes. "It isn't proper to have guests but I believe I'll invite Lady Aisely and her dear mother down for a long weekend. You must tell Caine we expect him to . . . why are you shaking your head at me?"

"You might as well save yourself the effort, Gweneth. Give it up. Caine won't be marrying Lady Aisely."

"It's a sound match, Henry," she argued. "Give me two good reasons why I cannot encourage this union?"

"Very well," he answered. "One, she doesn't have red hair."

"Well, of course she doesn't have red hair. She has beautiful blond hair. You know that well enough."

186

"And two," he continued, ignoring her befuddled look. "She doesn't have green eyes."

"Henry, you aren't feeling altogether well yet, are you?"

Henry's laughter echoed throughout the dining room. "Caine needs an enchantress. You'll have to accept it, my dear."

"Accept what?" she asked.

His slow wink left her more puzzled than ever. "I believe, Gweneth, that your breakfast will have to wait a while longer. You must go back to bed at once."

"I must?" she asked. "Why?"

The Duke leaned forward and whispered into his wife's ear. When he was finished with his explanation, his wife blushed.

"Oh, Henry," she whispered. "You really are feeling better."

Chapter Eleven

Jade returned to Caine's home a short time later. After handing the reins to Matthew, she rushed up the back steps to her bedroom. When she rounded the corner, she found Sterns standing like a centurian outside her bedroom door.

He did a double take when he spotted her. Then he folded his arms across his chest. "You're suppose to be inside your bedroom, mi'lady."

She decided to take the offensive. She'd make him do the explaining. "And what are you suppose to be doing?"

"I'm guarding the door."

"Why?"

"So you won't leave."

"But I already left," she countered with a soft smile. "Sterns, I do believe your time is too valuable to be guarding an empty room."

"But mi'lady, I didn't know it was empty," he protested.

She patted him on his arm. "You may explain this to me later, sir. Now please move out of my way. I really must change out of this riding garment and go help Caine."

She scooted past the disgruntled-looking servant and shut

the door on his protests. In little time at all, she'd changed into a dark green gown and hurried downstairs by way of the main staircase.

Sterns was now guarding the front door. The set of his jaw told her he was going to be difficult. "You may not go outside," he announced in a voice that would have chilled a polar bear.

She wasn't at all intimidated. She gave him a wide smile. "I can and I will," she answered.

"My lord is most insistent that you remain inside."

"I'm just as insistent that I go outside."

In answer to that challenge, Sterns leaned against the door and slowly shook his head.

Jade decided to turn his attention. "Sterns? How many servants are there in residence here?"

He looked surprised by her question. "We're only half staffed now," he answered. "There are five of us in all."

"Where are the others?"

"In London," he answered. "They're helping to clean the town house."

"But I thought it was destroyed in the fire," she said.

"It wasn't as bad as all that," he said. "The side's been boarded up and now there's only the smoke damage to be righted. While the workers repair the structure, the servants are cleaning the inside."

"I'm wondering, Sterns, if the servants here can be trusted."

He rose to his full height before answering. "Mi'lady, all the servants are trustworthy. They are all loyal to their employer."

"You're certain?"

He took a step away from the door. "Why are you so interested in . . ."

"You'll be having two guests in the next few days, Sterns, but no one must tell that they're here. Your staff must keep silent."

"The Marquess hasn't mentioned any guests to me," he argued, seeming mildly injured.

Jade rushed past him and threw the door wide. "Caine doesn't know about the visitors just yet," she said. "That's the reason he hasn't told you. It's going to be a surprise, you see."

She could tell from his befuddled expression that he didn't see. "I just thought you'd like to be forewarned so you could have the guest chambers made ready," she explained. She picked up her skirts and started down the steps. "Now quit frowning, Sterns. I shall tell Caine you tried to keep me inside."

"And I shall inform mi'lord that you weren't in your room," he called out.

Jade found Caine going through the remains of what had been his stables. Only smoldering embers remained. The destruction was absolute.

The horses, she noticed, were now housed in a large rectangular corral the men had just put together.

Caine's white shirt was covered with soot. "Have you collected all your horses?" she asked when she reached his side.

He slowly turned to look at her. The scowl on his face could very well start a fresh fire. His tone, however, was deceptively mild when he said, "All but the one you borrowed."

"Borrowed?" she asked, feigning innocence.

"Go and wait for me in the drawing room," he commanded.

"But Caine, I want to help."

"Help?" He almost lost his temper then and there. "You and your men have helped enough." Several deep breaths later, he said, "Go back inside. Now."

His roar accomplished his goal. Jade immediately turned around and hurried back to the house. She could feel Caine's stare on her back and wouldn't have been surprised if her gown had caught fire. The man was spitting-embers angry.

It would be pointless to try to reason with him now. She'd have to wait until his anger had dissipated just a little.

When she reached the bottom step, she turned back to him. "Caine? If you must stay outside, don't be such a bloody easy target."

Sterns rushed down the stairs, grabbed hold of her elbow, and whispered, "Do as he orders, Lady Jade. You don't want to prod his temper now. Come along inside now," he added as he assisted her up the stairs. "I don't believe I've ever seen mi'lord in such a rage."

"Yes, he is in a rage," Jade whispered, irritated by the tremor in her voice. "Sterns, do you think I might have a cup of tea? This day seems to have gone completely sour," she added. "And it's not even half done."

"Of course I shall fix you some tea," Sterns rushed out. "Mi'lady, I'm certain the Marquess didn't mean to raise his voice to you. Once he gets over his anger, I'm certain he'll apologize."

"He might not ever get over his anger," she muttered.

Sterns opened the front door for her, then followed her inside. "The stables weren't even a month old," he said.

Jade tried to pay attention to what Sterns was saying, but Caine's words kept echoing through her mind. You and your men have helped enough. Yes, those were his very words. He knew about Matthew and Jimbo. But how? she wondered, and more importantly, what else did he know?

While Sterns went to see about her tea, Jade paced the confines of the large drawing room. She opened the pair of French doors at the end of the room to let in the fresh spring air. It was a precautionary measure as well, for if Caine was bent on killing her, she'd have a possible escape.

"Nonsense," she muttered as she resumed her pacing. Caine would never raise his hand against her, no matter how angry he became. Besides, he couldn't possibly know the full truth.

The front door suddenly bounded open. It banged against the interior wall twice before it was slammed shut.

Caine had arrived.

Jade rushed over to the gold brocade settee, sat down, and folded her hands in her lap. She forced a serene smile on her face. He wasn't going to know she was shaking. No, she'd go to her grave before she'd let him know he had her worried.

The doors to the drawing room flew open next. Caine filled the entrance. Jade couldn't hold her smile once she saw his expression. He looked ready to kill. Why, he was so furious, he was actually trembling.

"Where did you go this morning?" he roared.

"Don't take that tone of voice with me, sir. You'll make me deaf."

"Answer me."

She glared at him because he'd ignored her order and had shouted once again, then said, "I went to visit your dear papa."

That announcement took a little of the bluster out of him. Then he shook his head. "I don't believe you."

"I'm telling you the truth," she stated.

Caine walked into the room and didn't stop until he towered over her. The tips of his boots touched the hem of her gown. He loomed over her like an avenging god. Jade felt trapped. In the back of her mind she knew that he wanted her to feel that way. "I'm sorry you don't believe me, Caine, but I did go to see your father. I was very concerned about him, you see. Sir Harwick mentioned he wasn't feeling well and I thought a nice chat would lighten his mood."

She stared down at her hands while she made that confession.

"When did you set the fire, Jade?"

She looked up at his face then. "I didn't set any fires," she announced.

192

"The hell you didn't," he roared. He turned away from her and walked over to the hearth. He was so furious, he didn't trust himself to stand close to her.

She stood up, folded her hands in front of her, and said, "I didn't set your stables on fire, Caine."

"Then you ordered one of your men to do it. Now I want to know why."

"What men?"

"The two bastards who've been hanging around here since the day we arrived," he answered.

He waited to hear her denial. She had given him nothing but lies since the moment they met. He realized that now.

"Oh, those two men," she answered. She lifted her shoulders in a delicate shrug. "You must mean Matthew and Jimbo. You've met them, have you?"

His anguish was almost unbearable now. "Yes, I've met them. They were two more lies, weren't they?"

She couldn't look at him now. God help her, she was finally seeing the man she'd read about in the file. Cold. Methodical. Deadly. The descriptive words hadn't been exaggerated after all.

"Matthew and Jimbo are fine men," she whispered.

"Then you don't deny . . ."

"I won't deny anything," she answered. "You're putting me in an impossible position. I have given my word and I can't break it. You'll just have to trust me a while longer."

"Trust you?" He roared the words like blasphemies. "I will never trust you again. You must think I'm a fool if you believe I would."

She was terrified of him now. She took a deep breath, then said, "My problem is very delicate."

"I don't give a damn how delicate your problem is," he roared. "What in God's name is your game? Why are you here?"

He was back to shouting at her. Jade shook her head at him. "I will tell you only that I'm here because of you."

"Answer me."

"Very well," she whispered. "I'm here to protect you."

She might as well have told him she'd come from the heavens for all the attention he gave that statement of fact. "I want the real reason, damn it."

"That is the real reason. I'm protecting you."

Sterns appeared at the opened doorway with a silver tray in his hands. He took one look at his employer's face and immediately turned around.

"Shut the doors behind you, Sterns," Caine ordered.

"Don't you raise your voice to Sterns," Jade demanded in a near shout of her own. "He has nothing to do with this and you shouldn't take your anger out on him."

"Sit down, Jade." His voice was much softer now, far more threatening, too. It took all Jade's determination not to do as he ordered.

"You probably kick puppies when you're in a foul mood, don't you?"

"Sit down."

She glanced over to the doorway, judging the distance to safety, but Caine's next words changed her mind. "You wouldn't make it."

Jade turned back to Caine. "You aren't going to be at all reasonable about this, are you?"

"No," he answered. "I'm not going to be reasonable."

"I was hoping that we could have a quiet discussion after you've calmed down and . . ."

"Now," he countered. "We're going to have our discussion now, Jade." He wanted to grab hold of her, shake her into answering all his questions, but he knew if he touched her, he might kill her.

His heart felt as though it had just been torn in half. "Pagan sent you, didn't he?"

"No."

"Yes," he answered. "My God, the bastard sent a woman to do his work for him. Who is he, Jade? Your brother?"

She shook her head and backed away from him. "Caine, please try to listen . . ."

He started after her, then forced himself to stop. "All of it . . . lies, isn't that right, Jade? You weren't in any danger."

"Not all of it lies," she answered. "But you were the primary target."

He shook his head. She knew then he wasn't going to believe anything she told him. She could see the pain, the raw agony in his eyes.

"He sent a woman," he repeated. "Your brother's a coward. He's going to die. It will be fitting justice, won't it? An eye for an eye, or in this instance, a brother for a brother."

"Caine, you must listen to me," she cried out. She wanted to weep because of the torment she was causing him. "You have to understand. In the beginning, I didn't know what kind of a man you were . . . Oh, God, I'm so sorry . . ."

"Sorry?" he asked, his voice flat, devoid of all emotion.

"Yes," she whispered. "If you'll only listen . . ."

"Do you think I'm going to believe anything you tell me now?"

Jade didn't answer him. Caine seemed to be staring through her. He didn't say anything for a long time. She could almost see the fury building inside of him.

She closed her eyes against his dark expression, his anger, his hatred.

"Did you let me make love to you because Pagan ordered you to?" he asked.

She reacted as though he'd just struck her. "That would make me a whore, Caine, and I don't whore for anyone, not even my brother."

He didn't agree with her soon enough to placate her. Her eyes filled with tears. "I am not a whore," she shouted.

The sudden roar that came from the French doors turned both Caine's and Jade's attention. The bone-chilling sound was like a battle cry.

Jade recognized the sound. Nathan had arrived. The deception was finally over.

"Did you just call my sister a whore?"

The walls shook from the venom in Nathan's deep voice. Jade had never seen her brother so angry.

She took a step toward her brother, but suddenly found herself hauled up against Caine's side.

"Don't get in my way," he ordered, his voice mild, horribly calm.

"In the way of what?" she asked. "You aren't going to hurt my brother, Caine. I won't let you."

"Get your hands off her," Nathan roared. "Or I'll kill you."

"Nathan," Jade cried out. "Caine doesn't understand." She tried to push Caine's hands away from her shoulders. It proved impossible. His grip was as tenacious as seaweed.

She didn't know who looked more furious. Nathan's scowl was just as ugly as Caine's was, just as threatening. They were equally matched, these two giant adversaries. They were bound to kill each other if given the chance.

Nathan looked like a pirate, too. His long, dark brown hair fell way past his broad shoulders. He was dressed in snug black britches and wore his white shirt opened almost to the waist. Nathan wasn't quite as tall as Caine was, but he was certainly just as muscular.

Yes, they would kill each other. Jade frantically tried to think of a way to ease the situation while the two men took each other's measure.

"I asked you a question, you bastard," Nathan shouted again. He took a threatening step forward. "Did you call my sister a whore?"

"He didn't call me a whore," Jade shouted when Nathan reached for the knife in his waistband. "He doesn't know about Colin. I kept my word not to tell him."

Nathan hesitated. Jade pressed her advantage. "He thinks you killed Colin. He has it all figured out, Nathan."

Nathan's hand moved back to his side, away from his dagger. Jade went weak with relief. "He has, has he?" Nathan drawled out.

Caine stared at the intruder, knowing now there couldn't be any doubt that the pirate was Jade's brother. They both had the same green eyes.

"Damn right I figured it out," Caine suddenly roared. "You're Pagan and you did kill my brother."

She pushed away from Caine and took a step toward Nathan. Caine roughly shoved Jade behind his back. "Don't try to go to him, Jade."

"Are you trying to protect me from my own brother?" she asked.

Caine didn't answer her.

"Did he touch you?" Nathan shouted the question as though it was a blasphemy.

"Nathan, will you quit that topic?" she cried out. "Now isn't the time to discuss such a personal matter."

"Be silent," Caine commanded.

Jade grabbed hold of the back of his shirt when he started forward. The action didn't waylay him. Caine kicked the ornately carved tea cart out of his path and continued toward his prey. "Damn right I touched her," he roared. "Wasn't that all part of the plan, you bastard?"

Nathan let out a roar, then rushed forward. The two men were like bulls charging at each other.

"No," Jade screamed. "Nathan, please don't hurt Caine. Caine, you mustn't hurt Nathan either . . ."

She quit her pleas when she realized they weren't paying any attention to her.

Caine got in the first toss. He literally threw Nathan up against the wall. A lovely painting depicting the Thames in earlier, cleaner times fell to the floor with a loud thud. Nathan finished the destruction of the artwork when he put his foot through it in an attempt to slam his knee into Caine's groin.

He was determined to make a eunuch out of him. Caine easily blocked the blow, however, then threw Nathan up against the wall again. Jade's brother landed the first good punch, though it was most assuredly by foul means. Caine had Nathan by his neck and was just about to smash his fist through the back of his skull when his attention was caught by the man standing in the doorway. His hold immediately slackened. Nathan pressed his advantage. He slammed his fist into Caine's jaw.

Caine shook off the blow as insignificant, then shoved Nathan against the wall again.

"Colin?"

The name came out in a strangled whisper of disbelief. His mind couldn't accept what he was seeing. His brother was alive. Colin was leaning against the door frame, grinning that lopsided grin of his that was so familiar, so boyish . . . so Colin. He looked thin, terribly thin, but very much alive.

Caine was so stunned he didn't realize he was strangling Nathan until he heard him gasping for air. As soon as he lessened his grip, Nathan tore free and hit him again. Caine ignored the blow and finally let go.

Almost as an afterthought, Caine slammed his elbow into Nathan's ribs, then took a step toward Colin.

"Honest to God, Colin, I'm going to kill your brother," Nathan shouted. "Do you know what he's done to my sister? He . . ."

"Nathan, you don't have to tell Colin," Jade cried out. "Please," she added. "For once, try to be a gentleman."

Colin slowly pulled away from the door. He used his cane to aid him as he made his way over to his brother. Caine was shaking with emotion when he wrapped his arms around his little brother. "My God, you're really here. I cannot believe it."

"I'm so damned happy to see you, Caine," Colin said. "I

know you're surprised. I'll explain everything. Try not to be too angry with me. I wouldn't let anyone tell you. I wanted to explain first. They're evil men. You would have gone charging in . . ."

Colin didn't seem to have the strength to go on. He sagged against Caine, giving him most of his weight. Caine continued to hold him close while he waited for his brother to regain his composure. "Take your time, Colin," he whispered. "Just take your time."

When Colin nodded, Caine stepped back to have another look at his brother. The dimple was back in Caine's cheek and tears had formed in his eyes. "Colin, you look like a pirate, too," he announced. "Your hair's as long as Pagan's," he added with a nod and a scowl in Nathan's direction.

Nathan scowled back. "I haven't told him anything, Colin," Nathan said. "But your astute brother has it all figured out. He knows I'm Pagan and I sent my little sister to whore for me."

Jade wished the floor would open up and swallow her whole. Her face felt like it was on fire. "Nathan, if Caine doesn't kill you, I very well might," she threatened.

Colin was staring at her. When he started laughing, she knew exactly what he was thinking. "Didn't I tell you . . ." he began.

"Colin, do sit down," she commanded. "You must get your weight off that leg. It's too soon for you to be walking."

Colin wasn't about to forget Nathan's horrid comment. "I knew you and Caine would . . ." He let out a sigh. "I did warn you, didn't I?"

"Colin, I don't want to hear another word about Caine and me," she shouted. "It's over, finished. Do you understand? Where is Winters?" she added in a rush, hoping to turn his attention. "The physician should be at our side."

"Winters was with you?" Caine asked.

"Pagan convinced him to take care of me aboard the

Emerald," Colin explained. He hobbled over to the settee
and sat down. "He was a little resistant at first, but Pagan
can be very persuasive. And in the end, I think Winters had
the time of his life."

"Well, where is he?" Jade asked.

"We let him go home," Colin answered. "Now quit
fretting. It's just going to take time for the leg to heal."

Jade pushed a pillow behind Colin's back, then propped
his feet up on a large round footstool.

"I believe I will order some refreshments for you, Colin,"
she said. "You look too pale to me. The walk from the drive
tired you out, didn't it?"

She didn't give him time to answer, but picked up her
skirts and started for the drawing room doors. Caine
blocked her path. "You aren't going anywhere."

She refused to look up at him as she tried to move around
him. Caine took hold of her arm. The grip was stinging. "Sit
down, Jade."

"Jade?"

Colin said her name in a surprised whisper.

"I have allowed Caine to call me by my given name."

"Allowed?" Nathan asked.

"What do you call her?" Caine asked his brother.

"She has several nicknames," Colin answered. "I call her
Red most of the time, don't I, Jade?"

When she nodded, Colin continued on. "Nathan calls her
Brat all the time. He has a particular fondness for that
nickname."

His slow wink increased Jade's blush. "Black Harry calls
me Dolphin," Colin went on to explain. "It's meant as an
insult, too."

Nathan shook his head. "Dolphins are gentle, Colin. It
wasn't meant as an insult."

Caine let out a weary sigh. "Who is Black Harry?"

It was suddenly hitting him full force, this amazing
miracle. He found his strength deserting him. Caine dragged

Jade over to the wingback chair that faced the settee, sat down, and forced her with his hold to sit on the arm.

He stared at his brother all the while. "I still cannot believe you're alive," he said.

"You have Pagan to thank for that," Colin replied. "And I can't believe you're so calm. I was certain you'd go into a rage when you found out I made Jade promise not to tell you. Caine, there's so much I have to explain. First, however, I do believe Nathan's sister has something she wants to tell you."

Jade was shaking her head vehemently. "I have nothing to say to him, Colin. If you feel like enlightening him on all the facts, do so after I've left."

Caine wasn't paying any attention to her rantings. He let go of her arm, leaned forward, his elbows resting on his knees, and said, "I want you to tell me who did this to you. Give me the name, Colin. I'll do the rest."

Jade took advantage of Caine's inattention. She once again tried to leave. Caine never took his gaze away from his brother when he grabbed hold of her hand. "I believe I mentioned that you aren't going anywhere."

Nathan looked incredulous. "Why haven't you put your knife through him yet?"

She shrugged before answering. "Colin would have been upset."

"What's taking Black Harry so long?" Nathan asked Colin then. He strolled over to the settee, took his place next to Colin, and propped his feet up on the same wide stool.

"He'll be a while yet," Colin explained. "He lost his spectacles."

Both men started laughing. Jade was horrified. "Black Harry's here? In England?"

Her voice shook. Only Nathan seemed to understand the reason for her distress. "He is," he announced in a hard voice. "And when I tell him . . ."

"No, Nathan, you mustn't tell him anything," she cried

out. She tried to get out of Caine's grasp. He tightened his hold in reaction.

"Who is Black Harry?" Caine asked, ignoring Jade's struggles.

"He's the uncle," Colin answered. "He took care of Jade after her father died."

Caine was trying to filter all this information through his mind. The way Jade had reacted to the news that Harry was here indicated she was afraid of him.

"How long was she with him?" he asked Colin.

"Years," Colin answered.

Caine turned to Nathan. "Where the hell were you when she was growing up? Out robbing people blind?"

"Damn it, Colin, a man can only take so much," Nathan muttered. "If he keeps it up, I'm going to kill him, even if it means losing your friendship."

Colin was still too exhausted from the walk to take part in the conversation. He wanted to rest for just a few more minutes before he started his explanation. With a loud yawn meant to draw attention, he said, "No one's going to kill anyone until this has all been straightened out." He leaned back against the cushions and closed his eyes.

A loud commotion drew everyone's attention then. Caine looked up just in time to see a large flower pot fly past the windows to the terrace. The pot crashed against the stone wall. A sharp blasphemy followed the splintering noise.

"Harry's here," Colin drawled out.

Caine continued to stare at the entrance, thinking to himself that he was prepared for just about anything now. Nothing more could ever surprise him again.

He was, unfortunately, mistaken. The man who finally strutted across the threshold was so outrageous looking, Caine almost laughed.

Harry paused, put his big hands on his hips, and glared at his audience. He was dressed all in white, with a wide red sash tied around his pot-bellied waist. His skin was bronzed by the sun, his hair was silver as clouds. Caine judged his age to be near fifty, perhaps a bit more.

This one could give children nightmares for months. He was amazingly ugly, with a bulbous nose that covered most of his face. His eyes were bare slits, due to the fact that he was squinting fiercely.

The man had flair, he'd give him that much. He literally swaggered into the drawing room. Two men rushed ahead of him, moving objects out of his way. Two more filed in behind. Caine recognized the last two. They were Matthew and Jimbo. Both of their faces were covered with fresh bruises Caine had inflicted when he'd had his little talk with them.

"It's getting damned crowded in here," Caine stated.

Jade jerked her hand away from his hold and rushed over to Black Harry. She threw herself into his arms and hugged him tightly. Caine noticed Harry's gold tooth then. When he smiled down at Jade, one of the front teeth gleamed in the light.

"Oh, Uncle Harry, I've missed you," she whispered.

"Of course you missed me," the elderly man grumbled. "I'm going to beat you good though," he added after he'd given her another hug of affection. "Have you gone completely daft, girl? I'll be hearing every spoiled morsel of this tale, and then I'm going to beat the daylights out of you."

"Now, Harry," Jade said in a voice meant to soothe. "I didn't mean to upset you."

Harry let out a loud snort. "You didn't mean for me to find out, that's what you didn't mean to do," he countered. He leaned down and kissed her loudly on the top of her head.

"That one be Caine?" he asked, squinting at the man in question.

"He is," Jade answered.

"He ain't dead."

"No."

"You done your task well then," Harry praised.

"He will be dead soon enough if I get my way," Nathan drawled out.

"What's this mutiny I'm hearing?"

"Harry?" Jade asked, tugging his attention back to her.

"Yes?"

She leaned up on tiptoe and whispered into his ear. Harry frowned during the telling.

When she was finished, he nodded. "I might be telling, and then again, I might not. You trust this man?"

She couldn't lie. "I do."

"What does he mean to you, girl?"

"Nothing," she blurted out.

"Then look at me eyes," he ordered. "You're talking to the floor and that tells me something tricky's going on."

"There's nothing tricky," she whispered. "I'm just glad this deception is over."

Harry didn't look convinced. "Then why'd you bother watching out for him if he meant nothing to you?" he prodded, sensing she wasn't telling him the full truth.

"He's Colin's brother," she reminded her uncle. "That is the only reason I bothered."

Harry decided to wait until they were alone before he forced the truth out of her. "I'm still not understanding," he bellowed. He was squinting in Caine's direction now. "You should be kissing Pagan's feet to my way of thinking," he added. "Your sorry brother's alive, ain't he?"

"Now that you're here, we can sort all this out, Harry," Colin called out.

Harry grunted. He looked back down at Jade. "I'm still going to beat you bloody, girl. Do you doubt me?"

"No, Harry, I don't doubt you," she answered. With an effort, she hid her smile. In all their time together, Harry had never, ever harmed her. He was a kind, gentle man with a soul so pure, so white, God was surely smiling down at him with pride. Harry liked to threaten all sorts of horrid punishments when there was an audience listening. He was a pirate, he would often remind her, and appearances had to be kept up.

Caine had started out of his chair when Harry made his first threat, but Colin motioned to him to sit down again. "Bluster," he'd whispered to his brother.

"Get me a chair, men," Harry shouted. He continued to squint at Caine as he walked over to the hearth. Both Colin and Nathan got their feet and the stool out of his way just in the nick of time. While Jade helped resettle Colin, Harry stood in front of the hearth, his hands clasped behind his back.

"You don't look anything like Dolphin," he remarked. He grinned, displaying his lovely tooth again, then added, "You and your puny-arsed brother are both homely as sin. Only family resemblance I can see."

Caine didn't think the man could see much of anything, but he kept that opinion to himself. He looked over at Colin to see how he was responding to that insult. Though Colin's eyes were once again closed, he was smiling. Caine concluded Harry's thunder was all for his benefit.

One of his men carried a big chair over to the hearth, and when Harry was settled, Jade walked over to stand behind him. She put her hand on Harry's shoulder.

"You wear spectacles, me boy?" Harry asked Caine.

Caine shook his head. "Anyone here wear them? One of your servants perchance?"

"No," Caine answered.

"Uncle, do you know where you lost your last pair?" she asked.

"Now, lovely, you know I don't remember," he answered. "If I did, I wouldn't have lost them, now would I?"

Harry turned back to Caine then. "There be a village close by?"

Colin started laughing. Even Nathan broke into a grin. Caine didn't have the faintest idea why they were so amused.

"There is a village close by," Colin said.

"No one was asking you, you twit. Go back to sleep, Dolphin. It's all you're good for," he added with a wink.

Harry turned to his cohorts and bellowed, "Men, you know what to do."

The two unsavory-looking men lounging by the terrace doors both nodded. Just as they turned to leave, Jade prodded Harry's shoulder. "Oh, all right, girl," he muttered. "No pillaging, men," he shouted then. "We're too close to home."

"Aye, Black Harry," one of the men called out.

"Did they jump to do my bidding?" Harry asked Jade in a whisper.

"They did," she answered. "As quick as lightning."

Harry nodded. He clasped his knees with his hands and leaned forward. "Now then, I was hearing talk of mutiny when I came inside. You'd think this was a time for rejoicing, but I ain't hearing any cheering. You hearing any cheering, girl?"

"No, Harry."

"Could it be that the Dolphin's such a bother, you ain't glad to have him back?" he asked Caine. "Can't say I blame you. The boy can't even play a decent game of chess."

"I was half out of my mind when we last played," Colin reminded him.

Harry snorted. "You only got half a mind, twit."

Colin grinned. "Caine? Do you know why this sorry piece of flesh is called Black Harry?"

"I'll be telling it," Harry announced. "It's because I got me a black heart."

He made that statement as a boast, then waited a full minute for Caine to appreciate his explanation. "I gave myself that nickname. It's fitting, ain't it, girl?"

"Yes, Uncle, it's very fitting. Your heart's as black as night."

"It's good of you to say so," Harry replied. He reached up and patted her hand. "As soon as me men get back from their errand, I'm leaving for the Wharf. I could use a spot of supper to hold me over."

"I shall see to it at once," Jade said. She immediately moved toward the doors, deliberately making a wide path of Caine's chair. When she reached the entrance to the foyer, she turned back to her uncle. "Please don't let Nathan and Caine fight while I'm gone, Harry."

"I wouldn't be caring," Harry called out.

"But I would care," she returned. "Please, Harry?"

"All right then, I won't let them fight."

As soon as the door shut behind Jade, Harry whispered, "She's a piece of work, that one. I should have cut her face years ago. She's too pretty for her own safety. 'Tis the reason I had to leave her behind so many times. Couldn't trust me men when my back was turned."

"She's so pretty," Nathan snapped, "that some dishonorable men would take advantage."

"Let it go for now, Nathan," Colin interjected. He opened his eyes and looked at Caine. "My brother's an honorable man."

"Like hell," Nathan growled.

Caine wasn't paying any attention to the conversation now. He'd homed in on Harry's casually stated comment that he'd left Jade behind. Where did he leave her? Who watched over her when he was away? There sure as hell hadn't been a woman there, or she would have known a little more about the facts of life.

"What's all this talk about?" Harry demanded, drawing Caine's attention again.

"Although it isn't in your nature, I'm asking you to be patient, Harry," Colin requested. "There's been a little misunderstanding, that's all."

"Clear it up quick then," Harry ordered.

"Damn it, Colin, I know all I need to know," Nathan said. "Your brother's a bastard . . ."

"You were born out of wedlock, son?" Harry interrupted. He looked absolutely thrilled by that possibility.

Caine sighed. "No, I wasn't born out of wedlock."

Harry didn't even try to hide his disappointment, another fact that made absolutely no sense to Caine.

"Then you can't be going by that nickname," he instructed. "Only those born with the stigma can boast of it. A man's only as good as his nickname," he added with a nod.

"Or a woman," Colin interjected.

Caine looked incredulous. Colin tried not to laugh. "Harry? Tell him about Bastard Bull," he suggested.

"Colin, for God's sake," Caine began.

"In time, Caine," his brother whispered. "I need a little more time to gather my thoughts."

Caine nodded. "All right," he said. He turned to Harry then. "Tell me about Bastard Bull."

"He weren't a bastard after all," Harry stated with a scowl. "He just said he was so he could sign on with us. He knew the store I put in nicknames. When we found out he'd lied, we tossed him overboard with the garbage."

"They happened to be in the middle of the ocean at the time," Colin drawled out. "Pagan wouldn't let him drown, though."

"How very considerate of you," Caine muttered to Nathan.

"Now there was this other bloke, a good, strong man . . ."

Caine let out a long sigh. He leaned back in the chair, closed his eyes, and decided he was going to have to wait until all this ridiculous talk about nicknames was finished. Colin seemed to be enjoying the conversation and he had asked for time. His brother looked half asleep now . . . and so damned pale.

For a good ten minutes or more Harry continued with his

dissertation. When he finally finished, Nathan said, "Jade has a special nickname, too."

"I'll be telling it," Harry stated. "I'm the one who came up with the special name, after all."

Nathan nodded. "All right, Harry, you tell it."

Everyone was watching Caine now. If he'd bothered to open his eyes, he would have seen their smiles.

Caine was having difficulty holding onto his patience. "And what is her special nickname, Harry?" he finally asked, his tone weary.

"Well now, me boy," Harry drawled out. "We like to call her Pagan."

Chapter Twelve

He didn't take the news at all well. For the longest time, he simply refused to believe Jade could possibly be Pagan. Only a man could get away with such daring feats, only a man.

Colin, Harry, and Nathan were all watching him closely. When he shook his head in denial, they nodded in unison.

"I can see you're having trouble accepting this," Colin said. His expression was sympathetic. "But it is true, Caine. Harry gave her that nickname years ago because . . ."

"I'll be telling it," Harry interrupted. "It was the color of her hair, son. As red as hell's fire it was when she was a youngster."

It was apparent from the look on Caine's face that he still didn't accept. Harry thought he didn't understand the reason for her special nickname. "She was as wild as the devil back then, too," he explained. "Just like a pagan baby, she was."

Caine's expression slowly turned from disbelief to fury. Both Colin and Harry became uneasy. Only Nathan seemed to be enjoying the moment. "Would a man be apt to leave a rose behind, Caine?" he asked, hoping to rub salt in his wounds. "That's the work of a woman. It's amazing to me that no one's figured it out by now. Don't you agree, Colin?"

"Yes," Colin answered, his gaze directed on his brother. "Amazing."

It was the last remark anyone made for a long while. Harry and Nathan waited for Caine to come to terms with the truth.

Colin knew his brother far better than his friends did. He patiently waited for the explosion.

Jade was in the dining room helping Sterns set the table. As soon as the butler took one look at her face, he knew something was wrong. She looked as pale as the linen tablecloth.

She wouldn't tell him anything but explained that her uncle had arrived and that he and his four men would require supper before they left. She also insisted upon using the finest crystal. Sterns went into the kitchens to order the meal, throwing both the cook and her assistant, Bernice, into a frenzy, and then returned to the dining room.

He found Jade examining a large oval silver platter. "Uncle would like this," she remarked. "The design is quite magnificent."

Sterns nodded. "A gift from the King," he explained. "When the Marquess was knighted, Colin threw quite a bash in his honor. The King showed up and gave him that platter. If you turn it over, you'll see the inscription."

Jade shook her head. She thrust the platter into Sterns' hands. "Hide it."

"I beg your pardon?"

"Hide it, Sterns," she repeated. She looked around the room, then asked, "Are there any other special things Caine would rather keep?"

"The silver tea set on the side bar," he said. "I do believe it has special meaning to mi'lord."

"Did the King give him that, too?"

211

"No, the set came from his grandmother."

"Hide it as well, Sterns. Put the things under Caine's bed. They'll be safe there."

"Mi'lady?" Sterns asked. "Are you feeling ill?"

"No."

"You look ill," Sterns announced. "And you're walking around as though you're in a trance. I know something's wrong . . ."

Jade walked over to the door, then turned back to Sterns. "You have been very kind to me, sir. I will always remember that."

Sterns looked startled. Jade was about to close the door behind her when Caine's command reached her.

"Jade!"

The bellow made the crystal goblets rattle. Jade showed no reaction to the summons, but Sterns jumped a foot.

"I believe your employer has just heard some distressing news," she said. "I had hoped that my uncle would wait . . . it doesn't matter."

Sterns followed her into the entrance. When she started up the stairs, he called out to her. "I believe mi'lord would like you to go to him, Lady Jade."

She continued up the stairs. "I would be happy to stand by your side," he promised. "I know his temper can be frightening at times."

Sterns waited until she was out of sight, then rushed inside the drawing room.

The butler had difficulty maintaining his steely composure when he spotted Colin. "My God, is that you, Colin?" he stammered out.

"Hello, Sterns," Colin said. "It's good to see you again. Are you still ordering your lord around?"

Sterns was slow to recover. "I give it my best," he whispered.

"Is this one a servant, Caine?" Harry asked.

"He's a dictator, not a servant," Colin announced with a grin.

Sterns turned to the older man with the obvious poor eyesight. He tried not to gape.

"Is me supper ready yet?" Harry bellowed.

Sterns decided this one had to be Jade's uncle. The stranger sitting next to Colin was too young. "It is almost ready," he told him before finally turning to Caine. "I must speak to you at once in the foyer, mi'lord. It is a most important matter."

"Not now, Sterns," Caine said, his tone weary. "Talk to me later."

"Perhaps you didn't hear me," Sterns countered. "There is a problem that must be resolved immediately. It concerns Lady Jade."

Caine wasn't at all surprised. "What's she burning now? The kitchens?"

"Mi'lord, this isn't the time for jests," the butler snapped.

"Do I look like I'm jesting, Sterns?"

The butler folded his arms across his chest. "Lady Jade isn't burning anything at the moment," he said. "She's leaving."

That announcement got just the reaction Sterns was hoping for. He moved out of his lord's way when he bounded to his feet, and nodded with satisfaction when Caine roared, "The hell she is!"

The butler waited until his employer had left the room, then turned back to Jade's uncle. "Dinner will be served in just a moment," he announced, his haughty tone of voice fully restored.

Caine took the stairs two at a time. His heart was pounding. The thought of her leaving him was untenable. For the first time in his life, he was in a panic. He didn't like the feeling at all.

As soon as he threw the door open to her bedroom, he saw

her. The panic left in a rush. He slammed the door shut behind him and leaned against it.

He took a deep breath to try to calm himself. She was pretending he wasn't there. She stood by the side of the bed, folding a gold-colored gown. Her satchel was open and nearly filled to the top.

"You might as well quit packing," he said, amazed that his voice sounded so forceful. "You aren't going anywhere."

Jade turned to confront him. She was determined to give him a piece of her mind before taking her leave, but when she caught his expression, her heart fell to her stomach and she couldn't remember any of the words she wanted to say to him.

He was so furious, the muscle in the side of his jaw flexed. She stared at it in fascination while she tried to find her courage again.

"I'm never going to let you leave me, Jade," he said. "Never. Do you hear me?"

She thought everyone in the village was hearing him. Her ear rang from his roar. It took all her strength to stand up to him. She slowly shook her head. "You called me a whore," she whispered.

The anguish in her voice got through to him. Some of his anger eased away. "No, I did not call you a whore."

"You thought it," she countered. "You were about to shout it to the world."

"I wasn't," he returned. "Jade, we have more important issues to discuss now."

She let out a gasp. "More important than calling me a whore?"

He moved away from the door and started toward her. She immediately backed up a space. "Don't come near me. I never want you to touch me again."

"Then you're going to be damned miserable for the rest of your days, Jade. I'm going to be touching you all the time."

"You don't really want me," she shouted. "You want the

vulnerable, weak woman I pretended to be, Caine. You don't know the real me. No, you don't," she continued when he shook his head at her. "I'm really very strong, determined, too. I just pretended to need you, you daft man, so that you would feel honor bound to stay by my side. I used all the ploys a weak woman would use, too. Yes, I did! I complained at every opportunity, and I wept whenever I needed to get my way."

He grabbed hold of her and jerked her up against him. "I'm leaving," she cried out. "Can't you get that through your thick . . ."

"You're staying."

"I hate you," she whispered before she burst into tears.

He rested his chin on the top of her head. "No, you don't hate me," he whispered.

"I hate everything about you," she wailed between racking sobs. "But most of all I hate the way you contradict me."

"Jade?"

"What?"

"Are your tears a pretense now?"

She couldn't quit crying long enough to give him a clear answer. "They most certainly are," she stammered out. "I never, ever cry," she added a moment later. "Only weak women cry."

"But you're not weak, are you, love?" he asked. His smile was gentle, his voice as well, but his grip continued to be as strong as iron, even after she quit her struggle to get away from him.

He wanted to hold her in his arms for the rest of his days. "Jade?"

"What now?"

"I love you."

She didn't respond to his vow, but started trembling. He knew he was terrifying her. "You're the most confusing woman," he whispered on a sigh. "God help me, I do love you, though."

"I won't love you," she stammered out. "I don't even like you. I won't trust you either." She ended her list of what she wouldn't do with a loud hiccup.

Caine wasn't the least upset by her denials. "I love you," he said again. "Now and forever."

He was content to hold her while she wept. Lord, she did have a store of tears locked inside her.

They must have stood there a full ten minutes before she was able to regain her composure.

She wiped her cheeks on the lapels of his jacket, then pulled away from him. "You'd better go back downstairs," she whispered.

"Not without you," he countered.

"No," she replied. "Nathan and Harry would know I'd been crying. I'm staying here."

"Jade, you can't put off . . ." He stopped in midsentence, then asked, "Why does it matter if they know you've been crying or not?"

"I wouldn't be what they expect me to be if I cried," she answered.

"Try to explain what you meant by that remark?" he asked gently.

She gave him a disgruntled look. "Appearances have to be kept up, Caine."

She walked over to the bed and sat down. "I don't want to talk about this." She let out a sigh, then added, "Oh, very well. I'll meet you downstairs . . ."

He was shaking his head at her. "I'll wait for you."

"You don't trust me?"

"No."

He waited for her temper to explode. She surprised him, however, when she merely shrugged. "Good," she said. "Don't trust me, Caine. I'm going to leave at the first opportunity. I won't stay here and wait for you to leave me. I'm not a fool."

He finally understood. She couldn't hide her fear or her vulnerability from him now. "And you're absolutely certain I would leave you, aren't you, Jade?"

"Of course."

She replied with such candor that he wasn't certain how to proceed. "Even though I've just told you that I love you, you still . . ."

"Nathan and Harry love me, too," she interjected.

Caine gave up trying to reason with her now, guessing it would do his cause little good. He decided he'd have to wait and find another way around her shields.

Caine suddenly wanted to go downstairs and kill both Nathan and Harry. He sighed instead. He couldn't undo the past for her. No, he could only give her a secure, safe future.

"I would never abandon . . ." he stopped himself, then said, "Very well, Jade. You may leave me whenever you want."

Her eyes widened over that announcement. She looked like she was going to start weeping again, too. Caine felt like an ogre. "Any time you want to leave, do so."

She turned her gaze to her lap. "Thank you."

"You're welcome," he drawled out. He walked over to her, pulled her to her feet, then tilted her head up. "Just one other little detail," he added.

"Yes?"

"Every time you leave, I'm going to come after you. There isn't any place you can hide, Jade. I'll find you and drag you back here. This is where you belong."

She tried to push his hand away from her chin. "You'd never find me," she whispered.

He could hear the panic in her voice. Caine leaned down and kissed her. He missed her mouth completely when she jerked away from him, then captured her soft lips by cupping the sides of her face and holding her still.

His tongue took possession then. He growled low in his

throat when she pinched him, then deepened the kiss. Her tongue finally rubbed against his own, her resistance spent. She wrapped her arms around his waist and melted against him.

"I love you," he told her again after he'd lifted his head away from her.

She promptly burst into tears again. "Are you going to do that every damned time I tell you I love you?" he demanded.

He was more amused than exasperated with her. She shook her head. "You don't understand yet," she whispered. "It hasn't settled in, Caine."

"What don't I understand?" he asked, his voice filled with tenderness.

"You don't understand what I am," she cried.

Caine let out another sigh. He took hold of her hand and dragged her out of the room. They were halfway down the stairs to the foyer when he finally answered her. "I understand, all right. You're mine."

"I hate your possessiveness, too," she told his back.

Caine paused at the door to the drawing room, then let go of her hand. "If you try to move away from me while we're in there, I swear to God I'll embarrass the hell out of you. Got that?"

She nodded. When he started to open the door, he noticed the change that came over her. Gone was the vulnerable woman he'd just held in his arms. Jade looked quite serene. Caine was so astonished by the change in her, he had to shake his head.

"I'm ready now," she announced. "But if you tell Harry we slept together . . ."

"I won't," he interjected before she could get herself all worked up again. "Unless you leave my side, of course."

She gave him a quick glare, then forced a smile on her face and strolled into the room.

The talk stopped as soon as she and Caine entered. Jade

sat on the arm of the chair adjacent to the hearth and motioned for him to take the seat.

"Is my supper near to ready?" Harry asked her.

"In just another minute or two," Jade answered. "I insisted on the best for you, Uncle. It takes a little longer."

Harry beamed at her. "I'm the lucky one, having you to take care of me, Pagan," he crooned.

"Don't call her Pagan."

That command came out in a harsh whisper. Jade shivered over the anger in Caine's voice.

Nathan grinned while Harry squinted at Caine. "Why the hell not? That's her name," he argued.

"No, her name is Jade," Caine snapped out.

"My name is Pagan."

Her voice had turned as hard as ice. "I'm sorry you don't like it, Caine, but that's . . ."

She quit her explanation when he took hold of her hand and started squeezing.

"He still doesn't believe it," Harry said.

Jade didn't answer her uncle, but she secretly believed he was right. Caine certainly wouldn't be holding her hand if it had all settled in. "He believes all women are weak, Uncle," she whispered.

Harry snorted. He was about to launch into several of his favorite stories about his Pagan's special abilities when the men he'd sent to the village returned from their errand.

The men lumbered over to Harry's side.

"Well? What have you got for me, men?"

"Eleven pair," the shorter of the two seamen announced.

While Caine watched in growing astonishment, spectacles of every size and shape were dropped into Harry's lap. The old man tried on the first pair, squinted at Caine, then took the spectacles off and tossed them over his shoulder.

"Won't do," he muttered.

The ritual was repeated again and again, until he tried on

the eighth pair. Then he let out a happy sigh. "These do," he announced.

"Uncle, try the others on," Jade suggested. "There might be another pair that will do just as well."

Harry did as she suggested, then tucked another pair in his pocket.

"You did your task well, men. I'm proud of you."

Caine's head dropped forward. The picture of how Harry's men had come by the spectacles forced a reluctant smile.

"Half of England will be squinting before Harry goes home," Colin predicted with a deep chuckle.

"You being insulting, boy?" Harry asked.

"No, just honest," Colin answered.

Sterns opened the doors then and announced that dinner was now ready to be served.

Harry bounded out of his chair. Nathan and Colin moved out of his way just as he kicked the footstool out of his path. "Are you coming with me, girl?" Harry asked as he charged past Jade.

Caine increased his grip on her hand. "No, Uncle, I'm staying here," Jade called out. "I have a little explaining to do. Enjoy your meal with your men."

As soon as Harry left the room, Jade motioned for the men to follow. Jimbo looked like he wanted to argue with that command. His expression bordered on hostility. His target was Caine.

Jade simply stared at Jimbo. The silent message got through and the big man hurried out of the room.

"Shut the doors behind you," she called out.

"I might not be able to hear you if you call out," Jimbo argued.

"You'll hear me," Jade promised.

"You'll hear me too," Nathan drawled out. "I can take care of my sister, Jimbo."

"That's still to be proven," Jimbo muttered loud enough

for everyone to hear. He gave Caine one last glare, then shut the doors.

"Are you rested enough to explain this problem to Caine? I really would like to get this over with, Colin, so I can leave."

Caine gave her hand another good squeeze.

"Yes, I'm rested enough," Colin said. He turned to Nathan, received his nod, then turned his attention back to Caine. "When I was in my last year at Oxford, a man by the name of Willburn approached me. He was from the War Office and he was recruiting men to do some undercover work for England. Our country wasn't officially at war with France yet, but everyone knew it was coming. Anyway, Willburn knew you worked for Richards. I was still sworn to secrecy. I should have wondered at the time why I couldn't discuss my duties with you, Caine, but I didn't. You never talked about your work, and I figured that was the way it was supposed to be. In all honesty, I think I was enamored with this spy business." His expression became sheepish when he added, "I saw myself as England's savior for a while, anyway."

"How did you meet Nathan?" Caine asked.

"Almost a year after I'd started working for Willburn. We were paired together then. He was recruited in much the same way I was. Eventually Nathan and I became good friends." He paused to smile at his friend. "Nathan's a hard man to like."

"I've noticed," Caine said.

"Get on with it, Colin," Nathan ordered.

"It took a long time to win Nathan's trust, almost another full year working together as a matter of fact. He didn't confide in me in all that time. Then, on a trip back from France, he told me about the letters Pagan had found."

Colin shifted positions, grimacing in pain. Nathan caught the expression before anyone else did and immediately righted the stool for his friend. With a gentleness surprising in such a large man, he lifted Colin's injured leg, slipped a cushion under the heel, then asked, "It's better now?"

"Yes, thank you," Colin answered. "Now where was I?"

Caine was watching Nathan. He could still see the concern in Nathan's eyes. He suddenly realized he couldn't hate the man after all.

That revelation was one hell of a disappointment. Caine wanted to hate him. The bastard had deserted his own sister, left her on her own to fend for herself. He was the reason Jade had so many shields guarding her heart, the reason she had had so much pain.

Yet Colin was alive.

"Caine?" Colin asked, drawing his brother back to the discussion. "Do you believe it's possible for a government to operate within a government?"

"Anything is possible," Caine answered.

"Have you ever heard of the Tribunal?" Colin asked. His voice had dropped to a whisper.

Both Colin and Nathan exchanged a nod. They were prepared to hear Caine's denial. Then they were going to knock the breath out of him with the facts they'd uncovered.

"Yes, I've heard of the Tribunal."

Colin was astonished. "You have?"

"When?" Nathan demanded. "How?"

"There was an investigation immediately after your father's death, Nathan. The Earl was linked to all sorts of subversive activities. His lands were confiscated, his children left in poverty . . ."

"How do you know all this?" Nathan asked.

Caine looked at Jade before answering. "When she told me who her father was, I asked Lyon to make some inquiries."

"Who is this Lyon?" Nathan asked.

"Our friend," Colin answered.

"Can he be trusted?" Nathan asked.

"He can," Colin answered before his brother could. "Caine, that was a safe bet. Lyon wouldn't ask the wrong people the way I did."

Jade's back started aching from her uncomfortable position. She eased her hand away from Caine's, somewhat surprised when he gave her her freedom. She knew better than to try to leave, though. If Caine was anything, he was reliable. He would embarrass her just as he threatened.

She moved to the chair Harry had vacated, and sat down.

"Lyon didn't ask anyone any questions," Caine explained. "He simply looked the information up in the files."

"He couldn't have," Jade interjected. "My father's file was missing."

Caine raised an eyebrow over that telling remark. "And how would you know if it was missing or not?"

She daintily shrugged. "Because I took it," she admitted.

"You what?"

"Caine, the file isn't the issue now," she rushed out, hoping to placate his rising temper.

"Then how did Lyon . . ." Nathan began.

Caine continued to frown at Jade when he answered her brother. "Richards was Lyon's director as well as mine. He had his own records. Lyon read those files."

"Was my father vindicated after the investigation?" Nathan asked.

"No," Caine answered. "He wasn't condemned either, Nathan. There wasn't enough proof."

"There is now," Jade whispered.

"Proof to vindicate your father?" Caine asked.

"No, proof to condemn him. I read Papa's letters."

The sadness in her voice tore at his heart. Caine still wanted to throttle her for deceiving him, but he also wanted to be kissing her at the same time.

"Caine, how can you be smiling now?" Colin asked. "This isn't . . ."

"Sorry," Caine answered, unaware he had been smiling. "I was sidetracked."

He stared at Jade while he made that admission. She stared at her hands.

"Continue, Colin," Caine ordered then, turning his attention back to his brother.

"Right after their father's funeral, Pagan . . . I mean, Jade, left with Black Harry. The Earl trusted Harry completely."

"That's difficult to believe," Caine interjected.

"Harry's a good man," Jade said. "He has a pure heart."

"I'm sure he does," Caine agreed. "However, you mentioned that there was another close friend, a woman by the name of Lady Briars, who would have been more than willing to take you and Nathan into her home. I just don't understand why your father would have chosen a thief over . . ."

"It was a question of trust," Nathan explained. "My father had turned his heart against England, Caine. He didn't think either one of us would be safe here. Harry was our best bet."

"Why didn't he think you'd be safe?"

"The letters," Colin answered. "The Earl kept all the ones he received from the other two. Nathan's father's operative name was Fox, and he was one of the three in the Tribunal. The other two were called Ice and Prince."

"My father was a very idealistic man," Nathan interjected. "In the beginning, I think he saved all the letters for future generations. He believed he was doing something . . . heroic for England. Things soured fast, though. Soon enough it became only for the good of the Tribunal. Anything was just, as long as it furthered the scope of their power."

"It was a slow metamorphosis," Colin said. "The first letters were signed with the closing, 'for the good of England.'

Then after the tenth, or perhaps the eleventh letter, the closing changed."

'To what?" Caine asked.

"They started using the phrase, 'for the good of the Tribunal,'" he answered. "Ice was the first to sign his letter that way, and the other two followed suit. Their corruption was complete by that time."

"They started acting independently long before that, Colin," Nathan remarked.

"The end justified their means," Colin explained to Caine. "As long as they believed that what they were doing aided their country, they could justify anything."

"Very like your attitude, Jade," Caine announced.

She was so startled by that comment, her eyes widened. "No, not at all like my attitude," she argued. "Caine, I'm nothing like my father. I don't approve of what he did. It's sinful to admit, but I don't have any feelings for him, either. He chose his path."

"Your father's lands were confiscated, his fortune taken away," Caine said.

"Yes," she agreed, wondering what he was leading up to with that remark.

"It's the reason you steal from the wealthy, Jade. I'd say you're getting even."

"I'm not!"

Her shout told him he'd rattled her with that opinion. "Power corrupts," he said. "Absolute power corrupts absolutely."

"You needn't quote Machiavelli to me, Caine. I will agree that the Tribunal was after absolute power."

"You were on the same path."

"I'm not," she cried out.

"Was, Caine?" Colin asked.

"Was," Caine announced. His voice was hard.

"Then you . . ." Colin began.

"Not now, Colin," Caine ordered.

"What are you talking about?" Jade asked. "I've never been after power."

Caine ignored her protest. "Tell me the rest of this," he ordered Nathan.

"Our father had a change of heart," Nathan said. "His conscience began to bother him when his director, a man named Hammond, was sanctioned."

"Sanctioned?" Colin scoffed. "What a pleasant word for such a foul deed."

"Hammond was director over all three," Nathan interjected. "There was Ice, Prince, and Fox. Anyway, in the beginning, they did whatever they were ordered to do. It wasn't long, though, before they started acting independently. Hammond was beginning to get wise to their doings and the three were certain he was growing in his suspicions. Ice came up with the idea that they sanction him."

"My father didn't want to kill Hammond," Jade said. "Papa was on his way to London to warn the director when he was killed. At least that's what we've been able to piece together."

"Who was killed? Your father or Hammond?" Caine asked.

"Our father," Nathan answered. "He had sent Hammond a note telling him that he had to meet with him as soon as possible, that it was an urgent, life-threatening matter."

"And how were you able to piece that together?" Caine asked.

"Hammond showed me the note at my father's funeral," Nathan replied. "He asked me if I knew anything about this urgent problem. I didn't know anything, of course. I'd been away at school. Jade was too young to understand."

"Our father confided in Harry and gave him the letters he'd saved."

"And Harry told you everything when you were older?" Caine asked Jade.

She nodded. She refused to look at him and kept her gaze directed on her lap.

"Harry wanted Nathan to go with us. Father had a ship and Harry was bent on becoming a pirate. Nathan wanted to finish school. He thought Harry was taking me to an island in the south and that I'd be safe until he could come and fetch me."

"When I started hearing about the escapades of a pirate named Pagan, I have to admit I never once considered that it might be Harry," Nathan interjected.

"Why didn't you come for Jade?" Caine asked.

"He couldn't," Jade answered before her brother could. "Harry and I were never in one place long enough. Besides, Nathan had his own problems then. Father's enemies knew he'd saved the letters. They were desperate to find them. Once Nathan's rooms had been searched, they left him alone . . . for a time anyway, until we started a fresh investigation of our own."

"The letters were with you?" Caine asked. "Or did Harry hide them somewhere safe?"

"We kept them on the *Emerald*," she answered.

"I want them," Caine demanded. "Is this vessel near enough to send one of the men? Or perhaps . . ."

He stopped his question when she shook her head. "There isn't any need to fetch them. I can tell you the contents."

"Word for word," Colin said. "Pagan need only read something once, and it's committed to memory for the rest of her life."

If Caine thought that talent odd, he didn't mention it. Jade was thankful he remained silent.

"Pagan, recite the letters for Caine," Nathan suggested.

"If you call her Pagan one more time, I'm going to beat the hell out of you."

Nathan scowled at Caine a long minute, then gave in. "All right," he snapped. "I'll call her Jade, though only because I don't want anyone hearing her nickname."

"I don't give a damn what your reasons are, just do it," Caine grated out.

"Hell, Colin, I'm trying to be accommodating, but I swear to God I'm going to knock the arrogance out of him when this is over and done with."

Jade believed a fight was imminent. She drew everyone's attention by beginning her recitation. The telling took over thirty minutes. She didn't leave a word out. And when she was finished, no one said a word for a long while. Everyone was slowly filtering through the information she'd just related.

Then Colin spoke. "All right then," he began, his voice filled with enthusiasm. "That very first letter was addressed to Thorton . . . that's Nathan and Jade's father, of course, and it was signed by a man named William."

"They hadn't been assigned their operative names yet," Jade volunteered.

"Yes," Colin agreed. "Then Thorton became Fox, and William became Prince. Ice is another matter, though. We don't have any clues as to his . . ."

"Colin, we can speculate about his identity later," Nathan interrupted.

Colin nodded. "I went to Willburn and told him all about the letters, Caine. Nathan and I decided we had to trust him. He was our director, after all, and he'd taken good care of us. To this day, I still don't believe he was involved with the Tribunal."

"You're an innocent," Nathan muttered. "Of course he was involved with the bastards."

"You'll have to prove it to me first," Colin argued. "Only then will I believe."

Nathan shook his head. He turned back to Caine. "We were sent to the south on what we now know was a setup. We were supposed to meet with two informants at the harbor. It was a trick, of course. Before we knew what was happening, we had both been bound and gagged, and tossed into the warm waters."

"You aren't going to tell all of it, are you?" Jade asked. "There isn't any need, Colin."

Neither Nathan nor Colin picked up on the fear in her voice. Caine did, and immediately glanced over to look at her.

"Get on with it, Colin," Nathan muttered.

Jade, Caine noticed, was now clenching her hands together. He decided then that she must have witnessed something that had terrified her.

"I was the first to go into the waters," Colin said, drawing Caine's attention again. "After they'd made long, shallow cuts on my legs with their knives, they tossed me off the pier. Nathan understood what they were up to, though I thank God now that I didn't understand at the time. I thought I still had a chance, you see."

Colin's expression had taken on a gray cast. Nathan looked just as grim.

"Because Shallow Wharf was close by, we spent several days with Jade and Black Harry. Colin didn't know she was Pagan then, of course, and he developed quite a crush on my little sister," Nathan continued.

"Yes, I did," Colin agreed. He turned to wink at Jade. "I'll still have you, Jade, if you'll only give me a chance."

She blushed while she shook her head at him. "You were quite impossible."

"Colin followed her around like a puppy," Nathan said. "When he realized she wasn't at all interested, he was so disappointed I had to take him drinking."

"I fell in love with two other ladies that night, Nathan," Colin remarked.

"They weren't ladies," Jade remarked.

"No, they weren't," Nathan agreed. "How can you even remember, Colin? You were sotted, man."

Colin laughed. "I remember everything," he boasted.

Caine held his patience. He could tell, from their dark expressions, that they needed to jest with each other in order to get through their memory.

Jade didn't have as much patience. "Tommy and I followed Nathan and Colin when they went to keep their appointment. They were so secretive about their plans, I became very curious. I also had this feeling that something was amiss."

"Who is Tommy?" Caine asked.

Jade literally bounded out of her chair and hurried across the room. "Nathan, you finish this story while I see to refreshments. I'm tired of talking about this."

Nathan started to call out to her but Colin stayed the action by putting his hand on his friend's arm. "It's still difficult for her," he whispered.

Nathan nodded.

"Of course it's difficult for her," Caine interjected, his tone harsh. "My God, she must have watched you . . ."

"She didn't watch," Nathan whispered. "As Colin was explaining, I knew what their plan was as soon as they cut Colin's legs. I put up a struggle when they tried to use their blades on me, ended up getting shot for my trouble. My shoulder was on fire when I went into the water."

"They cut us to draw the attention of the sharks, of course. The harbor is always full of the scavangers because of all the garbage that's thrown in. The blood did draw them, like flies to a carcass."

Colin could see that Caine's patience was wearing thin. His brother was leaning forward in his chair with a grim look on his face. "Bear with us, Caine. This isn't a pleasant memory for us."

Nathan nodded. "It was just past sunset," he began.

"I could still see their fins though," Colin interjected.

Caine was sitting on the edge of his chair. He now

understood the reason for Jade's nightmares. She dreamed about sharks. My God, the terror she must have endured made his heart pound.

"Pagan told Tommy to fetch a boat, then she took his knife and came into the waters after us. The men who'd put us there were sure we were done for and had already left. Pagan . . . I mean, Jade, got to me first. I was closer, I guess. Anyway, she pulled me toward the boat. A shark got a fair nibble out of my leg when they were hauling me in. Tommy lost his balance and fell overboard. He never resurfaced."

When Colin paused and turned to Nathan, his friend took up the telling.

"I still don't understand why, but the sharks kept away from me. They were in a frenzy and Tommy had become their target. Jade had gotten Colin into the boat by then."

"I tried to help," Colin whispered. His voice was hoarse. "But I passed out. The next time I opened my eyes, I was on the *Emerald*. The oddest-looking man I'd ever seen was trying to press me into a game of chess. Honest to God, Caine, I wasn't sure if I was in heaven or hell. Then I saw Nathan sleeping on the cot next to me. I saw his sister, too, and I suddenly remembered everything. It seemed to me that it had all just happened, but I found out I'd been ill for quite some time."

Caine leaned back in his chair in an attempt to ease the tension in his shoulders. He took several deep breaths, then noticed Colin and Nathan were doing the same thing.

"Did she know . . . when she went into the water, did she know there were sharks?"

"Oh, yes," Nathan whispered. "She knew."

"My God, the courage that must have taken . . ."

"She won't talk about it," Colin interjected.

"She dreams about it."

"What?" Nathan asked.

"She has nightmares," Caine explained.

231

Nathan's brother slowly nodded.

"Matthew and Jimbo wanted to go after the bastards who'd tried to kill us, of course," Colin said. "Jade wouldn't let them. She had good reason, though. She wanted the men to report back to their superior that we were both dead. Jade felt it was the only way to keep us safe. It was the right decision, I think. Nathan and I are content to stay dead for a while longer, until we find out who in hell is behind this treachery."

"Hell, Caine, we were sanctioned by our own government," Nathan muttered.

"No," Caine countered. "Your government didn't even know you worked for them. Did you ever report to Richards or his superiors? Were you ever acknowledged . . ."

"Go ahead and say it," Colin interrupted.

"All right," Caine replied. "You worked for the Tribunal."

"I knew you were going to say that," Colin whispered.

"You can't be certain," Nathan argued.

"Richards didn't know until he was informed of your deaths that you worked for the department, Nathan. He's investigating now."

"Then he'll be killed," Nathan predicted.

"He's quietly investigating," Caine qualified.

"Damn, I know I've made mistakes," Nathan muttered. "I almost got you killed, Colin. I never should have involved you in this."

Colin shook his head. "We're partners, remember?" He turned back to his brother and said, "Do you really believe Richards can be trusted?"

"I trust him with my life. Jade's going to have to give him the letters as soon as possible, or recite the contents to him."

"We can write copies," Colin suggested. "That way, the originals stay safe. No one will find the *Emerald.*"

"The ship was named for her, wasn't it?" Caine asked. There was a hint of a smile on his face now. "I should have guessed that sooner. Her eyes are the color of emeralds, especially when she's angry."

"Yes, Harry named the ship after her," Colin said. "Can you understand now why you became the target?"

Caine nodded. "Yes. I was searching for Pagan. The Tribunal couldn't take the risk of me finding the pirate and gaining the truth."

"You're still at risk, Caine," Colin reminded him.

"But not for long," Caine countered. "I have a plan."

Colin grinned at Nathan. "I told you he'd have a plan." He couldn't keep the relief out of his voice.

Jade walked back into the room. She looked much calmer now, almost serene. She wouldn't look at him, Caine noticed, didn't spare him a single glance as she made her way back over to the chair in front of the hearth and sat down.

"Sterns has ordered two rooms made ready for you and Nathan," she told Colin. "As soon as yours is ready, you must go upstairs and rest."

"Are you certain we should stay here?" Nathan asked. He nudged Colin in his side. "My country home is in a very remote area. I just finished the remodeling before our last assignment," he added with a glance in Caine's direction. "We'd be very comfortable there."

Colin grinned. "I've heard so much about this palace of yours I know each room by heart. That's all you ever talked about."

"Well, then, you have to agree with me. I have to say, Caine, that it's the most beautiful house in all of England now . . . Jade, why are you shaking your head at me? You don't think my house is grand?"

She gave him a quick smile. "Oh, yes, Nathan, your house was very grand."

Nathan looked startled. "Was, you say?"

"I'm afraid I have some disappointing news, Nathan."

Her brother leaned forward. "How disappointing?" he asked.

"You see, there was this fire . . ."

"A fire?" He sounded as if he were choking on something. Colin resisted the urge to slap him on his back.

"It was a rather large fire, Nathan."

Her voice reeked with sympathy. Nathan winced. "How large, Jade?"

"Your grand house was burned to the cellars."

She turned to Caine while Nathan muttered several obscenities. "I told you he'd be disappointed."

Nathan looked a little more than just disappointed, Caine decided. Jade's brother looked as though he wanted to kill someone. Since Caine had felt much the same reaction when his new stables were destroyed, he found himself in sympathy with Nathan.

Nathan took a deep breath, then turned to Colin. He sounded as if he were whining when he said, "I'd just finished the last damned room."

"Yes, he had," Jade interjected, giving her brother her full support. "The very last damned room."

Caine closed his eyes. "Jade, I thought it was all a lie."

"What was all a lie?" Colin asked.

"I didn't lie about everything," Jade interjected at the same moment.

"Exactly what didn't you lie about?" Caine demanded.

"You needn't take that tone with me, sir," she countered. "I only lied about witnessing a murder," she added with a nod. "It was the best I could come up with on the spur of the moment. At least, I think that's all I lied about. If I think of anything else, I'll mention it, all right? Now please quit your scowling, Caine. This isn't the time to be critical."

"Will you two save your arguing for later?" Nathan demanded. "Jade? Tell me how the fire started. Was someone careless with . . ."

"It was deliberate, not careless," Jade explained. "Whoever set out to burn your home, well, they certainly knew what they were about. They were very thorough. Even the wine cellar was destroyed, Nathan."

"Hell, not the wine cellar!" Nathan cried.

"I believe they were trying to destroy the letters," Jade said. "Since they couldn't find them when they pillaged the house, they . . ."

"They pillaged my house?" Nathan asked. "When?"

"The day before they burned it down," she answered. "Oh, dear, I just remembered," she added with a glance in Caine's direction. "I lied about falling down the stairs, too. Yes, I . . ."

Nathan let out a sigh, drawing her attention back to him. "When this is over, I will rebuild," he said. "What about the stables, Jade? Were they left intact?"

"Oh, yes, the stables were left untouched, Nathan. You needn't worry about that."

Caine was watching Jade. The worry in her gaze was so obvious, he wondered why Nathan hadn't noticed she hadn't finished giving him his disappointments yet.

"It's too bad about your house," Colin said.

"Yes," Nathan answered. "But the stables are all right. Colin, you should see my stock. There's one horse in particular, a fine Arabian stallion I paid a fortune for, but he was well worth the money. I named him Lightning."

"Lightning?" Colin asked, grinning over the absurd name. "Sounds like Harry had a hand in choosing that name."

"He did," Nathan admitted with a grin. "Still, it's fitting for the steed. He runs as fast as the wind. Only Jade and I can seat him. Wait until you see him . . ." Nathan quit his boasting when he noticed Jade was shaking her head at him again.

"What, Jade? Are you disagreeing that Lightning isn't as fast as the wind?"

"Oh, yes, Nathan, Lightning was as fast as the wind."

Nathan looked ready to weep. "Was?"

"I'm afraid I have a little more disappointing news for you, Nathan. There was this mishap and your fine horse was shot between his lovely brown eyes."

Caine had leaned forward in his chair again. The ramifications of what she was telling her brother had just hit him full force. "You mean to say you weren't lying about that, either?"

She shook her head again.

"What the hell!" Nathan shouted. "Who shot Lightning?"

She glared at Caine. "I told you he was going to be disappointed," she muttered.

"That sure as certain isn't my fault," Caine muttered. "So you can quit glaring at me so intently."

"Did Caine shoot him?" Nathan roared.

"No," Jade rushed out. "He just didn't believe you'd be so disappointed. I hadn't even met Caine then."

Her brother fell back against the cushions and threw his hand over his eyes. "Is nothing sacred?" he bellowed.

"Apparently Lightning wasn't," Caine interjected dryly.

Nathan glared at him. "He was a damned fine horse."

"I'm sure he was," Caine said before turning back to Jade. "If you're telling me the truth about this, then it can only mean . . ."

"I really would appreciate it if you'd quit insulting me, Caine," she snapped.

"Jade always tells the truth," Nathan defended.

"Really?" Caine drawled out. "I haven't seen that side of her yet. From the moment I met her, she's done nothing but lie. Haven't you, sweet? All that's going to change now though, isn't it?"

She refused to answer him.

"Sweetheart, why don't you give Nathan the rest of the bad news?"

"The rest? My God, there's more?"

236

"Just a little bit more," she answered. "Do you remember your lovely new carriage?"

"Not my carriage, Jade," Nathan protested with a low groan.

She turned to Colin while Nathan went through his list of expletives again. "You should have seen it, Colin. It was splendid. The interior was so large and comfortable. Nathan had the backs of the seats done in such soft leather."

Colin was trying to look sympathetic. "Was?" he asked.

"Someone torched it," Jade announced.

"Now why would anyone want to destroy a perfectly good vehicle?"

Caine answered that question. "Your sister has left out an important detail," he stated. "She happened to be inside when it was set on fire."

Colin was the first to react to that statement. "My God, Jade. Tell us what happened."

"Caine just did tell you," she said.

"No, tell us exactly how it happened," Colin insisted. "You could have been killed."

"That was their intent," she said, her voice tinged with exasperation. "They meant to kill me. After your house was destroyed, the carriage was made ready and I set out for London. I wanted to find you, Nathan . . ."

"How many men went with you?" Caine interrupted to ask.

"Hudson sent two men with me," she answered.

Caine shook his head. "I thought you told me you'd only been back in England two weeks," he said.

"Well, actually, it was a little longer," she hedged.

"How long?"

"Two months," she admitted. "I did have to lie about that."

"You could have told me the truth."

He was getting angry. She was too irritated to care. "Oh? And would you have believed me if I'd said I was Pagan and that I had just snatched Winters, given him to Nathan, and was now trying to . . . Oh, what's the use. You wouldn't have listened to me."

"Wait a minute," Nathan interrupted. "Who is Hudson, Jade? You said Hudson sent two men with you, remember?"

"He's the butler Lady Briars hired for you."

Nathan nodded. "And then what happened?" he asked.

"We were just outside London when those same three men trapped us. They'd blocked the road with fat tree branches. I leaned out the window to see what was going on when I heard the shouting. Someone hit me then, Nathan, on the side of my head. It fairly knocked the wind out of me. I must have fainted, though I'm embarrassed to admit to that possibility." She turned to look at Caine. "It isn't at all in my nature to swoon."

"Jade, you're digressing," Caine reminded her.

She gave him a disgruntled look, then turned back to her brother. "The interior of the carriage was ripped to shreds. They'd used their knives on the fine leather. I smelled smoke and of course got right out."

"They were hunting the letters?" Colin asked.

"You just opened the door and climbed out?" Nathan asked at the very same moment.

"Yes and no," Jade answered. "Yes, I do believe they thought I might have hidden the letters behind the leather, and no, Nathan, I didn't just open the door. Both sides were blocked shut with more branches. I squeezed through the window. Thank heavens the frame wasn't as durable as you believed. Actually, Nathan, now that I have time to reflect upon it, I think you paid entirely too much for that vehicle. The hinges weren't at all sturdy and . . ."

"Jade."

"Caine, don't raise your voice to me," Jade instructed.

"That was a close call," Colin interjected.

"I was very frightened," Jade whispered. She turned to

look at Caine. "There isn't any shame in admitting I was afraid."

Caine nodded. Her tone of voice suggested she was challenging him to disagree with her. "No, there isn't any shame in being afraid."

She looked relieved. Did she need his approval, then? Caine wondered about that possibility a long minute, then remarked, "Now I know how you got those bruises on your shoulders. It was when you squeezed through that window, wasn't it?"

"How the hell do you know if she has bruises on her shoulders or not?" Nathan roared his question, for he'd only just realized the significance of Caine's remark.

"I saw them."

Nathan would have gone for Caine's throat if Colin hadn't thrown his arm in front of his chest. "Later, Nathan," he stated. "You and Caine can settle your dispute later. It looks like we're going to be guests for a long while."

Nathan looked like he'd just been told he had to swim with the sharks again.

"You'll put yourself and Colin in danger if you leave," Jade said. "It would be too dangerous."

"We have to stay together," Colin added.

Nathan reluctantly nodded agreement.

"Caine?" Colin asked. "When you went after Pagan, you put yourself in danger. The remaining members of the Tribunal couldn't risk the chance of you finding the pirate."

"There was the possibility that Pagan would be able to convince you that she didn't have anything to do with your brother's death. Yes, it was too much of a risk to take."

"And so you sent Jade to me," Caine interjected.

Nathan shook his head. "We didn't send her. It was her plan from start to finish and we were informed after she'd left. We weren't given a say in the matter."

"How are we going to get the hounds away from you?"

Colin asked. "You can't help us find the culprits as long as you're being hunted." He let out a long sigh, then muttered, "Hell, it's such a mess. How in God's name are we going to find the bastards? We have absolutely nothing to go on."

"You're wrong, Colin," Caine said. "We have quite a bit of information to start with. We know that Hammond, the Tribunal's director, was a legitimate department head. The three men he recruited were Ice, Fox, and Prince. Now only one or two are still living, correct? And one or both are Willburn's directors. Willburn, by the way, has to be leading a duel life. He must be working for our government as well as for the Tribunal."

"How do you figure that?" Nathan asked.

"When we received word of your deaths, my father and I were sent files filed with minor though heroic deeds you two had allegedly fulfilled for England. Willburn was protecting his backside, Colin, and neither file had any substantial information that could be checked out. Security was given as the reason, of course. By the way, you both were given medals for valor."

"Why did they bother?" Colin asked.

"To appease," Caine answered. "Our father's a duke, Colin. Willburn couldn't just let you disappear. Too many questions would be asked."

"What about Nathan?" Colin asked. "Why did they bother honoring him after his death? His father was already dead and there weren't any other Wakerfields with a title. Did they want Jade to be appeased?"

Caine shook his head. "You're forgetting Nathan's other numerous titles," Caine said. "He's also the Marquess of St. James, remember? The Tribunal must have considered all the ramifications if they made that barbaric faction suspicious."

"I did forget about the St. James men," Colin announced. He turned to grin at Nathan. "You don't talk much about that side of your family, Nathan."

"Would you?" Nathan replied dryly.

Colin laughed. "This isn't the time for levity," Jade muttered. "Besides, I'm certain all those stories about the St. James men are pure exaggeration. Why, underneath all that gruffness, they're really very kind men. Aren't they, Nathan?"

Now it was Nathan's turn to laugh. "In a pig's eye," he drawled out.

Jade gave him a good frown for being so honest. Then she turned her attention back to Caine. "Did you go to the ceremony honoring Colin and Nathan?" she asked. "Was it lovely? Were there flowers? Was it a sizable group . . . ?"

"No, I didn't attend the ceremony," Caine interrupted.

"Shame on you," she announced. "You missed your own brother's . . ."

"Jade, I was too angry," Caine interrupted again. "I didn't want to listen to speeches or accept any medals on Colin's behalf. I let my father have that duty. I wanted . . ."

"Revenge," Colin interjected. "Just like the time you went after the Bradley brothers."

After making that remark, Colin turned to explain the incident to Nathan. Jade grew impatient again. "I would like to get back to our original topic," she announced. "Have you come up with any solutions yet, Caine?"

He nodded. "I think I have a sound plan to take the jackals off my trail. It's worth a try, anyway, but that's only one threat. We still have to worry about Jade."

"What do you mean?" Colin asked.

"Colin, we're dealing with two separate issues here. I'm one target, yes. We must assume they know I won't give up looking for Pagan, their convenient scapegoat."

"But what does that have to do with Jade?" Colin asked. "They can't possibly know she's Pagan."

Caine let out a sigh before answering. "Let's start at the beginning. It's obvious that the other two members of the Tribunal knew Fox had saved the letters. Since they couldn't locate them, they did the next best thing. They used their man, Willburn, to recruit you, Nathan. What better way to keep an eye on Fox's son."

He didn't wait for Nathan to respond to that statement, but continued on. "I imagine your rooms at Oxford were searched more than once, weren't they?"

Nathan nodded. "They had to be pretty certain you had the letters. For a time, you were the only logical candidate. Your sister was too young, and Harry had already taken her away. Now then," he added with a nod. "No one could believe that Fox would have trusted Harry with the letters. His appearance alone would lead anyone to that decision. They couldn't know Fox had known Harry for some time either."

Jade felt like sighing with relief. Caine was being so logical now. She felt as though he'd just taken the burden away from all of them. From the look on his brother's face, she concluded that Colin was feeling much the same relief.

"And?" Nathan prodded when Caine remained silent.

"They waited," Caine answered. "They knew eventually the letters would surface. And that's exactly what happened. Harry gave the letters to Jade. She showed them to Nathan and he shared the information with you, Colin."

"We know all this," Nathan snapped.

"Hush, Nathan," Jade whispered. "Caine's being methodical now. We mustn't interfere with his concentration."

"When Colin told Willburn about the letters, he went to the Tribunal, of course."

"And so we were sanctioned," Colin said. "I trusted the wrong man."

"Yes, you trusted the wrong man."

"They're still after the letters," Nathan said.

Caine's nod was quick. "Exactly."

Colin sat up a little straighter. "Now that they think we're dead, Nathan, there can only be one other person who could have the damning evidence."

He turned to look at Jade. "They know you have them."

"They can't be certain," Jade argued. "Or they would have killed me," she added. "That's why they're still searching, why your lovely house was destroyed, Nathan, the reason your fine carriage was shredded too . . ."

"Jade, they don't have anywhere else to search. There's only one avenue open to them now," Nathan interjected.

"They'll try to take her," Colin predicted.

"Yes," Nathan agreed.

"I'm not going to let anyone near her," Caine announced then. "But I'm not convinced they're certain she has the letters. Either one of you could have hidden them before you were taken. It must be making them crazed, though, waiting for the letters to surface again. They're getting desperate, I would imagine."

"So what do we do?" Colin asked.

"First things first," Caine said. He turned to look at Jade. "Do you remember what you asked of me when you came into the tavern that night?"

She slowly nodded. "I asked you to kill me."

"You what?" Nathan roared his question.

"She asked me to kill her," Caine repeated, though he never took his gaze off Jade.

"But he declined my request," Jade explained. "I knew he would, of course. And just what does that have to do with your plan?"

The dimple was back in evidence when he grinned at her. "It's really very simple, love. I've changed my mind. I've decided to accommodate you."

Chapter Thirteen

"Pagan has to die," Caine said, his voice low, emphatic. "It's the only way." He stared at Nathan when he made that statement. Jade's brother was quick to nod agreement.

Jade bounded out of her chair. "I don't want to die," she cried out. "I won't have it, Caine."

"Now, Jade . . ." Nathan began.

"He's talking about the pirate," Colin explained. "He isn't really going to kill you, love."

Jade glared at Colin. "I know exactly what he's talking about," she snapped. "And I still won't have it. Do you have any idea how many years it's taken to build my reputation? When I think . . ."

The men were ignoring her now. Nathan and Colin were actually smiling. Jade gave up. She sat down again and turned to frown at Caine. "If you hadn't started your hunt to capture Pagan, none of this would be necessary now. This is all your fault, Caine."

"Jade, it's the only way," Nathan argued. "If Pagan dies, or rather, if the world believes the pirate is dead, then Caine would have to give up his hunt, wouldn't he? The Tribunal knows he fully believes Pagan is responsible for killing his brother, remember?"

She reluctantly nodded. "Then they'd leave Caine alone, wouldn't they? He'd be safe again?"

Nathan smiled. He turned to Caine. "This plan of yours solves more than one problem," he remarked with a telling glance in his sister's direction.

Caine nodded. "Jade, you're going to have to change a few of your ways. When Pagan dies, you aren't going to be able to . . ."

"It's my work," she cried out. "It's what I do best."

Caine closed his eyes. "Exactly what is it that you do so well?"

Nathan answered him. "Harry did the pirating," he explained. "Jade was always on board, but he was the leader back then. She took care of the land raids. She does have a special talent, Caine. There isn't a safe she can't open, a latch she can't trick loose."

"In other words, she was an adequate petty thief," Caine drawled out. He was frowning at Jade when he made that statement.

She took immediate exception to both his manner and his opinion. "I don't care what you think of me, Caine. The deception's over now and you'll never see me again, so it really doesn't matter to me . . ."

Jade stopped her tirade when Harry's bellow reached her. A woman's shrill scream came next. Jade assumed one of the servants was being terrorized. "If you'll excuse me for a moment?" she asked.

She didn't bother to wait for permission, but rushed out of the room. As soon as the door closed behind her, Caine turned to Nathan. "She'll figure it all out very soon," he announced. "But hopefully by then we will have staged Pagan's death and it will be too late."

Colin nodded. "Yes, she's bound to realize they know she's with you and that killing Pagan isn't going to make any difference now. You're both still in danger. Odd, but Jade's usually much quicker," he added. "How long do you think it will take for her to sort it all out?"

It was Nathan who answered. "She already has, Colin. Didn't you see the look of relief in her eyes. It was fleeting, but there all the same. Deep down, I think she wants it to be over."

"Wouldn't you?" Caine asked Colin. "How could any of you want to go back on the ocean again? Jade isn't capable of being very logical right now. She thinks she has to resume her former . . . duties," he whispered. "It's a way of proving herself, perhaps. Still, it doesn't matter what her motives are now. She needs someone to take the possibility away from her, to demand she quit."

"And that's you, Caine?" Colin asked.

"Yes."

Jade walked back into the salon then. Nathan turned to her. "Jade? I don't think you should leave with Jimbo and Matthew just yet. Wait until we've settled this problem."

"Do you mean wait until you've found the Tribunal?" She sounded appalled. "I can't stay here, not after . . ."

Caine glared her into forgetting her protest. Jade walked over to the side of his chair and stood there. Her hands were folded in front of her.

"What about Harry?" Caine asked Nathan. "Will he give us any problems?"

"Why would he?" Colin asked with another yawn. "He's retired now. Surely you've noticed there haven't been any ships pirated in a long while."

"I noticed," Caine returned. "Still, he might take exception to having his ship burned."

"No!"

Jade was so appalled by that suggestion, she had to sit down. She moved back to the chair and collapsed.

Nathan was sympathetic. "The *Emerald* has been home for Jade," he said. "Perhaps we could find another ship, paint it to look like the *Emerald,* and set fire to it. Harry would keep the real one safely hidden."

Caine nodded. "Can he see to this chore? There have to be witnesses to the ship's sinking, witnesses who'll testify they saw Pagan die."

"If it's all spelled out for him, yes," Nathan agreed.

"If he's wearing his spectacles," Colin interjected with a grin.

"I'll go and speak to him now," Caine announced.

Nathan stood up before Caine did. "It's time for you to get some rest, Colin."

Before Caine or his brother realized Nathan's intent, he'd lifted Colin into his arms. Nathan staggered under the weight, righted himself, and then started out of the room. Colin immediately started protesting.

"For God's sake, Nathan, put me down. I'm not an infant."

"Could have fooled me," Nathan returned.

Jade watched the two friends disappear around the corner, then whispered, "Nathan has taken good care of your brother, Caine."

Caine turned to look at Jade. She was staring at her lap. "So have you, Jade," he replied.

She didn't acknowledge that compliment. "He's very gentle, my brother. He hides behind his angry expression most of the time. His back is scarred from the beatings he's taken, Caine. He wasn't always away at school. He won't talk about that long time he was missing, won't tell me where he was. I only know that there was a woman involved in his torment. He must have loved her very much, I think, and she must have betrayed him, because now he tries to be so cold and cynical all the time. Colin was able to touch Nathan's heart, though. Your brother gives his friendship without restrictions. He saved Nathan more than once, too. My brother doesn't trust many people, but Colin is the exception."

"Does your brother trust you?"

The question startled her. "Oh, yes," she rushed out. She glanced up to look at him, saw the tenderness in his eyes, and wondered what had caused that reaction. "Colin could never have managed all those stairs. Nathan knew that. My brother didn't give him time to let his pride become dented."

"It might still be dented just a little," Caine drawled out. They could both still hear Colin shouting his objections.

Jade's smile was hesitant. She stood up, then clasped her hands behind her back while she stared at Caine. "Since I cannot leave England just yet, I believe I shall send a note to Lady Briars and request an invitation to stay with her."

"No."

"No? Why not?"

"Jade, I'm really getting tired of repeating myself. You're staying with me."

"Lady Briars would welcome me into her home. It would be much easier for you if I left."

"Why?"

"Because you're going to think this all through in that logical mind of yours and then you're going to decide you can never forgive me. That's why."

"Do you want me to forgive you?"

"Not particularly."

"You're lying again."

"Does it matter?"

"Yes, it matters. Jade, I told you I loved you. Doesn't that matter?"

"It matters," she whispered. When he took a step toward her, she moved away from the chair and started backing toward the doors. The look on Caine's face worried her. Retreat seemed the logical choice now. "Why are you looking at me like that?" she asked.

"You've deceived me, manipulated me, run me in circles, but all that's going to change now, isn't it?"

"So it's finally settling in, is it?" She backed up another space. "When you apply your logic, I'm sure you'll understand that everything I did was to protect you and your brother. First you have to get past your anger . . . and your pride."

"Is that right?"

"Caine, someday soon, I believe you'll actually thank me for this deception. Besides, it's over now, finished."

He slowly shook his head. He smiled too. Jade didn't know what to make of that reaction. Because she didn't dare take her gaze away from him, she didn't look behind her and suddenly found herself backed up against the corner of the wall. She'd misjudged the distance to the entrance by several feet.

She was trapped. His smile widened, indicating he was well aware of her predicament and was thoroughly enjoying it.

"It's done," she stammered out.

"No, it has only just begun, sweet." His hands slammed against the wall on either side of her face.

"You're referring to this hunt for the Tribunal, aren't you?"

He slowly leaned down. "No, I'm referring to you and me. Did you let me touch you because you were protecting me?"

"What a ridiculous question," she muttered.

"Answer me."

"No, of course not," she whispered. She stared at his chest while she admitted that fact.

"Was it out of guilt for deceiving me?"

"No," she cried out. She realized she sounded frightened and immediately changed her tone. "I never feel guilty about lying. I do it very well. I'm proud of my talent, not ashamed."

Caine closed his eyes and said a quick prayer for patience. "Then why did you let me touch you?" he demanded.

"You know why."

"Tell me."

"Because I wanted you to touch me," she whispered.

"Why?"

She shook her head, then tried to push his hand away. He didn't budge.

"You aren't leaving this room until you've given me the full truth. No more lies, Jade."

She stared at his chin now. "You ask too much of me."

"I ask only what I can give in return," he countered. "And we're going to stand here all day until . . ."

"Oh, all right," she replied. "I wanted you to touch me because you were such a kind, gentle man and I realized how much I . . . cared for you."

She looked up into his eyes then, for she needed to know if he was going to laugh or not. If he showed even a hint of amusement, she swore she'd use her fist on him.

He wasn't laughing. He did look pleased with her admission, arrogantly so, but she decided he was entitled to that much. "Caine, you weren't anything like the man I read about in your file. Even your director doesn't know the real you."

"You read my file?"

She decided she shouldn't have mentioned that fact when he grabbed hold of her shoulders and began to squeeze fresh bruises on her skin. "Yes, I read your file," she announced. "It took most of the night. You have quite a history."

He shook his head. He was more astonished than angry. "Jade, the file should have been sealed . . . locked away, the name wiped clean."

"Oh, it was, Caine. Yes, the security was actually quite good. No faulty latches on all the doors, sturdy locks on each cabinet . . ."

"Obviously the security wasn't good enough," he muttered. "You were able to get inside. You found and read my file. My God, I haven't even read it."

"Why would you want to read it?" she asked. "You lived

each event. The file only related assignments you'd handled. There wasn't much about your personal life. Why, the incident with the Kelly brothers wasn't even mentioned."

"Caine, why are you so upset?" she asked. She thought he might be trying to crush her bones now.

"You read everything? You know everything I've done?"

She slowly nodded. "You're hurting me, Caine. Please let go."

He put his hands back on the wall, blocking her exit again. "And yet, knowing all this . . . you still came looking for me. You weren't afraid?"

"I was a little afraid," she confessed. "Your history is most . . . colorful. And I was worried, yes, but after we met, I found myself doubting the accuracy . . ."

"Don't," he interrupted. "There wasn't any exaggeration."

She shivered over the briskness in his voice. "You did what you had to do," she whispered.

Caine still wasn't absolutely certain he believed her. "What was my operative name?"

"Hunter."

"Hell."

"Caine, do try to understand my position. It was necessary for me to find out everything I could about you."

"Why was it necessary?"

"You were in danger."

"Did it not occur to you that I could take care of any threats that came my way?"

"Yes," she answered. "It occurred to me. Still, I had made a promise to your brother and I was honor bound to keep you safe."

"Your word is very important to you, isn't it, Jade?"

"Well, of course it is," she countered.

"I still don't understand why you thought you needed to read my file."

"I needed to find your . . . vulnerability. Don't look at me like that. Everyone has an Achilles' heel, Caine, even you."

"And what did you find? What's my flaw?"

"Like your father, you have a reputation for being a champion of the weak. That isn't necessarily a flaw, but I used that part of your character to my advantage."

"By pretending to be in danger? Jade, you were in danger. Those events did take place. You . . ."

"I could have taken care of the threat on my own," she boasted. "Once I got away from Nathan's carriage, I went to Shallow's Wharf. Jimbo and Matthew were there, waiting for me. The three of us could have taken care of the problem."

"Perhaps," Caine said.

Since he was being so agreeable, and looking so distracted, she tried to duck under his arm. Caine simply moved closer to stop her. "You believed I was weaker and you therefore became my champion, my guardian angel," she finished.

"As it turns out, you were my guardian angel, too," he said.

"Does that injure your pride?"

"No," he answered. "Being manipulated has already done quite enough damage to my pride."

"You have enough arrogance to suffer this paltry blow," she whispered, a wisp of a smile in her voice. "You would have given your life to keep me safe. I heard you whisper that promise to me when you thought I was asleep."

"Damn it, Jade, was there ever a moment when you weren't deceiving me?"

She didn't answer him.

"Jade, I gave you my protection. Do you know what you gave me?"

"Lies," she answered.

"Yes, lies, but something else as well." He could tell by her

252

blush that she understood what he was saying. "What else did you give me?"

"Well, there was . . . that," she whispered. "I was a virgin . . ."

"You gave me your love, Jade."

She shook her head.

He nodded.

"I didn't, Caine."

"You did," he replied. "Do you remember what I told you that first night we made love?"

She remembered every word. "No," she said.

"You're lying again, Jade. You have a knack for remembering everything you read or hear."

"Just everything I've read," she whispered. She started struggling to get away from him. She was suddenly filled with panic.

Caine moved closer, until his thighs were touching hers. "Then let me remind you, my little deceiver," he whispered. "I told you that you were going to belong to me. Now and forever, Jade."

"You didn't mean it," she cried out. "I won't hold you to such a foolish promise, Caine." She closed her eyes against the memory of their lovemaking. "Now is not the time to . . . Caine, stop that," she rushed on when he leaned down and kissed her forehead. "I tricked you, lied to you. Besides," she added. "You didn't know I was Pagan. Anything you said that night must be forgotten."

"I don't want to forget," he said.

"Caine, I can't possibly stay with you. You don't even like me. I'm a thief, remember?"

"No, my love, you used to be a thief," he said. "But all that's finished. There's going to be some changes, Jade."

"Impossible. You'd never be able to make so many changes, Caine. You're too rigid."

"I was referring to you!" he shouted. "You're going to be making these changes."

"I won't."

"You will. You're giving it all up, Jade."

"Why?"

"Because I won't have it, that's why."

She didn't want to understand. "What I do is of no concern to you," she argued. "My men depend on me, Caine. I won't let them down."

"They'll have to depend upon someone else then," he bellowed. "Your thieving days are over."

Her ears were ringing, but she was suddenly too angry and too frightened to worry about that. "Once I leave here, you'll never see me again. Don't worry, I won't come back to rob you." She decided she was finished with this conversation. She shoved away from Caine, then saw Nathan and Black Harry standing in the entrance, watching her. She assumed they'd heard most of the conversation. She had been shouting, she realized, almost as loudly as Caine had. And this was all Caine's doing anyway. He'd turned her into a raving shrew.

"Why do you care what she does?" Nathan asked.

For Jade's benefit, Caine kept his expression mild, contained. "Nathan, I believe it's time you and I had our little chat. Jade, wait in the dining room with Harry. Sterns?" Caine added when the butler joined the group. "See that we aren't interrupted."

Black Harry seemed to be the only one who fully understood what was about to happen. "Just a moment, me boy," he said to Caine as he made his way past Nathan. He rushed through the drawing room, snatched the silver bowl from the top of the mantle, then hurried back to the entrance. "It would be a shame to have this ruined, now wouldn't it? I'll be taking it with me," he added when Jade started to protest. "Caine would want me to have it, girl, so quit your frowns."

Nathan had moved into the drawing room. With a

whispered nod of good luck, Sterns dragged Jade out of the room and shut the doors.

"What do they have to talk about?" Jade asked Black Harry. "They don't even know each other."

The crash cleared up her confusion. "My God, they're going to kill each other," she cried out. "Harry, do something."

Jade gave that command while she tried to push Sterns out of her way. Harry rushed over and put his arm around her shoulders. "Now, girl, they've been itching to get at each other since the moment they met. Let them alone. Come along with me back to the dining room. Cook's about to do us with dessert."

"Harry, please!"

"Come along," Harry soothed. "Me men are waiting on me."

Her uncle gave up trying to persuade her to join him when she started in shouting. The sound didn't bother him much at all, considering all the noise coming from the drawing room. "You always were a mite stubborn, girl," he muttered as he moved back to the dining room. The cherished silver bowl was tucked under his arm.

A pounding began at the front door just as the dining room doors shut behind Harry. Sterns was immediately torn between duties.

"Will mi'lady please see who's come calling," he shouted so she could hear him above the noise.

Sterns' arms were folded across his chest. His back rested against the doors. Jade moved to stand beside him, then imitated his stance. "Mi'lady will guard these doors while you go see who it is."

The butler shook his head. "You cannot trick me, Lady Jade. You're wanting to get inside with the Marquess."

"Of course I want to go inside," she argued. "Caine's fighting with my brother. One's bound to kill the other."

Another loud crash shook the walls. Sterns decided one of the two men had thrown the settee against the wall. He mentioned that possibility to Jade. She shook her head. "Sounds more like a body hitting the wall, Sterns. Oh, please . . ."

She didn't bother to continue pleading with him when he shook his head.

The front door suddenly opened. Both Jade and Sterns turned their attention to the two guests who just walked inside.

"It's the Duke and Duchess of Williamshire," Sterns whispered, appalled.

Jade's manner immediately changed. "Don't you dare move away from these doors, Sterns."

She rushed across the foyer and made a curtsy in front of Caine's parents. The Duke of Williamshire smiled at her. The Duchess was barely paying her any notice, for her attention was centered on the entrance to the drawing room. Another loud blasphemy radiated through the doors. Caine's stepmother let out a small gasp.

"You took her innocence, you bastard."

Nathan's bellowed accusation echoed throughout the foyer. Jade felt like screaming. She suddenly hoped Caine would kill her brother.

Then she remembered their guests. "Good day," she blurted out. She had to shout so the Duke and Duchess would hear her. She felt like a simpleton.

"What is going on here?" the Duchess demanded. "Sterns, who is this lady?"

"My name is Lady Jade," she blurted out. "My brother and I are friends of Caine's," she added.

"But what is going on inside the drawing room?" the Duchess asked.

"A little dispute," she said. "Caine and Nathan, my brother, you see, are having a rather spirited debate about . . ."

She looked over at Sterns for help while she frantically tried to think of a plausible explanation.

"Crops," Sterns shouted.

"Crops?" The Duke of Williamshire asked, looking thoroughly puzzled.

"That's ridiculous," the Duchess announced. Her short blond curls bobbed when she shook her head.

"Yes, crops," Jade stated. "Caine believes the barley and wheat should be planted only every other year. Nathan, on the other hand, doesn't believe a field should go fallow. Isn't that right, Sterns?"

"Yes, mi'lady," Sterns shouted. He grimaced when the sound of glass shattering pierced the air, then said, "My lord feels quite strongly about this issue."

"Yes," Jade agreed. "Quite strongly."

The Duke and Duchess were staring at her with incredulous expressions. They thought she was crazed. Her shoulders slumped in defeat. "Upstairs, if you please."

"I beg your pardon?" the Duchess asked.

"Please come upstairs," Jade repeated.

"You want us to go upstairs?" the Duchess asked.

"Yes," Jade answered. "There's someone waiting to see you. I believe he's in the second room on the right, though I can't be certain."

She had to shout the end of her explanation as the noise had once again risen to ear-piercing dimensions.

The Duke of Williamshire came out of his stupor. He clasped Jade's hands. "Bless you, my dear," he said. "It's so good to see you again," he added. "You kept your word. I never doubted," he added. He realized he was rambling and immediately forced himself to calm down. "Come along, Gweneth. Jade wants us to go upstairs now."

"You know this woman, Henry?"

"Oh, dear, have I given myself away?" Henry asked Jade.

She shook her head. "I've already told Caine I came to see you," she said.

Henry nodded, then turned back to his wife. "I met this lovely young lady early this morning."

"Where?" Gweneth asked, refusing to let him tug her toward the steps. "I'll hear your explanation now, Henry."

"She came to see me in my study," Henry said. "You were still sleeping. Now come along, sweet. You'll understand after you've . . ."

"Henry, she has red hair!"

"Yes, dear," Henry agreed as he prodded her up the stairs.

Gweneth started to laugh. "And green eyes, Henry," she shouted in order for her husband to hear her. "I noticed her green eyes right off, Henry."

"How very astute of you, Gweneth."

Jade stared after Caine's parents until they'd reached the hallway above the stairs. "The fat's in the fire now, isn't it, Sterns?"

"I do believe that is a most accurate evaluation, mi'lady," Sterns agreed. "But have you noticed the blessed lack of noise?"

"I have," she replied. "They've killed each other."

Sterns shook his head. "My employer would not kill your brother," he said. "I believe I shall fetch the decanter of brandy for the two gentlemen. I imagine they're quite parched by now."

"Not parched," Jade wailed. "Dead, Sterns. They're both dead."

"Now, mi'lady, one must always look on the bright side."

"That is the bright side," she muttered. "Oh, go and fetch the brandy then. I'll guard the doors."

"I trust you to keep your word," he announced.

She didn't want to go inside now. She was furious with Caine and her brother, and so humiliated because the Duke and Duchess of Williamshire had strolled right into the middle of the brawl, she wanted to weep.

And just what did she care what Caine's parents thought about her? She was leaving, and that was that. She would have gone upstairs to pack her satchel then and there but she didn't want to take the chance of running into the Duchess again.

When Sterns returned with the crystal decanter and two glasses, Jade opened the door for him. Both she and the butler stopped when they saw the destruction. The lovely room was in shambles. Jade didn't think there was a single piece of furniture left intact.

Sterns found the two men before Jade did. His initial surprise wore off much faster, too. The butler straightened his shoulders and proceeded over to the far wall, where Caine and Nathan were seated on the floor, side by side, their backs propped up by the wall.

Jade stumbled after the butler. Her hands flew to cover her mouth when she looked at the two warriors. Neither looked victorious. Caine had a jagged cut on his forehead, just above his right eyebrow. Blood trickled down the side of his face, but he seemed to be oblivious to his injury. God's truth, he was grinning like a banshee.

Nathan looked just as defeated. There was a deep cut in the corner of his mouth. He held a handkerchief against the injury, and damned if he wasn't grinning, too. The area around his left eye was already beginning to swell.

Jade was so relieved to see that neither Caine nor Nathan appeared to be near death's door, she started trembling. Then, in a flash of a second, that surge of relief turned to raw anger. She became absolutely furious.

"Have you two gentlemen resolved your dispute?" Sterns inquired.

"We have," Caine answered. He turned to look at Nathan, then slammed his fist into his jaw. "Haven't we, Nathan?"

Nathan hit him back before answering. "Yes, we have." His voice was gratingly cheerful.

"You children should be sent to your rooms," Jade snapped. Her voice shook.

Both men looked up at her, then turned to look at each

other. They obviously thought her insult was highly amusing because they both burst into laughter.

"Your brother sure hits like a child," Caine drawled out when he could control himself.

"Like hell I do," Nathan countered. "Hand me the brandy, Sterns."

The butler knelt down on one knee and handed each man a glass. He then filled each goblet with a full portion of the rich liquid.

"Sterns, are you thinking to get them drunk?" Jade asked.

"It would be a marked improvement, mi'lady," Sterns replied dryly.

The butler stood up, bowed, and then slowly scanned the ruins. "I believe I was correct, Lady Jade. It was the settee that hit the wall."

Jade stared silently at the remains of what used to be a tea cart.

"Sterns, leave the bottle," Caine instructed.

"As you wish, mi'lord. Would you like me to assist you to your feet before I leave?"

"Is he always this proper?" Nathan asked.

Caine laughed. "Proper? Never, not Sterns. If I'm a minute late for supper, he eats my portion."

"Promptness is a quality I've still to teach you, mi'lord," Sterns said.

"You'd best help him to his feet," Nathan said. "He's as weak as a . . . child."

The two men started laughing again. "You'd best assist him, Sterns," Caine said. "He suffered more blows than I did."

"You never give up, do you, Caine?" Nathan asked. "You know good and well I won this fight."

"Like hell," Caine argued, using Nathan's favorite expression. "You barely scratched me."

Jade had heard enough. She whirled around, determined to get as far away from the two imbeciles as possible. Caine reached out and grabbed the hem of her gown. "Sit down, Jade."

"Where?" she cried out. "You've destroyed every chair in this room."

"Jade, you and I are going to have a little talk. Nathan and I have come to an agreement." Caine turned to Nathan. "She's going to be difficult."

Nathan nodded. "She always was."

Caine put his goblet down on the floor, then slowly stood up. "Nathan?" he said as he stared at the woman glaring so prettily up at him. "Think you can crawl out of here and give us a few minutes' privacy?"

"Crawl, my arse," Nathan growled as he stumbled to his feet.

"I don't want to be alone with you," Jade interjected.

"Too bad," Caine countered.

"Your parents are upstairs," she said when he tried to take her into his arms.

She waited for that statement to get a proper reaction and was unhappy to see that Caine didn't seem the least bit bothered. "They heard all the noise," she said then. "Sterns told them you were disputing the issue of crops."

"The issue of crops?" Caine asked Sterns.

The butler nodded, then turned to walk out of the room with Nathan at his side. "The rotation of crops, to be more specific, mi'lord. It was the best I could think of given the circumstances."

"They didn't believe him," Jade whispered, sounding as though she were confessing a grave sin.

"I would imagine they wouldn't," Caine answered dryly. He noticed that she suddenly looked close to tears.

"And that upset you, Jade?"

"No, that doesn't upset me," she cried out. She was so angry with him she couldn't even come up with a suitable insult. "I'm going up to my room," she whispered. "I need a few minutes of privacy."

She didn't mention she was going to pack her belongings, certain Caine or Nathan would try to waylay her. She simply wasn't up to another confrontation.

Without a hint of a farewell, Jade turned and hurried out of the room. Lord, how she wanted to weep. She couldn't, of course, until after she'd had a long talk with her uncle. Harry needed to understand. She didn't want him to worry about her.

She found Harry in the dining room, carefully examining the silver collection. He tucked a fork in his sash when she called out to him, then turned to smile at her. "I'm taking all the silver with me, girl. Caine would want me to have it for my collection."

"Yes," she answered. "I'm certain he would want you to have it. Uncle? I need to speak to you alone, please."

The men immediately filed out into the hallway. Jade sat down next to her uncle, took hold of his hand, and quietly told him what she was going to do. She also told him about the last two weeks, though she deliberately left out mention of her nightmares and her intimacy with Caine. Both of those facts would only upset Harry. Besides, he couldn't do anything about either now. No, he couldn't ward off her nightmares, and he couldn't make her quit caring about Caine.

Her uncle grunted several times during her explanation, but finally agreed. He didn't have any doubts in his mind that she'd be able to take care of herself. She was his protégée, after all, and as good as the best of them.

"I'll be waiting for you at the cottage," he promised. He pulled her over to kiss her cheek, then said, "Watch your backside, girl. Vermin like to sneak up on a person. Remember McKindry."

She nodded. Harry was referring to the pirate who'd marked her back with his whip. He had been vermin and he had snuck up behind her. Her uncle liked to use that memory as a lesson. "I'll remember," she promised.

Jade left her uncle taking inventory of Caine's possessions and went upstairs to pack. She passed Colin's room on her way to her own. The door was closed, but she could hear the Duke's booming laughter interspersed with his wife's loud, inelegant sobs. Colin's mama was obviously overcome with emotion and was probably weeping all over her son.

Colin's safety wasn't her concern any longer. She'd finished her task, she told herself. It was over now, finished.

Jimbo and Matthew were waiting for her in the hallway. Jimbo handed her the farewell gift she'd asked Harry to have him fetch.

"We'll be going with you, won't we?" Matthew asked, his voice a low whisper.

Jade nodded. "I'll meet you out back."

"I'll get Caine's horses ready for the ride," Jimbo whispered.

"A man can get himself hung for stealing a horse," Matthew interjected. His wide grin indicated he thought that was quite all right.

"Caine won't tell anyone," Jimbo argued. He took hold of Jade's satchel and started after his friend. "It's a shame, that. How we ever going to keep up appearances if no one . . ."

His sentence faded away as he turned the corner. Jade immediately went to Caine's bedroom. She placed the long-stemmed white rose on his coverlet. "I am Pagan," she whispered.

It was done. She turned to leave, then spotted Caine's black robe draped over the back of a chair near the window. On impulse she folded the garment and tucked it under her arm. His scent was on the robe, faint, but there still, and she wanted something to hold during the nights ahead, during the dark nightmares, to comfort her.

It was time to leave.

Both Caine and Nathan thought Jade was resting in her room. Caine had wanted to chase after her, but Nathan convinced him that his sister needed time alone to calm her temper.

"You might not have noticed yet, Caine, but Jade isn't one to take orders easily," Nathan explained.

Since Caine had more than noticed this, he didn't bother to comment.

The talk then turned to the problems at hand. Harry was dragged away from his inventory to add his suggestions. Jade's uncle had a quick mind. Caine watched him closely and came to a remarkable conclusion. Harry was civilized. He naturally kept that discovery to himself, for he guessed Harry would take grave exception to being confronted with the truth.

Uncle Harry did grumble about the fact that he was going to have to burn a ship. "It's a waste of good timber," he muttered. "Still, it could be worse. I might have to be burning my lovely *Emerald,*" he added. "Aye, it could be worse. I'd just as soon put a stake through me heart than damage my baby's ship. The *Emerald's* been home to Jade and me all these many years."

Before Caine could comment on Harry's remarks, the uncle surprised him by adding that he was in full agreement that his baby get out of her present line of work.

A good two hours passed before their plans were set to everyone's satisfaction. Harry strolled back into the dining room.

"He's bent on eating you out of house and home," Nathan drawled out. "He'll steal you blind, too," he added with a grin. "Harry likes to keep up appearances."

"He can have whatever he wants," Caine returned. "Jade's had quite enough time to calm her temper, Nathan. It's high time your sister and I had our talk."

"If you lecture her, you'll only . . ."

"I'm not going to lecture her," Caine replied. "I'm simply going to tell her what my expectations are."

"Sounds like a lecture to me," Nathan drawled out.

Both Nathan and Caine walked into the foyer just as the Duchess was coming down the winding staircase. Both men stopped to watch her. Caine's stepmother was smiling, but also dabbing at the corners of her eyes with her lace handkerchief. She'd obviously had quite a good cry.

Gweneth almost lost her balance when she spotted Nathan. She grasped the banister and let out a soft gasp of surprise. She quickly regained her composure, however, and continued down the steps. When she reached the foyer, she moved to Caine's side. "Is he the pirate friend of Colin's?" she whispered.

Nathan heard her. "I'm not the pirate, Pagan, madam, but I am a friend of your son's."

Nathan assumed his voice had been a little too harsh for her liking when she grabbed hold of Caine's arm and moved closer to his side. Her dark brown eyes widened, too, but she valiantly held her smile.

"You look very like a pirate," she announced. She adjusted the folds of her pink gown as she waited for his reply.

"Have you seen many, madam?" Caine asked.

"No, I've never seen a pirate," she confessed. "Though this gentleman certainly fits the picture of one in my mind. I believe it's because of the length of his hair," she explained after turning back to look at Nathan. "And the scar on your arm, of course."

"He's also covered with blood," Caine drawled out.

"That, too," his stepmother admitted.

He'd meant the remark as a jest, but her expression had become so solemn, he knew she didn't understand he was teasing her. "Pirates do like to brawl," she added with a nod.

"Madam, didn't Colin explain that . . ." Caine began.

"My son insists upon keeping Pagan's true identity a secret," she interrupted. "Still, I'm not completely obtuse," she added with a meaningful glance in Nathan's direction. "I've been around the corner once or twice. I know who Pagan is," she added with a nod. "Henry also knows."

"Henry?" Nathan asked.

"My father," Caine explained.

"Henry's never wrong, dear."

She'd made that statement to Nathan. He found himself nodding in agreement. "Then I must be Pagan," he announced with a grin. "If Henry's never wrong."

She smiled over his easy acceptance. "Do not worry, sir, for I shall guard your secret. Now where is that lovely young lady I was so horribly rude to, Caine?"

"You're never rude, madam," Caine interjected.

"I didn't properly introduce myself," she argued. "Now where is she?"

"Upstairs, resting," Nathan answered. "Why do you ask?"

"You know perfectly well why," she answered. Her exasperation was obvious.

"I do?" Nathan asked.

"I must apologize for my behavior, of course, but also I must thank her for all she's done for this family."

"Nathan is Jade's brother," Caine said.

"I knew that," she answered. "His green eyes gave him away, of course."

The Duchess walked over to the man she believed was the infamous pirate. "Lean down, dear boy. I must give you a kiss for being such a loyal friend."

Nathan was a bit disconcerted. Caine's stepmother had sounded like a commander when she gave her order. He suddenly felt as awkward as a schoolboy and didn't have the faintest idea why.

He did, however, do as she asked.

The Duchess kissed Nathan on both cheekbones. "You need to wash that blood away, my dear. Then Henry will give you a proper welcome into the family."

"Will he kiss him, too, madam?" Caine drawled out. He was thoroughly enjoying Nathan's obvious discomfort.

"Of course not," his stepmother answered.

"Why would he want to welcome me into the family?" Nathan asked.

The Duchess smiled, yet didn't bother to explain herself. She turned back to Caine. "I should have realized Lady Aisely wasn't going to do."

"Who is Lady Aisely?" Nathan asked, trying to catch the drift of this conversation.

"A ball of fluff," Caine answered.

The Duchess ignored that insult. "Henry realized right off. The green eyes, you see. And the red hair, of course." She patted her blond curls and looked over her shoulder at Nathan. "Henry's never wrong."

Nathan found himself agreeing once again with the woman. He still didn't have a clue as to what she was babbling about, but he found her loyalty to her husband quite honorable.

"Henry's infallible." Caine said what Nathan was thinking.

"My baby's terribly weak," the Duchess remarked. "And as thin as a reed." She started toward the dining room. "I'm going to find Sterns. Colin needs a good hot meal."

Because Caine was in a hurry to get to Jade, he forgot all about Harry and his men. Nathan was more astute. He thought about warning Caine, or mentioning the guests to his mother, then decided he'd just wait and see what happened. Besides, Caine was already halfway up the stairs, and the Duchess had already turned the corner.

Nathan started counting. He'd only reached the number five when a shrill scream filled the air.

The noise stopped Caine. He turned around and found Nathan lounging against the door frame again, grinning broadly.

"What the . . ." Caine began.

"Harry," Nathan drawled out.

"Hell," Caine returned as he started back down the stairs. "Harry."

The Duchess was screaming like a wild woman now. "Damn it, Nathan," Caine roared. "You could have reminded me."

"Yes," Nathan replied. "I could have."

Just as Caine reached the bottom step, his father appeared at the top. "What in God's name is going on?" he shouted. "Who is making all that noise?"

Nathan answered before Caine could. "Your wife, sir."

Caine paused to glare at Nathan, then turned to his father again. He was torn between going to his stepmother's assistance, and preventing his father from doing murder.

The chilling look in his father's eyes convinced him to handle him first. There was also the fact that even though Harry was probably scaring the Duchess out of her wits, Caine knew he wouldn't really hurt her.

Caine grabbed hold of his father's arm when he reached him. "Father, it's quite all right, really."

Henry didn't look at all convinced. "Your wife has just met Black Harry," Nathan interjected.

Caine's father pulled away from his son's grasp just as the dining room doors bounded open. Everyone turned to watch the unsavory-looking men filing past.

Black Harry was the last in the procession. He was dragging the Duchess in his wake.

Nathan started laughing. Caine shook his head. The Duke's full attention, however, was centered on the giant of a man with the gleaming gold tooth who was now swaggering toward the front door. A large silver bowl was tucked under the man's arm.

Henry let out a roar and started forward. Both Nathan and Caine blocked his path. "Father, let me take care of this, please," Caine asked.

"Then tell him to unhand my wife!" his father bellowed.

"Henry, do something," Gweneth cried out. "This . . . man believes I'm going with him."

Nathan took a step forward. "Now, Harry, you can't be taking . . ."

"Get out of my way, son," Caine's father snapped.

"Father, Harry's a friend," Caine countered. "He's Jade's uncle. You owe this man a debt for helping with Colin."

Henry paused to give his son an incredulous look. "And Gweneth is payment for this debt?"

"Let me handle this matter," Caine demanded once again.

Before his father could argue with him, Caine turned. "Harry," he called out.

Black Harry whirled around and hauled the Duchess up against his side. Caine noticed his grim expression, of course, but also the definite sparkle in his eyes. Appearances, he thought to himself. And pride. Both needed to be upheld.

"I'll be taking her with me," Harry announced to his audience. His men nodded their agreement. "Caine would want me to have her."

"No," Caine replied. "I don't want you to have her."

"You being inhospitable, boy?"

"Harry, it isn't possible for you to take her."

"It's a fair exchange," Harry stated. "You're determined to have my girl, now aren't you?"

Caine nodded. "I am."

"Then I'm taking this one," Harry countered.

"Harry, she's already taken," Caine argued. He turned to his stepmother then and said, "Madam, please quit shouting. It's difficult enough to negotiate with this stubborn pirate. Nathan? If you don't quit laughing, I'm going to bloody your nose again."

"What's this woman to you, Caine?" Harry asked. "You just called her madam. Now what the hell does that mean?"

"She's my father's wife."

"But she ain't your mama?"

"She's my stepmother," Caine qualified.

"Then it shouldn't matter to you if I take her or not."

Caine wondered what Harry's real game was. "She has been like a mother to me," he said.

Harry frowned, then turned to his pretty captive. "Do you call him son?"

The Duchess lost her outraged expression and slowly shook her head. "I didn't believe he would wish me to call him son," she answered.

"He ain't your favorite," Harry announced.

The Duke of Williamshire quit trying to get past Caine. His stance became relaxed. A hint of a smile turned his expression. He understood at last what this was all about, for he remembered Jade's instructions about loving his children equally. She must have mentioned her concern to Harry.

"I don't have a favorite child," Gweneth cried out. "I love all my children."

"But he ain't yours."

"Well, of course he's mine," she snapped.

The Duchess didn't look frightened now, only furious. "How dare you suggest . . ."

"Well now, if you'd call him son," Harry drawled out, "and if he called you mother, then I couldn't be taking you with me."

"For heaven's sake, Gweneth, call Caine son!" Henry roared, trying to pretend outrage. He was so pleased inside over this surprising development, he wanted to laugh.

"Son," Gweneth blurted out.

"Yes, Mother?" Caine answered. He was looking at Harry, waiting for his next rebuttal.

Harry let go of his hostage. His chuckle was deep as he turned and walked out the doorway.

While Gweneth threw herself into her husband's arms, Caine followed Harry outside. "All right, Harry, what was that all about?"

"My reputation," Harry drawled out after his men had taken their leave. "I'm a pirate, if you'll remember."

"What else?" Caine asked, sensing there was more to tell.

"My girl worried about Colin being the favorite," Harry finally admitted.

Caine was astonished by that statement. "Where did she get that idea?"

Harry shrugged. "Don't matter where she got it," he replied. "I don't want her worrying, no matter what the niggly reason be. You're going to have to ask me for her, you know. You'll have to do it proper, too, in front of me men. It's the only way you're going to be getting her, son." He paused to grin at Caine, then added, "Course you're going to have to find her first."

A feeling of dread settled in Caine's bones. "Hell, Harry, she isn't upstairs?"

Harry shook his head.

"Where is she?"

"No need to shout, son," Harry answered. "Can't tell you where she is either," he added. He waved his men away when they started toward him, then said, "It would be disloyal."

"My God, don't you . . ."

"I'm wondering to meself why you haven't noticed both Matthew and Jimbo are missing," he interrupted. "That's telling, ain't it?"

"She's still in danger."

"She'll do all right."

"Tell me where she is," Caine demanded.

"She's running from you, I imagine."

Caine didn't want to waste any more time arguing with Harry. He turned around and almost ripped the hinges off the door as he pulled it open.

"Where you going, boy?" Harry called out.

There was more than a thread of amusement in the old man's voice. Caine wanted to kill him. "Tracking, Harry."

"You any good at it?"

Caine didn't bother to answer that question.

"She's led you a merry chase with her little deception, now hasn't she? I'd have to say she did a fair job of impressing you," Harry called out at Caine's back.

Caine turned around. "What's the point, Harry?"

"Well now, I'm thinking to meself it's about time you did a little impressing of your own, assuming, of course, that you're up to it."

Caine took the steps to his bedroom two at a time. He was pulling his shirt over his head by the time Nathan caught up with him.

"What's happening now?" Nathan demanded.

"Jade's gone."

"Damn," Nathan muttered. "You going after her?"

"I am."

"I'll go with you."

"No."

"You could use my help."

"No," Caine snapped. "I'll find her."

Nathan reluctantly nodded. "You any good at tracking?"

Caine nodded. "I'm good."

"She left you a message."

"I saw it."

Nathan strolled over to the side of Caine's bed and lifted the long-stemmed white rose from the pillow. He inhaled the sweet fragrance, then walked over to the window to look outside.

"Is she in love with you?" Nathan asked.

"She is," Caine answered. His voice lost its brittle edge. "She just doesn't know it yet."

Nathan tossed the rose back on the bed. "I'd say Jade was telling you goodbye when she left you the rose."

"No."

"She might be reminding you who she is, Caine."

"That's part of it," Caine said. He completed his change of clothes, stomped into his boots, and started for the door.

"Then what's the rest?" Nathan asked as he trailed after him.

"Harry's right," Caine muttered.

"What?"

"She's trying to impress me."

Nathan laughed. "That, too," he agreed.

Caine bellowed for Sterns as he bounded down the stairs. The servant appeared at the doorway to the drawing room. "Lyon will find Richards for us," Caine said. "When the two arrive, make them wait until I get back, no matter how long it takes."

"What if your friend can't find Richards?" Nathan asked.

"He'll find him," Caine answered. "I probably won't be back before tomorrow morning," he said. "Take care of things while I'm gone, Sterns. You know what to do."

"Meaning the guards, mi'lord?"

Caine nodded. He started for the door, but Sterns' question stopped him.

"Where are you going, mi'lord?"

"Hunting."

The door slammed shut.

Chapter Fourteen

Matthew and Jimbo appeared to be as weary as Jade was by the time they reached their destination. It had been decided that they would spend the night in the isolated inn Harry frequented when he was on the run. Jade had insisted they take a roundabout way there, adding two more hours' travel, just as an added precaution against being followed.

The innkeeper was a friend of Black Harry's, a little on the disreputable side as well, and therefore never asked unnecessary questions. If he thought it odd a finely dressed young lady was traveling with two men who looked like they'd cut a man's throat for two pence, he certainly didn't remark upon it.

Jade was given the center bedchamber above the stairs. Jimbo and Matthew took the rooms on either side of her. Since the walls were paper-thin, neither man worried that anyone would be able to breach their temporary fortress. The steps were so old and rickety, a mouse would have made noise.

Jade soaked in a hot bath, then wrapped herself in Caine's robe. She was stiff and out of sorts by the time she went to bed. Her injury from the pistol shot was almost completely healed now, but it still itched something fierce.

Jade fell asleep saying a prayer that the nightmare would not visit her tonight, worrying she might cry out and cause Matthew and Jimbo alarm.

The air turned chilly during the night. Jade burrowed under the covers. She never felt Caine climb into the bed beside her. When he put his arm around her and gently pulled her up against his side, she let out a soft sigh and snuggled closer to his familiar warmth.

Moonlight filtered through the small window. He smiled when he saw she was wearing his robe. Then he slowly slipped the garment off her. That task completed, he removed her knife from under the pillow, then began to nibble on the side of her neck.

She was slow to wake up. "Caine?" she whispered, her voice a sleepy blur.

"Yes, love?" he whispered in her ear before his tongue swept inside to tease. She started shivering. It was just the reaction he wanted.

His hand moved down her chest, circled her navel, then trailed a hot path to one of her breasts.

She sighed again. He was so warm, smelled so wonderful, and oh, how he was making the cold disappear.

Caine continued to stroke her while he waited for her to realize where she was. He was ready to silence her if she tried to call out.

The awakening came like a bolt of lightning. The palm of his hand cut off her gasp. "Now, sweetheart, if you yell, I'll have to hurt Matthew and Jimbo when they come charging in here," he whispered. He rolled her onto her back, then covered her with his body. "You wouldn't want that, would you?"

She shook her head. Caine slowly eased his hand away from her mouth.

"You're naked."

"So are you," he whispered back. "Convenient, isn't it?"

"No."

"Yes," he answered. "And it feels good, doesn't it?"

It felt marvelous. She couldn't admit that, however. "How did you get in here?"

He kissed her chin in answer to that question. Jade prodded his shoulder. "Caine, what are you doing here?"

"Impressing you, sweetheart."

"What?"

"Keep your voice down, love," he cautioned. "You don't want to wake up the boys."

"They aren't boys," she stammered out. She sounded breathless. The hair on his chest was tickling her breasts, making her nipples hard. She didn't want him to move away from her, though, and that honest admission made her frown. Lord, she was confused. "Impressing me, Caine?" she whispered. "I don't understand what you mean."

"Of course you do, sweet," he answered. He kissed the bridge of her nose. "God, I love your freckles," he said with a low groan. He kissed her long, hard, and when he was finished, she was clinging to his shoulders.

She recovered much quicker than he did. "Have you come to say goodbye then?" she asked him in a ragged whisper.

Her question was meant to rile him. The defenses again, he thought to himself. "No, I didn't come to say goodbye," he answered, determined not to get angry. "I came to make love to you."

He grinned after making that promise. Jade's heart started pounding. It was the damned dimple, she told herself. It was too irresistible to ignore . . . and so appealingly boyish. He didn't feel like a boy, though. No, he had the body of a fit man, a warrior with sleek iron-hard muscles. She couldn't stop herself from rubbing her toes against his legs.

"Someday, my love, you're going to understand just how

much I care for you. You're my light, my warmth, my other half. I only feel alive when I'm with you. I love you."

He kissed her again, then whispered, "One day, you'll tell me you love me, too. For now I'll be content to hear you say you want me."

She shook her head. Caine could see the fear in her eyes, the confusion. His smile was filled with tenderness when he pushed her legs apart and settled himself between her silky thighs. He rubbed his hard arousal against her softness. "You do want me, love."

She closed her eyes with a telling sigh. Caine nibbled at her lips, tugging on her lower lip until she finally opened for him, then thrust his tongue inside to duel with hers.

"Caine, what are you . . ."

He silenced her with another long kiss, then whispered, "It's called pillaging, Jade."

"It isn't."

"Harry would be proud," he drawled out. His mouth was now placing wet kisses on the smooth, sensitive skin below her chin. She couldn't quit trembling.

"You're mine, Jade. The sooner you understand that, the better it will be for you."

"And then what, Caine?" she asked.

He lifted his head to stare down into her eyes. He could see the fear there, and the vulnerability. "You learn to trust me," he whispered. "And then we live happily ever after."

"No one lives happily ever after."

"We will."

She shook her head. "Get off me, Caine. You're . . ."

"Solid, love," he interrupted. "Steadfast, too. I won't leave you."

The promise was given in a fervent whisper. She pretended not to understand. "Of course you won't leave me. I'm leaving you."

"I love you, Jade."

Her eyes filled with tears. "You'll get tired of me. I won't change, not for you, not for anyone."

"All right."

Her eyes widened. "All right?"

He nodded. "If you want to stay a thief, so be it. I won't get tired of you, no matter what you do. And I'll never leave you."

"You won't be able to help it."

Caine kissed her brow, then said, "I can see it's going to take a little time for me to convince you. Will you give me at least two months?"

"Caine, I don't think . . ."

"You owe me, Jade."

"I what?" She sounded outraged. "Why would you believe I owe you anything?"

"Because you deceived me," he explained. "You caused me endless worry, too. And there I was, minding my own affairs that night in the tavern when you . . ."

"I also saved your brother," she interrupted.

"Then there's the issue of my wounded pride, of course," he drawled out. "A man shouldn't be made to feel he's been manipulated."

"Caine, for heaven's sake."

"Promise me you'll stay with me for two more months or I'm going to make so much noise when I pillage you, both Matthew and Jimbo will come running."

That odious threat got her full attention. The determined look in his eyes told her he meant what he threatened, too. "You should be ashamed of yourself."

"Promise me, Jade. Now."

His voice had risen and she clamped her hand over his mouth in retaliation. "Will you explain how you settled on two months instead of one, or three, or . . ."

He shrugged. She feigned irritation. "And during those two months you'll probably be dragging me to your bed every single night, won't you?"

"I will," he answered with a grin. "Do you know, whenever I look at you, I get hard?" He shifted positions and pressed against her. "Can you feel how much I want you? You make me ache to be inside you."

His honesty made her blush. "You shouldn't say things like that," she whispered. "And I shouldn't listen."

"You like it," Caine told her. His mouth covered hers and his tongue slid inside to taste her again. Jade didn't protest. She wanted him too much to stop now. She moved against him, then froze when the bed made such a loud, squeaky noise.

"We can't . . ." The denial came out with a groan.

"We can," he said, his voice a husky caress.

He silenced her worries with another kiss while he stoked the fire in her. Jade forgot all about Matthew and Jimbo. Caine was making her burn and all she could concentrate on was finding release from the sweet agony.

His fingers drove her wild. She was wet, hot, ready, knew she was going to die from the pressure building inside her. Her nails dug into his shoulder blades. She would have shouted for him to come to her if his mouth hadn't covered hers. Caine kept the torment up until she took him in her hands and tried to bring him inside her. He threw the coverlet off the bed, then followed it down to the floor with Jade protected in his arms. He cushioned the fall, taking most of the force on his back. Jade was sprawled on top of him. She tried to roll to her side, but Caine held her tight. "Take me inside you now, love," he whispered as he pushed her thighs apart to straddle him.

She was trembling too much to help. Caine took over. He held her by the sides of her hips and slowly eased into her. He let out a low groan of raw pleasure. She whimpered at the same moment.

When he was deep within her, he twisted her hair around his hands and pulled her down for another hot kiss.

The mating rhythm took over. Caine's discipline deserted

him. His thrusts became more powerful, more determined. "Take me to heaven again, Jade," he whispered when he was about to spill his hot seed inside her. "I'll keep you safe."

Jade found her release seconds later. She arched against Caine, squeezed him tight, biting her lip to keep herself from crying out, and then collapsed on top of him.

Her face was buried in the crook of his neck. They were both covered with a sheen of perspiration. Jade tasted his skin with the tip of her tongue while she waited for her heart to slow down. She was too exhausted, too content, to move. Caine held her close. She could feel his heart pounding against her own.

"What are you thinking, Jade?" he asked.

When she didn't answer him, he pulled on her hair. "I know you found fulfillment. Are you going to deny it now?"

"No," she whispered shyly.

Caine moved to his feet in one fluid motion with Jade in his arms. When they were both back in bed and under the covers, she tried to turn her back to him. He wouldn't allow her retreat, but forced her to face him. "Well?" he demanded.

"Well, what?" she asked, staring into those dark eyes that made her feel fainthearted.

"I'm good, aren't I?"

The dimple was back in his cheek. She couldn't help but smile. "Good at what?" she asked, pretending innocence.

"Pillaging."

She slowly nodded. "Very good," she whispered.

"And did I impress you?" he asked.

"Perhaps just a little," she answered. She let out a gasp when the palm of his hand pressed against the junction of her thighs. "What are you doing?"

"Impressing you again, sweetheart."

The man was as good as his word, Jade decided a long while later. And he had far more stamina than she did. When he finally rolled away from her, she felt like a limp rag.

She fell asleep with Caine holding her close, whispering words of love.

She didn't have any nightmares that night.

By noon, they were back at Caine's house. Matthew and Jimbo couldn't leave for Shallow's Wharf quickly enough. They were both mortified by their slip up of the night before. They'd obviously underestimated the Marquess. Matthew didn't think he'd ever live down the disgrace; though, of course, Jade promised not to tell anyone he'd been caught so unaware.

Hell, Caine had prodded him awake, and how in God's name such a big man was able to get into his room without making a sound still baffled him.

As soon as they returned to Caine's home, Jade changed her gown and then went to Caine's study to make copies of the letters for him. She listened to him explain his plan. She argued something fierce about trusting Richards, but agreed that Lyon could hold a confidence.

"When you meet Richards, you'll like him as much as you like Lyon," Caine replied. "You'll trust him as much, too."

She shook her head. "Caine, I like Lyon, yes, but that isn't the reason I trust him. No, no," she continued. "Liking and trusting are two different kettles of fish."

"Then why do you trust Lyon?" he asked, smiling over the censure in her tone.

"I read his file," she answered. "Do you know, in comparison, Caine, you've led the life of a choirboy."

Caine shook his head. "I wouldn't mention reading his file to him," he advised.

"Yes," she agreed. "He'd probably get as prickly as you did when I told you," she added. "Lyon's file is just as fat as yours, but he didn't have a special name."

Caine looked thoroughly irritated with her. "Jade, exactly how many files did you read?"

281

"Just a few," she replied. "Caine, I really must concentrate on these letters. Please quit interrupting me."

The library door opened then, drawing Caine's attention. Nathan walked inside. "Why hasn't anyone tried to get to you, Caine, since you've been here? It's damned isolated, and I would think . . ."

"Someone did try to get to Caine the day we arrived, Nathan," Jade said without looking up.

When Jade didn't continue, Caine filled Nathan in on the details of the failed attempt.

"Nathan, how nice you look," Jade said, completely turning the topic when she glanced up and saw his handsome shirt and pants.

"That shirt looks damned familiar," Caine drawled out.

"It's yours," Nathan answered with a grin. "Fits well, too. Colin has also borrowed a few of your things. We hadn't packed sufficiently when we were tossed into the ocean. Why hasn't anyone tried to get to you since that first day?" he added with a scowl.

Nathan started to pace the room like a tiger. Caine continued to lean against the edge of the desk. "They have."

"What?" Nathan asked. "When?"

"They have not," Jade interjected. "I would have known."

"In the past ten days, four others have tried."

"And?" Nathan asked, demanding more of an explanation.

"They failed."

"Why wasn't I informed?" Jade asked.

"I didn't want to worry you," Caine explained.

"Then you had to have known Matthew and Jimbo were here," Nathan said.

"I knew," Caine answered. "I left them alone, too, until they burned down my stables. Then I had a little talk with them. Couldn't you have come up with another plan to keep me busy while you went to see my father?"

He was getting all worked up again. Jade guessed he still wasn't over the fire yet. Sterns had said the stables were brand new. "I should have been more specific with Matthew," she announced. "I left the diversion up to him. Still, he was very creative, effective, too. You were busy."

"You took a needless risk going off on your own like that," he snapped. "Damn it, Jade, you could have been killed!"

He was shouting at her by the time he'd finished that statement. "I was very careful," she whispered, trying to placate him.

"The hell you were!" he roared. "You were damn lucky, that's all."

She decided she needed to turn his attention. "I'm never going to finish this task if you two don't leave me alone." She tossed her hair over her shoulder and returned to her letter writing. She could feel his glare on her. "Why don't you both go see how Colin's doing. I'm sure he'd like the company."

"Come on, Caine. We've just been dismissed."

Caine shook his head. "Promise me you won't take needless risks again," he ordered Jade. "Then I'll leave."

She immediately nodded. "I promise."

The anger seemed to drain out of him. He nodded, then leaned down to kiss her. She tried to dodge him. "Nathan's here," she whispered.

"Ignore him."

Her face was bright red when he lifted his mouth away from hers. Her hands were shaking, too. "I love you," he whispered before he straightened up and followed Nathan out of the room.

Jade stared at the desktop a long while. Was it possible? Could he really love her? She had to quit thinking about it in order to calm the trembling in her hands. Richards and his friend wouldn't be able to read the letters otherwise. Besides, it didn't matter if he loved her or not. She still had to leave him. Didn't she?

Jade had worked herself into a fine state of nerves by the time dinner hour was over. Nathan had decided to eat his supper upstairs with Colin. She and Caine, and Sterns, of course, ate at the long table. They got into a heated debate about the separation between church and state. In the beginning, when Caine stated he was in favor of the separation wholeheartedly, she took the opposite opinion. Yet when he deliberately argued the opposing view, she was just as vehement in her rebuttal.

It was a thoroughly invigorating argument. Sterns ended up acting as referee.

The debate made Caine hungry again. He reached for the last slice of mutton only to have it snatched out of his reach by Sterns.

"I wanted that, Sterns," Caine muttered.

"So did I, mi'lord," the butler answered. He picked up his utensils and proceeded to devour the food. Jade took sympathy on Caine and gave him half of her portion.

Both Sterns and Caine looked at each other when the sudden pounding on the front doors echoed through the room. Caine lost the staring contest. "I'll get it," he announced.

"As you wish, mi'lord," Sterns agreed between bites of his mutton.

"Be careful," Jade called out.

"It's all right," Caine called back. "No one could have gotten to the doors without my men noticing."

A good ten minutes elapsed before Sterns finished his second cup of tea. "I believe I shall go and see who's calling," he told Jade.

"Perhaps it's Caine's papa."

"No, mi'lady," Sterns countered. "I have ordered the Duke and Duchess to stay away. It would draw suspicion if they began to pay daily visits to their son."

"You really ordered them?" she asked.

"But of course, Lady Jade." With a formal bow, the butler left the room.

Jade drummed her fingers on the table until Sterns returned.

"Sir Richards and the Marquess of Lyonwood have arrived," he announced from the doorway. "My lord is requesting both brandy and you in the library."

"So soon?" she asked, clearly startled. She stood up, smoothed the folds of her gold-colored gown, then patted her hair. "I wasn't ready to meet anyone," she said.

Sterns smiled. "You look lovely, mi'lady," he announced. "You'll like these visitors. They're good men."

"Oh, I've already met Lyon," she replied. "And I'm certain I'll like Richards just as much."

As she started for the door, her expression turned from carefree to fearful.

"There's really nothing to be concerned about, mi'lady."

Her smile was radiant. "Oh, I'm not worried, Sterns. I'm preparing."

"I beg your pardon?" he asked. He followed after her. "What are you preparing for, mi'lady?"

"To look worried," she answered with a laugh. "And to look weak, of course."

"Of course," Sterns agreed with a sigh. "Are you ill, Lady Jade?"

She turned to look at him when she reached the library door. "Appearances, Sterns."

"Yes?"

"They must be kept up. Do the expected, don't you see?"

"No, I don't see," he answered.

She smiled again. "I'm about to give Caine his pride back," she whispered.

"I wasn't aware he'd misplaced it."

"I wasn't either, until he mentioned it to me," she replied. "Besides, they're only men, after all."

She took a deep breath, then let Sterns open the door for her. She stood just inside the entrance, her head bowed, her hands folded together in front of her.

Sterns was so surprised by the sudden change in her demeanor, his mouth dropped open.

When Caine called out to her, she visibly jumped, as if his command had the power to terrify her, then slowly walked into the study. The one called Richards bounded to his feet first. He was an elderly man with gray hair, a gentle smile, and a round belly. He had kind eyes, too. Jade acknowledged the introduction by making a perfect curtsy.

She then turned to greet Lyon. When he stood to his full height, he fairly towered over her. "It is good to see you again, Lyon," she whispered, her voice little more than a faint shiver.

Lyon raised an eyebrow in reaction. He knew she was a timid creature, but he thought that she had gotten over her initial reaction to him the first time they'd met. Now, however, she acted afraid again. The contradiction puzzled him.

Caine was sitting behind his desk. His chair was tilted back against the wall. Jade sat down on the edge of the chair adjacent to the desk, her back ramrod straight. Her hands were clenched in her lap.

Richards and Lyon both resumed their chairs across from her.

Caine was watching Jade. She appeared to be terribly frightened. He wasn't buying it for a minute. She was up to something, he decided, but he would have to wait until later to question her.

Richards cleared his throat to get everyone's attention. His gaze was centered on Jade when he said, "I cannot help but notice, my dear, how worried you seem to be. I've read the letters your father saved, but before I ask you my questions, I want to make it perfectly clear that I don't hold you in less esteem because of your father's transgressions."

She still looked like a trapped doe, but she managed a timid nod.

"Thank you, Sir Richards," she replied in a bare whisper. "It is kind of you not to blame me. I was worried that you might condemn me."

Caine rolled his eyes heavenward. Richards, a man rarely given to showing any affection, was now clasping Jade's hands. The director looked like he wanted to take her into his arms and offer her solace.

She did appear to be very vulnerable. Caine suddenly remembered that that same expression had been on her face when she'd stared at him in the tavern. She'd appeared vulnerable then, too.

What was her game?

"Neither one of us condemns you," Lyon interjected. He, too, leaned forward, bracing his elbows on his knees. "You have had a difficult time of it, Jade."

"Yes, she has," Sir Richards agreed.

Caine forced himself not to smile. Both his superior and his friend were falling under Jade's spell. He thought Lyon should have known better. After all, he'd met Jade before. Still, her manner now, added to his earlier thought that she was terribly timid, obviously convinced Lyon that she was sincere.

"Are you up to answering a few questions now?" Richards asked.

Jade nodded. "Would it not be better to have Nathan answer your questions? Men are so much more logical. I'll probably make a muddle out of it."

"Jade." Caine said her name as a warning.

She turned to give him a tremulous smile. "Yes, Caine?" she asked.

"Behave yourself."

Richards turned to frown at Caine. Then he returned his attention to Jade.

"We'll ask Nathan our questions later. If it isn't too

painful to recount, please tell us exactly what happened to you from the moment you arrived in London."

Jade nodded. "Certainly," she agreed. "You see, this all begins with the letters. My Uncle Harry was given a packet of letters by my father. Just two days later, Father was killed. Harry took me away on his ship then. He saved the letters, and when he felt the time was right, he gave them to me. I read them of course, then showed them to Nathan. My brother was working with Colin at the time, and he confided in him. Now then," she continued in a brisker tone. "As Caine has probably told you, both Colin and Nathan were . . . attacked. The villains thought they'd done them in, and . . . Pagan decided to let the hired thugs return to London to report their success."

"A sound decision," Richards interjected.

"Yes," Jade said. She turned to frown at Caine. "The plan was very simple. Pagan snatched a physician to take care of the injuries, and it had been decided that when Colin was well enough to travel, he would tell his brother, Caine, about the letters and ask his assistance."

"What happened to sour this plan?" Richards asked.

Jade frowned at Caine again. "He soured it," she announced. "Pagan had been made the scapegoat for Nathan and Colin's deaths, as you know, and Caine decided to seek vengeance. His timing couldn't have been worse. The remaining members of the Tribunal couldn't take the risk of Caine finding the pirate and having a talk with him. So Caine had inadvertently put himself in danger."

"It wasn't inadvertent," Caine interjected.

She shrugged. "Colin had made Pagan promise not to tell Caine anything. His brother knew Caine would . . . charge right in, you see, and Colin wanted to explain everything. In truth, I do believe Colin wasn't thinking the thing through, but he was in terrible pain at the time and he seemed obsessed with protecting Caine. Pagan agreed, just to placate Colin."

"And where do you fit into this scheme?" Lyon asked.

"Nathan is my brother," Jade answered. "I returned to England and went to stay at his country estate. There were several of Pagan's men with me. They took turns watching out for Caine. Several attempts were made to get him, and it was then decided that I would find a way to get Caine away from his hunt. Two days before I was supposed to leave, a series of incidents took place. On the first morning, when I was taking my usual walk, I came upon three men digging up my parents' graves. I shouted, for I was in a rage, you see, over what they were doing. I drew their notice, of course. One of the villains shot at me. I ran back to Nathan's house to get help."

"Weren't Pagan's men still guarding you?" Richards asked.

Jade shook her head. "They were all needed to keep Caine safe. Besides, I had Nathan's butler, Hudson, and the other servants to assist me."

"And then what happened?" Lyon asked.

"It was too dark for the servants to go to the graves. It was decided to wait until morning. That night, the house was pillaged," she continued. "I slept through, however, and never heard a sound. Even my bedchamber was turned upside down."

"You must have been drugged," Richards announced.

"I can't imagine how it done if I was drugged," Jade said. "The following morning, I rode one of Nathan's mounts back to the graves to see if any evidence had been left. Nathan's butler, Hudson, was having a difficult time believing me, you see, and I wanted to convince him. As it turned out, I never made it to the graves. The villains were obviously waiting to intercept me. They killed Nathan's horse. I went flying to the ground."

"Good Lord, you could have been killed by the fall," Richards said.

"I was most fortunate, as I only sustained a few bruises,"

she explained. "I went running back to the house, told Hudson what had happened. He sent men to chase after the villains. When they returned, they told me they couldn't find any evidence of foul play. The horse had vanished. I'm not certain how that was accomplished. Caine said it would take more than three men to lift it into a wagon and cart it away."

She paused to shrug, then continued. "I decided to go to London with all possible haste and immediately ordered the carriage made ready. Yet, as soon as we'd traveled down the first hill, the coachman shouted that there was a fire. We could see the smoke. I returned to the house just in time to witness the full fire. Poor Nathan's house was gutted to the ground. I then ordered Hudson and the other servants to go to Nathan's London residence, then once again set out for my own destination."

"And where was that?" Lyon asked. "Were you also going to Nathan's town house?"

Jade smiled. "No, I was going to a tavern called the Ne'er Do Well. I had a plan, you see, to get Caine away from his hunt."

Lyon nodded.

"I don't understand," Richards interjected. "What exactly was this plan? Caine isn't one to be easily fooled, my dear."

"I'll explain it all later," Caine interjected. "Let her finish with this now."

"On the way to London, the carriage was waylaid. I was hit on the side of my head. The blow made me sleep, and when I awakened, I found that the carriage had been torn apart. I was able to squeeze through the window after I'd widened the frame with the heel of my boot."

"And then?" Richards asked.

"I walked."

"All the way to London?" Lyon asked.

"No," Jade answered. "Not all the way. I was able

to . . . borrow a horse from a way station. It was unattended. The owner was probably inside having his supper."

Jade finished her accounting a few minutes later. She never mentioned the fact that she was Pagan, and Caine assumed he would have to be the one to tell Sir Richards and Lyon.

Just what was her game? Lord, by the time she'd finished her recitation, she was dabbing at the corners of her eyes with Richards' handkerchief.

The director was obviously shaken by her explanation. He leaned back in his chair and shook his head.

"Do you know who the other members of the Tribunal are?" Jade asked him.

"No."

"But you knew Hammond, didn't you?" she asked. "I understood that the two of you started out together."

"Yes, we started out together," Richards agreed. "Yet after a number of years, my dear, we were each given a different division within the War Department. Hammond had so many young men under his direction back then. He ran his own section. I met quite a few eager young saviors, but certainly not all of them."

"We have several telling clues," Lyon interjected. "It shouldn't take us long to find out the truth."

"The first letter was signed by a man named William. They hadn't been assigned their operative names yet. Hell, that's the most common name in England," Caine added. "How many Williams work for the War Office?"

Jade answered his question. "Actually, there were only three in Hammond's files."

Everyone turned to look at her. "Pagan read the files," she whispered. She blushed, then added, "It was necessary. There's William Pryors, William Terrance, and William Clayhill. All three worked for your department, Sir Richards. Two are still alive, though retired from duty, but William Terrance died four years ago."

"You're certain of these facts?" Lyon asked.

"How did Pagan get to our files?" Richards was obviously disconcerted. "By God, no one can get through our security."

"Pagan did," Caine said. He took over the conversation then, explaining in more detail how the pirate had set out to protect him. He told them about Colin's and Nathan's near miss with the sharks, too. When he was finished, no one said a word for a long while.

Jade was gripping her hands together. It wasn't a pretense now, but the memory of the sharks that made her so agitated.

"Three eager young men, bent on saving the world," Richards whispered. "But the lust for power became more important."

Jade nodded agreement. "Did you notice, sir, that the first letters were signed with the wording, 'for the good of England,' but as time went on, and they grew more and more bold, they changed the wording?"

"I noticed," Sir Richards muttered. "'For the good of the Tribunal' was how they signed their notes," he added. "And that does say it all, doesn't it. There can be no misinterpretation here."

"Her father was killed by the two others when he refused to go along with their plans, and then Hammond was murdered," Caine said.

Richards nodded. "We must find the other two," he muttered. "Lord, there's so much to take in." He let out a weary sigh, then said, "Well, thank God Pagan seems to be on our side. When I think of all the damage he could do with those files, my blood runs cold."

"Oh, Pagan's very honorable," Jade rushed out. "Most thieves are, sir. You mustn't worry that the information will fall into the wrong hands."

"Did that bastard read my file?" Lyon demanded.

Caine didn't answer him. He didn't think there was any reason to share the truth with his friend. It would only upset him.

"The very fact that there were sharks in those waters," Richards whispered, changing the topic. "Do you realize the courage it must have taken . . ."

"Have you finished your questions?" Jade interrupted.

The director immediately reached out and patted her hands again. "We've exhausted you, haven't we, my dear? I can tell how distressing this is for you."

"Thank you for your consideration," she whispered. She stood up and didn't protest at all when Richards embraced her.

"We'll find the culprits, I promise you," he said.

Jade hid her hands in the folds of her gown, then walked over to Lyon. He immediately stood up. She leaned against him. "Thank you, Lyon, for helping us. Please give my love to Christina. I cannot wait until I can visit with her again."

She turned back to Richards and hugged him again. "I forgot to thank you as well," she explained.

She pulled away from the director, bowed, and turned to leave the room.

"Jade?"

"Yes, Caine?"

"What was all that about?"

She turned around to smile at him. "You said a man's pride is very important, didn't you?"

"I did."

"You also said that when a man is manipulated or deceived, his pride suffers, too."

"I did say that." He leaned forward. "And?"

"Well, if others were also . . . fooled . . . friends who have earned their own legends and England's respect, then wouldn't the blow be less painful?"

He finally understood. His wink was slow, his grin arrogant. "I shall go and ask Colin and Nathan to join you now," Jade announced before she left the room. The door closed softly behind her.

"What was she talking about?" Richards asked.

"A personal matter," Caine answered. He turned to Lyon then. "Well? What do you think of her now?"

His friend refilled his goblet with more brandy before he answered. "She's still damned beautiful," he said. "But I'm once again thinking she's awfully timid. Must come from being around you."

Caine laughed. "You're back to thinking she's timid?"

"What am I missing, Caine?" Lyon asked, genuinely perplexed. "What's the jest you find so amusing?"

"Put aside this talk about women," Richards ordered. "Now, son, you must promise me something."

"Sir?" Caine asked.

"Have you actually met this Pagan fellow?"

"I have."

"When this is finished, you must find a way for me to meet him."

Caine leaned back in his chair. Jade had been right. She had just given him his pride back.

"I must meet Pagan," Sir Richards demanded again.

Caine nodded. "Sir Richards, you just did."

Chapter Fifteen

Jade, come back here." Caine shouted that order while his two friends were trying to absorb the news he'd just given them.

When she didn't respond to his summons, Caine called for Sterns. The butler must have been standing right outside the door, for he immediately rushed inside the library. He bowed to his employer, a courtesy he never ever extended when they were alone, and then asked, "You wished something, mi'lord?"

"Bring Jade back here," Caine ordered.

"I believe she heard your bellow, mi'lord," Sterns announced in that highbrow voice of his, "She has declined the invitation to rejoin you, however. Was there something more you wanted?"

Caine wanted to strangle Sterns, but he pushed the notion aside. "Bring her to me. Drag her in here if you have to, but bring her to me. That's what I want, Sterns."

The butler nodded, then left on his errand. Caine turned back to his friends. He lost some of his irritation when he saw Lyon's grin. His friend seemed to be taking the news of Pagan's identity much better than Sir Richards was. The director still looked quite stunned.

"Hell, Caine, I should have guessed," Lyon said. "She was so timid . . . yes, I should have known, all right. You aren't one to be attracted to . . . and Christina did say that I should look below the . . ."

"Son," Sir Richards interrupted Lyon's rambling. "This isn't the time for jests. We've a serious matter here."

Jade opened the door in the middle of Richards' protests. "I was fetching Nathan and Colin for you, Caine. What is it you wanted?"

"Give them back, Jade."

His voice had the bite of a pistol shot in it. Jade pretended innocence. "Whatever are you talking about?" she asked. She pressed her hand to her bosom in mock fear and fluttered her eyelashes at him.

He wasn't at all impressed. "You know damned good and well what I'm talking about," he roared. "Give them back."

"Caine, it isn't polite to raise your voice to me in front of visitors," she instructed. Her voice had risen an octave. "It's plain rude."

"They know who you are."

"They know?"

She marched over to the front of his desk and glared at him. Her hands were planted on her hips now. "Exactly what do they know?"

"That you're Pagan."

She let out a gasp. "Why don't you just post it in the dailies?" she shouted. "Then you wouldn't have to spend so much time . . ."

"I had to tell them," Caine interjected.

"You could have waited until after I'd left."

"Since you aren't leaving, that wasn't possible, now was it?"

"My God, it's really true?" Richards interjected in a near shout of his own.

Jade glanced over her shoulder to frown at the director. "No," she snapped. "It isn't true."

"Yes," Caine countered. "It is."

"Damn it, Caine, don't you know how to keep a secret?" She didn't give him time to answer that question but turned to leave.

"I told you to give them back, Jade."

"Why?"

"These men happen to be my friends," he answered. "That's why."

"Caine, if you can't rob from your friends, who *can* you rob?" she asked.

He didn't have a ready answer to that absurd question.

"You did say it was all right for me to continue my work," she reminded him. "Have you already gone back on your word?"

He couldn't believe she had the audacity to look so outraged. Caine didn't dare stand up, certain the urge to grab her and try to shake some sense into her would be too overwhelming to ignore.

Jade turned to look at Lyon. "When I give my word, I never break it," she stated.

Caine took a deep breath, then leaned back in his chair. He stared at Jade long and hard.

She glared back.

With the crook of his finger, he motioned her closer. When she'd reached his side, he said, "I meant what I said. You may continue with your work."

She was totally perplexed. "Then why are you making such a fuss over . . ."

"You may continue to rob," he interrupted. "But every time you take something, I'm going to give it back."

Her gasp nearly knocked her over. "You won't."

"I will."

"But that's . . . ridiculous," she stammered. "Isn't it?"

He didn't answer her. Jade looked over at Lyon for help. His grin told her she wouldn't be getting any assistance from him. Sir Richards was still looking too flabbergasted to intervene.

She was on her own, she decided, just as she'd always been. "No."

"Yes."

She looked as though she wanted to weep. "Now give them their . . ."

"I switched them," she announced. "May I leave now?"

Caine nodded. He waited until Jade had reached the door, then called out, "Jade, you may leave this room, but don't you dare try to leave this house. I'll only come after you if you do. You wouldn't want to inconvenience me again, now would you?"

She didn't answer that question. Caine knew she was furious with him, though. The door almost flew off its hinges when she slammed it shut behind her.

"She's got a bit of a temper," Caine announced. His grin suggested he didn't mind that flaw much at all. "Have you recovered yet, Richards?" he asked then.

"I have," Richards agreed.

"But you never once considered . . ."

"No, no," Richards returned.

Caine nodded with satisfaction. "It's good to know my own superior was taken in. I do believe my pride has been fully restored."

Nathan and Colin walked into the library then. Colin used his cane and Nathan's arm for assistance.

"Quit treating me like an infant," Colin muttered, as Nathan helped him ease into a chair.

"You are an infant," Nathan drawled out. He pushed a footstool in front of the chair, then propped Colin's foot on it.

Nathan stood to take his measure of the two men watching him. Caine made the introductions. He shook their hands, then sat on the arm of Colin's chair.

"Jade wants me to ask you what time it is," Nathan stated then.

The director looked puzzled by that request, then shrugged. "I'd say it was going on nine, wouldn't you, Lyon?"

Lyon was more astute than his superior. He lifted the timepiece from his waist pocket. He laughed then, a full booming sound that filled the room. "I believe this one is yours, Richards. You have mine. She did embrace both of us."

Richards was duly impressed. "I certainly misjudged her," he announced. "You saw her make the switch, didn't you, Caine. That's why you called her back."

Caine shook his head. "No, I didn't," he admitted. "But when she embraced each of you, I knew she was up to something. She doesn't usually show such affection to strangers."

"No, she doesn't," Nathan agreed.

Caine looked at Lyon. "The woman has led me in circles. She's determined to make me a madman."

"I'd say she's already accomplished that goal," Nathan drawled out.

"This sounds familiar to me," Lyon said. He smiled, remembering the bizarre circumstances leading up to his marriage. "I've been led in a few circles by Christina, too. Tell me this, Caine. What did you do while she was leading you?"

"Same thing you did," Caine answered. "I fell in love with her."

Lyon nodded. "God help you now, friend. It isn't going to get any easier after you've married her. When is the wedding, by the way?"

"Yes, Caine, when *is* the wedding?" Nathan demanded.

"There damned well will be a wedding." Colin made that statement of fact. He was frowning intently at his brother.

"Yes," Caine answered. "There will be a wedding."

"Sounds to me as if you don't have any choice, son," Sir Richards interjected. "Will you say your vows with a pistol aimed at your back?"

"If a pistol is needed, it will be aimed at Jade's back, not mine," Caine countered. "I still have to convince her that I mean what I say. Hell, I'll probably even have to get down on one knee in front of her men."

Even Nathan smiled over that picture. Colin scoffed. "Jade won't make you kneel before her," he said.

"No, but Black Harry sure as hell will," Caine replied.

"Who is Black Harry?" Richards asked.

"Nathan, you start explaining," Caine announced. "While I go after Jade."

"She's gone?" Nathan asked.

Caine stood up and started for the door. "Of course she's gone. I never make the same mistake twice, Nathan. I'll be back soon."

Since Caine was already wearing his riding britches and boots, he went directly to the corral housing the horses.

The speckled mare was missing. "How many men do you have trailing her?" he asked the stablemaster.

"Three at the back door chased after her," the servant answered.

Caine bridled his stallion but didn't bother with the saddle. He grabbed hold of the black mane and mounted the steed in one quick motion.

He trailed her to the cabin on the edge of his property. She was standing next to the creek, watering her horse.

Caine broke through the trees, then goaded his mount into a full gallop. Jade heard the sound of pounding hooves. She turned to run into the woods. Caine's stallion never broke stride as he leaned down and lifted her into his arms. He slammed her bottom down in front of him, turned direction and headed back toward home.

He didn't say a word to her, nor she to him, and he didn't slow his pace until they'd reached their destination.

Sterns was waiting at the front door. Caine dragged Jade up the steps. "Lock her in her room!" he roared. "Post two guards below her windows and two more outside the door."

He didn't let go of Jade until he'd dragged her inside the house and bolted the door behind him.

He kept his expression as ugly as he could manage until he was once again inside the library. When he was back in his chair behind his desk, he let himself smile.

"I assume you found her," Nathan said.

"I did," Caine answered. "Impressed the hell out of her, too. Now catch me up on what you've told my friends," he ordered.

The talk returned to the letters and the men didn't finish formulating their plans until well past eleven. Richards and Lyon were given chambers in the North wing. Both appeared to be reluctant to say goodnight.

Richards insisted on taking the copies of the letters to bed with him. "There's information still to be ferreted out," he announced.

No one argued with the director. Caine went directly to Jade's room. He dismissed the guards, unlocked the door, and went inside.

Jade was reading in bed. She wouldn't look at him, but kept her gaze on the book she held in her hands.

"You need more light if you're going to read," Caine announced. "The fire needs to be stoked, too. It's damned cold in here."

She didn't even look up at him. "It's ridiculous to pretend I'm not here," he told her, his exasperation obvious in his tone.

"As ridiculous as giving back everything I take?" she countered, her attention focused on her book.

Caine added two more candles to the bedside table. He went to the hearth next. "Where's Sterns?" he asked.

"Sterns has gone to bed," she answered. "You'd make a good butler, Caine. Your man has trained you well."

He didn't jump to the bait. "You're spoiling for a fight, sweetheart, but I'm not going to accommodate you."

"I'm not spoiling for a fight," she snapped. She slammed her book shut while she watched him add another fat log to the embers.

In the firelight, his skin looked as bronzed as a statue. His shirt was opened to the waist, his sleeves rolled up to his elbows. The fabric was stretched tight across the back of his shoulders, showing the splay of muscle there when he reached for the iron staff to prod the fire into a full blaze.

She thought he was the most appealing man in all the world.

Caine turned, still bent on one knee, and smiled at her. The tenderness in his gaze tugged at her heart. He was such a good man, a trusting man, a loving man.

He deserved better than the likes of her. Why didn't he realize that obvious fact?

Tears welled up in her eyes and she started trembling. It was as though the blankets had suddenly turned into snow. She was freezing . . . and terrified.

Don't ever let me leave you, she suddenly thought. Make me stay with you forever.

Oh, God, how she wanted to love him, to lean on him.

And then what would she become, she asked herself, when he left her. How in God's name would she survive?

The change in her was startling. Her face had turned the color of her white nightgown.

"Sweetheart, what's the matter?" he asked. He stood up and walked toward the bed.

"Nothing," she whispered. "Nothing's wrong. I'm just cold," she added in a stammer. And afraid, she wanted to add. "Come to bed, Caine."

She desperately needed to hold him close. Jade added to the invitation by pulling the covers back for him. Caine ignored her request. He went to the wardrobe, found another blanket on the top shelf, then draped it over the other covers on the bed.

"Is that better?" he asked.

"Yes, thank you," she answered, trying not to sound too disgruntled.

"If you aren't too tired, I want to ask you a few questions," he said.

"Ask your questions in bed, Caine," she suggested. "You'll be more comfortable."

He shook his head, then sat down in the chair and propped his feet up on the foot of the bed. "This will do," he said then, trying his damnedest not to smile.

She wanted him, perhaps even as much as he wanted her. And by God, she was going to have to tell him so.

Jade tried to hide her irritation. The man was as dense as rain. Didn't he realize she wanted to be held? She'd told him she was cold, damn it. He should have immediately taken her into his arms, then kissed her of course, and then . . .

She let out a long sigh. Caine apparently didn't realize what she needed when he started in with his questions about the stupid files again.

It took all her determination to hold onto her concentration. She had to stare at her hands so his heart-stopping smile wouldn't detract her.

"Jade?"

"Yes?" She looked startled.

"I just asked you if you read the files on our Williams," he said.

"They aren't our Williams," she replied.

She gave him an expectant smile, waiting for his next question.

Caine's smile widened. "Are you going to answer me?" he asked.

"Answer what?"

"You seem preoccupied."

"I'm not."

"Sleepy then?"

"Not at all."

"Then answer my question," he instructed again. "Did you read the files . . ."

"Yes," she interrupted. "You want to hear them, don't you?"

"Yes, I do," he answered. "Was there something else you wanted to do?" he asked.

The blush came back to her cheekbones. "No, of course not," she answered. "All right, Caine, I'll tell you . . ."

A knock sounded at the door, interrupting them. Caine turned just as Nathan peeked inside.

When Jade's brother saw Caine lounging in the chair, he frowned. "What are you doing here, Caine?"

"Talking to Jade," Caine answered. "What do you want?"

"I couldn't sleep," Nathan admitted. He strode over to the hearth and leaned against it. Nathan was barefoot and shirtless now. Caine saw the scars on Nathan's back, of course. He didn't mention them, but he wondered how Nathan could have survived such a beating.

"Here's Caine's robe, if you're cold, Nathan," Jade said. She pointed to the empty chair on the other side of the bed. "You'll catch a chill if you don't cover up."

Nathan was in an accommodating mood. He put Caine's robe on, then sprawled out in the chair.

"Go back to bed, Nathan," Caine ordered.

"I want to ask my sister a couple of questions."

Nathan had left the door opened. For that reason, Sir Richards didn't bother to knock when he reached the room. The director was dressed in a royal blue robe that reached his bare feet. He looked positively thrilled to see the gathering.

Jade pulled the covers up to her chin. She looked at Caine to see his reaction to this invasion.

He looked resigned. "Pull up a chair, Sir Richards," Caine suggested.

"Be happy to," Richards replied. He smiled at Jade then. "I couldn't sleep, you see, and so I thought I'd look in on you and . . ."

"If she was awake, you were going to question her," Caine guessed.

"This isn't at all proper," Richards said as he dragged a chair close to the bed. His chuckle indicated he didn't mind that fact at all. "Nathan?" he added then. "Would you mind fetching Lyon for us? By now he'll have a few questions of his own."

"He might be sleeping," Jade said.

"I could hear him pacing in the chamber next to mine. This Tribunal has us all rattled, my dear. It's quite a lot to take in."

Nathan returned with Lyon by his side. Jade suddenly felt ridiculous. She was in bed, after all, and dressed only in her nightgown. "Why don't we go down to the library to discuss this?" she suggested. "I'll get dressed and . . ."

"This will do," Caine announced. "Lyon, Jade's going to give us the files on the Williams."

"Do I have to repeat every word, Caine?" she asked. "It will take days."

"Start with just the pertinent facts," Richards suggested. "Lyon and I are going back to London tomorrow. We'll read the files from start to finish then."

Jade shrugged. "I'll start with Terrance then," she announced. "The dead one."

"Yes, the dead one," Lyon agreed. He leaned against the mantel and smiled encouragement.

Jade leaned back against the pillows and began her recitation.

Lyon and Richards were duly impressed. When they got over their initial astonishment, they took turns interrupting her to ask specific details on certain missions William Terrance was involved in.

She didn't finish with the file until two in the morning. She couldn't quit yawning either, a hint of the exhaustion she was feeling.

"It's time we all took to our beds," Sir Richards announced. "We'll start in again come morning."

The director was following Lyon and Nathan out of the room when Jade called out to him. "Sir Richards? What if the William you're looking for isn't one of the three in the files?"

Richards turned back to her. "It's just a starting place, my dear," he explained. "Then we begin the cross-check, read through each and every file the superiors in every department kept. It will take time, yes, but we will persevere until we get to the bottom of this."

"There couldn't be a chance they're both dead now?" Jade asked.

She looked so hopeful, Richards hated to disappoint her. "I'm afraid not," he said. "Someone wants those letters, dear. At least one of the two remaining members of the Tribunal is still very much alive."

Jade was relieved to be alone with Caine again. She was exhausted, worried, too, and all she wanted was for him to take her into his arms and hold her close. She pulled back the covers for Caine, then patted the sheet.

"Goodnight, Jade," Caine said. He walked over to the bed, leaned down, and gave her a horribly chaste kiss, then blew out the candles on his way to the door. "Pleasant dreams, sweetheart."

The door closed. She was astonished he'd left her.

He didn't want her any longer. The thought was so repugnant to her, she pushed it aside. He was just angry with her still because he'd had to chase after her again, she told herself . . . he was tired, too, she added with a nod. It had been a long, exhausting day.

Damn it, the man was suppose to be reliable.

She didn't have pleasant dreams. She was drowning in the blackness, could feel the monsters circling her as she went down, down, down . . .

Her own whimpers awakened her. She instinctively turned to Caine, knowing he'd soothe away her terror.

He wasn't there. She was wide awake by the time she'd made that determination, and shaking so much she could barely get the covers out of her way.

She couldn't stay in bed, but went to the window and stared out at the starless night while she contemplated her bleak situation.

She didn't know how long she stood there, worrying and fretting, before she finally gave in. She was going to have to go to him.

Caine woke up as soon as the door opened. Since it was dark, he didn't have to hide his smile. "I don't know how to dance, Caine," she announced.

She slammed the door shut after making that statement, then walked over to his side of the bed. "You might as well know that right off. I can't do needlework, either."

He was resting on his back with his eyes closed. Jade stared at him a long minute, then prodded his shoulder. "Well?" she demanded.

Caine answered her by pulling the covers back. Jade pulled off her nightgown and fell into bed beside him. He immediately took her into his arms.

The shivers vanished. She felt safe again. Jade fell asleep waiting for Caine to answer her.

He woke her up a little past dawn to make love to her, and when he was done having his way with her and she having her way with him, she was too sleepy to talk to him. She fell asleep listening to him tell her how much he loved her.

The next time she was nudged awake, it was almost noon.

Caine was doing the nudging. He was fully dressed and sweetly demanding she open her eyes and wake up.

She refused to open her eyes, but tried to kick the covers away and make him come back to bed. Caine insisted on holding the covers up to her chin. She didn't understand why he was being so contrary until she finally opened her eyes and saw Sterns standing at the foot of her bed.

She took over the task of shielding her nakedness then. Jade could feel her face turning crimson. It would be pointless to try to bluster her way through this embarrassment. "Oh, Sterns, now you're ashamed of me, aren't you?"

The question came out in a wail. Sterns immediately shook his head. "Of course not, mi'lady," he announced. "I'm certain my employer dragged you into his bed," he added with a nod in Caine's direction.

"By her hair, Sterns?" Caine asked dryly.

"I wouldn't put it past you, mi'lord."

"He did," Jade announced, deciding to let Caine take all the blame. "You mustn't tell anyone," she added.

Sterns' smile was gentle. "I'm afraid there isn't anyone left to tell."

"Do you mean Sir Richards and Lyon know?"

When Sterns nodded, she turned to glare up at Caine. "You told them, didn't you? Why don't you just post that in the dailies too?"

"I didn't tell," Caine countered, his exasperation obvious. "You didn't shut your door when you . . ." He paused to look at Sterns, then said, "When I dragged you in here. They noticed the empty bed on their way downstairs."

She wanted to hide under the covers for the rest of the day.

"Jade? Why is my silver under my bed?"

"Ask Sterns," she said. "He put it there."

"It seemed an appropriate place, mi'lord," Sterns announced. "One of your guests, the big man with the gold tooth, certainly would have taken a liking to the silver.

Mi'lady suggested a safe haven for the pieces once I'd explained their special meaning to you."

She thought he might thank her for saving his treasures. He laughed instead. "Come downstairs as soon as you're dressed, Jade. Richards wants to start questioning you again."

Sterns didn't leave the room with his employer. "The Duchess has sent over several gowns belonging to one of her daughters. I believe the fit will be close, mi'lady."

"Why would she . . ."

"I requested the clothing," Sterns announced. "When I was unpacking your belongings, I couldn't help but notice there were only two gowns."

She looked as though she were going to protest, but Sterns didn't give her time. "The selection is hanging in the wardrobe. Cook will act as your lady's maid. I shall go and fetch her immediately."

It wouldn't do her any good to argue with him. Sterns had turned from butler to commander. He selected the garment she'd wear, too—a deep, ivory-colored gown with lace-embroidered cuffs. The gown was so elegant looking, Jade couldn't resist.

There were undergarments as well. Though Sterns didn't make mention of them, he put the silk treasures on the foot of her bed, next to the thin-as-air stockings and matching ivory-colored shoes.

Jade was washed and dressed in the finery a scant fifteen minutes later. She sat in a straight-backed chair while Cook pulled on her hair. The elderly woman was tall and rotund. Her salt and pepper hair had been clipped into short, bobbing curls. She attacked Jade's hair as if it were a side of beef. Still, Jade would have put up with the mild discomfort for the rest of the day if it would put off having to face Lyon and Sir Richards again.

The meeting couldn't be avoided, however. "You're a looker, you are," the servant announced when she'd finished her task. She held up a hand mirror and gave it to Jade. "It's a simple braid, but those little wisps of curls along the sides of your face soften the look. I would have put it up in clusters atop your head, mi'lady, but I fear the weight would have toppled you over."

"Thank you so much," Jade replied. "You've done a splendid job."

Cook nodded, then hurried back downstairs. The meeting couldn't be avoided any longer. Caine would only come and fetch her if she stayed closeted in his room. When Jade opened the door, she was surprised and irritated to find two guards in the hallway. Both men looked a little undone by the sight of her. Then one stammered out what a fair picture she was. The other blurted out that she looked just like a queen.

Both guards followed her downstairs. The dining room doors were closed. The bigger of the two men rushed ahead to see them opened for her. Jade thanked the man for his consideration, then straightened her shoulders and walked inside.

Everyone was seated at the long table, including Sterns. And everyone, including the rascal butler, was staring at her.

All but Colin stood up when she entered the room. Jade kept her gaze on Caine. When he moved to pull out the chair adjacent to his, she slowly walked over to his side.

He leaned down and kissed her brow. Nathan broke the horrid silence. "Get your hands off her, Caine."

"My hands aren't on her, Nathan," Caine drawled out. "My mouth is." He kissed Jade again just to goad her brother. Jade fell into the chair with a sigh.

Sterns saw to her breakfast while the men continued their discussion. Sir Richards sat at one end of the long table, Caine at the other. When her plate had been taken away, Sir Richards called everyone to attention. She realized then that they had all been waiting for her.

"My dear, we've decided that you must come to London

with us," Sir Richards announced. "We'll keep the security tight," he added with a glance in Caine's direction.

Richards then pulled the pen and ink well close. "I'd like to make a few notes while I question you," he explained.

"Sir? Why must I come to London?" Jade asked.

The director looked a little sheepish now. Lyon, Jade noticed, was grinning.

"Well, now," Richards began. "We need to get in the file room. If I request the keys during working hours, my name will have to go into the entry book."

"They want to go during the night," Colin interjected. "Without keys."

"You did say you'd broken into the building once and read the files," Richards reminded her.

"Three times," Jade interjected.

Sir Richards looked as if he wanted to cry. "Is our security so puny then?" he asked Lyon.

"Apparently," Lyon returned.

"Oh, no," Jade said. "The security is very good."

"Then how . . ." Richards began.

Caine answered. "She's better than good, Richards."

Jade blushed over the compliment. "Sir Richards, I understand your need for secrecy. You don't want the Tribunal knowing you're hunting them, but I believe they probably know already. They've sent men here. Surely they saw you and Lyon arrive and reported back . . ."

"No one who was sent by the Tribunal has returned to report to anyone," Lyon explained.

"But how . . ."

"Caine took care of them."

Jade's eyes widened over Lyon's statement. He sounded so certain. She turned to look at Caine. "How did you take care of them?"

Caine shook his head at Lyon when he thought his friend might explain. "You don't need to know," he told Jade.

"You didn't kill them, did you?" she whispered.

She looked frightened.

"No."

Jade nodded, then turned to look at Lyon again. She noticed his exasperated expression but decided to ignore it. "He didn't kill them," she announced. "Caine doesn't do that sort of thing any longer. He's retired."

She seemed to want Lyon's agreement. He nodded, then knew his guess had been correct when she smiled at him.

"Jade?" Colin asked, drawing her attention. "You can stay with Christina and Lyon when you reach London. Caine will stay in his town house, of course . . ."

"No," Caine interrupted. "She stays with me."

"Think of the scandal," Colin argued.

"It's almost summer, Colin," Caine countered. "Most of the *ton* is away from London now."

"It only takes one witness," Colin muttered.

"I've said no, Colin. She stays with me."

His hard voice didn't suggest his brother continue the argument. Colin sighed, then reluctantly nodded agreement.

Jade wasn't certain she understood. "What did you mean by one witness?"

Colin explained. Jade looked appalled by the time he'd finished telling her the damage that could be done by one malicious gossiper. Sterns sat down next to Jade, patted her hand, and said, "Do look on the bright side, mi'lady. Mi'lord won't have to post it in the dailies now."

She turned to glare him into silence. Sterns couldn't be intimidated, though. He squeezed her hand. "Do not fret, dear lady. It has all been arranged."

She didn't know what he was talking about but his grin suggested he was up to something. Sterns turned her attention, however, by arrogantly motioning to his empty tea cup. She immediately went to fetch a fresh urn.

As soon as she'd left the room, Sterns turned to Caine. "Your guests should be arriving in half an hour's time."

"Guests? We can't be having any bloody guests," Colin bellowed.

Nathan nodded. "Damned right we can't. Caine, are you out of your mind to invite . . ."

Caine was staring at Sterns. "I didn't invite anyone," he said. A hint of a smile turned his expression. "Why don't you tell us who these guests are, Sterns?"

Everyone was staring at the elderly man as though he'd just grown another head. "I have taken the liberty of inviting your parents, Jade's uncle and cohorts, and one additional guest."

"What the hell for?" Nathan demanded.

Sterns turned to smile at him. "The ceremony, of course."

Everyone turned to look at Caine. His expression didn't tell them anything.

"The license, Sterns?" Caine asked in a blasé tone of voice.

"Secured the day after you signed the request," Sterns answered.

"Isn't this man your butler, Caine?" Sir Richards asked.

Caine wasn't given time to answer that question, for Nathan blurted out, "She'll argue fierce."

Colin agreed. "I don't think Jade has come to terms with her future just yet."

"I'll persuade her," Caine announced. He leaned back in his chair and smiled at his butler. "You've done well, Sterns. I commend you."

"Of course I've done well," Sterns agreed. "I've seen to everything," he boasted.

"Oh?" Nathan asked. "Then tell us how Caine's going to convince Jade?"

In answer to that question, Sterns removed the empty pistol he'd concealed in his waistband. He dropped the weapon in the center of the table.

Everyone stared at the pistol until Sterns broke the silence again. He addressed his remarks to Richards. "I believe I overheard you suggesting the pistol be aimed at Lady Jade's shoulders, or was I mistaken?"

The laughter was deafening. Jade stood at the door, the urn in her hands while she waited for the men to calm down.

She then poured Sterns his tea, put the urn on the sideboard, and returned to her seat. She noticed the pistol in the center of the table, but when she asked what it was doing there, she couldn't get a decent answer. The men had all started laughing again.

No one would explain. Jade guessed someone had told a bawdy jest and they were too embarrassed to share it with her.

Jade was ready to return to their plans. Caine surprised her by suggesting she return to her room.

"Why?" she asked. "I thought we were going . . ."

"You need to pack your things," Caine said.

Jade nodded. "You just want to tell more of your jests," she announced before she took her leave.

They were all smiling at her like happy thieves looking over their booty. She didn't know what to make of that. The two guards were waiting for her in the foyer. They helped her carry the gowns Sterns had placed in Caine's wardrobe down to her chambers, then waited outside in the hall while she packed.

When she was finished with her task, she sat down by the window and began reading the book she'd only half finished two nights ago.

A short time later, there was a timid knock on the door. Jade closed her book and stood up just as Black Harry came into the room.

She was clearly astonished to see him. Her uncle was carrying a dozen long-stemmed white roses. "These are for you, girl," he announced as he shoved the bouquet into her arms.

"Thank you, Uncle," she replied. "But what are you doing here? I thought you were going to wait for me at the cottage?"

Harry kissed her on the top of her head. "You look fit,

Pagan," he muttered, completely ignoring her question. "Caine should be wearing my clothes this proud day."

"Why should Caine wear your clothes?" she asked, thoroughly confused now. She'd never seen her uncle act so nervous. He looked terribly worried, too.

"Because my shirt is the very color of your pretty gown," Harry explained.

"But what does . . ."

"I'll be telling it in my own good time," Harry blurted out. He hugged her close, squishing the flowers in the process, then stepped back. "Caine asked me if he could wed you, girl."

Harry took another precautionary step back after making his announcement, fully expecting an explosion. He got a dainty shrug instead. He noticed, though, that she was gripping the flowers tightly. "Watch for thorns, girl," he ordered.

"What did you tell him, Uncle?" she asked.

"He asked me real proper," Harry rushed out. "I could have had him down on one knee," he added with a nod. "He said he would, if it be needed to win my permission. He said it loud and clear right in front of me men, he did."

"But what did you tell him?" she asked again.

"I said yes."

He took another hasty step back after telling her that. She shrugged again, then walked over to the side of the bed and sat down. She put the bouquet of roses on the coverlet beside her.

"Why aren't you getting your temper up, girl?" Harry asked. He rubbed his jaw while he studied her. "Caine said you might be resistant to the notion. Ain't you angry?"

"No."

"Then what is it?" he demanded. He clasped his hands behind his back while he tried to guess her reasons. "You care for this man, don't you?"

"I do."

315

"Well then?" he prodded.

"I'm afraid, Uncle."

Her voice had been a bare whisper. Harry heard her but was so astonished by her admission, he didn't know what to say. "You're not," he stammered.

"I am."

He shook his head. "You ain't never been afraid of anything before." His voice was gruff with affection. He went to the bed, sat down beside her on top of the flowers, and awkwardly put his arm around her shoulders. "What's different now?"

Oh, yes, she wanted to shout, I've been afraid before . . . so many times, so many near mishaps, she'd lost count. She couldn't tell him, of course, for if she did, he'd think he'd failed her.

"It's different because I'll have to give up my work," she said instead.

"You know it's time, what with me retiring and all," he countered. "I've hid it from me men, girl, but my eyes, well, I ain't seeing as proper as I used to. They'll balk at following a blind pirate."

"Then who will they follow?" she asked.

"Nathan."

"Nathan?"

"He wants the *Emerald*. It belonged to his father, after all, and he has that little business to take care of. He'll make a fine pirate, girl. He's learned how to be real mean."

"Yes, he would make a good pirate," she admitted. "But Uncle Harry, I can't be the kind of woman Caine wants."

"You are the woman he wants."

"I'll make so many mistakes," she whispered. She was on the verge of tears and was valiantly trying to keep her emotions controlled for Harry's sake. "I don't know how to do all the things a proper wife should know how to do. I'm no good with a needle, Harry."

"Aye, you're not," Harry admitted bleakly, remembering the time she tried to mend his sock and stitched it to her gown.

"I can't dance," she added. She looked so forlorn when she'd made that confession, Harry threw his arm around her shoulder and hugged her. "All the fine ladies of the *ton* know how to dance," she ended on a wail.

"You'll learn," Harry predicted. "If you want to learn."

"Oh, yes," she admitted in a rush. "I've always wanted . . ."

Now she sounded wistful. Harry didn't know what was going on inside her mind. "What?" he asked. "What have you always wanted?"

"To belong."

The look on his face indicated he didn't understand what she was talking about.

"Are you wishing now I'd given you to Lady Briars? She would have taken you, girl. Why, she fought me something fierce for you, too. She's the reason we snuck off real quiet-like right after your father's funeral. I guessed she'd come back with the authorities and try and steal you away from me. I weren't your legal guardian, if you'll remember. Still, your papa wanted you to get away from England."

"You kept your word to my father," she interjected. "You were very honorable."

"But are you wishing now I wasn't so honorable back then?"

She shook her head. For the first time in all their days together, she was seeing Harry's vulnerability. "I cannot imagine my life without you, Harry. I would never wish that things had been different. You loved me as though I were your very own daughter."

Harry's arm dropped to his side. He looked dejected. She put her arm around his shoulders, trying now to comfort him. "Uncle, Lady Briars would have taught me all the rules, yes, but she couldn't have loved me the way you did. Besides, you taught me far more important rules. You taught me how to survive."

Harry was quick to perk up. "I did," he admitted with a grin. "You had the makings though. I've never seen such a natural thief or a born liar in all my days. I'm right proud of you, girl."

"Thank you, Uncle," she replied, blushing over his praise. Harry wasn't one to give idle compliments and she knew he spoke from his heart.

His expression soured, however, when he returned to her initial remark. "Yet you didn't think you belonged? You did say you wanted to belong, girl."

"I meant to be a proper wife," she lied. "That's what I meant by belonging now."

"You weren't speaking plain enough, girl," Harry announced. He looked relieved. "As for me, I've always wanted to be a grandpapa."

She started to blush. "I don't know how to have babies either," she wailed.

Harry had meant to lighten her mood. He realized he'd taken the wrong approach. "Hell, no woman knows how until the time comes, girl. Tell me this. Do you love Caine? He says you do."

She skirted his question. "What if he gets tired of me? He'll leave me then, Harry," she whispered. "I know he will."

"He won't."

"He needs time to realize . . ." She paused in midsentence. "That's it, Harry. If the courtship is long enough, perhaps he'll realize he's made a mistake." She smiled then. "And during that time, in case he isn't making a mistake, I could try to learn all that would be required of me. Yes, Uncle, that's it. Caine's being very honorable now, trying to do the right thing . . ."

"Well, now, girl," Harry interrupted. "About this lengthy courtship plan . . ."

"Oh, Harry, that is the only answer," she interrupted. "I'll insist on a year. I'll wager he'll agree right off."

She was so pleased with her decision, she rushed out of the room. Harry adjusted his ill-fitting spectacles on the bridge of his nose, grabbed the bouquet and tucked it under his arm, and chased after her.

"Wait up," he bellowed.

"I must talk to Caine at once," she called over her shoulder. "I'm certain he's going to agree."

"I'm just as certain he ain't going to agree," Harry muttered. "Girl, hold fast. There's still a bit of the telling I have to do."

She'd already reached the foyer by the time Harry reached the landing above. "They're in the drawing room," her uncle shouted as he lumbered down the stairs.

Jade came to an abrupt stop when she opened the doors and saw the gathering. Harry caught up with her and forced her hand on his arm. "We're doing this proper, girl," he whispered.

"Why are all these people here?" she asked. She looked at the group, recognized everyone but the short, partially bald-headed man standing by the French doors. He held a book in his hand and was in deep conversation with the Duke and Duchess of Williamshire.

Caine was standing by the hearth, talking to Lyon. He must have sensed her presence, for he suddenly turned in midsentence and looked at her.

His expression was solemn.

He knew at once by her puzzled expression she didn't understand what was going on. Caine braced himself for the fireworks he was sure were about to erupt, then walked over to face Jade.

"I ain't had time to finish explaining," Harry said.

"I can see you haven't," Caine interjected. "Jade, sweet, we're going . . ."

"I'll be telling it," Harry insisted.

He clasped Jade's hand flat on his arm so her nails wouldn't do injury, then said, "There ain't going to be a year's courtship, girl."

She continued to stare up at him with that innocent, angelic gaze. Harry tightened his hold on her hand. "But there's going to be a wedding."

She was beginning to understand, Harry guessed, when he noticed her eyes were turning the color of emeralds again.

She was trying to tug her hand away. Harry held tight. "When is this wedding?" she asked in a hoarse whisper.

Harry grimaced before answering. "Now."

She opened her mouth to shout her denial, but Caine moved closer, blocking her view from the audience. "We can do this the easy way, Jade, or the hard way. You call it."

She shut her mouth and glared up at him. Caine could see how frightened she was. She was in a near panic. She was actually shaking. "The easy way is for you to walk over to the minister and recite your vows."

"And the hard way?" Jade asked.

"I drag you over there by your hair," Caine told her. He made sure he looked as if he were up to that task, too. "Either way, I win. We are getting married."

"Caine . . ."

The fear in her voice tore at his heart. "Decide," he ordered, his voice hard. "Easy or hard?"

"I won't let you leave me," she whispered. "I won't! I'll leave you first."

"What are you stammering about, girl?" Harry asked.

"Jade? Which is it?" Caine demanded again, ignoring both her protest and Harry's interference.

Her shoulders sagged. "Easy."

He nodded.

"I'll be walking her over to the preacher man," Harry announced. "Nathan," he called out. "You can trail behind."

"In just a minute," Caine ordered.

While Jade stood there trembling with panic and Harry stood there giving the Duchess downright lecherous looks, Caine went over to the minister and spoke to him. When he was finished, he handed a piece of paper to the man.

All was finally ready. Colin stood up at his brother's side, supported by Caine's arm. Jade stood beside Caine. Harry had to support her.

Jade repeated her vows first, a breach from tradition Caine had insisted upon. He stared at his bride while he repeated each of his vows. He let her keep her gaze downcast until he reached the end of the litany. Then he tilted her chin up and forced her to look at him.

She looked so scared, so vulnerable. Her eyes glistened with tears. He loved her so much. He wanted to give her the world. But first he had to gain her trust in him.

The minister closed his book, opened the sheet of paper in his hand, and began to read. "Do you promise to stay with your wife for as long as you shall live? Do you give your word before God and these witnesses that you will never leave her until death do you part?"

Her eyes had widened during the minister's questions. She turned and saw the paper he was holding.

"I do," Caine whispered when Jade turned back to him. "And now the last," Caine directed the minister.

"This is highly irregular," the minister whispered. He turned to address Jade. "And do you promise to tell your husband you love him before this day is out?"

Her smile was radiant. "I do," she promised.

"You may kiss the bride," the minister announced.

Caine happily obliged. When he lifted his head, he said, "You're mine now."

He pulled her into his arms and hugged her tight. "I never make the same mistake twice, sweetheart," he whispered.

"I don't understand, Caine," she replied. She was still on the verge of tears and was desperately trying to maintain her composure. "Then why didn't you have the minister make me promise not to leave you? Don't you believe I'd honor my vows?"

"Once you give your word, I know you won't break it," he answered her. "But you have to give it freely. When you're ready, you'll tell me."

He wasn't given any more time to talk to her, for the crowd of well-wishers moved in on them to offer their congratulations.

Harry stood in the corner with his men, dabbing at his eyes with the edge of his sash. Caine's mother seemed genuinely happy to have Jade in the family. Of course she didn't know her new daughter-in-law was a common thief, Jade reminded herself.

"Will your uncle be visiting you often?" Gweneth asked after giving Harry a quick glance.

"He lives a fair distance from England," Jade explained. "He'll probably come just once a year."

Caine heard the last of Jade's explanation, saw his mother's quick relief, and started to laugh. "My mother's a little nervous around your uncle," he said.

"Oh, you shouldn't be," Jade countered. "Harry is really a very kind man. Perhaps if you got to know him better . . ."

Caine's mother looked absolutely appalled by that suggestion. Jade didn't know what to make of that. "That was Harry's idea a while back," Caine explained. "He wanted to get to know my mother a whole lot better."

Since Jade hadn't witnessed Harry trying to drag the Duchess out the front door, she didn't understand why his mother was looking so horrified. She didn't understand Caine's amusement, either.

"Now, son, this isn't the time . . ."

"You called him son," Jade blurted out. "And you called her mother, didn't you?"

"He is my son," Gweneth announced. "What else would I call him, dear? I have his permission."

Jade was so pleased, she couldn't quit smiling. "Oh, I misunderstood," she whispered. "I thought he only called you madam, and that you never, ever called him son. I wanted him to belong . . . yes, I was mistaken."

Neither Caine nor his mother set her straight. They smiled at each other.

"Where's Henry?" Gweneth suddenly asked. "Harry's coming over here."

The Duchess picked up her skirts and went running toward her husband before Caine or Jade could stop her.

"You were worried I didn't belong?" he whispered.

She looked embarrassed. "Everyone should belong to someone, Caine, even you."

Harry shoved the bouquet of roses in her hands. "These will be the last roses Jimbo's going to fetch for you, girl, so you might as well enjoy them." He thought his announcement might have sounded surly, so he gave her a kiss on her forehead. Then he turned to Caine. "I need to give you the telling about the fire we got planned for the ship," he said. "The painting should be done by tomorrow."

"If you'll excuse me, I want to talk to Nathan," Jade said. She noticed her brother standing all alone on the terrace.

Caine listened to Harry as he outlined his plans, but he kept his gaze directed on his bride all the while. Jade faced her brother and spoke to him a long time. Nathan nodded several times. His expression was serious. He looked startled, too, when Jade pulled one of the roses from her cluster and held it out to him.

He shook his head. She nodded.

And then he smiled at his sister, accepted the rose, and pulled her into his arms.

For the first time since Caine had met Nathan, he was seeing the real man. He was completely unguarded now. The look on his face as he held his sister close was filled with love.

Caine didn't intrude. He waited until Jade moved away from Nathan and walked back to his side.

Harry and his men were all watching Nathan now. When Jade's brother lifted the rose in the air, a resounding cheer went up. The men immediately went to Nathan. Both Jimbo and Matthew pounded him on his back.

"What is that all about?" Caine asked Jade. He put his arm around her and pulled her into his side.

"I gave Nathan a wedding present," she told him.

Her eyes sparkled with merriment. He was sidetracked by the sudden desire to kiss her. "Well?" she asked when he just stared down at her so intently. "Don't you want to know what I gave him?"

"A rose," he whispered. He leaned down and kissed her brow. "Love, let's go upstairs for a few minutes."

The urgency in his voice, added to the look on his face, left her breathless. "We can't," she whispered. "We have guests. And we have to go to London," she added with a nod.

Caine let out a long sigh. "Then quit looking at me like that."

"Like what?"

"Like you want to go upstairs, too," he growled.

She smiled. "But I do want to go upstairs."

He kissed her then, just the way he wanted to, using his tongue in erotic love play, pretending for just a moment that they were really all alone.

She was as limp as lettuce when he lifted his head back. Lord, how he loved the way she responded to him.

324

He remembered the promise she'd given the minister then. "Jade, wasn't there something you wanted to say to me?" he gently prodded when her glazed expression began to fade.

"Yes," she whispered. "I wanted to tell you I gave Nathan a white rose."

She looked so sincere, he knew she wasn't jesting with him. He decided then he'd have to wait until they were alone before nagging her into admitting she loved him. Damn, he needed to hear her say the words.

"Do you understand the significance, Caine?"

He shook his head. "I gave him my name," she explained.

He still didn't understand. "He's going to look damned silly answering to your name, sweetheart."

"Pagan."

"What?"

She nodded when he looked as if he wanted to argue with her. "Nathan's going to be Pagan now. It was my gift to him."

She looked so pleased with herself, he felt guilty for arguing. "Jade, Pagan has to die, remember?"

"Just for a little while," she replied. "The men have a new leader, Caine, Nathan wants the *Emerald*. He has business to take care of."

"What business?"

"He has to fetch his bride."

That statement did get a reaction. Caine was stunned. "Nathan's married?"

"Since he was fourteen," she returned. "By the King's command."

"Where's his wife?" Caine asked.

She laughed, delighted by his astonishment. "That's the business he has to attend to, Caine."

He started to laugh. "Do you mean to tell me Nathan lost his wife?"

"Not exactly," she answered. "She ran away from him. Now can you understand why he's so cranky?"

Caine nodded. "Sweetheart, how many other secrets have you still to share with me?"

She wasn't given time to mull that question over. Sir Richards interrupted with the reminder that it was time they left for London.

"Jade, you'd better change into your riding garments," Caine instructed. "We won't be taking the carriage."

She nodded, quickly said her farewells, and went upstairs to change. Sterns carried her satchel downstairs to give to the stablemaster so he could secure it on the back of her horse.

Caine was just putting his jacket on when she walked into his room. He'd already changed into snug-fitting fawn-colored britches and dark brown Hessian boots. He wore the same white shirt but had removed the cravat.

"I'm ready," she called out from the doorway to get his attention.

"It's a hell of a way to begin our marriage," Caine muttered.

"We could have waited," she replied.

He shook his head. "No, we couldn't have waited."

"Caine? Why couldn't we have taken the carriage?"

"We're taking the back way, through the woods, starting out in the opposite direction, of course, and then circling. We're going to sneak up on London, sweet."

She smiled. "Just like McKindry," she announced.

Caine slipped the long knife into one boot, his attention turned to his task, and asked, "Who's McKindry?"

"The man who used the whip on me," Jade answered. "Don't forget your pistol, Caine."

"I won't," he answered. He turned to look at her. "McKindry's the bastard who marked you?" he demanded.

"Don't look so angry, Caine, it was a long time ago."

GUARDIAN ANGEL

"How long ago?"

"Oh, I was eight, perhaps nine years old at the time. Harry took care of McKindry. And it was a very good lesson for me," she added when his expression turned murderous.

"What lesson?"

"McKindry sneaked up behind me," she explained. "After that, every time Harry left me, his very last words were, always, remember McKindry. It was a reminder, you see, that I must always be on my guard."

What the hell kind of a childhood was that? he asked himself. Caine kept his anger hidden. "And how often did Harry leave you?" he asked, his tone mild. He even turned toward the wardrobe so she wouldn't see his expression.

"Oh, all the time," she answered. "Until I was old enough to help, of course. Then I went with him. Caine, you'd really better hurry. Sir Richards will be pacing. I'll go downstairs . . ."

"Come here, Jade."

His voice was a hoarse whisper, his expression solemn. Jade was thoroughly confused by his behavior. She walked over to stand in front of him.

"Yes, Caine?" she asked.

"I want you to remember something else besides McKindry," he said.

"What?"

"I love you."

"I could never forget you love me." She reached up and gently brushed her fingertips down his cheek.

She tried to kiss him then, but he shook his head. "I also want you to remember something else," he whispered. "Remember your promise to me that you're never, ever going on the ocean again."

Her eyes widened. "But I didn't promise you . . ."

"Promise me now, then," he ordered.

"I promise."

327

She was looking quite stunned. Caine was satisfied by that reaction. "I'll tell Harry he'll have to come to England if he wants to see you. We won't be going to him. I'll also tell him I made you promise me. He won't argue over that."

"How long have you known, Caine?" she asked.

"That you're afraid of the water?"

She timidly nodded. "Since the first nightmare," he explained. He took her back into his arms. "You've been worried, haven't you?"

"A little," she whispered. Then she shook her head. "No, Caine, I wasn't just a little worried. I was terrified. Harry wouldn't understand."

A long ponderous moment passed before she whispered, "Caine, do you think me a coward for being afraid of the water?"

"Do you have to ask me that question?" he replied. "Don't you already know the answer, Jade?"

She smiled then. "No, you don't believe I'm a coward. I'm sorry for insulting you by asking. I'm just not use to admitting . . ."

"Sweetheart, Poseidon wouldn't go back in the water if he'd been through your terror."

She started to laugh and cry at the same time. She was so relieved he'd just taken her burden away, she felt positively light-headed. "Nathan's stronger than I am," she said then. "He's going on the waters again."

"Nathan isn't human, love, so he doesn't count," Caine replied.

"Oh, he's human, all right. If I tell you a secret, will you keep it? You won't torment my brother with . . ."

"I promise."

"Nathan gets seasick."

Caine laughed. "He's going to make a hell of a pirate then," he drawled out.

"I love you."

She'd blurted out her confession, her face hidden in the lapels of his jacket.

He quit laughing. "Did you say something?" he asked, pretending he hadn't heard her. He nudged her chin up and stared down into her eyes.

It took her a long time to get the words out again, and every ounce of courage she possessed. Her throat tightened up, her heart hammered a wild beat, and her stomach felt like it was tying itself in knots.

She wouldn't have been able to tell him if he hadn't helped. The look on his face was so filled with love, it made some of the panic ebb away. The dimple did the rest. "I love you."

He felt relieved, until she burst into tears again. "Was that so difficult? To tell me you loved me?"

"It was," she whispered while he kissed her tears away. "I'm not at all used to telling what's in my heart. I don't believe I like it at all."

He would have laughed if she hadn't sounded so damned vulnerable. He kissed her instead.

"You didn't like making love the first time, either," he reminded her before kissing her sweet mouth once again.

Both of them were shaking when they drew apart. He would have dragged her over to the bed if Sir Richards' bellow hadn't interrupted them.

They sighed in unison. "Come along, sweetheart. It's time to go."

He started out the doorway, tugging her by her hand.

Lyons and Richards were waiting for them in the foyer. The time for gaiety was quickly put aside. They walked in silence through the backwoods where Matthew and Jimbo waited with their horses.

Caine took the lead. Jade was next in line, with Lyon responsible for protecting her back. Sir Richards trailed last.

Caine was cautious to the point of fanaticism. The only

time they stopped to rest was when he backtracked on his own to make certain they weren't being followed. Still, Jade didn't mind the inconvenience. She was comforted by his precautions.

Each time Caine left, Lyon stayed by her side. And every time he talked to her, the topic was always about his file. It was apparent he was concerned about someone else getting hold of it.

She suggested he steal his own file so that he could gain peace of mind. Lyon shook his head. He tried not to smile as he explained it wouldn't be ethical. There might also come a time, he added, when someone would question one of his missions. The file couldn't be destroyed or stolen, for the truth was his protection.

Jade didn't argue with him, but she decided the file would be much better protected in his home than in the War Office. She made the decision to take care of that little chore on her own.

By the time they reached the outskirts of London proper, the sun was setting. Jade was exhausted from the long ride. She didn't protest when Caine took her into his lap. She rode the rest of the distance with his arms wrapped around her.

And all the while she kept thinking to herself that Caine was such a solid, reliable man. A woman could depend on him.

She was just drifting off to sleep when they reached his town house. Caine went inside first, curtly dismissed his servants for the night, then took Jade into the library. The scent of smoke was still in the air, and most of the walls were still blackened from the fire, but the servants had done a good job righting the damage. The town house was sound enough to live in.

When Lyon and Richards joined Jade and Caine, Richards said, "We'll leave as soon as it goes completely dark."

"It would be safer if we waited until midnight," Jade interjected. "There are two guards until then."

"And what happens at midnight?" Sir Richards asked.

"Only one guard stays during the blackest hours of the night," she explained. "His name is Peter Kently and he's always half-sotted by the time he takes over the watch. Now, if we wait until half past, he'll have finished the last of his bottle, and he should be fast asleep."

Sir Richards was staring at her with his mouth gaping wide. "How did you . . . ?"

"Sir, one must always be prepared for any eventuality if one is going to be successful," she instructed.

While Sir Richards sputtered about the lack of morals in government workers, Lyon asked Jade about the locks. "The back door is a piece of work," she announced. Her eyes sparkled with merriment, for she was obviously warming to her topic.

"A piece of work?" Caine asked, smiling over her enthusiasm.

"Difficult," she qualified.

Sir Richards perked up considerably. "Well, thank God something's up to snuff."

She gave him a sympathetic look. "Difficult, Sir Richards, but not impossible. I did get inside, if you'll remember."

He looked so crestfallen, she hastened to add, "It took quite a long while that first time. Double locks are rather tricky."

"But not impossible," Lyon interjected. "Jade? Just how long did it take you that first time?"

"Oh, five . . . perhaps as many as six minutes."

Richards hid his face in his hands. Jade tried to comfort him. "There, there, Sir Richards. It isn't as bad as all that. Why, it took me almost an hour to get inside the inner sanctuary where the sealed files are kept."

The director didn't look as if he wanted to be comforted

now. Jade left the men to their plans and went to the kitchens to find something to eat. She returned to the library with an assortment of food. They shared apples, cheese, cold mutton, day-old bread, and dark brown ale. Jade took her boots off, tucked her feet up under her, and fell asleep in the chair.

The men kept their voices low while they talked about the Tribunal. When Jade awakened several hours later, she saw Caine was rereading the letters she'd copied.

He had a puzzled look on his face, his concentration absolute, and when he suddenly smiled and leaned back in his chair, she thought he might have sorted through whatever problem he'd been contemplating.

"Have you come to any conclusions, Caine?" she asked.

"I'm getting there," Caine answered, sounding positively cheerful.

"You're being logical and methodical, aren't you?" she asked.

"Yes," he answered. "We take this one step at a time, Jade."

"He's a very logical man," she told Lyon and Sir Richards. Caine thought she sounded like she was making an excuse for a sorry flaw. "He cannot help himself," she added. "He's very trusting, too."

"Trusting?" Lyon snorted with laughter. "You can't be serious, Jade. Caine is one of the most cynical men in England."

"A trait I developed by running with you," Caine drawled out.

Jade was amazed by Lyon's comments. He sounded so certain. Sir Richards was nodding too. She turned to smile at Caine, then said, "I'm honored then that you trust me."

"Just as much as you trust me, sweetheart," he answered.

She frowned at him. "And just what is that supposed to mean?" she asked. "Are you being insulting?"

He grinned. Jade turned to Lyon. "Do you have any idea how maddening it is to be married to someone who's so damned logical all the time?"

Caine answered her. "I haven't the faintest idea."

She decided to quit the topic. She eased her feet to the floor, grimacing over the discomfort that movement caused her backside. If she'd been all alone, she would have let out a loud, unladylike groan. "I'm not at all accustomed to riding for such long hours," she admitted.

"You did well today," Lyon praised. He turned to look at Caine. "When this is finished, Christina and I will give a reception for the two of you."

"That would be fine," Caine interjected. "You know, Lyon, Jade and Christina are really quite alike."

"Is she a thief then?" Jade asked before she could stop herself. Her voice was filled with enthusiasm. "We got along quite well right from the start. No wonder . . ."

"Sorry to disappoint you, love, but Christina isn't a thief," Caine said.

She looked crestfallen. Lyon laughed. "Christina isn't very logical either, Jade. She comes from a rather unusual family. She could teach you all sorts of things."

"God help us," Caine interjected, for he was very familiar with Lady Christina's unusual background. Lyon's wife had been raised in the wilderness of the Americas by one of the Dakota tribes.

Jade misunderstood Caine's reaction. "I'm certain I'm a quick study, Caine. If I apply myself, I could learn everything Christina would like to teach me."

She didn't give him time to argue with her. "I'm going to change my clothes. We must leave soon."

Caine, she noticed, was glaring at Lyon when she took her leave. Jade quickly changed into her black gown. She carried a cloak with her. The hood would shield her brightly colored hair in the lamplight.

They walked most of the way to the War Office. The building was across town, but they used the hired hack for only half the distance. When they reached the alley behind the building, Jade moved to Caine's side. She took hold of his hand while she stared up at the top floor of the brick structure.

"Something's wrong, Caine."

"What?" Sir Richards asked from behind her back. "Your instincts, my dear, or . . ."

"There's a light in the third window on the right," she explained. "It shouldn't be showing any light."

"Perhaps the guard at the entrance . . ."

"The entrance is on the other side," Jade interrupted. "That light comes from the inner office."

Caine turned to Lyon. "If someone's in there going through the files, he'll use the back door when he leaves."

"Let him pass when he does," Sir Richards directed. "I'll follow him."

"Do you want me to go with you?" Lyon asked. "If there's more than one . . ."

Richards shook his head. "I'll see who the leader is and follow that bloke. You're needed here. We'll meet back at Caine's, no matter what the hour."

They moved to the shadows a fair distance from the back door, then patiently waited. Caine put his arm around Jade's shoulders and held her close.

"You don't want me here with you, do you, Caine?" she whispered when his grip became almost painful.

"No, I don't want you to be here," he answered. "Jade, if there's trouble inside . . ."

"Lyon will take care of it," she interjected before he could finish his thought. "If there's any killing done, God forbid, then Lyon should be the one doing it. He's used to it."

Lyon heard her announcement and raised an eyebrow in reaction. He wondered if she'd read Caine's file all the way through. It was a fact that Caine was every bit as capable as Lyon was.

Their whispers stopped as soon as the back door squeaked open. While they watched, two men scurried outside. In the moonlight, Jade could see their faces clearly. She couldn't contain her gasp. Caine clamped his hand over her mouth.

The second man out turned and locked the door. How had he secured the keys? Jade wondered. She held her silence until the men had turned the corner. Sir Richards left to follow them.

Then she turned to Caine. "The security is deplorable," she whispered.

"Yes," he agreed. "You recognized them, didn't you?"

She nodded. "They are two of the three men who waylaid Nathan's carriage. The bigger of the two is the one who hit me on the head."

The look on his face frightened her. She thought he might very well go after the two men then and there. "Caine, you must be logical now, please. You can't chase after them."

He looked exasperated with her. "I'll wait," he said. "But when this is over . . ."

He didn't finish that statement, but took hold of her hand and led her over to the door. With the special tool Harry had given her for her tenth birthday, she was able to get the lock undone in quick time. The second latch took only a few minutes longer.

Lyon went inside first. Jade followed, with Caine taking up the rear. She nudged Lyon out of the way and took the lead. They went up to the third floor by way of the back steps. Jade remembered the squeak in the fourth rail on the second staircase, motioned for both men to avoid it, then felt Lyon's arms on her waist. He lifted her over the step and put her down. She turned to smile her appreciation before continuing on.

The guard wasn't sleeping at his post behind the desk in

the outer office. He was dead. Jade saw the handle of the knife protruding from his shoulders. She took a quick step back. Caine's hand immediately covered her mouth again. He must have thought she was going to cry out.

Through the glass window of the door, they could see two shadows. Caine pulled Jade over into the corner, motioned for her to stay there, and then followed Lyon into the inner office. She was impressed by their silence. The two of them would make proper thieves, she decided.

They were taking too long, though. She stood there with her back pressed against the cold wall, wringing her hands together while she waited. If anything happened to Caine, she didn't know what she would do. Until she had to leave him, of course, she qualified in her mind . . . God help her, she needed him.

She didn't realize her eyes were squeezed shut until she felt Caine's hand on her shoulder. "Come on, we're alone now."

"What about the men inside?" she whispered. "And for heaven's sake, lower your voice. We're at work now."

He didn't answer her. Jade followed Caine inside the sanctuary, tossed her cloak on the nearest desk while Lyon added another candle to the lights.

She noticed the two men on the floor in the corner then. She couldn't contain her gasp. "Are they dead?" she asked.

She couldn't quit staring at the bodies sprawled atop each other. Caine moved to block her view. "No," he said.

Her relief was obvious. "Jade, didn't any of your men ever have to . . ."

"They most certainly did not," she interrupted. "I would have had their hides. Killing wasn't allowed. Now quit talking so much, Caine. You must hurry. If they wake up, they'll shout an alarm."

"They won't wake up for a long while," Caine said. He pulled out a chair, gently pushed her down into it. "You rest. This is going to take some time."

"Rest while I'm at work? Never." She sounded appalled by his suggestion.

"Terrance's file is missing," Lyon announced, drawing their attention. He was bent over the file drawer, smiling broadly. "Interesting, wouldn't you say?"

"The lamplighters probably think it's very interesting, too," Jade snapped. "Do keep your voice down, Lyon."

"Yes, it is interesting," Caine said quietly in answer to Lyon's remark.

"Then we can leave now?" Jade asked, glancing over at the two men on the floor once again.

"Jade, why are you so nervous?" Caine asked. "You've been in and out of this room several times before," he reminded her.

"I was working with professionals then," she announced.

Lyon and Caine shared a smile. "She's worried about us," Lyon said.

"No," Caine countered. "That would be insulting if she . . ."

She couldn't believe he was daring to tease her now. "Of course, I'm worried. You two aren't even proper apprentices. Even an imbecile would know that now isn't the time for idle chitchat. Do get on with it."

"She is insulting us," Lyon drawled out. He started to laugh, but her glare changed his mind.

The men turned serious then. They labored over certain files for two long hours. Jade didn't interrupt. She didn't dare rest, either, for she was determined to keep on her guard in case of intruders.

"All right, we're finished," Caine said as he slammed the last file shut.

Jade stood up and walked over to the drawer. She took the folder from Caine, turned, and put it back in its proper place. Her back was to the men and it didn't take her any time at all to remove both Caine's and Lyon's fat files.

She turned around, determined to have it out with them

then and there if they offered one word of protest. Luck was on her side, however, for the men had already moved to the outer office.

"Aren't you going to go through their pockets?" she called out. She pointed to the sleeping men.

"We already did," Caine answered.

Jade wrapped the files in her cloak. She blew out the candles and followed the men downstairs. Since they were all alone inside the building, she guessed they didn't need to be quiet. Each was taking a turn muttering expletives. Caine's, she noticed, were every bit as colorful as Lyon's were.

"I am never taking either one of you on another raid again," she muttered. "I wouldn't be surprised if the authorities were waiting for us outside."

Neither Caine nor Lyon paid any attention to her ramblings. She soon became too weary to lecture them anyway.

Sir Richards was waiting for them in the alley. "There's a hack waiting four blocks over," he announced before he turned and took the lead.

Jade stumbled when they rounded the corner. Lyon grabbed her, lifted her into his arms. She thought he might have felt the folders when he transferred her into Caine's arms, then decided he hadn't noticed after all when he grinned down at her and turned to take up the rear guard.

She fell asleep in the vehicle with the cloak clutched to her breasts. It was such a comfort to realize she didn't have to worry. As long as Caine was nearby, she felt safe, protected. For the first time in a good long while, she didn't have to remember McKindry. Caine would keep his guard up for both of them. He'd never make a proper thief, of course, but he certainly wouldn't let the evil McKindrys of the world sneak up behind them, either.

She found herself in Caine's bed when she woke up. He was trying to pry her cloak away from her. "Are they waiting for you downstairs?" she asked in a sleepy whisper.

"Yes, they are. Sweetheart, let me help you . . ."

"I can undress myself," she said. "Do you need me . . ."

She was going to ask him if he needed her to go downstairs with him, but he interrupted her. "I'll always need you, Jade. I love you."

He leaned down and kissed her. "Go to sleep, sweetheart. I'll join you as soon as we've finished."

"I don't want to need you."

She blurted out that confession in a voice filled with panic. Caine's smile was almost sympathetic. "I know, love, but you do need me. Now go to sleep."

She didn't understand why, yet found she was comforted by his contradiction. He was so sure of himself, so confident. It was a trait she couldn't help but admire.

Jade let out a loud sigh. She was simply too tired to think about the future now. She hid the files, took her clothes off, and fell back into bed. She thought she very well might have the horrid nightmare again, then realized she wasn't dreading it as much as before.

She fell asleep hugging the promise Caine had given her. She would never have to go near the ocean again.

Caine didn't come to bed until after seven in the morning. Jade opened her eyes just long enough to watch him pull back the covers and stretch out beside her. He hauled her up against his side, his arm wrapped tightly around her waist, and was snoring like a drunk before she got settled again.

She went downstairs around noon, introduced herself to Caine's London staff, and then went into the dining room to have breakfast.

Caine suddenly appeared at the doorway, dressed only in a pair of light-colored britches. He looked exhausted, angry, too, and when he crooked his finger at her she decided not to argue.

"Come here, Jade."

"Did you get up on the wrong side of the bed, Caine?" she

asked as she walked over to face him. "Or are you always this surly when you first wake up?"

"I thought you'd left."

Her eyes widened over that confession, but she wasn't given time to think about it too much. Caine lifted her into his arms and carried her back upstairs. She realized just how furious he was when she noticed the muscle in the side of his jaw was flexing. "Caine, I didn't leave you," she whispered, stating the obvious. She reached up to caress his cheek, smiling over the stubble there. "You need a shave, husband."

"That's right, I am your husband," he grated out. He tossed her onto the bed, took his pants off, and stretched out beside her, facedown, with his arm anchored around her waist. She was fully clothed; he was stark naked.

She would have laughed over the absurdity of her circumstances if the fullness of what he'd just implied hadn't settled in her mind. How dare he not trust her? She was furious. She would have given him a good piece of her mind, too, if he hadn't looked so damned peaceful. She didn't have the heart to wake him up.

The lecture would have to wait until later. She closed her eyes, selected a book from her memory, and reread it in her mind while she patiently waited for Caine to get the rest he needed.

He didn't move until almost two that afternoon. He was in a much better frame of mind, too. He smiled at her. She glared at him.

"Why don't you trust me?" she demanded.

Caine rolled onto his back, stacked his hands behind his head, and let out a loud yawn. "Take your clothes off, sweetheart," he whispered. "Then we'll discuss this."

Her gaze moved down his body to his obvious arousal. She blushed in reaction. "I think we should discuss it now, Caine," she stammered out.

He pulled her on top of him, kissed her passionately, and

then ordered her to take her clothes off again. Odd, but she didn't mind obeying his command now. He was such a persuasive man. Demanding, too. She climaxed twice before he finally filled her with his seed.

She could barely move when he finally moved away from her. "Now what was it you wanted to discuss?"

She couldn't remember. It took them another hour to get dressed, for they kept stopping to kiss each other. It wasn't until they were on their way downstairs that Jade remembered what it was she wanted to lecture him about.

"Haven't I proven myself to you?" she asked. "You should trust me with all your heart."

"You don't trust me," he countered. "It works both ways, Jade, or not at all. You've made it clear you'll leave me at the first opportunity. Isn't that right, love?"

He paused on the bottom step and turned around to look at her. They were eye to eye now. Hers, he noticed, were cloudy with tears.

"I don't wish to talk about this now," she announced, struggling to maintain her composure. "I'm hungry and I . . ."

"It gives you the edge, doesn't it, wife?"

"I don't understand what you mean," she returned. Her voice shook. "What edge?"

"In the back of that illogical mind of yours lurks the possibility that I'll eventually leave you," he explained. "Just like Nathan and Harry did. You're still afraid."

"I'm afraid?" she stammered out.

He nodded. "You're afraid of me."

He thought she'd argue over that statement of fact. She surprised him by nodding. "Yes, you make me very afraid," she admitted. And I can tell you, sir, I don't like that feeling one little bit. It makes me . . ."

"Vulnerable?"

She nodded again. He let out a patient sigh. "All right, then. How long do you suppose it's going to take you to become unafraid?" His voice was so gentle, his expression so serious.

"How long before you get tired of me?" she asked, her fear apparent.

"Are you deliberately misunderstanding?"

"No."

"Then in answer to your absurd question, I will never get tired of you. Now tell me how long it will take you before you trust me?" he ordered again. His voice wasn't at all gentle now. It was as hard, as determined as his expression.

"I told you I loved you," she whispered.

"Yes, you did."

"I repeated the vows before you and God." Her voice had risen an octave. He could also see her panic, her insecurity.

"Well? What more do you want from me?"

She was shouting now, wringing her hands together. Caine decided she still wasn't ready to surrender whole-heartedly.

He felt like an ogre for upsetting her. "Jade . . ."

"Caine, I don't want to leave you," she blurted out. "I do trust you. Yes, I do. I know you'll keep me safe. I know you love me, but there's a part of me that still . . ." She stopped her explanation and lowered her gaze. Her shoulders slumped in dejection. "Sometimes the feelings locked inside me since I was a little girl do get in the way of being logical," she admitted a long minute later. "I suppose you're right. I'm not at all logical about this, am I?"

He pulled her into his arms and held her close. The hug was more for his benefit than hers. In truth, he couldn't stand to see the torment in her eyes.

"I want to tell you something, sweetheart. The first time you tried to leave me . . . when Harry told me you'd left, it threw me into a panic. I've never had such a god-awful feeling before, and I sure as hell hated it. Now I'm beginning to realize that you've lived with that feeling a long time, haven't you?"

She mopped her tears away with his shirt before she answered. "Perhaps."

"And so you learned how to make it completely on your own," he continued. "You've been teaching yourself not to depend on anyone else. I'm right, aren't I?"

She shrugged against him. "I don't like talking about this," she whispered, trying to sound disgruntled and not terrified. "I love you with all my heart," she added when he squeezed her. "And I know you love me now, Caine. Yes, I'm sure of that."

Neither said a word for a long while after she'd made that statement. Jade used the time to calm her racing heart. He used the silence to think of a logical way to ease her illogical fears.

"What if we make this a short period?" he suddenly blurted out.

"What?" She pulled away from him so she could see his expression. Surely he was jesting with her.

The look on his face indicated he was quite serious. "You want to make our marriage a short union? But you just told me you loved me. How can you . . ."

"No, no," he argued. "If we just make this commitment to each other for six months' time, if you can just promise me you'll stay with me for that length of time, won't some of your panic ease away?"

He sounded so enthusiastic, looked so arrogantly pleased with himself. She realized then he was quite sincere in this absurdity. "You already said you'd never leave me. Now you're telling me six months . . ."

"I won't ever leave you," he snapped, obviously irritated she wasn't embracing his plan wholeheartedly. "But you don't believe I mean what I say. Therefore, you have only to promise to give me six months, Jade."

"And what about you, husband? Does this promise hold for you as well?"

"Of course."

She threw herself back into his arms so he couldn't see her smile. She didn't want him to think she was laughing at him. Odd, too, but she suddenly felt as though a weight had been lifted from her chest. She could breathe again. The panic was gone.

"Give me your word, wife."

The command was given in a low growl. "I give it," she replied.

"No," he muttered. "It won't work. It's too short a time," he added. "Hell, if I ever forgot, you'd be gone before I . . . I want a full year, Jade. We'll start from the day we were married. I won't ever forget our anniversary."

He squeezed her shoulders when she didn't answer him quickly enough. "Well? Do you promise not to leave me for a full year?"

"I promise."

Caine was so relieved, he wanted to shout. He'd finally come up with a way to keep her happy. He'd just given her the edge he was certain she needed. "Say the words, wife," he ordered, his voice gruff. "I don't want any misunderstandings."

The man really should have become a barrister, she decided. He was so logical, so clever, too. "I'll stay with you for one year. Now you must promise me, husband."

"I won't leave you for one full year," he announced.

He tilted her chin up with his thumb. "You do believe me, don't you?" he asked.

"Yes, I do."

"And you're relieved, aren't you?"

She didn't answer him for a long minute. The truth wasn't at all slow in coming, either. It hit her like a warm bolt of sunshine, filling her heart and her illogical mind all at once. He would never leave her . . . and she could never leave him. The vulnerable childlike feelings hidden inside her for so many years of loneliness evaporated.

"Sweetheart? You are relieved, aren't you?"

"I trust you with all my heart," she whispered.

"You aren't in a panic now?"

She shook her head. "Caine, I want to tell . . ."

"I took the panic away, didn't I?"

Because he looked so supremely pleased with himself, she didn't want to lessen his arrogant satisfaction. A man had to have his pride intact, she remembered. "You have made me sort this all out in my mind," she whispered. "And yes, you have taken my panic away. Thank you, Caine."

They shared a long sweet kiss. Jade was shaking when Caine lifted his head away. He thought his kiss had caused that reaction.

"Do you want to go back upstairs, love?" he asked.

She nodded. "After you've fed me, Caine. I'm starving."

He took hold of her hand and started for the dining room.

"Do you know, husband, I have the oddest feeling now."

"And what is that?" he asked.

"I feel . . . free. Do you understand, Caine? It's as though I've just been let out of a locked room. That's ridiculous, of course."

Caine held out the chair at the table for her, then took his own. "Why is it ridiculous?"

She immediately looked disgruntled. "Because there isn't a locked room I can't get out of," she explained.

Caine ordered their breakfast, and when Anna, the servant, had left the room, he asked Jade to tell him about some of the adventures she'd had. "I want to know everything there is to know," he announced.

"You'll only get angry," she predicted.

"No, no," he argued. "I promise I won't get angry, no matter what you tell me."

"Well, I don't mean to boast," she began. "But I do seem to have a natural ability for getting in and out of tight spots. Uncle Harry says I'm a born thief and liar," she added.

"Now, sweetheart, I'm sure he didn't mean to criticize you," Caine replied.

"Well, of course not," she returned in exasperation. "Those were compliments, husband. Uncle's praise meant all the more to me because he doesn't usually give compliments to anyone. He says it isn't in his nature," she added with a smile. "Harry worries that others will find out the truth about him."

"And what might that truth be?" Caine asked. "That he's actually a little civilized after all?"

"How did you guess?"

"From the way you turned out," he explained. "If he was such a barbarian, you wouldn't have become such a lady."

She beamed with pleasure. "It is good of you to notice," she whispered. "Uncle is very intelligent."

"He's the one who taught you how to read, isn't he?"

She nodded. "It proved fortunate, too, for his eyes started failing him. At night I would read to him."

"From memory?"

"Only when there weren't any books available. Harry stole as many as he could get his hands on."

"The way he speaks," Caine interjected. "That's all part of his deception, too, isn't it?"

"Yes," she admitted. "Appearances, after all. He doesn't even use proper grammar when we're alone, fearing he'll slip up in front of his men, you see."

Caine rolled his eyes. "Your uncle became a bit of a fanatic about his position as leader, didn't he?"

"No," she argued. "You misunderstand. He enjoys the deception, Caine." She continued to talk about her uncle for another few minutes, then turned the topic to some of her most memorable escapades. Because he'd promised not to get angry, Caine hid his reaction. His hands were shaking, though, with the true need to wring good old Uncle Harry's neck, by the time she'd finished telling him about one particularly harrowing incident.

He decided he didn't want to know all about her past after all. "I think I'd better hear these stories one at a time."

"That's what I'm doing," she countered. She paused to smile at the servant when the woman placed a tray of crusty rolls in front of her, then turned back to Caine. "I am telling them one at a time."

Caine shook his head. "I mean I want you to tell me one every other month or so. A man can only take so much. I promise you I'll be thinking about the story you just told me a good long while. Hell, Jade, I can feel my hair turning gray. You could have been killed. You could have . . ."

"But you aren't getting angry," she interjected with a smile. "You did promise."

Caine leaned back in his chair. "I think we'd better change the subject. Tell me when you realized you love me," he commanded. "Did I force you?"

She started to laugh. "You can't force someone to love you," she said. "I believe, however, that when I read your file, I was already falling in love with you."

She smiled over the astonished look on his face. "It's true," she whispered.

"Jade, I'm not very proud of some of the things I had to do," he said. "You did read the entire file, didn't you?"

"I did," she answered. "You were determined, methodical too, but you weren't inhuman about it. In every accounting, you were always so . . . reliable. People depended upon you and you never let them down. I admired that quality, of course. And then I met you," she ended. "You were a little like McKindry, because you snuck up behind me and stole my heart before I even realized what was happening. Now you must tell me when you realized you loved me."

"It was during one of our many heated debates," he said.

It was her turn to look astonished. "We never debated," she said. "We shouted at each other. Those were arguments."

"Debates," he repeated. "Loud ones but debates all the same."

"Are you telling me you fell in love with my mind first?"

"No."

She laughed, delighted by his honesty.

"Shouldn't your man be here with us? It might look suspicious if he stays in the country, Caine."

"Sterns never comes to London with me," he explained. "Everyone knows that. Sterns hates London, says it's too cluttered."

"I miss him," she admitted. "He reminds me of you. Sterns is most opinionated—arrogant, too."

"No one understands why I put up with him," Caine said. "But if the truth were out, I don't understand why he puts up with me. He's been like a shield to me, especially when I was a lad. I did get into quite a bit of mischief. Sterns softened the telling, though. He pulled me out of certain death several times, too."

Caine told her a story about the time he almost drowned in a boating incident and how Sterns had saved him only to toss him right back in the waters to learn the proper way to swim. Both of them were laughing by the time Caine ended the tale, for the picture of the sour-faced butler in full clothing swimming alongside his small charge was quite amusing.

Jade was the first to grow somber. "Caine, did you and your friends come to any conclusions last night after I went to bed?"

"The man Richards followed home was Willburn. Do you remember Colin told us that Willburn was his director and how he confided in him?"

"Yes, I remember," she replied. "Nathan said he never trusted Willburn. Still, my brother doesn't trust anyone but Harry and Colin, and me, of course."

"Colin was wrong, Jade. Willburn did work for the Tribunal. He's now employed by the one remaining member."

Before she could interrupt him, he continued. "We're pretty certain William Terrance was the second man. Since he's dead, and your father too, that only leaves the third. Richards is convinced Terrance was called Prince. That leaves Ice unaccounted for."

"How will we ever find Ice? We really don't have much to go on. The letters were very sparse with personal information, Caine."

"Sure we do, sweetheart," he replied. "In one of the letters, there was mention that Ice didn't attend Oxford. Also, both Fox and Prince were surprised when they met Ice."

"How did you gather that bit of information?"

"From one of the remarks made by your father to Prince in the third . . . no, the fourth letter."

"I remember," she countered. "I just didn't think it significant."

"Richards believes Ice could very well be a foreigner."

"And you?" she asked.

"I'm not convinced. There are other important clues in those letters, Jade. I just need a little more time to put them all together."

She had complete faith in his ability to sort it all out. Once Caine put his mind to a problem, he would be able to solve it.

"Richards put a watch on Willburn. He thinks he might lead us to Ice. It's a start, but I'm not putting my money on it. We have other options, too. Now, sweetheart, I don't want you to leave this town house, no matter what the reason, all right?"

"You can't leave either," she returned. "Agreed?"

"Agreed."

"Whatever will we do to keep ourselves occupied?" she asked with as much innocence in her tone as she could manage.

"We could do a lot of reading, I suppose," he drawled out.

She stood up and went to stand behind his back. "Yes, we could read," she whispered as she wrapped her arms around his broad shoulders. Her fingers slipped inside the top of his shirt. "I could learn how to embroider," she added. "I've always wanted to learn that task." She leaned down and nibbled on his earlobe. "But do you know what I want to do most of all, husband?"

"I'm getting a fair idea," he answered, his voice husky with arousal.

"You know? Then you'll teach me?"

"Everything I know, sweetheart," he promised.

He stood up and took her into his arms. "What will we do for music?" she asked.

If he thought that an odd question, he didn't say so. "We'll make our own music," he promised. He dragged her by the hand into the foyer and started up the steps.

"How?" she asked, laughing.

"I'll hum every time you moan," he explained.

"Don't you think the drawing room will be better?" she asked.

"The bed would be more comfortable," he answered. "But if you're determined to . . ."

"Learn how to dance," she interjected. "That is what this discussion is all about, isn't it?"

She smiled ever so sweetly up at him after telling that lie, waiting for his reaction. She thought she'd bested him with her trickery. Caine, however, proved to be far more cunning than she was, more creative, too. He followed her into the drawing room, locked the doors behind him, and then proceeded to teach her how to dance.

It was a pity, but she was never going to be able to show off her new skill in public, for Caine and she would scandalize the *ton* with the erotic, absolutely sinful way he taught her how to dance. And though he was thoroughly logical in his explanation, she still refused to believe the ladies and gentlemen of the *ton* took their clothes off before they did the waltz.

Caine kept her entertained the rest of the day, but as soon as darkness fell, they had their first argument.

"What do you mean, you're leaving?" she cried when he put his jacket on. "We agreed that we wouldn't leave this town house . . ."

"I'll be careful," Caine interrupted. He kissed her on her forehead. "Lyon and Richards are waiting for me, sweet. I'm going to have to go out every night, I'm afraid, until we finish this. Now quit worrying and tell me you won't wait up for me."

"I will wait up for you," she stammered out.

"I know," he answered with a sigh. "But tell me you won't anyway."

She let him see her exasperation. "Caine, if anything happens to you, I'm going to be very angry."

"I'll be careful," he answered.

Jade chased after him to the back door. "You'll remember McKindry?"

He turned, his hand on the doorknob. "That's your lesson, sweetheart."

"Well, you can damned well learn from it, too," she muttered.

"All right," he answered, trying to placate her. "I'll remember McKindry." He turned and opened the door. "Jade?"

"Yes?"

"You will be here when I come home, won't you?"

She was amazed by his question, insulted, too, and she would have blistered him with a piece of her mind if he hadn't sounded so vulnerable. "Have I made you so insecure, then?" she asked instead.

"Answer me," he commanded.

"I'll be here when you come home."

Those parting words became their ritual. Each night, just as he was leaving, he would tell her he would remember

McKindry, and she would tell him she would be waiting for him.

During the dark hours of the night, while she waited for her husband to come home to her, she thought about his vulnerability. At first, she believed she was the cause. After all, she'd let him see her own insecurity often enough. But she sensed, too, that Caine's background was another reason for his own vulnerability. She couldn't imagine what his early life must have been like. Sir Harwick had called Caine's mother a shrew. She remembered he'd also said that the woman had tried to turn her son against his father. It couldn't have been a peaceful time for Caine.

The more she thought about it, the more convinced she became that Caine actually needed her just as much as she needed him.

That realization was a comfort.

Lady Briars sent several notes inviting Jade to visit. Caine wouldn't let her leave the town house, however, and sent word back that his wife was indisposed.

In the end, her father's dear friend came to see her. Jade's memory of the woman was hazy at best, but she felt horribly guilty about pretending to be ill when she saw how old and frail the woman was. She was still beautiful, though, with clear blue eyes and silvery gray hair. Her intellect appeared to be quite sharp, too.

Jade served tea in the drawing room, then took her place next to Caine on the settee. He seemed quite determined to participate in the women's conversation.

Both husband and wife listened to Lady Briars extend her condolences over Nathan's tragic death. Jade played the role of grieving sister well, but she hated the deception, for Lady Briars was so sincere in her sympathy.

"When I read about the tragedy in the papers, I was stunned," Lady Briars said. "I had no idea Nathan worked for the government doing such secretive work. Caine, I must tell you how sorry I was to hear your brother was also killed by that horrid pirate. I didn't know the lad, of course, but I'm certain he must have had a heart of gold."

"I never met Colin either," Jade interjected. "But Caine has told me all about him. He was a good man, Lady Briars, and he died for his country."

"How did Pagan become involved in this?" Lady Briars asked. "I'm still hazy on the details, child."

Caine answered her question. "From what the War Department was able to piece together, Nathan and Colin were waylaid when en route to investigate a highly secretive matter."

"Isn't it rather ironic that you two ended up together?" Lady Briars asked. There was a smile in her voice now.

"Not really," Caine answered. "Both of us missed the ceremony honoring our brothers," he explained. "Jade came to see me. She wanted to talk about Nathan and I guess I needed to talk about Colin. We were immediately drawn to each other."

He paused to wink at Jade, then continued, "I believe it was love at first sight."

"I can see why," Lady Briars said. "Jade, you've turned into a beautiful woman." She shook her head and let out a little sigh. "I never understood why your father's friend snatched you away so quickly after your father's funeral. I will admit I was going to petition the Crown for guardianship. I'd always wanted a daughter. I also believed you would have fared much better with me. Now, after visiting with you, well, I must concede that you were properly raised."

"Uncle Harry insisted we leave right away," Jade explained. "He wasn't our legal guardian and he knew you'd fight for Nathan and me."

"Yes," Lady Briars agreed. "Do you know, I feel in part responsible for Nathan's death. Yes, I do. If he'd come to

JULIE GARWOOD

live with me, I certainly wouldn't have allowed him to go off on those sea voyages. It was too dangerous."

"Nathan was a fully grown man when he made his decision to work for England," Caine interjected. "I doubt you could have kept him home, Lady Briars."

"Still," she countered. "I still don't understand why your father didn't consider me for guardianship . . ."

"I believe I understand," Jade said. "Harry told me that Father had turned his heart against England."

"I cannot imagine why," Lady Briars returned. "He seemed very content to me."

Jade shrugged. "We probably will never know his reasons. Harry believed Father was being chased by demons who lived in his head."

"Perhaps so," Lady Briars agreed. "Now enough about your father, Jade. Tell me all about your early life. We have so much catching up to do. What was it like living on this tiny island? Did you learn to read and write? How did you keep yourself occupied, child? Were there many functions to attend?"

Jade laughed. "The people on the island weren't part of society, Lady Briars. Most didn't even bother to wear shoes. I never managed to read or write because Harry couldn't find anyone who could teach me."

Jade told that lie because Caine had insisted no one know she'd conquered those skills. Every little edge would give them an added advantage, he'd explained. If everyone believed she hadn't learned how to read, then she couldn't have read the letters.

She thought that reasoning was filled with flaws, but she didn't argue with her husband. She concentrated on making up several amusing childhood stories to satisfy Lady Briars' curiosity. She ended her remarks with the admission that although it had certainly been a peaceful time, it had also been a little boring.

The topic returned to the issue of their recent marriage. Caine answered all of the woman's questions. Jade was amazed by the easy way he told his lies. He obviously had a natural talent, too.

Her father's old friend appeared to be genuinely interested. Jade thought she was a terribly sweet woman.

"Why is it you never married?" Jade asked. "I know that's a bold question, but you're such a beautiful woman, Lady Briars. I'm certain you must have set the young men scurrying around for your attention."

Lady Briars was obviously pleased by Jade's comments. She actually blushed. She paused to pat her hair before answering. Jade noticed the tremor in the elderly woman's hand then. The ravages of age, she decided as she waited for her to answer.

"I had my hopes set on your father for a long time, my dear. Thorton was such a dashing man. That special spark was missing, though. We ended up good friends, of course. I still think about him every once in a while, and I sometimes bring out some of the precious little gifts he gave me. I get quite maudlin," she admitted. "Do you have any special mementos to remember your father by, Jade?"

"No," Jade answered. "Everything that belonged to my father burned in the fire."

"Fire?"

"This is going to disappoint you, Lady Briars, but the lovely house you helped Nathan renovate caught fire. Everything was destroyed."

"Oh, my poor dear," Lady Briars whispered. "It has been a difficult time for you, hasn't it?"

Jade nodded agreement. "Caine has been a comfort, of course. I doubt I would have gotten through this last month without him at my side."

"Yes, that is fortunate," Lady Briars announced. She put her teacup down on the table. "So you say you don't have anything at all to remember your father by? Nothing at all? Not even a family bible or a time piece or a letter?"

Jade shook her head. Caine took hold of her hand and squeezed it. "Sweetheart, you're forgetting the trunk," he interjected smoothly.

She turned to look at Caine, wondering what his game was. Not a hint of her confusion appeared in her expression however. "Oh, yes, the trunk," she agreed.

"Then you do have something to remember your father by, after all," Lady Briars announced. She nodded in apparent satisfaction. "I was going to rush right home and go through my things to find something for you. A daughter must have a trinket or two from her father. Now, I remember a lovely porcelain statue your father gave me as a birthday gift when I turned sixteen . . ."

"Oh, I couldn't take that from you," she interjected.

"No, she couldn't," Caine said. "Besides, she has the trunk. Of course, we haven't had a chance to look inside yet. Jade's been so ill these past weeks with the worrisome fever."

He turned to smile at Jade. "My dear, what say we go over to Nathan's town house next week? If you're feeling up to the outing," he added. "We still have to settle her brother's affairs," he told Lady Briars.

Jade thought Caine had lost his mind. She smiled, just to cover her unease, while she waited for his next surprise.

It wasn't long in coming. "Perhaps you'd like to accompany us over to Nathan's place and have a look at the trunk with us," Caine suggested.

Lady Briars declined the invitation. She insisted that Jade come to see her soon, then took her leave. Caine assisted the frail woman into her carriage.

Jade paced the drawing room until he returned. "And just what was that all about?" she demanded as soon as he walked inside again.

He shut the doors before answering her. She noticed his grin then. Caine looked thoroughly pleased with himself.

"I didn't like lying to that dear woman one bit, Caine," she cried out. "Besides, I'm the accomplished liar in this family, not you. Why did you tell her there was a trunk, for heaven's sake? Were you thinking to make her feel better so she wouldn't have to give up any of her cherished possessions? Do you know, now that I reflect upon this, I don't like hearing you lie at all. Well?" she demanded when she needed to pause for breath. "What have you got to say for yourself?"

"The lie was necessary," Caine began.

She wouldn't let him get any further. "'No lie is ever necessary,'" she quoted from memory. "You told me that days ago. Remember?"

"Love, you're really upset because I lied?" he asked. He looked astonished.

"I most certainly am upset," she returned. "I've come to depend upon your honesty, Caine. Yet if you tell me the lie was really necessary, then I must assume you have a plan. Do you think Lady Briars might mention this imaginary trunk to someone? Is that it?"

She thought she had it all figured out. "No," he answered, smiling over the frown his denial caused.

"No? Then you should be ashamed of yourself for lying to that old woman."

"If you'll let me explain . . ."

She folded her arms across her chest. "This had better be good, sir, or I just might blister you."

He thought she sounded like her Uncle Harry now. She was certainly blustering enough to make him draw that conclusion. He laughed and took his disgruntled looking wife into his arms.

"Well?" she muttered against his jacket. "Explain, if you please, why you lied to a dear family friend."

"She isn't a dear family friend," Caine told her, his exasperation apparent in his tone of voice.

"Of course she is," Jade protested. "You heard her, husband. She has kept all the little presents my father gave her. She loved him!"

"She killed him."

Jade didn't react to that statement for a long, silent minute. Then she slowly lifted her gaze to stare into his eyes. She shook her head.

He nodded.

Her knees went weak on her. Caine had to hold her up when she slumped against him. "Are you trying to tell me," she began, her voice a mere thread. "Do you mean to say that Lady Briars is . . ."

"She's Ice."

"Ice?" She shook her head again. "She can't be Ice," she cried out. "For God's sake, Caine. She's a woman."

"And women can't be killers?"

"No," she returned. "I mean to say yes, I do suppose . . ."

He took mercy on her confused state. "All the clues fit, Jade. Now sit down and let me explain it to you," he suggested.

She was simply too stunned to move. Caine led her over to the settee, gently pushed her down on the cushions, and then settled himself next to her. "It's really very logical," he began as he put his arm around her shoulders.

A small smile tugged at the corners of her mouth. She was recovering from her initial surprise. "I knew it would be logical."

"I was suspicious when I reread the letters, of course. And I never make the same mistake twice, love, remember?"

"I remember that you like to make that boast whenever possible, husband, dear. Now explain to me what this mistake is that you didn't repeat."

"I thought Pagan was a man. I never once considered that

he could be a she. I didn't make that same error when I was hunting Ice."

"You are really convinced Lady Briars is Ice? How did you come to that conclusion?" she asked.

He wasn't about to let the topic completely turn just yet. "Jade? Did you ever consider that Ice could be a woman? Tell me the truth," he commanded in that arrogant tone she liked so much.

She let out a sigh. "You're going to gloat."

"Yes, I'm sure I will."

They shared a smile. "No, I never once considered that possibility. There, are you happy?"

"Immensely," he drawled out.

"Caine, you still have to convince me," she reminded him. "Lord, I'm still having difficulty believing this. Ice killed people and threatened to kill Nathan and me. Remember that one letter, where he told my father that if the letters weren't returned, he would kill us?"

"Not he, love," Caine replied. "She." He let out a long sigh, then added, "Jade, some women do kill."

"Oh, I know," she countered. "Still, it isn't at all lady-like."

"Do you remember in one of the earlier letters, when they were given their operative names, that Ice admitted to being furious over that name? That comment made me curious. Not too many men would care one way or the other. A woman would mind, though, wouldn't she?"

"Some might."

"There are more substantial clues, of course. Briars hired the full staff for Nathan's country home. They were her men, loyal to her. The fact that the house was pillaged told me they were searching. And guess where Hudson, Nathan's butler, turned up?"

"He's staying at Nathan's town house, isn't he? He's guarding it until we close it up."

"No, he's currently in Lady Briars' residence. I imagine we'll find that your brother's town house has been turned upside down by now."

She ignored his smile. "I never trusted Hudson," she announced. "The man kept trying to force tea down me. I'll wager it was poisoned."

"Now, Jade, don't let your imagination get the better of you. By the way, all those confusing incidents were Hudson's doing. They did dig up your father's grave on the off chance that the letters had been hidden there. They cleaned up the mess, too."

"Did Hudson shoot Nathan's fine horse?"

"No, Willburn did," Caine explained.

"I'm telling Nathan."

Caine nodded. "Hudson had the cleanup detail. You were right, by the way, a cart was used to carry the horse away. It must have taken seven strong men to lift the steed."

"How did you learn all this?"

"You're impressed with me, aren't you?"

He nudged her into answering. "Yes, Caine, I'm impressed. Now tell me the rest."

"My men have been ferreting out the facts for me so I can't take all the credit. The horse was found in a ravine almost two miles away from the main road."

"Just wait until I tell Nathan," Jade muttered again.

Caine patted her shoulder. "You can explain it all to him after this is finished, all right?"

She nodded. "Is there more to tell me, Caine?"

"Well, once I decided that Briars was certainly the most logical candidate, I looked into her background. On the surface, everything appeared to be above board, but the deeper I looked, the more the little oddities showed up."

"For instance?"

"She did a hell of a lot of traveling for a woman," he remarked. "For instance," he added before Jade could interrupt, "she went back and forth to France at least seven times that I know of, and . . ."

"And you thought that odd? Perhaps she has relatives . . ."

"No," he countered. "Besides, Jade, she did most of her traveling during war time. There were other telling clues."

"I do believe I'm married to the most intelligent man in all the world," she praised. "Caine, it's only just beginning to make sense to me. What do Sir Richards and Lyon have to say about your discovery?"

"I haven't told them yet," he answered. "I wanted to be absolutely certain. After listening to Briars' questions, I don't have any doubts left. I'll tell them tonight when I meet them at White's."

"What question did she ask that made you suspicious?"

"She asked you right away if you could read, remember? Considering the fact that most well-bred ladies in England have acquired that skill, I thought it was a telling question."

"But she knew I'd been raised on an island," Jade argued. "That's why she asked, Caine. She was trying to find out if I'd been raised properly without coming right out and . . ."

"She was also a little too interested in finding out what your father had left you," he interrupted.

Jade's shoulders slumped. "I thought she was sincere."

"We'll have to tighten the net around Nathan's town house," Caine remarked. "I only have two men guarding it now." He paused to smile at Jade. "Your poor brother will probably have his town house burned to the ground before this is over."

"You needn't look so cheerful over that possibility," she said. "Besides, Hudson has had ample time to find out there isn't any trunk." She let out a small gasp. "I have another disappointment for you, Caine. Lady Briars knows I was lying when I said I couldn't read. I believe she asked that question to find out if we might be on to her. Oh, yes, I do believe we've mucked it up this time."

Caine lost his smile. "What are you talking about? Why do you think Briars knows you were lying?"

"Hudson saw me reading almost every night," she rushed out. "After dinner, I'd go into Nathan's lovely study and read until I became sleepy. There were so many wonderful books I hadn't memorized yet. Hudson would light the fire in the hearth for me. I'm certain he told Lady Briars."

She patted his hand to soften his disappointment. "Now, what will you do?" she asked, certain he'd come up with an alternate plan of action in no time at all. Caine was simply too logical not to have covered every possibility.

"Eventually we'll be able to compare the handwriting, once we get the letters from the *Emerald*."

"We have a sample here," Jade said. "Lady Briars sent two notes requesting I call on her. I hate to disappoint you, but the handwriting didn't look at all familiar."

"I doubt she wrote those notes," Caine returned. "She's old, Jade, but she hasn't gotten careless yet. No, she probably had one of her assistants pen the letters."

"Would you like for me to steal . . ."

"I'd like you to stay here day and night," he stated. The suggestion was given as a command. "This is going to get sticky before it's finished. Everything I've gathered is actually circumstantial evidence in a court, Jade. I've still got some work to do. Now promise me you won't leave."

"I promise," she answered. "Have a little faith in me, husband. You know that once I give my word, I'll keep it. Please tell me what you have planned."

"Lyon's been itching to put a little pressure on Willburn. I think it's time he had his way. Willburn hasn't been at all accommodating thus far. We hoped he'd lead us to Ice, but he stays hidden behind his drapes all day. Yes, it's time we had a talk with him."

"I don't like the idea of you leaving every night, Caine. Until the ship is burned and the rumor of Pagan's death hits

London, I think you should stay home. I'll tell you this, sir, if the people in this town celebrate my death, I'm going to be very disappointed."

Caine's smile was gentle. "They would mourn," he promised. "Anyway, we'll never know. It isn't necessary to burn the ship now."

"Why?"

"Because I know who Ice is," he explained. "And she isn't going to quit coming after me, either. She knows we're on to her."

"Yes," Jade countered. "If you hadn't made me lie about not knowing how to read, she wouldn't be on to us, husband. See? That lie wasn't all for the good."

"Don't sound so smug, my love."

"Harry's going to be happy he doesn't have to burn a ship," she announced, ignoring his remark. "You will send someone to tell him, won't you?"

"Yes, I'll send someone to Shallow's Wharf," he replied. "You're going to have to tell me exactly where that is, Jade. It's an operative name for somewhere else, isn't it?"

Jade cuddled up against her husband. "You are so clever," she whispered. "You will be careful when you go out, won't you? She's on to us, all right. I don't want you turning your back on anyone, Caine. I have come to rely on you."

"And I have come to rely on you," he answered. His grin was telling. "This is sounding damned equal to me."

"It is equal," she said. "But you can pretend it isn't if it will make you feel better."

He ignored that comment and tickled the side of her neck instead. Jade shivered in reaction. "Do you feel like another dance lesson now?"

"Will I be on my knees again?"

"Didn't you like it, love? You acted like you did. Your mouth was so sweet, so . . . ."

"I liked it," she admitted in a rush.

"Can we?"

"Oh, yes." Her voice was breathless.

"Upstairs or here?"

"Upstairs," she whispered. She stood up and tugged on his hand. "But this time, Caine, I want to lead."

They spent the rest of the day in each others' arms. It was a blissful time that ended all too soon. Before she knew it, she was reminding him to remember McKindry and he was demanding her promise to stay put until he returned.

Jade was so exhausted, she slept quite soundly until an hour or so before dawn. She awakened with a start, then rolled on her side to take Caine into her arms.

He wasn't there. Jade rushed downstairs to check inside the library. Caine hadn't come back to her yet. Since he'd never taken this long before, she started worrying.

She'd worked herself into a frenzy when another hour passed and he still hadn't returned.

Her instincts were screaming a warning. Something was terribly wrong. The familiar ache had settled in her stomach just like in the old days when a plan would go amiss.

She had to be ready. Jade dressed in quick time, added a dagger to her pocket, the special clip to her hair, then resumed pacing again.

Caine had left two guards for her protection. One stood in the shadows outside the front door and the other guarded the back entrance.

Jade decided to talk to Cyril, the man guarding the front entrance. Perhaps he'd know what they should do. She opened the door just in time to see a man hand Cyril a piece of paper and then run away.

Cyril bounded up the steps two at a time. "It's a letter for you," he said. "At this hour of the night," he added in a near growl. "It can't be good news, mi'lady."

"I hope it's from Caine," she blurted out. "Come inside, Cyril. Bolt the door behind you. Something's wrong," she added as she tore the seal from the envelope. "Caine has never taken this long before."

Cyril grumbled his agreement. "Aye," he said. "I feel it in my gut."

"Me, too," Jade whispered.

As soon as Jade unfolded the sheet of paper, she paled. She recognized the script immediately. The note came from Ice.

"What is it, mi'lady?" Cyril asked. He spoke in a hushed tone, an oddity, that, for Cyril was a big man with a booming voice to match.

"Caine's in trouble," Jade whispered. "I have one hour to go to a building on Lathrop Street. Do you know where that is?"

"It's a warehouse if it's on Lathrop," Cyril answered. "I don't like this," he added. "I'm sniffing a trap. What happens if we don't go?"

"They'll kill my husband."

"I'll go fetch Alden," Cyril announced. He started toward the back door but stopped when Jade called out to him.

"I'm not going."

"But . . ."

"I can't leave. I have to stay here, Cyril. This could be a trick and I gave my word to Caine. No, I have to stay here. Do you know how late White's stays open?"

"It's closed for certain by now."

"Caine might have gone to have a talk with a man named Willburn. Do you know where he lives?"

"I do," the guard answered. "He's just six, perhaps seven blocks over."

"Send Alden over there now. Lyon and Caine might be having a visitation with the infidel."

"And if they aren't?"

"While Alden goes to Willburn's house, I want you to run

over to Lyon's residence. Now then, if Lyon isn't home, then go on to Sir Richards' town house. Do you know where those two men live?"

"Yes," Cyril said. "But who will guard you while we're tracking Caine down? You'll be all alone."

"I'll bolt the doors," she promised. "Please hurry, Cyril. We need to find Caine before the hour is up. If we can't find him, then I have to assume the note wasn't trickery."

"We'll hurry," Cyril promised on his way toward the back of the house.

Jade clutched the letter in her hands and stood in the center of the foyer a long while. She then went upstairs to her bedroom. She bolted the door behind her.

The pounding started on the front door just a few minutes later. She knew it wasn't Caine. He had a key, of course. The sound of glass shattering came next.

Had she inadvertently played right into their hands? Were they so certain she'd send the guards to look for Caine? Jade found solace in that possibility, for it meant Caine hadn't been taken captive after all.

She prayed she was right, prayed, too, that God wouldn't get angry with her. She was probably going to have to kill someone, and very soon, judging from the sounds of men lumbering up the steps.

Jade grabbed the pistol from the drawer of the nightstand on Caine's side of the bed, backed herself into a corner, and took aim. She decided she would wait until they'd broken the latch, then shoot the first man who entered the room.

Her hand was steady. A deadly calm came over her, too. And then the door was kicked open. A dark form filled the entrance. And still she waited, for she wanted to be absolutely certain it was her enemy and not one of Caine's hired men arriving to save her.

"Light a candle," the voice shouted. "I can't see the bitch."

Jade squeezed the trigger. She must have caught the man somewhere in the middle, for he let out a loud scream of pain as he doubled over. He fell to the floor with a loud thud.

She won that round, she told herself, though the battle went to Ice. Jade was surrounded by three men. When the first reached for her, she cut his hand with her knife. The second villain grabbed her weapon just as the third slammed his fist into the side of her jaw. The blow felled her to the floor in a dead faint.

Jade didn't wake up again until she was being carried inside a dark, damp building. There were only a few candles lighting the area but quite enough for Jade to see the crates stacked up along the stone walls. At the end of the long corridor stood a woman dressed in white. Lady Briars was there, waiting for her.

The man carrying her dropped her when he'd reached his leader. Jade staggered to her feet. She rubbed the sting in her jaw while she stared at her adversary.

The look in those eyes was chilling. "I understand now why you were given the name Ice," she heard herself say. "You don't have a soul, do you, Lady Briars?"

Jade was rewarded by a sound slap across her face. "Where are the letters?" Briars demanded.

"Safe," Jade answered. "Do you really believe stealing the letters back is going to save you? Too many people know what you've done. Too many . . ."

"You fool!" Briars shouted. There was such strength, such cruelty in her voice that Jade suddenly felt as though she were facing the devil. She resisted the urge to cross herself. "I will have those letters, Jade. They are my proof to the world of all the glorious feats I've accomplished. No one's going to deny me now. No one. In years to come, the world will realize what my Tribunal was able to accomplish. We could have ruled England, if I had chosen to continue with my work. Oh yes, I will have the letters back. They will be kept in a safe place until the time is right to reveal my genius."

She was mad. Jade could feel the goose bumps on her arms. She tried desperately to think of a way to reason with the woman before she finally came to the conclusion that the crazed woman was beyond any kind of reason. "If I give you the letters back, will you leave Caine alone?" she asked.

Lady Briars let out a high-pitched snicker. "If? Don't you have any idea who I am? You can't possibly deny me, Jade."

"Oh, I know who you are," Jade replied. "You're the woman who killed my father. You're the woman who betrayed her country. You're the foul creature who was born from the devil. You're the demented . . ."

She quit her tirade when Briars hit her again. Jade backed up a space, then straightened her shoulders. "Let Caine go, Briars, and I will get you the letters."

In answer to that promise, Briars turned to one of her cohorts. "Lock our guest in the back room," she ordered. She turned to Jade then. "You're going to be the bait, my dear, to get Caine here. He has to die," she added in a singsong voice. "But only after he's given me the letters, of course. Then I shall kill you, too, little Jade. Your father was the true traitor, for he turned his back against me. Me! Oh, how I wished I could have been there when his son died. You will have to make up for that regret, dear, dear child, by dying slowly by my hand . . . Get her out of here!" Briars ended in a near shout.

Jade felt like weeping with relief. They hadn't taken Caine after all. He would come for her, she knew, and there was still danger . . . but he was safe for the moment.

She actually smiled to herself when they led her to her temporary prison. They believed they had her now. They mustn't tie her hands, she thought to herself. Jade started whimpering so that her captors would believe she was frightened. As soon as they opened the door, she rushed inside, then collapsed on the floor in the center of the room, and began to cry.

The door slammed shut behind her. She kept up her wailing until the sound of footsteps faded. Then she took inventory. Moonlight filtered in through the gray filmed window. The opening was a good fifteen feet up. There was only one piece of furniture, an old scarred desk with only three legs, and they certainly knew she wouldn't be able to reach the window even if she stood on top of the desk.

Yes, they thought they had secured her inside. Jade let out a little sigh of pleasure.

She pulled the special clip from her hair that she used for just such an occasion, and went to work on the lock.

Because she was in such a desperate hurry to get to Caine before Briars' men did, she wasn't as quick as she would have been under calmer circumstances. It took her a little over ten minutes to work the lock free.

It was pitch black inside the warehouse proper. Even though Jade was certain Briars had taken all her men with her, she still made her exit as quietly as possible. Jade was completely disoriented when she reached the street. She ran in one direction for two long blocks before she got her bearings and realized she'd taken the wrong way.

Jade was in absolute terror now. She knew it was going to take her another fifteen minutes to reach home. While she ran, she made several fervent promises to her Maker. She gave him her word that she would never lie or steal again, if he would only keep Caine safe. "I know you gave me those special talents, Lord, and you know that once I give my word, I won't break it. I won't follow in my father's path, either. Just let me live long enough to prove myself. Please, God? Caine needs me."

She had to stop when the stitch in her side intensified. "If you'll only give me a little added strength, Lord, I won't use blasphemies either."

Odd, but the stitch in her side faded. She was able to catch her breath, too. That last promise must have been the one her Maker was waiting to hear, she decided.

"Thank you," she whispered as she picked up her skirts again and started running.

Jade didn't stop again until she reached the street their town house was located on. She kept to the shadows as she made her way toward the steps. When she spotted three men littering her stoop, she started running again. The men weren't in any condition to waylay her. They looked restful too, in their forced slumber.

Caine had obviously come home.

Jade couldn't remember the number of men Briars had with her. She began to fret again. Should she sneak in by way of the back door or should she boldly walk into the foyer and try to confront Briars once again.

The question was answered for her when Caine's bellow reached her.

"Where is she?" Caine roared through the door.

The anguish in his voice tore at Jade's heart. She pulled the door open and rushed inside.

They were all in the drawing room. Lyon, Jade noticed, was holding Caine by the shoulders. Briars stood in front of the two men. Sir Richards stood next to her. Both Cyril and Alden stood behind the director.

"She'll die of starvation before you find her," Briars shouted. She let out a snort of amusement. "No, you'll never find her." Never."

"Oh, yes, he will."

Briars let out a screech when Jade's soft voice reached her. Caine and Lyon both whirled around.

Caine simply stood there, smiling at her. She saw the tears in his eyes, knew her own were just as misty. Lyon looked as startled as Richards. "Jade . . . how did you . . . ."

She looked at Caine when she gave her answer. "They locked me in."

It took a full minute before anyone reacted. Lyon was the first to laugh. "They locked her in," he said to Caine.

Jade kept smiling until Caine walked over to her. When he reached out to touch her face with his fingertips, she burst into tears and ran up the stairs.

She went into the first bedroom, slammed the door shut behind her, and threw herself down on the bed. Caine was right behind her. He pulled her into his arms.

"My love, it's all over now," he whispered.

"I didn't leave you. I stayed right here until they came inside and dragged me away. I didn't break my word."

"Hush, Jade. I never thought . . ."

"Caine, I was so scared," she wailed against his chest.

"So was I," he whispered. He squeezed her tight, then said, "When Cyril told me . . . I thought you were . . . Oh, God, yes, I was damned scared."

She mopped her eyes on his jacket, then said, "You can't say damn anymore. We can't ever use another blasphemy, Caine. I promised God."

His smile was filled with tenderness. "I see."

"I would have promised anything to keep you safe," she whispered. "I need you so much, Caine."

"I need you, too, my love."

"We can't steal anymore, or lie, either," she told him then. "I made those promises, too."

He rolled his eyes heavenward. "And your promises are also mine?" he asked her. He hid his smile now, for she looked so sincere, and he didn't bother to mention to her that he'd never stolen anything before.

"Yes, of course my promises are also yours," she answered. "We are suppose to share everything, aren't we? Caine, we are equal partners in this marriage."

"We are equal," he agreed.

"Then my promises are also yours?"

"Yes," he answered. He suddenly pulled away from her.

The worry in his expression was obvious. "You didn't give up anything else, did you?"

He looked as though he dreaded her answer. She immediately guessed what he was thinking. "Like dancing?"

"Like making love."

She laughed, a full rich sound filled with joy. "Aren't they the same thing?"

"This isn't the time for jests, Jade."

"No, Caine, we didn't give up dancing or making love. I would never give a promise I couldn't keep," she added, quoting back his very words to her.

Caine wanted to tear her clothes off and make love to her then and there. He couldn't, of course, for there was still the mess to be cleaned up downstairs.

He wasn't able to spend much time with his bride over the next couple of days. He and Lyon were both occupied dictating their findings for their superior's records. Lady Briars was locked away in Newgate Prison. There was talk that she was going to be transferred to a nearby asylum, for the court had decreed that the woman was quite mad. Jade was in wholehearted agreement.

Caine was finally free to keep his other promise to Jade. They settled down to live a peaceful life together.

And just as he'd predicted, they did live happily ever after.

He was still terribly insecure, however. Jade did worry about that. On the morning of their first anniversary, he demanded she give him her pledge to stay for another year.

Jade thought the question was ill-timed, considering the fact that she was in the midst of an excruciating contraction. She gritted her teeth against the agony.

"Caine, we're going to have our baby," she said.

"I know, my love," he answered. He rolled to his side and gently rubbed her swollen abdomen. "I noticed quite a long time ago," he added just to tease her. He leaned down to kiss her damp brow. "Are you too warm, Jade?"

"No, I'm . . ."

"Give me your promise," he interrupted while he pulled the top cover away. "Then you can go back to sleep. You were very restless during the night. I think you stayed up too late talking with Lyon and Christina. I was glad to see them, of course, and I'm happy Christina wants to offer her services when the time comes, but I still insist that a physician be in attendance, Jade."

Jade was too exhausted to argue. She'd been having sporadic contractions during the long night. She didn't wake Caine, though. She was following her good friend's advice. Christina had suggested that it would be better if her husband weren't bothered until the very last minute. Husbands, Christina had explained, fell apart too easily.

Christina considered Jade her blood sister, ever since the night she handed her Lyon's file and told her to keep it safe. The two ladies trusted each other completely and spent hour upon hour telling each other favorite stories about their pasts.

Caine gently prodded his wife. "I want your word now."

As soon as the fresh contraction faded, she answered him. "Yes, I promise you. And, Caine, we're going to have our baby now. Go and wake Christina."

The babe Jade was certain was going to present himself at any moment didn't actually arrive for another three hours.

Through the intense labor, Caine remained as calm, as solid and dependable as Jade had expected. She thought then that Christina had been wrong. Not all men fell apart so easily.

Christina sent Caine down to the library when Jade's contractions became too unbearable for him to watch. Caine only lasted five minutes below the stairs, however, and was then back at Jade's side, clutching her hand in his and begging her forgiveness for putting her through this god-awful ordeal.

He was more hindrance than help, of course. He didn't

panic during the birthing, however, and just bare minutes later was holding his beautiful daughter in his arms.

Sterns couldn't restrain himself. As soon as he heard the lusty cries of the newborn, he bounded into the room. He immediately took the baby away from Caine, announced that she was indeed magnificent, and then proceeded to give her her first bath.

Christina took care of Jade. Caine helped her change the sheets and Jade's gown, as well, and when Christina told Caine he'd held up rather well, he actually managed a smile.

Caine was pale, his hands were shaking, his brow was drenched with sweat, he still couldn't speak a coherent word, but he had held fast.

Yet once the trauma was over, his discipline deserted him.

Christina had just left the room to give the wonderful news to her husband. Sterns was cuddling his new charge in his arms, and Jade was simply too weak to catch her husband.

"Is he all right?" Jade asked Sterns. She couldn't even find the strength to look over the edge of the bed.

"He swooned."

"I know he swooned," Jade replied. "But is he all right? He didn't hit his head on anything sharp, did he?"

"He's fine," Sterns announced. He hadn't bothered to look down at his employer when he made that pronouncement but continued to stare down at the beautiful infant. The look on his face was one of true adoration.

"Do help him up," Jade whispered. She was biting her lip to keep herself from laughing.

"He doesn't appear to be ready to get up just yet," Sterns announced. "The babe needs my full attention now. You've done very well, mi'lady, very well, indeed. I'm certain the Marquess will agree when he finishes his faint."

Jade beamed with satisfaction. Her eyes filled with tears. "You're never going to let him live this down, are you, Sterns?"

Caine groaned then, drawing her attention. "We must never tell anyone he swooned. He'd die of embarrassment."

"Don't worry, mi'lady," Sterns returned. "I certainly won't tell anyone. I promise."

She should have realized from the determined sparkle in his eyes that he wasn't going to honor his promise. Three days later, she read all about Caine's fainting spell.

The rascal butler had posted it in the dailies.

The Marquess of Cainewood took it all in stride. He didn't mind the jests from the well-wishers at all.

Nothing could rile his temper. After all, his mission had been successful. He'd hunted down the infamous pirate . . . and now she belonged to him.

The hunter was content.